Also by Kate Alexander

FIELDS OF BATTLE
FRIENDS AND ENEMIES

Paths of Peace

KATE ALEXANDER

Macdonald

A Macdonald Book

First published in Great Britain in 1984
by Macdonald & Co (Publishers) Ltd
London & Sydney

Reprinted 1985

Copyright © Tilly Armstrong 1984

British Library Cataloguing in Publication Data

Alexander, Kate
    Paths of peace.
    Rn: Tilly Armstrong   I. Title
    823'.914[F]   PR6051.L363

    ISBN 0 356 10342 0

Printed in Great Britain by
Redwood Burn Limited, Trowbridge, Wiltshire
Bound at the Dorstel Press

Macdonald & Co
London & Sydney
Maxwell House
74 Worship Street
London EC2A 2EN

A BPCC plc Company

Chapter One

There was a good turn-out from the village of Brinthorpe to watch Wally Carless take his daughter, Evelyn, to church to marry Terry Blackmore, but the women who gathered round the gate were nearly as interested in Evelyn's sister, Anne, newly returned from Canada, widowed and with a two-year-old daughter.

Wally and Beryl Carless had lived in Brinthorpe all their lives and the neighbours had seen their three children grow up. Anne had always been a handful – just as well she had married young. She had been the only girl from the village to marry one of the Canadian soldiers stationed nearby during the war and that had been an added interest. The previous autumn they had been appalled to hear that Anne had lost her young husband. 'After all that fighting over here,' they said, 'fancy him going and getting killed in Korea. It makes y'think, don't it?'

Now it was February 1951 and Anne was home, and meaning to stay it seemed, though Beryl was unable to satisfy the curious enquiries about her daughter's future.

'She's not told me what she means to do,' Beryl said. 'And what she thinks she's coming back to here I'm sure I don't know! Shortages, rationing, austerity. You'd think we'd be due for a bit of plenty considering we've had peace for the last six years, but not a bit of it!'

Anne arrived at the church on foot, leading Melanie by the hand, with her brother, Peter, following one step behind. Melanie was a beautiful child, there was no doubt about that. Thick black hair, very fine and straight, and big brown eyes. Beryl had let it out that Anne's husband had Red Indian blood in him and those of the village who could remember him, tall, dark and quiet-moving, thought that it showed in his baby daughter's colouring, though the delicate wild roses in her cheeks came from Anne.

Anne had always been the beauty of the family, a brown-haired, blue-eyed flower of a girl. She was taller than her elder sister, slimmer, better proportioned. Evelyn was inclined to drop her head into her shoulders; Anne walked proudly, straight as a young birch tree. Poor girl. Married at nineteen, a mother at twenty and widowed at twenty-two – what sort of a life was that?

As for Peter, the village had got used to him, though there were still one or two who shied away, fearing contact with someone who was not quite right in the head. Peter had gone off to the war a dashing young soldier, smart as paint, and had returned from a Japanese prisoner-of-war camp an empty shell of a man. The scars on his body spoke of beatings and torture, but Peter, it seemed, had no recollection of what had happened to him except for saying that he didn't want to go 'back in the box', whatever that might mean. His memory had gone and he was unable to work. At the time of Evelyn's marriage he had only just got past the stage of having to be put on the bus for the Hospital Rehabilitation Centre every day and met by his mother in the evenings. Only Wally and Beryl knew what a step forward it had been when Peter had started walking down to meet the bus on his own, and only Beryl still believed that one day he would be his old self again. Better, some thought, if he had been killed outright like his friend, Dave, but Beryl didn't see it that way. She seized on every little sign of returning normality and the way Melanie had taken to her uncle had been a promising development in Beryl's eyes. To Anne it seemed that what attracted Melanie to Peter was his childlike quality, but she kept that thought to herself.

Evelyn arrived at the church, in the white satin and lacy veil she had always wanted, amidst murmurs of approval. Anne effaced herself, giving Melanie's restlessness as her excuse for sitting in a back pew. Peter sat with her, partly to keep her company, but mainly so that he could be near the door in case the blind panic that sometimes came over him forced him to make a dash for the open.

Melanie stood on the seat, stamping on the wood with a satisfyingly loud noise and looking round with fascinated eyes at the strange building and all the people, but when the congregation knelt down to pray she wriggled away from Anne and had to be rescued from under the pew, flushed and dusty, with her lower lip jutting out ominously and tears threatening.

Peter took her on his knee. He pulled a large handkerchief out of his pocket and with a few quick twists turned it into a rabbit with large ears and a nibbling mouth which seemed intent on making a meal out of his other hand. Melanie broke into delighted giggles, her small body wriggling in excitement as the rabbit threatened her own button nose. One or two people in the congregation turned their heads to see what was going on.

'Take her out for me, Pete,' Anne whispered. 'Play with her in the churchyard.'

She was on tenterhooks for the rest of the ceremony, worrying in case he let Melanie wander off, but when they were assembling outside for the photographs Melanie ran forward, a posy of flowers in her hand, and presented them to her Aunt Evelyn in an unplanned gesture. There were shocked titters when it was realized that the flowers had been taken from nearby graves, but no one said anything and the charming moment was captured by the photographer.

It was still only February, mild for the time of year, but with rain threatening and a stiff breeze blowing across the fields, flattening the grass which had grown up amongst the leaning headstones. Evelyn's veil was lifted by the wind. She cried out as it caught against the rough stone wall of the church and her bridesmaids rushed to free it.

Anne, one hand restraining Melanie, the other clutching at her new, unseasonable straw hat, shivered in the wind, remembering as she did so that the snow had been four feet deep when she had left the ranch in Canada. It would be April before it finally disappeared, before the last of the ice on the rivers cracked and swirled away. There, the ground would be iron hard, gripped in winter; the sun might shine from a cloudless sky, but the air tore at the lungs and froze the hairs inside the nostrils. Here, for all the cold wind and grey sky, there was something in the air, a dampness, a hint of change which showed that the year had turned. The earth beneath their feet was soft and richly brown, and even in that bleak churchyard there was a feeling of life beginning to stir, with a few stray snowdrops appearing and a swelling of buds on the bare branches.

The church stood on rising ground at the eastern end of the village of Brinthorpe. The village houses marched towards it down one long street, broken half-way down by a crossroads where two public houses stood on diagonal corners. Between the crossroads and the church were the village shops – a greengrocer, a butcher, the General Stores and Post Office. There had once been a bakery, but now the old ovens were cold and the villagers relied on deliveries of factory-baked bread. There had been a blacksmith's forge, too, along the road called Burden Lane where the Carless family lived, but when it had fallen into disuse the premises had been snapped up by an executive from the steel works and converted into a smart house known, inevitably, as 'The Old Forge'.

Beyond the church, outside the village, the land fell away in flat, grassy meadows towards the Wallenshaw Beck. On the far side of the water stood the Wallenshaw Iron and Steel Works.

Apart from the vicar, the shopkeepers, and a few farmworkers, every man in Brinthorpe was employed in the steelworks, and had been for the past hundred years. The Works had been founded in 1870 by a local landowner, Ezekiel Smithson, exploiting the northernmost limit of a field of ironstone with an overburden of soft blue-grey lias clays and blown sand which, at that date, was worked with a pick and shovel. He built the Works by the side of the Wallenshaw Beck and ran a railway line to fetch in the ironstone from the south and coal from the Yorkshire coalfields in the north, and to take the billets and slabs from the rolling mills to the banks of the Humber.

When Ezekiel retired at the age of sixty-eight, he was succeeded by his son, Alexander. Alexander began by running the Works with all the vigour of his pioneering father, but the First World War dealt him a blow which both sapped him of his vitality and forced him to go on working long after he should have retired: his only son was killed on the Somme. Alexander struggled on until his seventieth year and then, having no natural successor, yielded control to a group which paid him the compliment of adding his name to that of the company, but had no other use for him.

The newly-merged company of Smithson, Venner and Tyndall Limited had substantial interests in iron and steel in Scunthorpe and Wales as well as at Wallenshaw. Like Alexander Smithson, the 'Venner' of the title had long since disappeared, but the Tyndalls came of a famous line of eighteenth century ironmasters and in 1951 one of them, Sir Frederick Tyndall, was on the Board of the parent company and also General Manager of Wallenshaw. Prior to the nationalization which the Labour Government (reluctantly, it was said by some) had just implemented, Fred Tyndall had been hot favourite to become the next Chairman of S.V.T. Ltd; now there was no telling what would happen.

The wedding party had gathered round the west door of the church. Anne yielded to Melanie's tugging hand and wandered round to the back, and stopped, looking towards Wallenshaw. During all her childhood she had taken it for granted, this powerful presence dominating the skyline to the east: the tall chimneys, the cooling towers, the gas holders, the blast furnaces, the long, solid mass of the rolling mills.

She had always known that her mother tried not to do her washing on the days when the wind blew from the east and arrived in Brinthorpe loaded with grit and dust; she knew the times of all the shifts; she was familiar with the distant clang of locomotives shunting their loads of iron and coal; she had leaned out of her bedroom window and seen in the dark across the Beck the glow of coke ovens disgorging their load of red hot coke. She knew, in theory, how iron ore was turned into steel and knew, too, that her father was one of the aristocrats who worked in the melting shop. She knew that making steel was a proper job for a man: hot, noisy, dirty and dangerous. The nonchalance with which the blast furnace operators ran the molten iron along sand channels in the floor and the crane drivers swung ladles of liquid steel from the melting shop to the pitside for teeming was the result of years of hard experience and an inborn respect for the nature of the materials with which they were working. There was no such thing as a trivial accident in a steelworks; it needed only a moment's carelessness to leave a man maimed or dead.

Anne heard her name being called and turned back towards the church. The best man, Terry's brother Jeff, was coming towards her.

'The photographer wants all the bride's family together,' he said. 'I've been sent to find you and to try to round up Pete. Do you think he'll stand still long enough to get his picture taken or will he imagine he's facing a firing squad?'

Something in her recoiled from his insensitivity and she let her distaste show in her reply.

'That's a heartless thing to say,' she said, and turned away before he could begin to justify himself.

Jeff took it up with her later, at the reception. The village hall had been laid out with trestle tables covered by Beryl's best tablecloths and one or two reluctantly borrowed from neighbours. The florist who had supplied the bouquets had contrived a flower arrangement for the top table, but apart from that Anne thought that the hall had a bleak look. It was better when it was filled up with guests, squeezing into place at the tables, and an excited buzz of conversation filled the air. The hot soup went down well after everyone had stood about outside for so long and if the cold meat with hot vegetables and pickles which followed lacked class at least it was satisfying, eked out with the inevitable Spam. There was white wine to drink with it, which none of them very much liked, but Evelyn had been so agitated at the idea of the men drinking beer at the table that Terry had let her have her way, passing the word round quietly amongst his mates that there was a keg of beer to be broached when the meal was over. After the fruit salad and jelly there were speeches and toasts and the cutting of the cake and then what all the women declared they were dying for – a good, hot cup of tea.

It was after they had finished eating and the last of the

facetious telegrams had been read out, when the chairs had been pushed back from the tables and people were beginning to roam around, that Jeff came up to Anne again.

'I upset you outside,' he said abruptly. 'I'm sorry. It was only meant as a joke.'

'A callous joke,' Anne said quietly.

'That's what Army life does for you.'

'You've been out of the Army for five or six years, haven't you?'

'Five. I got out in 'forty-six. Meaning I've had time to learn to be human again? Perhaps you're right. I've said I'm sorry.'

She could see that he expected her to accept his apology, that he was impatient with her for making an issue over his remark about Peter. He was older than Terry and Anne scarcely knew him, even though the Blackmores had lived in Brinthorpe all their lives, just like the Carless family. He had been called up in 1939 at a time when Anne was no more than ten years old, and he had spent most of the war in the Western Desert. She remembered that he had been decorated for bravery; there had been a report about it in the local paper, but she could not remember any of the details. Doing swift sums in her head she reckoned his age as around thirty. There was something about him that made him stand out from the other men. Not just that he was tall and well built and still carried himself like a soldier; something more than that: an air of authority, a decisive, almost arrogant manner.

'What have you been doing since you were demobbed?' she asked, feeling that she ought to make an attempt at conversation.

'First of all I went back to school.'

'You're joking!'

'I went up to Cambridge and got a degree in engineering.'

'I remember now,' Anne said slowly. 'You were the clever one.'

'That's me. Brains *and* brawn.'

And looks, too. He was very dark, almost swarthy, with a good, hard profile and a well-shaped head. He reminded Anne, just a little, of her dead husband. It was a painful recollection; she put it away from her and allowed herself to wonder why her sister had preferred the younger brother, who was only a pale copy of this forceful man. He looked down at her with a smile and Anne knew the answer: even if Evelyn had wanted Jeff, he had not been available. Jeff was very well aware of his own value and he was not likely to waste himself on a prim, conventional girl of only moderate attractions.

'What are you doing now?' Anne asked.

'I'm at Wallenshaw Works.'

'Didn't you want to break away?'

'I was a sponsored student. I owe the Company a year or two. Besides, there are opportunities for me at Wallenshaw.'

Wally was banging on the table with his beer glass.

'Ladies and gentlemen! We've had our toasts to the happy couple, and the best of luck to them, but this week's been a historical one for all of us that work in the steel industry, and I'd like to mark the occasion. You all know my views, 'cause I've never made no secret of them . . .'

'That you haven't!'

'Aye, well, I've always said the industry belonged to them that worked in it and now we've got nationalization pushed through at last we'll likely see some changes. I'll not ask anyone to drink to anything they don't believe in – and I know there's some as can't see farther than the end of their noses and don't agree with me – so what I'm going to ask you to drink to is – the future!'

They drank the toast, amidst some good-natured ribbing, but afterwards Anne looked at Jeff enquiringly.

'You don't look very enthusiastic,' she suggested.

'I'm a Labour voter, like your Dad, but if you ask me, this nationalization isn't going to stick. Support from the bottom is all very well, but I know for a fact that the new Iron and Steel Corporation isn't getting any co-operation from the people at the top, and the Tories have said all along that they'll denationalize if they get in again. I'll tell you one thing though, young Anne: if we manage to keep the industry nationalized then I'll be General Manager of Wallenshaw Works one day, but if it slips back into private hands then I reckon Jocelin Tyndall will pip me to the post.'

He raised his glass to her as if in salute and then he moved away. He had been smiling, but Anne had seen that he meant what he said. He didn't lack for ambition, that was certain, nor for audacity. She liked him for it, that assumption that anything was possible; it fitted in well with her own outlook on life, the adventurous spirit which had pushed her towards marriage with Mel, even though her own courage had faltered in the face of hardship and loneliness.

There was dancing in the evening to a local band, earnest young boys with slicked back hair and ambitions for the big time. Anne watched while Evelyn and Terry circled the floor. Evelyn was still wearing her wedding gown, but she would be leaving soon to change, then she and Terry would be back to say goodbye before they left for their fortnight on Jersey. Anne remembered, as if it had been something in another life, her own brief honeymoon, a weekend in a country pub. Not much glamour about it, but happiness . . . yes, they had been deliriously happy. She felt tears coming into her eyes and bent over Melanie to hide them.

Melanie was worn out, her eyelids drooping. Anne scooped her up, glad of the excuse to escape.

'Going already?' Jeff asked.

'I must put Melanie to bed,' Anne said.

She avoided looking at him, not wanting to draw attention to her distress, but she guessed he must have seen, because he reached out and took the baby from her arms.

'I'll walk home with you,' he said.

That was unexpected, and not altogether welcome. It would be noticed – and remarked on – Jeff Blackmore walking off with the young widow from Canada. Not much she could do about it though, not without making him think that she attached some importance to his offer.

She made an effort to seem offhand as they walked down the High Street.

'Good of you to help me,' she said. 'Melanie's getting heavy to carry.'

'She's a little beauty – like her mother,' Jeff said.

There was not much Anne could say about that either. They didn't speak again until they reached the Carless's front gate.

Jeff handed over the sleeping Melanie and asked, 'You're not coming back for the dancing?'

'No, I'll need to stay with the baby. I can say goodbye to Evelyn when she comes home to change.'

She had the front door open before Jeff said, 'We will dance together one of these days, Anne.'

There was more behind his words than a simple wish to be sociable, just as the way he was looking at her conveyed an interest that went way beyond the new family connection between them. The thought of another man being attracted to her, less than six months after her husband's death, was more than Anne could cope with, but the recollection of his interest would stay at the back of her mind. Such plans as she had made did not include remarriage, not yet, while she felt so raw, but if she did come round to it Jeff Blackmore had more to offer than any other young man in the village. He had a drive that most of them lacked and his education had given him the means to achieve his ambitions. He would soon be in a position to give Anne and, even more importantly, Melanie, the sort of life that Anne wanted for them.

*

When Anne eventually found a place to live – after months of searching – both her parents raised objections, Beryl to the cottage itself and Wally to the way Anne had obtained it.

'Writing and asking for favours,' he grumbled.

'Independence is all very well,' Anne retorted. 'But I've already spent six months chasing rooms where they didn't want Melanie and although you and Mum have been very good, having me here all this time, you must admit that it's not an ideal arrangement, not from anyone's point of view.'

'You're better off with us than stuck out there in the wilds,' Beryl said.

'It's only half an hour's walk to Brinthorpe and not much more to Upbridge, and the bus passes the end of the lane. Anyway, I mean to have a bike.'

'All very well in the summer, but you'll not do a ride like that in winter, not with snow on the ground. How did you come to hear the cottage was falling empty?'

'Jeff heard about it from someone at the Works.'

'Oh, aye. Been seeing him again, have you?'

'I bumped into him, quite by accident, when I was taking Melanie for a walk. I wrote to Sir Frederick as soon as I got home. I didn't say anything to you because I thought it was bound to be one more disappointment. The last thing I expected was that he would send his son round to see me.'

'I could have dropped,' Beryl said. 'Me in my old pinny doing the ironing and Mr Jocelin Tyndall comes to the door.'

'No call to be ashamed of that,' Wally put in quickly. 'Jocelin Tyndall's a decent enough chap, and he works for his keep, I'll say that for him, but he's no better than the rest of us, for all his father's the boss.'

'You were nice enough to him when he was here,' Beryl said.

'Aye, well, I had him under me in the melting shop when he was learning the trade. He did none so badly,' Wally admitted.

Sir Frederick Tyndall had read Anne's letter over the breakfast table. Anne had written to him at home because she suspected that if the letter went to the Works it would be opened by a secretary, who might use her own discretion to decide who dealt with it. Lady Tyndall, Jocelin and Tessa were all with him and, after he glanced through the letter, Sir Frederick looked up and enquired, 'Does anyone know a family called Carless?'

His wife, immersed in her own correspondence, shook her head without looking up, but Jocelin said, 'There's a Wally Carless in the melting shop.'

'That's the man. His daughter's written asking if she can rent Nanny Brewster's cottage. Does that mean you've persuaded Nanny to move out at last, Em?'

'I've talked her into going into an almshouse in Upbridge. So much more suitable, though I shan't believe she's really going until I've seen her installed,' Emmeline Tyndall said. 'Does this Carless girl really want that poky, out-of-the-way cottage?'

'The housing shortage is so bad that the young people are clutching at anything. She sounds like a deserving case: a widow with a small child. She says she worked for the company before her marriage and her father has been with us all his working life.'

'There's a brother, too,' Jocelin said. 'Brain-damaged after being in a Japanese prisoner-of-war camp.'

'But, Daddy, I wanted that cottage!' Tessa Tyndall exclaimed.

'What on earth for?' Fred Tyndall looked at his young daughter with frowning suspicion.

'To live in. You know you promised me I could be independent as soon as I was twenty-one . . .'

'Which you won't be for another three months. As for living in Nanny Brewster's cottage, it's out of the question.'

'I don't see why. It needs doing up and modernizing, I admit, but I was going to use the money Gran left me as soon as I could get my hands on it.'

'It'd be money down the drain. When I said you could be independent I was thinking of buying you a decent flat – in London, perhaps.'

'Shovelling me out of the way,' Tessa said bitterly. 'You don't want me at Wallenshaw, do you? It's so unfair; you don't mind Jocelin working for you.'

'Steel is a man's world. Because you were so keen I've taken you into the works . . .'

'A measly typing job!'

'Now that you've had some experience you could easily get a good secretarial post in Head Office – or you could have done a few months ago; what the situation will be under the present set-up I really don't know.'

'Jocelin will be a manager before he's thirty.'

'I *am* a qualified metallurgist,' Jocelin said mildly.

There was a strong likeness between the two Tyndall children. They were both tall, with a slender, elegant build they had inherited from their mother. They both had non-descript light brown hair, but Tessa lightened hers to honey-blonde. They had grey eyes and dark, arching eyebrows which could give them a supercilious look. Tessa seemed, on casual acquaintance, to have the more forceful character, but that was a deceptive impression. Jocelin, eight years the elder, was quiet, but whereas Tessa blustered, argued and threatened and sometimes got her own way by sheer persistence, Jocelin wore down opposition by the use of implacable patience, allied to his considerable mental powers. His father respected his ability, even though Jocelin sometimes baffled him. Fred Tyndall was closer in temperament to his daughter; anyone who was against him was almost bound to be in the wrong and he brushed their opinions to one side. But he was not an unperceptive man and he had noticed with a strange uneasiness that although he frequently pushed an argument with Jocelin to a successful conclusion, his son would merely say calmly, 'I think you will find I'm right' and change the subject as if he no longer found it worth arguing with his father. A cold young devil, Fred thought him, and yet when his rare anger was aroused you suddenly found you had a tiger by the tail. He'd go far, that was certain; if it wasn't for this bloody nationalization, Fred would have confidently predicted that he himself would be the next Chairman of Smithson, Venner and Tyndall Limited, and that one day in the future he would be succeeded by his son.

As for Tessa, her ambition to get into management in the steel industry seemed ludicrous to Fred. He had been tickled at first by the thought of having both a son and a daughter in the Works and he had indulged Tessa's whim by asking the Personnel Director to find an opening for her in one of the offices, but now it seemed that she was beginning to take it seriously and that was more than he had bargained for. It was not reasonable, the idea of any of his men taking orders from a woman. It was a passing fad which Tessa would grow out of. Once she had settled down with a husband and family she would look back and laugh at the days when she had been jealous of her brother because he was a natural to follow in his father's footsteps.

As far as Fred was concerned the question of the cottage was settled and his daughter's smouldering anger might have subsided if his wife had not enquired, 'Does this girl . . . what's her name . . . ?'

'Anne Hardwick.'

'Does she say how she came to hear that the cottage would be vacant? I haven't told anyone because although I think it's a foregone conclusion that Nanny will be accepted, the next meeting of the Almshouses Committee isn't actually until Friday. It would be embarrassing if the members heard that Nanny's old cottage was being disposed of before they'd given a decision.'

'She doesn't say. From Nanny herself perhaps.'

Tessa put her coffee cup down with a bang that made Emmeline Tyndall wince for her fine china.

'I told Jeff Blackmore,' she said. 'And if he passed it on to this Hardwick girl I'll . . . I'll *murder* him!'

'What were you doing, gossiping with Jeff Blackmore, may I ask?' her father demanded.

Tessa avoided looking at him. 'I did some typing for him. I'd just heard the news about Nanny. I was full of my idea of taking on the cottage. I asked him if he knew any reliable workmen who'd do some work on it for me. I didn't think he'd stab me in the back like this, the beast.'

'Serves you right for letting your tongue run away with you. There's no point in getting annoyed with Jeff,' Sir Fred said. 'Nothing would change my mind about giving you that cottage.'

He got up from the table and absently kissed his wife on the forehead as he passed her. 'I'm off to London. Back in time for dinner tomorrow night, Em. Jocelin, you'll have to give Tessa a lift to work this morning.'

'Do you want anything done about the cottage while you're away?' Jocelin asked.

'Yes, deal with it for me, will you? Tell the girl she can have it – provided Nanny gets her almshouse.'

After he had left Tessa turned her attack on her mother, but Jocelin cut her short.

'You won't get Dad to change his mind, no matter how much you storm. I'm leaving for work in ten minutes. Are you coming like that or are you going to get dressed?'

Lady Tyndall appeared to have been taking very little interest in the argument that had raged over her breakfast table, but Jocelin was not surprised when she asked, as soon as Tessa had flung out of the room, 'Who is Jeff Blackmore?'

'One of our sponsored students who didn't take up his grant

until after the war was over, which means he's been late qualifying. He's just about to be appointed Coke Ovens Manager; a very good man.' Jocelin paused and added deliberately, 'Very popular with the female staff.'

'Unmarried?'

'Mm, and apparently determined to stay that way. He loves 'em and leaves 'em.'

'The trouble with Tessa,' his mother said thoughtfully, 'is that she's not qualified for anything. And she won't *listen*. If she'd exerted herself she could have gone up to Cambridge, but she said she wanted *real* experience. Such nonsense! I tried to talk her into all sorts of careers, but the only thing she would agree to do was that secretarial course, and that was because your father put his foot down and said he wouldn't have her lolling around at home any longer. If only she'd been old enough to get into one of the Women's Forces during the war! She would have been in her element changing wheels on lorries like Princess Elizabeth, but in peacetime one really can't let her become a motor mechanic. Any other girl would be over the moon at the idea of being given a flat in London, but Tessa just looks blank and says she doesn't want to leave her horse!'

It was a conversation that came back to Jocelin after he had talked to Anne. His father would have written a letter, and probably left it to be signed by someone else; Jocelin, with his recent service in the Army still fresh in his mind, knew the importance of the personal touch. He valued Wally Carless's good opinion; something almost like affection had grown up between them since they had come to know one another in the steelworks, in spite of Wally's outspoken political views and Jocelin's attempts to defend the value of private enterprise. They had liked one another well enough to laugh about it and agree to differ and Wally spoke tolerantly of Jocelin as a likely young fellow, even after the long-awaited nationalization had taken place and been followed by fewer changes than Wally thought right.

Wally was as taken aback as his wife when Jocelin called at their house early one evening, especially when he heard the reason.

'Mrs Brewster's old cottage!' he exclaimed. 'As ramshackle a place as you'll find hereabouts. Your father ought to be ashamed of himself, letting an old woman live in such a place.'

'She's an obstinate old lady and she wouldn't move,' Jocelin said. 'But of course you're right, the place has running water laid on, but no gas or electricity. Nanny did her cooking on a coal-fired kitchen range and used oil lamps. One of the reasons I've come round to see your daughter is to make sure she knows what she's taking on.'

'I know all about it,' Anne said quietly. 'It would still be a place of my own.'

'What will people say, you going to live in a pig sty when you could be here in your old home?' her mother demanded.

'Mrs Brewster kept it clean enough until she broke her hip. The roof is sound and it's not damp. And it's cheap.' She looked enquiringly at Jocelin. 'That's right, isn't it? You'll not put the rent up?'

'Nanny lived rent free – which is one reason why she wouldn't move. The rent will, of course, be low, considering how few amenities you will have.'

'I'm not worried about that.'

He was impressed by her quiet determination. There was something of Wally's doggedness about her. An attractive girl, too. Anne had found time to have her hair cut short in a boyish style, and she was wearing navy-blue slacks and a white cotton shirt with the arms rolled up above her elbows. She looked very businesslike and capable but, in spite of her short hair and trousers, extremely feminine. Not at all like a bereaved young mother, though. Presumably she had had time to get over her husband's death. At the back of Jocelin's mind was the thought that she would probably not live alone in the Brewster cottage for long: she would get married again. He was taken by surprise when Anne disclosed the rest of her plan.

In response to Jocelin's diffident enquiry, 'You won't be lonely?' she replied, 'I want to be alone and quiet so that I can study.'

She glanced at her mother and father and Jocelin saw that she had kept them in the dark about what she meant to do.

'I've had plenty of time to think since I came back to England,' Anne said. 'By the time I married Mel the war in Europe was over so I never faced up to the idea that I might lose him, not until he joined up again, and even then I thought more about how I would feel than about the practical side of how I would manage with a baby to bring up. When he was killed in Korea I began to regret that I had no proper career to fall back on.'

'What work did you do before you were married?' Jocelin asked.

'I was in the Accounts Department at Wallenshaw and I liked it. I was always good at figures.'

He thought that she was going to ask him to find her a job, but Anne's plan was more far-reaching than that.

'I want to take the exams and become a properly qualified accountant,' she said. 'Not Chartered, or even Certified, I don't aspire to that, but I think I could manage to become a Company Accountant.'

'You'll never do it!'

The automatic, unthinking response from her mother brought a shade of annoyance to Anne's face.

'Yes, I will,' she said obstinately. 'But I need peace and quiet. I can't work for my exams in a room where Pete's using a fretsaw, Dad's listening to the football on the wireless, you're doing the ironing and Melanie is running around under my feet the whole time.'

'You've had me to help you with Melanie for the last few months,' Beryl said. 'You'll miss that.'

'I will,' Anne said quickly. 'But I've thought it all out. I can get Melanie into the nursery school in Upbridge and once that's fixed up I mean to look for a part-time job doing accounts. I'll get a bike and put a safe seat on the back for Melanie – you'd help me with that, wouldn't you, Dad? – and I'll ride into Upbridge every day, drop her off at school and go on to work. In the evenings I'll study.'

They could all see defects in her scheme, but Jocelin thought it wise to bring his visit to an end before a full-scale family argument developed. He hoped Anne would succeed, even though he was doubtful whether she would really carry it through to the end. He made a mental note to keep in touch, if only out of curiosity to see how she got on.

The dispute raged furiously after Jocelin had left. Anne was fully awake to something that Jocelin had realized, too: that Beryl and Wally were aghast at her wish to break out of the accepted mould. She had been married and widowed and she had a baby; her role now was to stay quietly at home and bring up her child. Possibly she might marry again; they would accept that and be relieved for her. What they could not understand was her desire to involve herself in long hours of lonely study in order to build a career, and a professional career at that. Beryl had nothing to say against her taking a job, something nice in a shop or an office, not too demanding, but bringing in a welcome income; the idea of spending years chasing after an elusive qualification was something she would have supported if Anne had been a man; in a young widow it seemed a freakish ambition.

The thing that silenced Beryl eventually was the fact that it was Jeff Blackmore who had told Anne about the cottage. He'd make a good husband, would Jeff, once he'd settled down; he was going up in the world and he might just fancy a girl like Anne. But she couldn't let even that go by without a word of warning as soon as she had Anne to herself.

'I suppose it was good of Jeff to tip you off about the cottage,' she said grudgingly. 'How did he know you were looking?'

'It's no secret. Evelyn may have told him.'

'More likely you told him yourself,' Beryl said drily. 'You've "bumped into him by accident" more than once, haven't you? He's seen to that. You want to watch your step with that one.'

'Mum, for goodness sake! Jeff and I scarcely know one another.'

'Keep it that way. He's run through most of the girls in Brinthorpe – silly clunches – though to give him his due he's not left any little mementoes behind him. They do say he's carrying on with a married woman in Upbridge now.'

'The local rumour factory's been busy, hasn't it?'

'We take an interest in our neighbours, that's all. I'm just telling you Jeff's not steady, not like Terry.'

'He's not dull like Terry either,' Anne retorted. 'I dare say the girls ran after him.'

'Aye, that they did,' her mother admitted. 'They've only got themselves to blame if they made it easy for him. He'd be a good catch, would Jeff Blackmore, but you'd need to keep him at arm's length till you got his ring on your finger.'

'Thanks for the advice, but I don't need it. I've got no designs on Jeff or any other man. I've told you, Mum, I'm going to make my own way in the world.'

Because she was feeling defiant about it Anne went out of her way to make sure she saw Jeff to thank him for his help.

'It'll be a few weeks before I can move in,' she concluded. 'Pete and Dad are going to help me paint the walls and do a few repairs first. I've got to get some furniture together, too.'

'Are you going to be too busy to come on the outing to the Festival of Britain?'

'I can't afford to go jauntering off to London!'

'Come as my guest.'

It took her breath away, that casually uttered invitation. She shook her head uncertainly.

'No . . . no, I couldn't do that, Jeff. Besides, there's Melanie . . .'

'Your mum would look after her, just for one night. It's down on Saturday and back on Sunday, you know. Terry and Evelyn are going.'

'Yes, but . . .'

'Do you want to go?'

'I do,' Anne admitted. 'I've hardly ever been to London and it sounds as if it would be fun. All the same, no. Thanks for asking me, but I can't possibly come.'

She thought she had made her refusal definite enough to put him off, but Jeff sensed the regret behind her words and he persisted.

'You could do with a spot of amusement. You've had a rotten time. I thought the other day when I saw you out with Melanie that you looked moped.'

'I'm not moped, I'm bored,' Anne retorted. 'That's why I'm glad I'll soon have a house of my own to look after, however small. I've got nothing to do at home. Mum doesn't like me in the kitchen. She'd even do Melanie's washing if I didn't keep it away from her. The only useful things I've done lately are mend Dad's socks and make myself a summer dress.'

'And where are you going to wear that if you don't come to the Festival? Come on, Anne; change your mind.'

He was watching her intently, aware that she was wavering, but Anne repeated obstinately, 'I can't let you pay for me.'

'Why not?'

It was an awkward question. Anne tilted her chin, looked him straight in the eye and spoke with a bluntness that surprised both her and Jeff.

'It wouldn't be suitable. You're an unmarried man and I'm a widow. If I let you spend money on me you might start thinking you had some rights over me, and I won't stand for that. I've heard too much about your way with women, Jeff Blackmore; I won't have it said you've made me one of them.'

For a moment his lips tightened into a thin line, but he spoke lightly enough when he answered her. 'The old women of the village have been gossiping, have they? You should know how they exaggerate. It seems a pity for a few silly stories to spoil your chance of a trip to London. Come anyway – and pay your own way, if you insist.'

'I'll think about it,' was all Anne would say.

She mentioned it at home the next day when Evelyn and Terry came to Sunday dinner, carefully suppressing Jeff's offer to pay for her. To her surprise, her sister urged her to join the party.

'It would do you good to get away for a couple of days,' Evelyn said. 'Don't you agree, Mum? Anne ought to have a change before she goes and hides herself away in that horrible little cottage.'

'Anne's place is at home looking after her baby,' Beryl said, but both sisters recognized this as her automatic response while she took time to think it over.

'Who else is going?' she asked.

Evelyn ran through a list of names. 'Lots of Anne's old friends,' she concluded.

Anne, looking up from coaxing Melanie to eat up her greens and potatoes, caught the meaning look that passed between the two women and bent over the baby again to hide a smile. The list had included the names of several unattached men. What Evelyn was trying to convey to her mother was that some of Anne's old boy friends were still available and they might do well to put her in the way of meeting them again.

'I suppose it wouldn't do any harm,' Beryl conceded. 'Wally, what do you say to you and me treating Anne?'

When Anne found herself sitting next to Jeff on the train to London the following weekend she told him about the conversation. She was glad that she had spoken to him so frankly when he had tried to persuade her to go on the outing. It had cleared the air between them and made it possible for her to say, 'If Ron and Doug and Bill knew that my Mum had them lined up as possible second husbands for me they wouldn't be charging down the corridor in search of beer, they'd be running for their lives, poor things.'

'Hasn't she got her eye on me, too?'

'She doesn't think you're steady,' Anne retorted.

'Steady as the Rock of Gibraltar,' Jeff insisted, but he was laughing in tacit admission that he was not the pillar of respectability that Mrs Carless demanded.

It was easy after that to fall in with Jeff's suggestion that he and Anne should stick together, since they both wished to avoid involvement with anyone else. They made up a foursome with Evelyn and Terry and explored the South Bank of the Thames where the new Festival Hall had been built and the temporary buildings and gardens had been laid out. The Festival was due to end in September and there were throngs of people intent on seeing it all before it finished.

'It's been a success,' Jeff said. 'A good omen. I think things are going to start getting better all round. If you've finished gawping at the Skylon, young Anne, I'll take you to Battersea Fun Fair.'

They lost Evelyn and Terry in the Fun Fair and although Anne suspected that it was not by accident it was done so adroitly that she could not be quite sure. In the whirling colours of the swings and roundabouts, the music, the shouts and laughter of the crowd Anne forgot for a short time that she was the mother of a young daughter, a woman determined on a career which would make a worthwhile future for the pair of them. Astride a painted ostrich, her full cotton skirt hitched up, her hair blowing in the breeze, she felt young and careless. For a few short hours the aching sense of loss she had carried with her unremittingly since Mel's death faded away. As for Jeff, he was behaving like a carefree boy; no one would have believed that he had just had his thirtieth birthday. It was part of his attraction, Anne decided, this ability to throw himself single-mindedly into whatever he was doing.

'This is my last fling before I settle down to my new responsibilities,' he said in response to a comment from Anne.

He took hold of her arm and began to guide her through the crowd towards the exit.

'Your promotion, you mean?' Anne asked. 'I heard about that from Terry. Congratulations.'

'It's a beginning.'

'Terry sees you as Chief Engineer at Wallenshaw one day.'

Almost under his breath Jeff said, 'I'm aiming higher than that,' but before Anne could pursue it he went on, 'Have you had enough? Do you want to go back to the hotel?'

'I'm tired and my feet ache, but I'm reluctant to say goodbye to it all,' Anne admitted. 'I'd like to see the Houses of Parliament lit up. Can we do that from here?'

'It's a little way down the river. We'll take a taxi.'

'Such extravagance!'

He took her on a rapid tour of the floodlit buildings and ended up by paying off the taxi on the Victoria Embankment.

'We can walk from here and you can have a last glimpse of the lights on the South Bank from this side of the river.'

They went and leaned on the parapet with the dark river flowing below them.

'Have you had a good time?' Jeff asked.

'Marvellous, but it's made me feel a bit sorry for myself. Looking back I realize now how little time I had for being young.'

'You're still young, for goodness sake!'

'In years perhaps, but you know what I mean, Jeff. The war was on all the time I was growing up. We were terribly confined by the blackout, the restrictions, the air raids. There was a lot of gaiety about if you were the right age and could shut your mind long enough to the horrors to enjoy it, especially if you were in the Forces, but I just escaped being called up. I was committed to Mel by the time I was eighteen, married by the time I was nineteen, a mother the following year.'

She said nothing about her widowhood, but he knew it was in her mind.

'I'm not going to let Melanie make the same mistake,' Anne said. 'She's going to have a good life and I'll make sure she has time to enjoy it before she ties herself down.'

The sound of music and voices came across the river from the South Bank; the reflections of the lights shimmered in the water. A river patrol boat went by, a vague dark outline, small and purposeful, and the noise of it disappearing towards the City seemed to leave Anne and Jeff more isolated. Jeff put his arm round Anne's shoulders.

'You ought to have worn a jacket,' he said, his hand sliding down her bare arm.

'I'm not cold,' Anne said.

'Then why did you shiver?'

Anne didn't answer. Jeff laughed under his breath and turned her towards him, feeling for her chin to make her look up. He felt very large and solid, holding her tightly against him with his other arm. Anne had a confused feeling of being stifled, of panic, and of a surge of excitement which made her tremble.

'No, Jeff,' she said uncertainly. 'I don't want . . .'

'Yes, you do.'

It was like being overwhelmed by an irresistible natural force. His body engulfed her, his mouth drained all her strength away. For a few moments she collapsed against him, one hand clutching convulsively at the loose material of his shirt near his shoulder, then Anne twisted her head to one side.

'Let me go.'

When he took his arms away she had to reach for the stone balustrade to steady herself. She moved a few steps away from him and stood leaning against the wall, looking down into the river.

'It'll be just a year next week since Mel was killed,' she said. 'I miss him, of course I do. Sometimes it's almost unbearable. But I don't want anyone else.'

'You can't go on living like that for the rest of your life.'

'All I know is, I don't want to get involved with another man, not yet, not when I'm just beginning to work things out for myself.'

'It was only a kiss.'

'Was it?' Anne asked. 'It seemed to me that you were trying to get me to commit myself to something more than that.'

'We're very alike in many ways, Anne. Two individuals with strong ideas of what we want out of life. Is there any reason why we shouldn't give one another a little pleasure along the way?'

'Once I give in to you, you'll dominate me,' Anne said. 'I don't want to be taken over.'

'Do you understand how alone you're going to be? I don't mean isolated because you'll be living in that cottage. You're trying to step outside the class you were born into, just as I have. Think, Anne, about the boys and girls you once knew who went on to higher education. How many of them have you seen in Brinthorpe since you came home? I'm one of the few who still lives in the village and I'm beginning to wonder whether I may not have to move. It's the attitude that stifles me. Your father, for instance, says he approves of a working class lad becoming a manager, but in his heart he thinks I've copped out. He'll feel the same about you if you become a professional lady.'

'What's that got to do with you trying to make love to me?'

'I'm telling you you'll be lonely – as I am myself sometimes.'

'Oh? What about your married woman in Upbridge?'

'Her husband came back.'

He was laughing, but Anne could tell that he was annoyed. She began to walk away, towards the lights and the traffic.

'Let's go back to the hotel. I'm tired.'

He said nothing more, but after a minute or two he took her arm and drew it through his and they went slowly back to the hotel, walking in step with a rhythmic harmony as troubling to Anne as his kisses had been.

Chapter Two

One of the things that went with Jeff's new job was a personal secretary.

'I've got three girls who might be suitable,' the Typing Pool Supervisor told him. 'One of them, I must warn you, is Tessa Tyndall, Sir Fred's daughter.'

'I don't want her. It would make life too difficult.'

'I think you should give her an interview. It would be diplomatic.'

He saw Tessa last of the three, having already made up his mind that the person for the job was a forty-year-old spinster with greying hair and a no-nonsense manner.

Tessa slouched in and sat down with none of the diffidence to be expected from an inexperienced typist. Nor did she wait for Jeff to open the interview.

'I've been wanting to see you,' she said. 'I'm absolutely furious with you for telling Mrs Hardwick about Nanny's cottage. I wanted it – I told you I did.'

'Anne needs it more than you do.'

Jeff leaned back in his chair, not unwilling to be sidetracked from pretending to consider her as a secretary.

'I need my independence,' Tessa said. 'You don't know what it's like at home. Jocelin is the blue-eyed boy and Tessa is the nuisance who won't settle down and do what's expected of her.'

'What do they want you to do?'

'Oh, have a London Season, dance with a lot of chinless wonders, marry one of them and start producing grandchildren.'

'The programme doesn't appeal to you?'

'Why should it? I was brought up with Wallenshaw on my doorstep just as much as Jocelin was. He'll run the show one of these days – and probably the rest of the Company as well. Not me, though. They expect me to take up interior decoration or . . . or flower arranging.'

'There's nothing to stop you studying metallurgy if you really want to,' Jeff pointed out.

Tessa huddled lower in her chair. 'I'm not brainy,' she admitted. 'I'd have to cram for ages if I wanted to get into a university.'

'You ought to meet Anne Hardwick. You've got a lot in common, except that she's going to buckle down and study accountancy. Does that appeal to you?'

'Ghastly figures. No, thank you.'

'What *do* you want?' Jeff asked, beginning to lose patience with her.

'I want people to say "there goes Tessa Tyndall",' she said slowly. 'Not "Fred Tyndall's daughter" or "Jocelin Tyndall's sister" – "Tessa Tyndall".'

There was something about the way she spoke that made Jeff look more closely at this sulky, immature girl with ambitions greater than her capacity.

'To be a person in your own right,' he said. 'Yes, I can sympathize with that. You'll have to find a line of your own, though. Get away from S.V.T., or at any rate from Wallenshaw.'

'Are you going to give me this job?' she demanded abruptly.

'No.'

He expected her to be annoyed, but Tessa looked up with a sudden wide grin that transformed her sullen face into something younger and more attractive.

'I'll say one thing for you, Jeff B!ackmore, you give a straight answer,' she said. 'I knew I hadn't got a chance. Oh, God, isn't life boring? If only I could have had Nanny Brewster's cottage at least it would have been an interest, doing it up.'

'Interior decorating?' Jeff enquired.

'That's right, laugh at me!'

She stood up and stretched, tall, slim, with the grace of a cat for all her deliberately bad posture, and insolent in her disregard for him.

'Have I been here long enough to make it look as if I've had a proper interview?' she demanded.

Jeff consulted his watch. 'Five minutes less than I gave the woman who's getting the job.'

'And have you got a reason for turning me down that won't make me look a fool?'

'I prefer to work with an older woman,' Jeff said solemnly. 'I'm not to be trusted with the junior typists.'

'So I've heard. I've been wondering when it was going to come round to my turn.'

There was an infinitesimal pause and then Jeff said deliberately, 'I'll take you to the pictures in Upbridge tomorrow night.'

She had not expected him to accept the challenge she had thrown out to him. For one moment she looked uncertain and then, seeing the smile on his face, she said with a coolness that tried to match his own, 'All right. Straight from work?'

'Seven o'clock in the Red Lion. I'll give you a drink and a sandwich first.'

By the time Jeff and Tessa met at the Red Lion it was known that the Government had decided to go to the country; there would be a general election on the 25th October.

Jeff mentioned it in passing as he and Tessa sat in the saloon bar of the Red Lion with their drinks and sandwiches on the table in front of them, and discovered that politics was yet another subject in which Tessa took no interest.

'Daddy will be pleased,' she said. 'He thinks the Conservatives will get in and he'll get back all his old splendour – not to mention his money. Actually, I can't say I've noticed that nationalization's made much difference, except to his temper.'

'We haven't had a chance to make it work,' Jeff said. 'Are you going to be campaigning for the Tory candidate?'

'No, I think he's a boring old trout. He's what Daddy calls a safe man, which means he always votes the way the Party wants. I shouldn't think he's ever had an original idea in his life.'

'What about the Labour man? I don't suppose you know him,' Jeff asked.

'I have met him. Had to, once he'd become our M.P. A scruffy little man on the make. I saw him weighing up everyone who was introduced to him to decide how useful they could be in pushing him a bit farther up the ladder.'

'I won't say you're wrong about that,' Jeff admitted. 'Still, a good campaigner, and he's had a hard fight to get where he is.'

'Fortunately I don't come of age until a couple of weeks after the election so I don't have to decide how to vote.'

'You could support the Liberal woman,' Jeff suggested.

'Lesbian cow.'

Jeff swallowed some beer the wrong way and choked.

'Good, I've managed to shock you,' Tessa said. She looked blandly satisfied. 'We're going to be late for the film if we don't hurry.'

He followed her out of the pub, aware that he had lost ground in the unspoken contest that was going on between them. He took a surreptitious look at her as they walked down the road. Most women had to increase their pace to keep up with him unless he remembered to walk slowly and take short steps, but Tessa's long legs adapted easily to the length of his stride. Every other girl he had known would have gone to some trouble to dress up even for a simple visit to the cinema with him; Tessa was wearing flat shoes, thick dark stockings, a plaid skirt, a sweater which clashed with it and a knitted beret. She looked as if she had picked out her clothes at random from a heap on the floor, and yet she had an air about her that Jeff could not analyse, any more than he could understand why he was bothering with her at all.

It was not because of her father; indeed, that relationship made him wary of her. It was something about Tessa herself. She was a mass of contradictions: only half-educated, in spite of her expensive school, but by no means a fool; apparently uninterested in any serious subjects, though Jeff suspected that was a pose she had taken up to avoid comparison with her brilliant brother; too lazy to work for what she wanted, yet cherishing high ambitions. He did not admire her looks;

Tessa's long, bony face had none of the prettiness Jeff expected in a girl, none of the beauty he recognized in Anne, but Tessa's body was beautiful and her sexual appeal was powerful.

'What was the name of that girl who was chained to a rock and had to be rescued from a dragon by the chap on a flying horse?' he demanded as they entered the cinema.

'Andromeda,' Tessa replied without hesitation. 'Why?'

'You remind me of her.'

'I can't stand passive heroines. I would have teamed up with the dragon. With his fire power and my connections we would have gone far.'

He took her home in his car after they left the cinema and, because he thought she expected it, because of a nagging curiosity about her response, he slipped his arm around her, pulled her close and kissed her. He meant it to be a casual, exploratory kiss, but Tessa twisted in his hold, put both arms round his neck and kissed him back long and expertly.

When she drew away from him Jeff said, with a thickness in his voice that betrayed his reaction, 'Your mother is right, you ought to be married.'

Tessa evaded his attempt to take hold of her again and opened the car door.

'At least there's one bloody thing I'm good at,' she said.

She got out and walked away, without a backward look.

Her offhand attitude tantalized Jeff, but he held back from suggesting another meeting, partly because of the Tyndall connection and partly from a suspicion that Tessa might turn him down, if only to rile him. Anne was the girl he ought to cultivate, Jeff told himself. She was his sort, and beautiful into the bargain; a far better proposition than Tessa, who had probably only gone out with him in the hope of annoying her father.

In any case, the next thing Jeff heard about Tessa was that she was off to London. In the Tyndall household the result of the October election had been received with relief, not least because Sir Frederick relaxed into a mood of jovial good humour. The Labour Party had been defeated and on 13th November nationalization of the iron and steel industry came to an end. The new Conservative Government set up the Iron and Steel Holding and Realization Agency to hold the unsold iron and steel assets and a start was made on returning the shares which had been taken over to private hands. Fred Tyndall not only gave his daughter a flat in Kensington for her twenty-first birthday, he added a car as a bonus, and Tessa disappeared to London to become a trainee personnel officer in the Head Office of S.V.T.

The only word Jeff had from her was an early Christmas card with a scrawled message, 'Still chained to my rock, but let out on a long leash. Love and kisses. Andromeda.'

Since she did not include her address and he had no intention of asking for it, Jeff was unable to reply. The mocking 'love and kisses' stung him, after the way she had walked away from him when he had kissed her. He tore the Christmas card into small pieces and threw it away. Goodbye Tessa. He would call in and see Anne on his way home that afternoon.

*

Anne had settled into the small cottage, but had only just begun to make it cosy against the winter. It was sparsely furnished, but she had new linoleum on the floor and some old rag rugs made by her grandmother, which Beryl had turned out of the attic. She hated them, but Anne liked their faded pinks and blues and was grateful for the warmth under her feet.

One of the things she dreaded was getting home and finding the place cold and uninviting, but on the evening when Jeff looked in to see her she had come in to find a bright fire glowing in the kitchen range. It was one of Pete's good days and he had been in to light her fire for her. Anne felt tears of thankfulness coming into her eyes as she recognized, not for the first time, the depth of his inarticulate affection for herself and Melanie.

She began to strip off Melanie's coat and leggings. Melanie flapped her hands in the air.

'My hands stingle, Mummy,' she said.

'Do they, darling?' Anne kissed her quickly on her cold, frost-reddened face. 'That's a very good word. My hands stingle, too. Can you put your slippers on yourself while Mummy gets the tea? Clever girl!'

She had given Melanie her boiled egg, read her a story and was getting her ready for bed when Jeff knocked. She was about to call out 'Come in' when it occurred to her that it might not be prudent to invite in an unknown caller on a dark December evening. To find Jeff outside was a surprise, but the important thing was to get him inside and shut the door before all the warmth rushed out.

'Come along in and sit down, Jeff, while I take Melanie upstairs. Say goodnight to your Uncle Jeff, Melanie.'

She picked up the little girl and Melanie leaned out from her arms and gave Jeff a wet kiss on his cheek.

'I've got a warm wabbit to take to bed with me,' she told him, holding up her hotwater bottle in its cuddly rabbit cover.

'Very fine,' Jeff responded. 'Hug him tight. It's a nasty cold night.'

When Anne came downstairs he was looking at the cottage door, which opened straight into the living room.

'You ought to have a chain on this,' he said.

'Oh, Jeff, no one ever comes up here.'

'All the more reason to have a chain. I'll bring one over and fit it for you at the weekend.'

'Good of you,' Anne said, giving in. 'Any special reason for coming to see me tonight?'

'No, I just happened to think of you and decided to drop in and see how you were getting on.'

Anne opened the oven door and peered in. 'I've got a stew simmering away in here,' she said. 'Do you want some?'

'I wouldn't say no.'

'Your mum isn't expecting you home for a meal?'

'Mum expects me when she sees me.'

'She puts up with a lot from you,' Anne commented, poking at the potatoes she had put to boil on the hob. There would not be enough for herself and Jeff, but it would take too long to add more. He would have to fill up with bread.

'I'm thinking of going into a flat of my own in Upbridge,' Jeff said.

'That doesn't surprise me. I only wonder you haven't done it before.'

'I've been saving up my money. What I want is going to set me back a cool three thousand.'

He watched Anne lifting the heavy stewpot on to the top of the range. 'Can I do anything?'

'You can lay the table and fill the kettle so that I can put it on the hob for hot water for washing up.'

'Sure I'm not in your way, turning up without warning like this?'

'It's nice to have some company.'

It was not until they were seated at the table with steaming dishes of stew in front of them that Jeff said, 'You haven't told me how you're getting on.'

'I've got a job. Part-time and not too demanding. I'm working at Durham's, the drapers, keeping the books, sending out bills, that sort of thing. I'm doing a correspondence course in accountancy and I've managed to wangle myself into classes at the Technical College two days a week. I ought to be going to evening classes really, but that's more than I can manage, so I talked the Principal into letting me join the day-time classes. Most evenings after I've put Melanie to bed I have a meal, like this, and then do a couple of hours studying.'

'It's a hard life,' Jeff commented.

'Not as hard as some. I've got it organized. I get up early and prepare as much of my evening meal as I can. By the time I get Melanie up this room is beginning to warm through so that we can have breakfast in comfort. One thing about this enclosed grate, the fire is completely safe and I can leave it in when we go out so that the place doesn't get really cold. Pete is very good about coming in and freshening up the fire in the afternoons. He'd been in today before I got home.'

'You're cycling into Upbridge every day?'

'Yes, with Melanie on the back. She loves it, bless her. I leave her at the nursery school and go to work or my class. I do my shopping at lunchtime and all my housework and washing at the weekend.'

She saw something she suspected was pity in his expression and tilted her chin. 'I'm loving it.'

'It'll snow in the New Year.'

'The farmer at the top of the lane keeps it open as much as he can. He says there's not been many winters he hasn't been able to run a tractor down to the main road. I'm getting in a store of dry goods and tins, just in case we're cut off.'

The coming of the snow was something she secretly dreaded. She didn't want to think about it. She would have liked to have got away from talking about her situation, but Jeff said, 'I'm thinking about another girl I know who's got a car, and a flat of her own, and no worries or responsibilities, and yet she never seems happy. I wonder how she'd cope with what you're putting up with.'

'If she'd got a baby to bring up she'd probably do the same as me,' Anne said. 'How was the stew? Did you have enough?'

'It was first rate. Very filling.'

'It was meant to be,' Anne said. She had a moment's regret as she realized that her meal for the following evening had gone, but she dismissed it. Jeff's company was welcome on that bleak night and there was a satisfaction to be found in feeding a man which she did not get from coaxing spoonfuls into Melanie's mouth.

'I've nothing fancy for afters,' she said briskly. 'A piece of jam tart and a cup of tea?'

'That'll suit me. You're a good cook, Anne.'

'Oh, aye,' Anne said, with exactly the ironic intonation in her voice with which her mother greeted any praise.

She was filling the tea pot from the big black kettle on the hob when Jeff came up behind her and put his arms round her waist. Anne put the kettle of hot water down carefully.

'None of that, Jeff,' she said. 'If that's what you've come round for, you can go right now.'

Jeff stepped back. 'Just trying to show you how much I admire you,' he said. 'More than that, I respect you.'

'You've got a right funny way of showing respect,' Anne said drily. 'Keep your hands off me, Jeff Blackmore, or you needn't come again.'

But he did come again, once to fit the chain on the door, and then late one evening near to Christmas, and this time he brought a doll for Melanie, a bottle of wine, a sprig of holly and a piece of mistletoe.

'I've come to wish you a Merry Christmas,' he announced.

'It strikes me you've been celebrating already. I'm not sure I'll let you in,' Anne said, observing his high colour and dishevelment.

'I made an early get away from the works party. By heck, there'll be some funny steel made tonight! What I could do with is a strong cup of tea.'

'You certainly could! All right, come in, but be quiet because I've only just got Melanie off to sleep. She's all excited about Father Christmas. Wanted to know if I was quite sure he'd know she'd be staying with Granny and Grandpa. Is that doll for her?'

'I won it in a raffle at the party. That's what gave me the idea of coming round. Just the thing for Melanie, I thought.'

'She'll love it. I'll hide it away. Thanks, Jeff, it was a kind thought. Here, drink this. There was a cup already in the pot.'

They sat in silence for a few minutes until Anne looked up and caught Jeff looking at her with a sheepish air that made her laugh.

'Feeling more sober?' she asked.

'I was all right. The cold air got hold of me, that's all.'

'Cold air, my foot! Too many pints of Batemans' Brown, that was your trouble. Have you had anything to eat?'

'I had a cheese sandwich mid-day. Some crisps and things at the party.'

'No wonder your head went round! Could you eat bacon and eggs?'

'I could that! Thanks, Anne. What about you?'

'I had a chop half an hour ago.'

By the time she had cooked him bacon and eggs Jeff had opened the bottle of wine.

'I would have thought that was the last thing you needed,' Anne said with strong disapproval.

'One glass won't hurt me, especially with food. I've got a head like iron in the ordinary way. Come on, Anne, drink a Christmas toast with me.'

She had no wine glasses, so they drank it from tumblers,

with Anne keeping a sharp eye on the amount Jeff poured into them. It was not a good wine and it had not benefited from being jolted around in Jeff's car and opened immediately after being out in the cold night air. Anne thought it sharp, unpleasant stuff, but to please Jeff she drank it down.

'Were all the nobs at the party?' she asked idly.

'Indeed they were. The outgoing Chairman of S.V.T., no less; and Sir Fred, looking like a cat that's been at the cream, so I guess they'll be announcing him as new Chairman soon; Lady Tyndall, His High and Mighty Lordship Mr Jocelin Tyndall and Her High and Mighty Ladyship Miss Tessa Tyndall.'

Jeff stopped. Tessa had ignored him. His face darkened and his hand clenched round the glass so hard that it came near to breaking as he remembered the way she had drawled 'How do you do?' and looked him in the face without a flicker of recognition.

'Are they really like that?' Anne asked. 'Snooty and stand-offish? I liked what I saw of Jocelin. He was really helpful to me over this cottage.'

'I dare say that pleased him, playing the Lord of the Manor.' Jeff struggled with himself and added reluctantly, falling back on the local idiom, 'He's none so bad, is Jocelin.'

'It's my belief you're jealous of him.'

'Aye, maybe. Because of the war we entered the Works at the same time. We've both been promoted recently. We're both on the way up and the nearer you get to the top the fewer places there are. I watch him like a hawk because I think he's got the edge on me, being Sir Fred's son. One of these days he'll inherit his dad's financial stake in the firm now that it's going back into private hands. That'll give him a seat on the Board. If I'm to get to be a director it'll have to be through merit.'

'All the more credit to you if you get there. You've set your sights high, haven't you, Jeff?'

'No harm in being ambitious.'

'Not unless you let it rule your life. When we ran races at school we were told not to look back over our shoulders to see if anyone was catching us up.'

'What I see is Jocelin Tyndall already ahead of me and drawing away into the distance,' Jeff retorted. He picked up the wine bottle. 'We might as well finish this, it'll not be worth keeping.'

'Not with you driving home tonight,' Anne said firmly, taking the bottle out of his hand.

'I could stay.'

He looked at her, half smiling and half serious, and Anne looked away, unable to meet his eye.

'No.'

'Why not, Anne?' Jeff took her hand in his, gently rubbing his thumb over the soft skin on the inside of her wrist. 'We'd be wonderful together. You know that as well as I do. And no one would know. I've moved into my flat in Upbridge. I'm independent. No one asks now where I've been if I don't come home all night.'

'How are you going to stop a three-year-old baby telling everyone that Uncle Jeff came to breakfast?'

Anne took his empty plate away from the table and carried it over to the sink. As she put it down her hands were trembling.

Jeff came up behind her and put his arms around her, pinning her against the sink. 'Is that your only objection? All right, let me stay for an hour. Just one short hour, Anne.'

She tried to twist away from him, but as soon as she turned he brought his mouth down on hers and it was the same as it had been in London, except that now she was more lonely than she had been then, further away from the anniversary of Mel's death, and living under conditions that reminded her constantly of her short married life. Somewhere at the back of Anne's mind a cold little voice told her that she was being a fool, but she could not entirely resist the throb of the blood in her veins as she let her mouth respond and her body grow pliant under his hands.

'That's better,' Jeff whispered in her ear. 'Come over to the fire.'

She let him lead her over to the circle of warmth, but when Jeff tried to draw her down on to his knee in her one armchair she shook him off. To give herself time to think Anne took the lid off the hob and picked up the scuttle full of coke to renew the fire. Jeff got up and took it away from her.

'Here, let me. It's too heavy for you.'

'I do it all the time,' Anne said.

That's what I need a man for, she thought bitterly. To carry my heavy loads and share my responsibilities, not just to pleasure me when he's been to a party and feels like having sex. She watched Jeff's easy strength as he lifted the heavy scuttle and put it down, and could have wept.

When he took her in his arms again she shook from head to foot, but this time she clung to him, giving him back kiss for kiss, twisting her fingers into the hair at the back of his head, undulating her body against his as Jeff's lips moved over her eyelids, her nose, her ear.

Jeff pulled back the neck of her sweater, brushing her soft skin with kisses. With his lips against the hollow at the base of her throat he said, 'Anne, I want you like hell. Undress for me, darling. Let me see you naked. Here in front of the fire. A few cushions. We can be perfectly comfortable.'

Anne shook her head slowly, but Jeff did not even see that last despairing effort at refusal. He was tossing cushions off the chairs on to the floor. I meant to be sensible, Anne thought. I didn't mean it to come to this. I can't stop now. And it isn't Jeff I can't stop, it's me.

When Jeff turned round and found her still standing passive and unmoving, where he had left her, he went to her and began to help her to undress, his hands moving unfalteringly over the fastenings. He's had plenty of practice, the voice in Anne's head reminded her: you fool, you fool.

He lowered her to the floor and knelt beside her, touching her gently, murmuring his pleasure as he cupped one breast in his hand. Then he left her to toss off his own clothes with impatient hands. Anne lay and watched him. He was powerfully built; a fine, vigorous man, and ready as a stallion to claim his mare. As he lowered himself towards her, Anne arched her body to meet him.

'I want you, too,' she answered him at last. 'Yes, I do. Oh, Jeff, be quick, be quick!'

He took her twice, once in the blind passion her cry had

engendered, and again before he left, more gently, using art and patience to bring her to a brilliant climax.

It was three o'clock in the morning when he went. Anne huddled a few clothes round her and went with him to the door. A quick, chilly kiss and he was gone. She put the chain on the door with stiff, awkward fingers and stood leaning against it listening to the sound of his car disappearing down the valley.

She had been too proud to cry in front of him. Now, looking round the disordered room, she savoured to the full the depths of her folly. She stumbled on one of the cushions and automatically picked it up and dropped it on the chair. The fire was nothing but a dull glow, the lamp was guttering. The cloth was still on the table. In the sink the greasy frying pan, Jeff's used plate and two wine glasses sticky with dregs waited to be washed up. She had to be up by half past six and out of the house by eight o'clock. Her body seemed strangely heavy. Her breasts felt bruised and her thighs were sticky.

The water in the kettle was still warm. Anne put the dirty dishes on one side and used it to wash herself. And all the time as she soaped and dried herself, tears of exhaustion and humiliation ran in an unceasing stream down her face.

When Anne got home the following evening a sheaf of flowers had been laid on her doorstep. A dozen red roses. There was a card with them, 'Thank you, darling. Love, J.'

At that moment she hated him. Expensive, out-of-season, give-away flowers. How was she to explain them if anyone came round? And the message. Patronizing. A form of words he thought he ought to use to a woman whose body he'd had. There was only one word in it she would have valued, if he had meant it; but what Jeff felt for her was not love, any more than what she felt for him was.

She was tempted to put the roses straight into the dustbin, but Melanie was already saying, in pleased surprise, 'Pretty flowers', and the scent of them was sweet as she took off the cellophane wrappings. Anne cut the ends and stuck them in a jug for lack of a proper vase and something in her was fiercely pleased when the buds darkened and dropped without even coming into full flower.

*

Anne and Melanie spent the whole of Christmas week back home once more with Wally and Beryl. Anne saw nothing of Jeff though she expected to bump into him every time she went out into the village street, since he must surely be visiting his mother. It was not until New Year's Eve that they met again at Evelyn and Terry's house when the two families united to see in the New Year. All through the evening Anne and Jeff avoided one another, and Anne raged inwardly at the prudent way Jeff guarded his eyes. When she carried Melanie upstairs to be put down to sleep she half expected to find him lurking on the landing, but he had not followed her.

As the largest and darkest man present, Jeff was sent outside to be the first-footer. When he was let in as midnight struck, his face flushed from the cold, a few drops of rain shining in his hair, Anne felt a thrill of pride. He was a magnificent-looking man and he had chosen her. What galled her, and made her despise herself, was that Jeff showed no sign of wanting to claim her openly. Why not? While all around her kisses and good wishes were exchanged, Anne asked herself whether she would accept Jeff if he asked her to marry him, and the answer was that she would.

Physically they were well suited, that side of their marriage would present no difficulties, and in other respects why shouldn't Anne make Jeff a good wife? She was good-looking, intelligent, had already proved herself as a home-maker. And yet she knew in her bones that it was a question Jeff would never ask.

Little Melanie might be a stumbling block, except that Jeff seemed carelessly fond of her. Perhaps he sensed that Anne doubted whether the passion that had raged between them would last. It was not the same as the sweet, romantic love she had experienced in her early days with Mel. This was a devouring sexual hunger that frightened her by its intensity. She had been swept away by it once, and could be again, if she did not hold on to her resolve not to form one of Jeff's harem. She deserved something more than that, for Melanie's sake as well as her own. Fidelity, for one thing, and the formal bond of marriage. As for the career about which she had talked so emphatically, Anne knew that she would throw up her plans in order to marry Jeff if he asked her. But he was not going to ask her.

They could not avoid exchanging a kiss. Jeff's lips brushed over hers. Only they knew that his hand on her arm was gripping it to the bone.

As he released her he said very softly, 'When are you going back to the cottage?'

'The day after tomorrow.'

On Thursday as soon as it grew dusk Anne put the chain on the door. She waited, every nerve strung taut, but Jeff did not come. The following night she took the same precaution, put out the lamp early and went to bed, intending him to find the cottage in darkness. Braced for the sound of his car turning into the lane, she could not sleep, even after hours of lying awake and knowing that the time had long since gone past when Jeff might have visited her. Had he repented, as she had done, of that one tumultuous night? She had not thought so on New Year's Eve.

He came on Saturday, in the middle of the evening. Melanie was asleep and Anne was washing up after her evening meal, listening to a programme on the battery wireless which had been her Christmas present from Wally and Beryl. Above the sound of the music she heard a car come up the lane and stop. Anne dropped the tea towel and went quickly across the room, intent on keeping him out, but when the cold links of the chain were in her hand she waited, leaning against the door. She had been alone with Melanie all day, and Melanie, a little spoilt after all the petting she had received over Christmas, had been difficult to amuse. Because they had been away Anne had had less housework and washing to do and she was not as exhausted as she often was on Saturday nights. She would have welcomed some adult conversation, but it was the memory of Jeff's lovemaking that held her trembling with indecision as his car door slammed and the sound of his footsteps approached.

Anne thrust the chain into place as Jeff reached the door. She knew he must have heard it go home.

'It's me, Anne – Jeff,' he said. 'Let me in.'

Anne backed away from the door. 'Go away, Jeff,' she said.

'Come on, Anne. Don't be daft, girl. Let me in. It's beginning to snow.'

'Then you'd better get home,' Anne said, gathering strength now that she had rebuffed him once.

'I can't talk to you through the door. Open it up and tell me what's wrong.'

She opened the door a crack, but without taking off the chain. It made her feel ridiculous, peering at Jeff through a narrow slit. He stood there, big and smiling and impatient, sure that she was going to relent. Behind him she could see in the shaft of light a few snow flakes swirling against the black sky.

'If I let you in you'll take it for granted that you're going to make love to me,' she said.

'And why not? Wasn't it good enough for you last time?'

'It's not the way I want to live, carrying on a hole-in-the-corner affair with you.'

She was holding her breath. If at that moment Jeff had said that he loved her, that he wanted to bring it out in the open, that he would make her his wife, Anne would have opened the door and thrown herself into his arms. But Jeff, after a moment's pause, descended to coaxing.

'Come on, love. You don't mean it. You're too much of a woman to live alone, and I'm the man for you, you know that as well as I do.'

He slipped a hand through the narrow opening and tickled her under the chin, an insinuating, teasing little caress which made Anne's nerves crawl with desire for him, until the sensation was swept away by a wave of indignation. How dare he treat her like some mindless little kitten.

'You're not coming in and that's flat,' she said. 'Take your hand away or I'll shut it in the door.'

He still didn't believe her, but he withdrew his hand and the next moment he was looking at the door which had been slammed in his face and listening to the sound of the key being turned in the lock.

Jeff turned away, as puzzled as he was indignant. What

reason did Anne have for sending him packing? He had believed that she was as keen to continue their affair as he was. She had been magnificent, once she had got over her first reluctance, on that one night they had had together. How could she pretend to be unwilling for a repeat performance? What did she want from him? A wedding ring?

As he started up the car Jeff considered that possibility. She came from a conventionally respectable background; she might feel that having shown him what she was made of she could bargain her way into a permanent arrangement. If so, she had mistaken her man. It was not what Jeff wanted. He supposed he would get married – one day – but not to Anne. He was looking for something different; he was not sure what it was, he only knew that it was not Anne.

He turned his car out of the lane and drove along the road towards Upbridge, going slowly because of the snow which drove into the windscreen and blocked the wipers. A mile down the road he saw a car drawn up by the side of the road. A figure stepped forward and flagged him down, a woman. As he slowed down Jeff saw that it was Tessa Tyndall.

'Oh, it's you,' she said, as he wound down the side window. 'I've been incredibly stupid and run out of petrol. Do you carry any spare?'

'No.'

'You'll have to drive me home then.'

She put her hand on the door, but Jeff did not unlock it.

'Come on,' Tessa said impatiently. 'I'm freezing.'

'I don't pick up strange women in my car at night.'

'I'm not a stranger, am I? Come on, Jeff, don't play games. Hardly anyone comes along here at this time. What do you expect me to do?'

'Walk.'

She jumped backwards with a startled yelp as he put the car in motion. Glancing in the rear view mirror he could just see her, standing in the middle of the road, unable to believe that he meant what he said.

Jeff drove half a mile down the road to a point where it curved to the left then, out of sight of Tessa, he stopped and waited. It was twenty minutes before she came along, limping in flimsy shoes, a fur jacket huddled round her shoulders. Jeff opened the door and the light inside his car came on. Tessa climbed in beside him and slumped down in the seat.

'I could bloody kill you,' she said.

'Don't swear at me. If you ask me for a favour say "please". And next time we meet at a Works party say "Hello, Jeff", not "How do you do" in that nimmy-pimmy voice.'

He started the car. There was a long silence and then, unexpectedly, Tessa began to laugh.

'You've got the nerve of the devil,' she said, with more admiration than rancour. 'I've ruined these shoes, my feet are wet and I'm freezing. I could do with something to warm me up. How about buying me a drink? Please.'

'I've got a bottle of rum in my flat,' Jeff said. 'That'll warm you.'

Chapter Three

The snow that fell on the night of Jeff's visit was no more than
a flurry. Anne and Melanie treated it as a joke, sliding down
the hill on the bicycle and only just managing to scoop up a
handful for a snowball.

'Not a bit like the snow in Canada,' Anne told her daughter.
'Do you remember?'

Melanie said 'Yes', but Anne saw that she had no real
memory of the deep soft snow covering the prairie.

The following week there was a heavier fall and it was no
longer funny. Anne woke early and the cold clear light reflected
on the ceiling warned her what to expect when she pulled back
the curtains. Outside the world was white, all the normal
features of the landscape merging into unfamiliar mounds and
hollows. Every fence post had a round cap of snow and the
branches of the trees were etched in black and white against
a sullen yellow sky.

Anne went downstairs and lit the fire, automatically following her usual routine. She washed and dressed and laid the
table for breakfast. Melanie came thumping down the stairs,
still in her pyjamas, one arm in and one arm out of her
dressing gown.

'Mummy, mummy, snow, snow, snow!'

She held her arms out wide, trying to convey the immensity
of the snow.

'Yes, lots of snow,' Anne agreed. 'Come here and let me
wash your face.'

They had their breakfast. Anne hesitated with her hand on
the teapot and then made herself a cup of instant coffee and
drank it black, hoarding the milk for Melanie, just in case

there was any trouble about getting into town for a fresh supply.

That was the moment when she faced up to the realization that it was going to be difficult to get out of the cottage and down the lane.

'We'd better start early today,' she said. 'Mummy will have to push the bike until we get down to the main road. Come on, let's dress you up warm.'

The door of the cottage opened inwards and with it came a drift of snow which had to be scraped up and thrown outside before Anne could go out to the bicycle shed. The snow on the path outside was just over her ankles, which did not seem too bad, but in places where it had drifted it was knee high. And there was more to come, she thought, looking at the threatening sky.

With Melanie strapped in to the box seat on the back of the bicycle Anne struggled out of the gate and into the lane. It was hard going because the snow clogged the spokes of the wheels. Melanie was singing a meaningless little song,

'Lots of snow, lots of snow,
Lots and lots and lots and lots and lots and lots . . .'
She swayed happily from side to side.

'Keep still,' Anne said. 'Don't make it more difficult for me.'

'Is it like Canada, Mummy?'

'It's drier in Canada and colder. The snow is like powder. And the sun shines. This is nasty, wet stuff.'

She spoke in short gasps as she pushed through the snow lying on the uneven surface. The lane was no more than a cart track and deeply rutted. The narrow wheels bit through the soft snow into the concealed ruts beneath. Melanie was having a bumpy ride. Anne's arms and shoulders ached, trying to keep the bicycle upright. She veered towards what seemed like a smoother patch, but instead of the hard surface of the lane her foot met no resistance. She plunged down, waist high in a snow-filled ditch. The bicycle skidded away on its side, wheels spinning, with Melanie still strapped into her seat.

For a moment Anne was too shocked to move, then she heard Melanie crying and calling to her and she floundered out of the ditch and crawled towards her. Melanie had fallen in soft snow and she was more frightened than hurt. Her small face was scarlet, her mouth was wide open and she was bawling furiously.

'Darling, are you all right?' Anne's hands felt her anxiously. 'Poor baby, I'm sorry.'

Melanie cried all the more loudly, refusing to respond to Anne's hugs and kisses. Laboriously Anne clambered to her feet and righted the bicycle. Once she was upright again Melanie's tears began to subside.

'We can't go on,' Anne said. 'We'll have to go home again, Melanie.'

'No school?' Melanie asked, her mouth drooping ominously.

'No school for you and no work for me,' Anne said. 'Now don't start crying over that, please. You'll have Mummy to play games with you all day.'

It was even harder pushing the bicycle up hill. Anne admitted to herself now that she had been a fool to set out. How had she expected to get home in the dark, pushing all the way, and with the possibility of more snow? She had wanted to prove that all the people who had told her she would never last out the winter in the cottage had been wrong. Pride, that's what it had been, and pride had been her downfall.

She made hot Bovril for them as soon as they got in. There was a dull ache in her side and she guessed she had wrenched her muscles. No use paying much attention to it because there were chores which had to be done. She brought in as much coke as she could manage and filled every receptacle she could find with water in case the pipes froze. They would be down to tinned milk by the end of the day and she had little in the way of fresh fruit or vegetables, but there were plenty of substitutes in her store of food.

'We shan't starve,' she said aloud. 'Sausages for dinner, Melanie; we'd better eat those up first. Bangers and mash and baked beans.'

The day passed successfully. Anne, exercising a skill her Canadian mother-in-law had taught her, baked some bread and the warm, yeasty smell filled the kitchen. Melanie played with her games and toys. Anne grinned ruefully to herself as she heard her telling her doll earnestly, 'Mummy didn't *mean* to frow you in the snow, darlin'.'

Towards evening a wind got up. Anne pulled back the curtain and looked out. An impenetrable curtain of snow was swirling between the cottage and the fields beyond.

The next morning there was no question of leaving the house. Anne even had difficulty in getting the door open. She shovelled the snow away from the step, wondering why she was bothering, since she had no intention of going anywhere and was not likely to have any visitors. The wind had dropped and the sky had cleared to a misty blue with a weak sun shining through.

'Can I make a snowman?' Melanie demanded.

Anne hesitated, but the fresh air would be good for them and the exercise might loosen up her stiffening muscles. She cleared a larger space and they built up a mound of snow with a smaller round on top and decorated the face with pieces of coke for eyes and a nose. Anne refused to allow him any clothes, in spite of Melanie's conviction that snowmen wore scarves, but she made him a paper hat and skewered it to his head with a sliver of wood.

'Mummy, there's a man on sticks,' Melanie said.

Anne, her attention given to the snowman, responded absentmindedly, 'What, darling?'

'Sticks. A man on sticks.'

Anne looked where Melanie was pointing. Coming towards them across the snow-covered field was a man on skis.

'He's ski-ing,' she told Melanie. 'What a good idea. That's what we ought to learn to do.'

They stood and watched him. Melanie waved excitedly.

'He's coming to see us,' she said. 'Is it Father Christmas, Mummy?'

'No, ducky, you don't get Father Christmas twice in one year. It's . . . well, what do you know, it's Mr Tyndall.'

Jocelin Tyndall, in black trousers and a scarlet, hooded anorak, with a pack on his back, was not unlike a modern Santa Claus, she thought in amusement, and Melanie was right, he was coming to see them.

'I used to do this for Nanny Brewster,' Jocelin Tyndall

explained as he removed his skis and took the pack off his back. 'I've brought you a few supplies, just in case you weren't prepared for being snowed in.'

'Melanie thought you were Father Christmas, and it seems she was right,' Anne said, watching him pile up food on the kitchen table.

'I got to know the things Nanny valued most over the years and I've brought the same for you. Brussels sprouts, onions, carrots, some stewing steak, cooking apples, butter, bread, eggs and milk.'

'You must be pretty confident about your ski-ing to carry eggs!' Anne commented.

'I picked them up from the farm at the top of the road. If you are in any real difficulty they are prepared to put you up for a few nights, provided I can get you up there. What about it?'

'I'd rather manage here. I've got a good stock of food and fuel. Not that the things you've brought won't be a help,' she added hastily.

'I thought perhaps some sweets might be welcome for the little girl,' Jocelin said with a diffidence Anne found endearing.

She looked at the expensive box of chocolates and suppressed a smile, or thought she had, but Jocelin noticed the small twitch of her lips.

'Are they wrong for her?' he asked.

'A bit sophisticated for a three-year-old,' Anne admitted. 'But very much appreciated by her mum! It must have taken all your ration for the month.'

'I never use my sweet ration. I believe Mum exchanges the coupons for sugar for jam-making. There, that's everything. Now, is there anything I can do for you before I go? Anything heavy you need shifting? Anything else I can bring you if the snow persists?'

'Oh, I do hope it won't!' Anne exclaimed. 'I really ought to make a push to get into work. Did they say at the farm whether they were going to try to open up the lane?'

'They're working on it from their end, but it's a slow process.'

'I tried to get out yesterday,' Anne told him. 'We had a tumble in the ditch.'

'Any harm done?'

'I pulled a muscle or something,' she admitted, putting her hand to her side. 'If you could fetch me in some more coke I'd be grateful.'

She watched him with a certain degree of disbelief as he shovelled coke and carried it indoors. The Tyndall family had always been like the inhabitants of another world to Anne. The sight of Jocelin Tyndall doing her menial tasks made her feel that everything had gone topsy-turvy.

He made very little of it, working quickly and with a strength she would not have suspected. When they had met over the negotiations for the cottage she had thought him a languid specimen, with his long, elegant limbs and quiet speech, but now she saw that what Jocelin had was control. He exerted himself just as much as was necessary for the task in hand. She had sensed it as he had skied down the hill towards her. No spectacular swoops and flurries of snow, just an easy bending of knees and hips, a curve across the white hillside, and he was at the door, without having made any apparent effort.

A disciplined man, and not only in a physical sense; he would think in the same way, logically and dispassionately, until the problem in hand was solved. Anne remembered that Jeff had spoken of him as a rival. At first sight it seemed to her that Jocelin had all the advantages, in spite of Jeff's ability and cleverness, and yet . . . Jeff was ideally suited to his environment; he had a toughness which it was difficult to believe that this man, with his diffidence and his mouse-brown hair falling into his eyes, could match. If they moved up the ladder together they might make an ideal team, complementing one another's qualities. Jocelin would see that, but would Jeff? It was all or nothing for Jeff.

'Anything else?' Jocelin asked.

'Nothing, except that I'd like to get a message to my mum to let her know I'm all right.'

'I'll see to that.' He glanced round at the warm, cluttered kitchen. 'You certainly look comfortable enough.'

It occurred to Anne belatedly that she ought to offer to pay for the food he had brought them, but as soon as she mentioned it she saw from his surprise that she had made a mistake. She saw, too, that although he had not expected payment he was afraid of offending her by refusing to take her money.

'Look, we're being silly,' Anne said abruptly. 'I've no objection to accepting it as a present if that's what you intended. But you must take something in return; stay and have dinner with us. We're having home-made vegetable soup, scrambled eggs on toast and rice pudding – with stewed apple now that you've brought us some.'

He accepted, apparently with pleasure. Too polite by half, Anne thought to herself. No need to look that delighted at an invitation to share a nursery meal with a three-year-old girl.

Conversation was limited by the necessity to see that Melanie was eating properly. As usual, Anne's food cooled on the plate while she attended to her daughter, but fortunately Melanie was behaving well, fascinated by this strange man at their table.

'You're not my Uncle Pete,' she told him.

'No,' Jocelin agreed.

'This is Mr Tyndall,' Anne informed her.

'Mr Trindle,' Melanie said.

'Tyndall.'

'I *said*. Mr Trindle walks on sticks.'

'He's a very clever man. Eat up your rice pudding and then you can have one of the beautiful chocolates Mr Tyndall brought you.'

It was better when Melanie, her mouth wiped and her pinafore removed, was allowed down from the table to play on the floor at their feet.

'Coffee?' Anne asked. 'Only instant, I'm afraid. I miss my Canadian coffee.'

'Did you enjoy living in Canada?' Jocelin asked.

'Not much,' Anne admitted. 'But the circumstances were not ideal. If Mel – my husband – had lived and we'd got over the difficult times while Melanie was tiny and we hadn't any money then I think I could have learned to love it. The fault was more in me than in Canada; I wasn't ready for it.'

'Is Melanie named for the two of you?' he asked with a smile.

'Yes, it was Mel's idea. If she'd been a boy she would have been Melvin, after him.'

'It's a pretty name and she's a beautiful little girl.'

'She's very like her father.'

Jocelin glanced at her, but made no comment, although the thought in his mind was that Melanie got her looks from her mother, too.

He looked at his watch and Anne asked, 'Do you have to go?'

'I've got a quarter of an hour. I'll ski straight down to the Works.'

'That'll make them stare,' Anne said, amused by the thought of the man on the gate watching Mr Jocelin Tyndall arriving in this unorthodox way.

'They're used to my small eccentricities. I'm working odd hours at the moment because we're experimenting with oxygen lancing, as perhaps you already know.'

Anne shook her head. 'I don't know a lot about steelmaking,' she admitted. 'I know about how we dig the ore out of the ground, turn it into pig iron and then melt it down again to turn it into steel, but that's about as far as my knowledge goes.'

'You should be ashamed of yourself, with the most fascinating industry in the world on your doorstep and a first class steelmaker in your own home! Well, I won't bore you with technical details, but just to save your face in case your father talks about it I'll tell you that we're using oxygen in the ladle as a desiliconizing agent before the charge is placed in the furnace and the results so far are encouraging; up to thirty per cent output gains – and we can do with all the advantages we can get.'

'Business is good at the moment, isn't it? Wallenshaw is working at full capacity – that's something I have heard my dad say.'

'There's a boom in steel, partly because of the Korean War,' Jocelin admitted. 'There's bound to be a downturn in a few years' time. That's when the works with the technical innovations will come into its own, or so I maintain. I'd like to see a lot of money spent on bringing Wallenshaw up to date.'

'Sir Frederick will be able to fix that,' Anne said. 'He is going to be the new Chairman of S.V.T., isn't he?'

'Yes, it was announced yesterday. I'd like to think he'll still see it my way when it comes to investment in Wallenshaw, but you get a different perspective when you get to the top of the mountain. Company strategy may dictate something different.'

'So my dad was right when he said we'd be better off under nationalization!' Anne said.

Jocelin looked up quickly from his coffee cup and saw that she was teasing him, but he chose to answer her seriously.

'I sometimes wonder whether these people who favour nationalization have followed it through to a logical conclusion,' he said. 'From a Company point of view Wallenshaw still performs a useful function, but if you look at the steel industry in Britain as a whole it might be better to close it.'

'*Close* Wallenshaw? You can't mean it!'

'Think about it. It's a medium-size nineteenth century works in dire need of modernization and all the current thinking is towards economy of size. It's isolated and yet it's close to another major steelmaking centre. As long as that complex belongs to a separate company, and as long as we can hang on to our markets, then Wallenshaw is a viable concern. But suppose we were all under one ownership and a decision was made to go in for major development at Scunthorpe? It would have to be at the expense of works like Wallenshaw.'

'You've shaken me,' Anne said. 'I've never thought of it in that way before. But there's nothing else at Wallenshaw! What would all the people do?'

'Ah, now we're into the realm of social policy and I haven't got time to deal with that today.'

He got up, laughing at her worried face. 'It's not going to happen overnight; it may not happen at all. That's why I'm fighting to prove the advantages of oxygen steelmaking. And why we're putting in the new sinter plant. Jeff Blackmore is in charge of that. He's related to you in some way, isn't he?'

'My sister is married to his brother.'

'That's right, there's a brother. I can't remember his name, but he's a salesman.'

'Terry.'

'My Uncle Terry and my Uncle Jeff and my Uncle Pete and my Uncle Trindle,' Melanie said from the floor with a certain consciousness of her own cleverness.

'You're showing off,' her mother told her. 'I'm sorry, Mr Tyndall. She thinks all grown-ups are either aunts or uncles.'

'Count me as an honorary uncle,' Jocelin said. 'Now I really must go. Goodbye, Mrs Hardwick, and thank you for giving me lunch. It's saved me a double journey.'

Anne and Melanie went to the door to see him off. The sun was stronger and the haze had cleared from the sky; there was a trickle of water from the pile of snow Anne had cleared, giving some hope of a thaw. She picked up Melanie to stop her from running outside and stood with her in her arms, conscious from the way Jocelin looked at them that they made an appealing picture, outlined in the doorway.

Anne was thoughtful as she carried Melanie back indoors and then began washing up. It was interesting, what Jocelin Tyndall had been telling her, but it showed up her ignorance. He was right, she ought to know more about the great steelworks on the other side of the Beck, but her father had rarely talked about his work, thinking rightly that her mother would not understand, and Anne doubted whether he had ever given much thought to the economies of running Wallenshaw, not beyond being pleased when production was good and sales were up, giving him the chance to earn some overtime. Presumably Jeff would understand all the implications of what Jocelin had been saying, but Jeff would never talk to her in that way. That was partly her own fault, Anne admitted. If she had bothered to question him he might have talked about his work. Not now, though. She had treated him badly, leading him on and turning him down, and Jeff was not likely to forgive that, otherwise he might have been the one struggling through the snow to make sure she was all right.

Anne's hand hovered over the expensive chocolate box. As she selected one and bit into it she wondered whether Jocelin had really been so naïve as to believe that they would appeal to a three-year-old – or had it been a subtle way of giving Anne a present?

The promise of a thaw came to nothing. It froze hard in the night and the going underfoot the next morning was even more treacherous than it had been the previous day. It was another twenty-four hours before the lane was cleared sufficiently for Anne to make her way out on to the road, with Melanie saying anxiously, 'Don't spill me, Mummy.'

Her reception when she got to work was as cool as the temperature outside. Her services were needed, it was pointed out, particularly at that time, with the sales on. However, it was recognized that she had particular difficulty in getting into Upbridge and it was agreed that her absence would be overlooked – that time.

That night it snowed again and once more Anne and Melanie were confined to the house, this time for three days. Anne knew what was going to happen. On a day of ankle-deep slush and drenching rain she struggled into Upbridge and found that she had lost her job.

The cottage was cheap and Anne could afford to live there on her widow's pension alone, but she needed the stimulus of going out to work each day, of meeting other people and exercising the practical side of the theory she was learning, keeping the books of the shop.

She gritted her teeth when her mother pointed out that she had always said it was a mistake to go and live in the old cottage.

'I've made it comfortable,' Anne said. 'It feels like home. I'd be reluctant to give it up.'

'Home! You've never had what I'd call a proper home, not since you got married. Married quarters in Germany, a cabin in the wilds of Canada and now a run-down old cottage. I'm ashamed to tell people you're living there and that's flat.'

'We can't all have a semi-detached villa with china ducks on the wall.'

'Sneering at your sister now, are you? Evelyn's got a very nice home, modern, convenient and tasteful. You'd take it over fast enough if it was offered to you, especially being only five minutes from the bus stop. Are you managing all right for money?'

'I get by.'

Beryl fidgeted with the edge of her apron. 'Your dad's being doing overtime. We could help if you needed any extra.'

'Thanks, Mum. No, it's not the money I'm missing, it's the work and the company.'

'Jeff hasn't been to see you lately?'

'No.'

'No need to prim up your mouth like that. I know well enough he was visiting you, round about Christmas time. He must have come twice at least, to give Melanie that doll and to fix that chain on the door, and I was told his car was seen turning up your lane another time you didn't think fit to mention.'

She paused expectantly, but Anne refused to make any comment.

'All fizzled out, has it?' Beryl asked. 'Pity. He would have been ideal for you, having a bit of education to go with your fancy ideas.'

'I thought you didn't approve of his morals?' Anne said.

'He's a man,' Beryl said tolerantly. 'He'd settle down if he had a wife and family.'

'Have you got the local paper?' Anne asked. 'I want to have a look at the job advertisements.'

Beryl looked dissatisfied, but she handed the *Upbridge Chronicle* over to Anne.

'It's full of bits about the King,' she said. 'Poor man, very sad him going off like that. It's going to seem strange, having a queen. There's a few jobs advertised at the back, but I don't know that there's anything to suit you. Pity you didn't do shorthand and typing, like Evelyn. Plenty of office jobs about.'

'There are plenty of accountancy jobs, too,' Anne said. 'But they all want people with qualifications, which I'm a long way from getting. Never mind, something will turn up. I'm not really bothered, just a bit bored. I'd better take Melanie home before it gets dark.'

'I can hear your father stirring upstairs. Wait ten minutes and let him see his grand-daughter.'

'Do you mind being on your own when Dad's on nights?' Anne asked curiously, thinking of her own solitary evenings.

'I've got Pete,' her mother pointed out. 'He's been so much better lately. I won't say like his old self, but brighter, more cheerful, and talking more.'

'I've certainly appreciated the way he's come up to my place and lit the fire for me this winter.'

'And it was entirely his own idea. He wouldn't have been capable of that a year ago. It fretted him dreadfully, not being able to come through the snow, but his chest was that bad with the bronchitis I wouldn't let him out of the house.'

'Of course not. Hello, Dad! Had a good sleep? I hope my noisy daughter didn't wake you up?'

Wally, still flushed from sleep, shook his head. 'It takes more than a little 'un like her to disturb me when I've been working all night.'

'Grandpa, you *snore!*' Melanie informed him.

'So your Granny tells me. How are you, then? Still going to school?'

'Yes, but not when it snows. I drewed a picture of Uncle Trindle on sticks and my teacher did think it was Father Christmas, so there!'

'Who the heck's Uncle Trindle?' Wally demanded.

'Mr Tyndall,' Anne said. 'I told you about him coming over on skis. It made a great impression on Melanie.'

'It would. He told me he'd seen you. He asked after you last night, as a matter of fact.'

'How's the experiment with the oxygen injection going?'

'It's past being an experiment now. It's working a treat. Did he tell you about that? Funny bloke, you'd think he'd know it wouldn't interest a woman.'

'I was interested,' Anne said mildly, but she let it go.

'You'll not forget it's Evelyn's wedding anniversary next week,' her mother said. 'I've got her a nice card. You can put your name to it as well if you like.'

'No, I'll get one of my own when I go to my class tomorrow.'

The fact that she had been home a year and achieved so little weighed on Anne's spirits. She was still taking Melanie to the nursery school on the days when she had classes and fending off questions about when she was going to get another job. She was glad to be spared the ride into Upbridge on the other days of the week, but it left her with time on her hands and Melanie to amuse. She was bored and lonely, just as everyone had said she would be, but she would have bitten her tongue out rather than admit it.

She saw nothing of Jeff. She told herself that it was what she had intended, to make a complete break, but the truth was that she would have welcomed him on his own terms if he had chosen to pay her a visit.

By the time he did find his way back to the cottage again one Sunday afternoon Anne was too strung up to be welcoming.

'If I was given to reading the tea cups I would have known I was going to have a visit from a dark stranger,' she said.

'What did you expect?' Jeff retorted. 'I'm not used to having doors slammed in my face.'

'They've all made it easy for you, haven't they? All those other women.'

'If you want the truth, yes. So there's no reason for me to waste time on a girl who plays at being hard to get. Except . . .' He moved closer to her. 'Except that we did have something special, you and me, Anne.'

His arms closed round her and Anne lifted her face, but almost as soon as their lips touched she broke away again.

'No, Jeff, please. Not in front of the baby.'

'She wouldn't notice!'

'Don't you believe it! Besides, I haven't really changed my mind. I still think I'll be a lot happier if I keep you at arm's length.'

'I could coax you round if I tried,' Jeff said, watching her.

'That's why I shut the door on you,' Anne said.

She made an effort to regain her composure, moving away from him, sitting down at the table, picking up the sewing she had been doing when he had knocked at the door.

'What brings you round today?' she asked.

'A message from your mum. She saw me in the village and asked me to call in on my way back to Upbridge. I could hardly tell her you weren't likely to let me in. She says Mr

Rogers at the General Store has already got someone to help in the shop so you needn't bother to go and see him.'

'That's a relief,' Anne said. 'He wanted someone full time, which wouldn't fit in with my plans at all.'

'You still cling to this idea of qualifying as an accountant?'

'Certainly! Let me tell you, I'm one of the stars of the class.'

He picked up one of the text books that was lying on the table.

'*Book-keeping and Accountancy Practice*. Dry stuff.'

'Not to me,' Anne said.

She hoped she made it sound convincing, but if she was to be really truthful she would have had to admit that it was a dreary business, studying alone.

They both turned round and looked out of the window as another car drew up outside.

'Two cars in one afternoon! The place is getting like Piccadilly Circus,' Anne said.

'Jocelin Tyndall,' Jeff said. 'I didn't know he was on visiting terms with you.'

'He's not. I mean, he came once before.'

'And got the door shut in his face next time, like me?'

'Don't be silly,' Anne said, but the sarcastic question had brought the colour into her face and she was very conscious of it as she opened the door to Jocelin.

The two men greeted one another with a certain reserve. They were friendly enough, but Anne had the feeling that Jocelin would not have come if he had known that Jeff would be with her, while Jeff had no intention of leaving until he had found out why Jocelin was there.

'I've come to talk to you about a job,' Jocelin said. 'It's rather confidential at the moment . . .' He glanced at Jeff.

It was the moment for Jeff to go, but he merely settled himself more comfortably in his chair and looked interested.

'I won't talk,' he said.

'Before the war S.V.T. had a Conference Centre and Training School at Swallow Park. It's taken us all these years to get it back from the War Office and put it in order again.'

'The Company stopped work on it when the Nationalization Bill went through in 1948,' Jeff said helpfully.

'That's true,' Jocelin admitted. 'However, if all goes well it will be re-opened this summer and we've started recruiting the staff. On the administrative side there's to be a bursar, a housekeeper and an administrative assistant who will help both of them. Would you like to be considered for that job?'

'I don't do shorthand or typing,' Anne pointed out.

'That's not what's required. You'd do things like checking the reservations for courses, help keep the accounts, wages and insurance for the domestic staff – that sort of thing.'

'I wouldn't have to live in?'

'If you got the job you could move into the Gate House. It's very tiny, just two up and two down, like this cottage, but it's got gas and electricity and it's close to a main road. It's an ugly little place – Victorian, like Swallow Hall – and it's not yet been redecorated, but it would be more convenient than this cottage.'

'I've become attached to the cottage,' Anne said, looking round the room she had worked to make homely.

'It's done as a stop-gap, but how often in the last six months have you wished you could walk down the road to the shops? And this isolation cost you your last job, didn't it?'

'What will you do with the Gate House if Anne doesn't take the job?' Jeff asked.

'It would probably be used for one of the ground staff.'

'Could I work part time?' Anne asked. 'I still want to go on with my accountancy course.'

'That would be something to negotiate with the Bursar. I very much hope that a chap who was in the Army with me is going to take that job.'

'Jobs for the boys . . . and the girls,' Jeff murmured.

'To a certain extent, yes,' Jocelin said evenly. 'I happen to think Brian Pitford would be a perfect choice for the post and I approached him to see if he was interested, but he will appear before a selection committee just like the other candidates, and I have no say in their decision. Mrs Hardwick's application will be considered in the same way.'

'It sounds like a job I could do,' Anne said.

'You ought to take time to think about it,' Jeff put in.

'The advertisement will be out on Wednesday,' Jocelin said.

'I've brought all the details and an application form with me. Try to get the form back by the end of the week. There's not a lot of time to spare. The official reopening is in June, but the Bursar and his staff will start work in April.'

He went soon after that, refusing Anne's slightly distracted offer of a cup of tea. He nodded to Jeff, saying, 'I'll see you tomorrow.'

'No, you won't, as a matter of fact,' Jeff said. 'I'm going up to London for a Technical Committee at the British Iron and Steel Federation.'

He leaned back in the armchair by the fire and asked, 'Can I deliver any messages to your family?'

For one moment it seemed to Anne that there was something more between the two men than the difference in temperament that made them incompatible. Jocelin seemed to stiffen, his grasp on the doorhandle tightened until his knuckles were white, but all he said, in a perfectly equable way, was, 'No, thank you. We keep in touch.'

Anne didn't like the way Jeff was smiling to himself when she went back to him.

'What are you up to?' she asked.

'Just testing the water. I should have known Jocelin would be on the ball. How do you come to be on such good terms with our Jocelin that he puts himself out to give you advance warning of a job and offers you a house to go with it?'

'He's been very kind,' Anne said stiffly.

'He has that! You'll have to be a bit careful about that Gate House, Anne. It'll be a tied house, you know. O.K. as long as you keep the job, but what will happen if you give it up? You could find yourself homeless again.'

'It's the best chance I'm likely to be offered.'

'Play your cards right and Jocelin might put you on his personal payroll.'

For one moment Anne did not grasp his meaning. When she did she felt anger and a sense of distaste. 'There's nothing like that between us, nothing at all,' she said.

'No? He didn't look very pleased to find me here.'

'I don't think he likes you.'

'You've got a point,' Jeff admitted. 'He likes you all right though. You watch your step, young Anne. I'm not the only one who'll think it a bit strange, Jocelin Tyndall taking such an interest in your welfare.'

'It's time you went,' Anne said coldly.

'It is if I'm going to drive down to London tonight. I don't have to. I could go in the morning if you'd make it worth my while to stay.'

Anne shook her head, refusing to look at him, afraid of what he might do to her with his dark, intent gaze.

'All right, if you don't want me then I'll go to someone who does. And I won't ask you again. If you want a man you'd better concentrate on Jocelin Tyndall.'

Chapter Four

Anne discovered that when Jocelin had told Jeff that she would have to compete for the administration post at Swallow Hall he had meant what he said. Having seen that she knew about it, he stood back and let her application go through the normal channels. Anne respected his scrupulousness, and yet it added to her nervousness: she felt that if she failed to get the job she would be letting him down.

She was elated to get an interview, still more pleased to discover that she had been put on the short list of three. There was a nerve-racking interval until Brian Pitford's appointment as Bursar was confirmed and then the three final candidates were interviewed by him. Anne caught a glimpse of the girl who preceded her. She looked awe-inspiringly efficient, older than Anne, and probably without the encumbrance of a young daughter, Anne thought gloomily.

Brian Pitford was a man of about fifty, on the short side, and with the taut look of a man who took trouble over keeping himself fit. His hair was carefully arranged to conceal a receding hairline. A middle-aged man who had not quite reconciled himself to his years, Anne decided. His manner was brusque at first, perhaps because he was more accustomed to dealing with men than with young women, but it seemed to Anne that he gradually warmed to her.

'You don't mention how you came to hear about this job,' he remarked, glancing through her application. 'Was it from the local paper?'

'Mr Tyndall told me about it,' Anne said.

'Jocelin?'

She caught a hint of surprise in his quick look at her –

surprise, and appraisal. If everyone was going to look like that when she mentioned Jocelin Tyndall she would just as soon not have the job, Anne thought rebelliously, but the moment passed and Brian Pitford did not refer to it again.

'I think you and I could work together, don't you?' he said at last. 'That last lady I saw . . .' he grimaced comically, '. . . she scared the daylights out of me. I'd prefer a little less efficiency – not that I think you'd be inefficient – and a little more human warmth.'

'Does that mean I've got the job?' Anne asked, trying to conceal her excitement.

'I think so. I'm supposed to make you wait for a formal letter, but I really don't see why you should be kept in suspense. Keep it to yourself until the offer comes through, of course. It wouldn't be fair to the other girls for them to hear unofficially that you had been chosen.'

He laughed suddenly. 'I hope Jocelin will be pleased.'

'That's not the reason why I've been successful,' Anne said quickly.

'No, no! I've decided on you because I think you're best for the job. But it does mean that he's got both his candidates into the posts he wanted for them. Quietly getting his own way, as usual.'

It was all very satisfactory, except that Anne could not help reflecting that Jocelin would not have made those remarks about one of the other candidates. Nor, she thought, would he have allowed himself the pleasure of giving her the news in person, as Brian Pitford had done.

As soon as she moved into the Gate House at Swallow Hall everything became easier for Anne. She could get Melanie to school in ten minutes, and if the weather was poor they could go by bus. Even better, she discovered that although Brian Pitford was in his fifties, he had married late and had two young children, one a year older and one a year younger than Melanie. The older child went to the same nursery school as Melanie and Mrs Pitford was perfectly prepared to collect both children and keep Melanie with her until Anne was free to call for her.

It meant that Anne no longer had to worry about being at

the school gate exactly on time each day; a quick telephone call to Moira Pitford and she could settle down to complete her work without keeping one eye on the clock. Once the college was officially open it made a great difference, particularly since it allowed her to slip into the lecture room occasionally if there was a talk that interested her. She rarely spoke, feeling that she was there on sufferance and must keep in the background, but as her confidence increased she began to ask questions over the lunch she shared with her new colleagues and was surprised to find her enquiries being taken seriously, so much so that they often led to heated debates which were only broken off when the bell for the afternoon session warned them that it was time to go.

One or two of the students attempted to get on a friendlier footing with her, but Anne fended them off with smiling regret at being unable to leave Melanie alone, although when she was invited to a farewell dinner at the end of the first management course she accepted, took Melanie to stay the night with her grandparents, and even bought a new dress.

There was a long driveway between the Gate House and Swallow Hall, but it was a bright, sunny evening and Anne did not mind the walk, especially since she had put on walking shoes and was carrying her high-heeled sandals in a bag. All the same, when Jocelin Tyndall's car drew up beside her she readily accepted the lift he offered.

'Am I allowed to tell you that you look remarkably pretty?' he enquired.

'Why not? It does a lot for my self esteem,' Anne said.

She smoothed down a fold of her ballerina-length taffeta skirt.

'It's such an age since I dressed to go to a party. I thought this frock looked rather good, but if it has *your* approval then I know it must be all right.'

It struck her as she spoke that it was extraordinary that she should be on such easy terms with Jocelin Tyndall, able to laugh at him, tease him a little, without any feeling of self-consciousness.

'You look very smart yourself,' she added with a feeling of recklessness.

'I had a shave and put on a clean shirt,' he said solemnly.

He was looking thinner, Anne suddenly thought. Was it the effect of the dark suit he was wearing, or had he really lost weight?

'Do you look after yourself properly now that your father is based in London and your mother is away so much?' she asked.

'Oh, yes! Mum always leaves stacks of food when she goes off on Mondays and there's a woman who comes in and heats things up,' he said with a vagueness that made Anne suspect that his meals were not very interesting to him.

His long face with its sharp, distinguished profile was looking amused. 'Are you trying to mother me, Mrs Hardwick?' he enquired. 'I assure you I am quite accustomed to fending for myself.'

'I suppose so,' Anne said.

She suspected that he thought her question foolish, but it must be a strange, lonely life he led, alone in a ten-bedroomed house for five days out of every week. What did he do for company? What were his interests? It struck her that she knew remarkably little about him. She was suddenly intensely curious about this cool, almost secretive man, who had shown her so much kindness.

Because of her new interest in him Anne made a point of being present the following week when Jocelin was a visiting speaker on a special short course for high level managers. She slipped into place as unobtrusively as possible, hoping that he would not notice her. Anne had become something of a connoisseur of lecturers in the last few months. She realized as soon as he began that Jocelin was first rate. His explanation of the new Linz-Donawitz steelmaking process which had been developed in Austria was so lucid that even Anne could grasp it, but even cleverer was the way he led into a discussion of the application of this new oxygen converter development in Great Britain and the limitations imposed by the fact that it did not deal successfully with ore from British fields. It became more of a debate than a lecture, with arguments raging across the floor on whether the industry would ever wholly abandon home-produced ore in favour of better quality imported ore which would make it possible to use the new process.

Jocelin leaned back against the edge of the table on the low platform and listened, with a slight smile on his lips. He looked towards the back of the room and caught Anne's eye and his smile deepened. At the first lull in the discussion he caught up the threads of what he had said, presented them with a resumé of the arguments they had themselves put forward and left them to draw their own conclusions.

Anne left the room as soon as he had finished speaking, but she loitered in the corridor and allowed Jocelin to catch up with her.

'Furthering your education?' he enquired.

'I often go to lectures,' she said quickly. She didn't want him to think she had gone in specially to hear him, even though that was exactly what she had done. 'You told me I ought to be ashamed of knowing so little about the steel industry,' she pointed out.

'Did I? I must be careful what I say if you take me so seriously. Did you understand it?'

'Yes, you made it very clear. In fact, it was a first-class lecture. Worrying, though.'

'It was meant to be. I'm an innovator, Mrs Hardwick. It grieves me to see the industry in this country standing still while the rest of the world forges ahead. I admit the L.D. process is still in its infancy, but there was a conference on it which was reported at length in *Stahl und Eisen* and yet most of those men in there are still not taking it seriously. They can't face the idea of the end of traditional open hearth steelmaking, and they certainly don't like to think of closing the U.K. ore fields.'

'I always thought that Wallenshaw's great strength was that it had everything that was needed to make steel, right through from digging the iron out of the ground to rolling the finished steel,' Anne said with a puzzled frown.

'Now that communications have improved and new ore fields are being developed a fully integrated steelworks relying on low-grade home ore isn't necessarily the most economic way of producing steel.'

'Do you really believe it would be a good thing for Wallenshaw to be dependent on imported ore?'

'It will come. We can't go on spending good money on driving out impurities we don't want when there's ore available which is something like ninety per cent pure. But you've heard me say all this in the lecture room.'

'I can't quite take it in,' Anne admitted. 'I'll try to keep an open mind.'

With a feeling that she wanted to impress him, she added, 'I'll get that copy of *Stahl und Eisen* out of the library and read the report of the conference.'

'You understand German?'

'I lived in Germany for nearly two years and there wasn't much for me to do except study the language. I used to be quite fluent. I dare say it'll come back if I try hard enough.'

Two days later, late in the afternoon, when Anne was playing ball in the garden of the Gate House with Melanie, Jocelin's car drew up in the driveway.

'I couldn't bear to think of you struggling through that technical report in German,' he said. 'Here, if you really want to read it I'll lend you my copy of the translation.'

He looked down at Melanie, bouncing her ball near his feet. 'My word, you've grown since I saw you last. I suppose everyone tells you that?'

'Yes,' Melanie agreed. 'I'm going to be four next week.'

'Really? Which day?'

'Thursday, I think,' Melanie said, glancing at Anne for confirmation.

'That's right, darling, the twentieth.'

'My own birthday is only two days before that, on the eighteenth,' Jocelin told Melanie. 'We're practically twins.'

'I *think* twins has to be *ezackly* the same age,' Melanie said carefully. 'Uncle Trindle, did you know that babies grow inside their mummy's tummies?'

'Er, yes, I had heard that,' Jocelin said gravely, but with an amused glance at Anne's embarrassed face.

'My sister is expecting her first baby,' she said. 'It seemed a good idea to give Melanie a little basic information, but I didn't bargain on her passing it on to everyone. She told the milkman yesterday. I didn't know where to look.'

'We're just going to have our tea,' Melanie said. 'You can come and have some too, if you like, Uncle Trindle.'

'I think you're old enough now to call Mr Tyndall by his proper name,' her mother said.

'I like being Uncle Trindle,' Jocelin objected. 'Could you really give me a cup of tea? I've just come from a committee meeting and I'm parched with thirst.'

'We're going to have it in the garden and then the birds can have the crumbs,' Melanie said.

He only stayed long enough to drink one cup of tea, but when Anne got up and went with him to the garden gate, he asked, 'What would Melanie like for her birthday?'

'I don't want her to get the idea that she only has to tell someone about her birthday and she'll get a present,' Anne objected.

'I'm an honorary uncle,' Jocelin pointed out. 'Come on, give me some ideas. I don't know much about small children.'

'A jig-saw puzzle – a simple one – or perhaps a book I could read to her,' Anne suggested.

'Has she got a dolls house?'

'Mr Tyndall, they cost a fortune! You mustn't think of anything like that.' Anne paused, looking thoughtful. 'Actually, I've just had a brilliant idea. I'll get Pete to make her one for Christmas. He'll love doing it and it will be better than anything I could buy in a shop.'

Jocelin's present was a book, delivered to Anne at the College. Melanie drew a picture of a strange pink animal, alleged to be a dog, and laboriously printed her name in straggling letters, to be sent to 'Uncle Trindle' as a thank you letter. It would have surprised Anne, it surprised Jocelin himself, that he kept it for weeks and felt an amused pleasure every time he looked at it.

He needed something to make him feel cheerful. The prevailing mood in the steel industry was one of cautious optimism. Output was up, sales were good, estimates of future demand were being revised upwards, but always with a warning that no one could count on the trend continuing.

Jocelin urged that this was the time to implement a programme of drastic reorganization, but he rarely got anyone to listen to him.

'There's plenty of modernization going on,' his father said impatiently. 'Most of the post-war plans have been completed and the industry is reaping the benefit.'

'Piecemeal methods of jacking up production. Oil firing has been a success, oxygen injection has been a success, there are improved rolling mills coming into operation. I admit all that. What I'm saying is that we're just putting patches on old fabric.'

'That's our way and I'm not sure it isn't best. Introduce innovations slowly and adapt to them as you go along. When you've been in the industry as long as I have you'll know that no process is as perfect as it's claimed to be on paper. Only when you start using it do you discover the snags.'

'Most of my ideas are likely to remain on paper,' Jocelin said ruefully. 'So we'll never know whether or not they would have worked, will we?'

'If you can tell me where to find the finance for your grand new ideas I might take them seriously,' his father said. 'I think it's time you stepped back and took a wider view . . .'

'That's what I am doing!' Jocelin protested. 'I'm the one who's arguing for rationalization of the whole British industry!'

'A look at the world picture, I mean. I'm sending you to America to have a look at the way they do things there.'

'I'm not sure the United States is a good model for us to follow.'

'You'll go – and that's an order from your Chairman. My God, I would have jumped at the chance at your age!'

Jocelin grumbled, but he took the trip to America. He had a suspicion that there was something in what his father said. He was getting too involved with Wallenshaw and that was a mistake for someone who knew in his heart that one day he would be responsible for the fortunes of a company with interests all over the country.

On an impulse he dropped in to say goodbye to Anne and Melanie before he went. He had always had an obscure feeling of responsibility for them, ever since Anne had first approached his father about the old cottage. They were an appealing pair, the young, good-looking widow and the lovely little girl. He admired Anne for her obstinate independence, her pride and courage. He found her physically attractive too, more than was quite comfortable. He wondered whether Anne was aware of it.

On the evening that he called he found her exhausted.

'I've been taking exams,' she explained. 'I'm sure I've done badly. I'm worn out.'

She cast a distracted look at the clock. 'Pete's collected Melanie from school for me. I can't think where they've got to. He sometimes takes her to play in the grounds, but he ought to have brought her home for tea by this time.'

'I've called at a bad time,' Jocelin said. 'I only looked in to say goodbye. I'm off to America tomorrow for three months.'

'How interesting for you. Could you spare the time to do something for me? Drive up to the house and ask if anyone has seen them. I mean, it's not like Pete. If I say I want him here with Melanie by five o'clock he's usually on the doorstep at five minutes to, and here it is nearly six and they're not back.'

Anne tried to speak lightly, but she was uneasy. She had come to think of her brother as reliable, but there were still times when he went off into a strange, dreamlike state, and other times when unreasoning panic overcame him and he had to get out of doors no matter where he was.

She saw from Jocelin's acute look that he had understood her fears. He touched her lightly on the arm as he moved towards the door.

'Try not to worry,' he said. 'You are far more likely to have heard if something *had* happened than if it had not.'

Jocelin did rather more than Anne had asked. He made enquiries at Swallow Hall, with no result, and he rang the headmistress of the nursery school and checked that Melanie had been collected by her uncle at the usual time. He also spoke to Moira Pitford who agreed that she had seen

Melanie and Peter walking off down the road together in a perfectly normal way.

Jocelin sat in thought for a minute or two. He hesitated to call in the police at this stage, especially without mentioning it to Anne, but he did telephone the local hospital and checked that there had been no casualties admitted that afternoon. The only other thing he could think of was that Peter might have taken Melanie to his own home, but Wally Carless was not on the telephone. Jocelin searched his memory, came up with the name of the local vicar and despatched him to visit the Carless home. It took twenty minutes to get his answer: Mrs Carless had not set eyes on her son since he set off to meet Melanie.

Jocelin went back to Anne, half expecting to find that the truants had turned up, but she was still alone and far more anxious than she had been when he left her.

'At least I know neither of them has been knocked down, thanks to you,' she said gratefully. 'I'm sure they'll turn up. I mustn't keep you any longer.'

'You don't imagine I'm going to leave you on your own?' He glanced at the clock. 'Give it another half hour and then I think you have no option but to inform the police.'

'But what can have happened . . . ?'

'Let's think about what we know. They left the school safely and were seen walking in this direction. What time should they have got back here?'

'Some time around three thirty.'

'And you had said Melanie must be home by five, so Peter would have had to think of some way of amusing her for an hour and a half. You say they sometimes played in the grounds of Swallow Hall?'

'Yes, hide-and-seek in the garden, things like that. He's always been so *good* with her!'

'Then the next thing to do is to search the grounds. Why didn't I think of that while I was up at the house? There are twenty students in residence, we can organize them to do the rounds. It's just possible Peter has had a fall or something and Melanie has stayed with him.'

'Or not been able to find her way home alone. She's so little.'

'We will find her. I promise you.'

She managed to smile, shakily but with real gratitude. 'I suppose I must stay here?'

'I'm afraid so. This is where they'll come to if they've merely wandered too far afield and if Melanie should come home alone she must find you here.'

The September evening would still be light for a couple of hours at least, Jocelin calculated. He gave one fleeting thought towards his own plans and then dismissed them from his mind. He had meant to catch a train that evening and stay the night in London before taking the flight to New York early in the morning, but he could make other arrangements.

There was one possibility he had not mentioned to Anne; even to think about it made him feel cold. She was a local girl, she must know about the old iron workings next to the grounds of Swallow Hall. Not deep pits like the coal mines, but not the modern open cast ore workings either; in earlier centuries the miners had worked the iron by means of shafts and galleries. It had never been an important deposit and the ore had long since been worked out, but the shafts were still there, fenced off and surrounded by warning notices. Jocelin had clambered over them himself; no doubt Peter Carless had done the same. It seemed unthinkable that he should have taken his small niece to such a dangerous place and yet, if the search round the gardens and fields failed, Jocelin knew that they must turn to the old drift mine.

*

When Peter collected Melanie from school it was a bright, sunny afternoon. The weather was still warm, with only a hint of autumn in the air. Melanie walked along by Pete's side, taking his hand to cross the road, talking eagerly about what she had done at nursery school that day.

'I made Mummy a picture,' she said. 'Look, flowers.'

'Very pretty,' Pete said. 'Shall I put it in my pocket for you?'

'No, 'cause it might get creased. I'll carry it.'

'Anne said we'd got to be home by five o'clock today,' Pete said. 'That's a long time yet. We can go across the fields and get into Swallow Hall the back way.'

'Let's go and see the farmer cutting the corn,' Melanie said.

'I expect he's finished.'

They left the road on the outskirts of Upbridge and struck out across the fields. Pete knew every inch of them and they had changed very little since he was a boy. As he had expected, the harvesting in the top field had been completed, except for carting away the bales of straw.

'We can play hide-an'-seek,' Melanie said.

She laid her drawing of a lop-sided vase of flowers down on the ground. Pete found a couple of stones and weighed it down to stop it blowing away.

It was a one-sided game, since Pete was clearly visible behind even the largest bale of straw, while Melanie could tuck herself down and hide completely. She gave herself away by delighted giggles when he failed to find her.

'Melanie, come and look at this,' Pete called to her. 'Quietly now.'

She came and crouched by his side.

'It's a harvest mouse,' Pete explained.

The tiny creature stayed completely still, sitting back on its haunches, its front paws raised, only its whiskers quivering. Melanie leaned towards it until their noses were almost touching.

'A little, little mouse,' she breathed. 'Does he like me?'

'He loves you.'

She moved her hand and, as if released from a spell, the mouse darted away.

'He thought you were going to catch him and shut him up,' Pete explained. 'You mustn't shut wild creatures up. Or anyone else.'

'I could draw a little mouse on the bottom of my picture for Mummy,' Melanie decided. 'Have you got a pencil, Uncle Pete?'

He found a stub of pencil in his pocket. 'We'll have to go soon,' he warned her.

'Not yet.'

'Anne said five o'clock and she expects us to be on time.'

'Mummy's doing exams,' Melanie said, drawing busily. 'She does very hard sums. When I go to proper school I'll do sums.'

Pete lounged by her side, chewing a piece of straw. He was not consciously thinking at all, but somewhere at the back of his mind was the memory, carefully suppressed, of another companion who had played in these fields with him. He sat up and threw away the straw, not knowing what it was that troubled him, only that unless he was careful something was going to start hurting him with a pain that was more than he could bear.

'There! Do you think Mummy will know that's a mouse?' Melanie asked.

'Unless she thinks it's an elephant,' Pete said. The bad moment had passed, he was back in the field with Melanie, there was nothing to be frightened about.

Melanie thought his remark was wildly funny. 'I'm going to hide again,' she said. 'Count a hundred and come and find me, Uncle Pete.'

'This is the last game,' he said. 'Don't lose your drawing.'

She ran away across the field, holding the piece of paper by the corner, enjoying the way it fluttered as she ran, but at the corner of the field it got away from her, floating in the breeze across the fence. Melanie turned to call to Pete, but then she saw that there was a gap in the fence; it would be easy to crawl through and get the picture back. She could hide on the other side, too, and he wouldn't know where to find her.

'. . . eighty-five, ninety, ninety-five, a hundred – coming!' Pete called, bringing his counting to a conclusion.

He searched the field from end to end, believing at first that she must be darting from one bale to another. But Melanie was not as clever as that, she always gave herself away and he caught her easily. She was not in the field.

Pete began to call to her, shouting that the game was over, that they must go home. There was no reply. A feeling of panic rose up in him, almost choking him, but he still kept his head. He walked round the edge of the field, calling out to her. On two sides it was open to other fields and there was no possibility of her hiding from him there; on the far side there was a line of trees, but there was also a deep ditch and a barbed wire fence and he could see no way she could have got through. On the remaining side were the old iron workings.

The flower picture had blown away again before Melanie could catch it and had caught on a branch of hawthorn, out of her reach. Pete saw it fluttering like a flag, like a signal. He saw, too, the broken fence and the crushed grass where Melanie's small body had bent it down as she crawled through. He made the hole larger and went after her.

He crawled over the ground, knowing its treacherous nature, and the wriggling motion on knees and elbows again touched off memories that were better forgotten. The jungle, the wicked, inpenetrable jungle, with silent enemies behind every tree. Pete put his head down on his hands, gasping for breath and at that moment he heard Melanie's voice calling to him.

'Uncle Pete, Uncle Pete, please come and find me!'

He moved forward until he found the place where the ground had crumbled away beneath her running feet.

'Melanie?' he called hoarsely.

'Uncle Pete, I fell in a nasty hole. Come and get me out, Uncle Pete.'

She sounded tearful, but she must be unharmed. The obvious thing to do was to leave her where she was and go for help, but she was so small, such a little thing to be left all on her own. Racked by indecision, Pete edged forward again, trying to discover where she was.

'Call out to me again Melanie,' he shouted.

'I want Mummy,' Melanie wailed.

She did not sound far away. Pete guessed that she had fallen through one of the air vents leading down into a passage and had lodged in it. What he needed was some rope, but there was none of that about. Wire from the fence? Not strong enough. He edged forward again and small stones from the edge of the hole cascaded downwards.

'The ground's falling on me,' Melanie said. 'Please get me out, Uncle Pete.'

Enraged by his own futility Pete stood up. 'I'm going to fetch help,' he called out.

'Don't go, don't go. Uncle Pete, Uncle Pete!'

The panic in her voice alarmed Pete. He took one unwary step forward and the earth at the edge of the shaft crumbled. He flung out his arms in an effort to save himself, but he was too late. In a rush of loose stones Pete hurtled down to join his niece. Half choked, she clutched at him blindly and the built up deposit of earth, supported on a dead gorse bush, on which her light body had been resting, gave way beneath them and they were swept another six feet below ground.

Melanie, clinging to Pete like a baby monkey to its mother, was less shaken than he was and although she was still terrified, she was reassured by his presence. The shaft through which they had both fallen had been straight, but the passage where they now rested was no more than a steep incline. By digging in his heels and scrabbling wildly with his hands Pete was able to stop them from sliding farther. He sat up. He was not badly hurt, but everything had gone dark. Pete looked up. The sky had disappeared.

To Pete it seemed that he was screaming, but no sound came from his agonized mouth. He was shut in. They had caught him again. This time there would be no escape.

Melanie tugged at his hand. 'Uncle Pete, I want to go home,' she said in a very small, uncertain voice.

Inside Peter Carless's disordered mind something lurched back into place, as if a cogwheel had slipped back on its ratchet. Outside was not the steamy jungle, not the dusty compound surrounded by wire, not the slit-eyed, yellow-faced guards; above him, if he could only get back to it, was sweet green grass and fields just come to harvest. He was in England. He was at home. And his companion was a small child. His niece. Anne's baby.

From somewhere he managed to find a voice to answer her. 'Don't you fret, lovey. I'll get you home all right. I just have to think for a minute.'

He crouched beside her, his knees bent, his head hunched

over them. He knew these workings, if he could only get his memory going again. He'd been all over them as a boy, in spite of threats and warnings. They'd been thrashed for it more than once, he and . . . Automatically his mind shut down as he approached the unmentionable name, but this time Pete found the strength to resist the merciful oblivion. He and Dave. He had explored the iron mine with Dave. With Dave. Twenty feet below ground, lost in impenetrable darkness, Pete rocked backwards and forwards in an agony of grief.

They had always been friends, even before they had started school on the same day at the age of five. They had fought, quarrelled and come back together again. They had got into mischief, sometimes into danger, and had shared the punishment. They had been rivals in the classroom, on the football pitch, on the running track, but always friends. They had smoked their first cigarette together, exchanged information on sex, drunk illicit beer behind the cricket pavilion. Dave had been the first to score with a girl, and had boasted unbearably about it. Once Pete had been able to report his own success they had become allies again, going to local dances and looking hopefully for girls who would let them go further than a quick kiss outside the front door. They joined the Army together and served in the same unit, sweating out the war in Burma, hating every moment of it, but still able to laugh together.

When Burma fell they were taken prisoner. From the first Dave had been in trouble. The Japanese despised their prisoners for surrendering and that influenced their attitude towards them. There were harsh punishments for insolence, and Dave was naturally cheeky. Pete warned him, his own officers warned him, but nothing suppressed Dave for long. They talked about escape, knowing that it was next door to impossible. Because he was alarmed by the way Dave was behaving Pete agreed to go through the wire with him, even though he knew in his heart that they wouldn't get away. Inevitably they were caught, dragged back to the camp, humiliated in front of their companions. They might have been shot, it was by no means unknown, but instead they were merely punished.

Pete resigned himself to working his way through the punishment period, but Dave could not accept it. The day came when he picked up a bowl of rice and plastered it all over the Japanese Commander's face, like a custard pie. And then, seeing the furious, spluttering face, covered in white mess, he had laughed.

This time the punishment was carried out away from the other prisoners, but they heard Dave's screams. It was two days before the Medical Officer was allowed to see him and he was so angry that he forgot discretion. Rumours of what had happened to Dave began to circulate.

Pete got the details out of a medical orderly. Both Dave's arms and legs were broken, he had been whipped until his back was raw, and he had been so badly mauled that the Medical Officer suspected that his spleen was ruptured. In that condition he had been pegged out on the ground and left in the broiling sun without food or water. He was still there and no representations from the British officers could shift the Japanese Commander's resolution to make an example of him.

That night Pete crawled out of his hut. Slithering along on his belly he made his way to where Dave was lying. He took with him a canteen of water and from time to time during the night he wet Dave's lips. When dawn came Dave was still alive, with the prospect of another day of torture under the sun. His condition was fearful, his open wounds crawling with ants. As the sun came up he turned his eyes towards Pete, mutely begging for release.

The guards were stirring. One of them came towards them and before he could raise the alarm Pete rushed him and tore his knife away from him. As the guard started to shout, Pete knelt above his friend. Then he killed him.

They said it was murder and that in England he would be hanged for it, but honourable death was too good for him, so they put him in the hot box, six foot by four foot of corrugated iron. And they put Dave's corpse in with him.

Melanie was moving against him, tugging at his arm.

'Have you thought, Uncle Pete?' she whispered. 'Can we go home now?'

Slowly Pete returned to the present. This cool, earth-smelling darkness was not the sun-scorched torture chamber where the heat drew sweat out of the body until the skin cracked and wild visions of fever swirled through the head.

Melanie's head butted against his chest. 'It's very dark,' she said. 'I'm not afraid of the dark, am I, Uncle Pete?'

Pete felt in his jacket pocket and found his lighter. By its small flame he saw not the green face and blackened lips of a putrefying corpse, but a small girl with jet black hair like a skein of silk, big brown eyes wide with shock, and the wild roses of England in her cheeks.

'I know my way out,' he said. His voice was hoarse, but he spoke steadily.

He knew exactly where they were. The map of the under-ground workings was as clear in his mind as if he had been there only yesterday. There was a passage, sloping down-wards with the fall of the land, about two hundred yards long. It led to the main tunnel and at the end of that there was a doorway, leading out to the bottom of the field. That was the way he and Dave had got in, long ago when they were boys.

He was afraid that the ground might have subsided, but the passage, once he had found it, was quite clear. There was room for Pete to crawl on his hands and knees; in places Melanie could have walked upright. But when they reached the exit he found not the broken door he remembered, but a stout new one. Their way out was barred.

For a moment Pete gave way to bitter anger. He thumped the door with his fists. It shook, but it did not give way.

'Why can't we go out?' Melanie asked. 'I do want my Mummy.'

She began to cry, not loudly, but in a subdued, tired way.

'What we're going to have to do is burn down that door,' Pete said.

He was afraid that the wood would be damp, but he had a refill of lighter fuel in his pocket and he dribbled that over the door before flicking the lighter. A quick, bright flame sprang up. Acrid smoke began to fill the tunnel, stinging their eyes and making them cough.

'Get back a bit and lie down on the floor,' Pete told Melanie.

The fire penetrated to the wood outside, dried in the sun, and burned more briskly. After five minutes Pete caught a glimpse of open sky; after ten minutes he moved forward and began kicking at the door. It crashed outwards, still burning. Pete took off his jacket, wrapped it round Melanie, picked her up and, bent double, rushed over the burning wood and out into the open air.

The grass outside was long and green, the sky was blue with a line of gold in the west as the sun went down; a late sky-lark twittered over their heads. Pete stood up and looked round.

'I'm free,' he said.

His legs would scarcely carry him, but Melanie was crying again, so he set her on his shoulder and set out for the Gate House.

Anne saw them coming and ran out of the house to meet them.

'Where have you been?' she cried out before she was near enough to see their scratches and bruises. 'Pete, I've been worried out of my mind!'

Then she realized his state of exhaustion and caught her breath. She held out her arms and Melanie tumbled into them.

'I fell down a nasty hole and Uncle Pete fell after me and it was all dark and horrid and you weren't *there*!' she said, her face crumpling up as she thumped her mother angrily on the chest.

'Poor baby! Never mind, darling, I've got you now. Pete, was it the old iron workings? Jocelin – Mr Tyndall – was just about to start a search there.'

Pete nodded. 'She got through the fence when we were playing in the top field.' He yawned hugely.

Jocelin had joined them. 'Never mind the explanations,' he said. 'Go inside and sit down. I'll go up to the Hall and call off the search and then I'll run your brother home, Mrs Hardwick.'

When he came back Anne said distractedly, 'You're going to America in the morning. All this running about, it'll upset all your plans.'

'I've still got time to throw a couple of shirts into a suitcase. I couldn't have gone without knowing what had happened, no one could.'

'Thank God it's turned out all right,' Anne said fervently. 'I'm more than grateful for everything you did.' She smiled shakily. 'Shall I wish you a happy Christmas now, three months in advance, or will you be back in England by then?'

'I hope to be back. I must be here by the beginning of January in any case, for the wedding.'

'Wedding?'

Jocelin looked surprised and, after a moment, worried. 'I assumed you knew. Jeff Blackmore is a friend of yours, isn't he? He's going to marry my sister.'

Chapter Five

———✦———

The wedding took place in London, much to the disappointment of the inhabitants of Brinthorpe, who had planned to gather outside the Parish Church in Upbridge for a satisfying stare at the bride.

'Mrs Blackmore's only set eyes on the girl once,' Beryl told Anne. 'Jeff did bring her over to see his mother on Christmas Eve, I'll say that for him, but from what I can gather she didn't stay long. Still, we'll hear all about the wedding from Evelyn, though how she dares travel to London, the size she is, I really don't know. Eight months gone! It's more than I'd have done.'

Anne, meeting Jeff at her sister's house when he called to see his brother about the arrangements, offered him her congratulations.

'Found what you want, have you, Jeff?' she asked with a touch of irony.

'She'll do,' Jeff said.

They looked at one another, a long, measuring glance, and then he said, as if it was dragged out of him, 'I'm in love with her.'

'I took that for granted, since you're going to marry her.'

'Her mother thinks I'm marrying the Tyndall name and a five per cent holding in S.V.T.'

'What about Sir Fred?'

'He likes me. Always has. We get on all right together.'

'That's good. I don't suppose it will hurt your career, being the Chairman's son-in-law.'

'That's what everyone keeps hinting, but it's not the only reason for marrying Tessa.'

He glanced over his shoulder, but Terry was fussing over Evelyn. 'It may have been what steered me towards her in the first place, but Tessa's got me hooked. I've been spending the night with her every time I went to London for the best part of a year.'

Something stirred in Anne's memory. 'Did Jocelin know that?' she asked.

'I think he suspected. None of his business. His sister was old enough to arrange her own life. She takes after Sir Fred. Jocelin is more like his mother. A cold fish.'

'He's been very kind to me,' Anne said quickly.

'There you are. Any other man might have looked for some return, but not our Jocelin.'

'Just because he hasn't got the morals of an alley cat doesn't mean he has no feelings,' Anne said.

She turned away, angry at having been drawn into a discussion about Jocelin. Jeff apparently didn't understand disinterested kindness. She was annoyed with herself, too, for not keeping her congratulations to a wish for his happiness and leaving it at that, but something about his complacent look had nettled her and his admission that he had been sleeping with Tessa made her seethe. He ought to have kept it to himself, and if the affair had been going on for a year then he must have picked up with Tessa as soon as Anne had started turning him down. That was why he had told her; he had wanted her to know that he had lost no time in filling her place and this girl, who had not shut doors in his face, was going to become his wife. The best of luck to her. She'd need to keep him on a pretty tight leash, for all he said he loved her.

Evelyn managed to get through the marriage ceremony and the reception in spite of her advanced pregnancy.

'It was a real Society wedding,' she said admiringly. 'I never thought much of Tessa's looks, the few times I saw her in Upbridge, but she has got style. Not pretty, you couldn't call her that, but striking-looking and when she holds herself up she's got a lovely figure. She wore white and gold brocade and she had two bridesmaids in dark blue velvet. The flowers were gorgeous, white and blue and yellow, all carried through to match in the church and at the reception. The Savoy! Never in my life did I think I'd be drinking champagne at the Savoy. They've gone to Switzerland for the honeymoon, you know. I thought it was a funny choice myself in the middle of the winter.'

'Tessa says she's going to teach Jeff to ski,' Terry put in. 'Let's hope he doesn't break a leg. A fine honeymoon that'd be!'

The elaborate wedding was considered a nuisance by the bridegroom and an enormous joke by the bride. Jeff would have preferred a quiet civil ceremony, but Tessa counselled him to let her mother have her head.

'It'll be a hoot,' she said. 'Me, swanning up the aisle in white brocade! But it will pacify Mummy. She's frightfully worried about me marrying into the proletariat, you know, and a conventional wedding with all the trimmings will quieten her poor nerves.'

Tessa had changed during the year since she and Jeff had first become lovers. She had dropped her surly manner and her disfiguring slouch. She had learned to make the best of her fine-skinned, bony face and she no longer disguised her full-breasted figure under sloppy jumpers.

'I didn't want all that fuss, but you did look marvellous,' Jeff told her after the wedding was over. 'I got quite a thrill when I looked over my shoulder and saw you coming towards me, all white and gold.'

'That's nice,' Tessa said. She spoke absentmindedly, still pottering about the hotel bedroom in her underclothes, while Jeff was already stretched out in bed waiting for her.

'Get a move on,' he said.

'Why? Our honeymoon isn't likely to produce any surprises, is it?'

'Being married might bring out reserves you didn't know I had.'

'Oh, in that case . . .'

She pulled her satin slip over her head and let it fall on the floor. The rest of her clothes followed in a careless heap.

'Untidy slut,' Jeff said as she slid in beside him.

'You like sluts. That's why you married me.'

'What beats me is why you married me,' Jeff said under his breath.

'This is one reason,' Tessa said, putting her arms round his neck. 'And the other one is that you're going to put me where I've always wanted to be. I may not be able to sit on the throne, but by God I'm going to be the power behind it.'

Jeff raised himself on one elbow to look down at her. 'Let's get one thing straight from the start,' he said. 'It's my career we're talking about, not yours. I'll take your advice, I'll take your money, but I won't take direction. And if I ever catch you being unfaithful to me I'll beat the living daylights out of you.'

'My he-man.' She sounded sulky, but after a moment she laughed and pulled him down to her again. 'All right, anything you say. Damn you, Jeff, I need you too much to make bargains with you.'

They returned to England and started house-hunting. Anne heard that they were negotiating for a large house not far from Swallow Hall. Tessa's money would pay for that, presumably. Anne wondered briefly how Jeff would square that with his pride, and then dismissed them from her mind.

She had plenty of other things to occupy her. She had got through her first-year examinations successfully, but she was having to study hard to keep going and the work seemed less congenial than it had once been. Her job at the college was growing more demanding, too. She seemed to be everlastingly dashing from one place to another.

Melanie, after a short spell of refusing to be left alone in the dark which had been resolved by giving her a nightlight, had suffered no ill effects from her adventure in the old mine, but as she grew older she seemed to need more of Anne's attention rather than less. To Anne it began to seem as if her life consisted of cooking, washing, housework, study, a demanding job, and nothing but the conversation of a four-year-old girl to lighten her leisure time.

At the end of January Anne was involved in the disaster which overtook the Lincolnshire coast. On a night of high tide the sea defences were breached and the sea roared in, engulfing reclaimed land, sweeping away walls, fences, roads and, in some cases, even houses. Wallenshaw, Brinthorpe and Upbridge were all too far from the coast to be affected, but twenty homeless people were taken into Swallow Hall and although it was supposed to be a temporary measure some of them were forced to stay for six weeks.

It was Anne who knew that there were camp beds, left over from the wartime occupation of Swallow Hall, stored in the attic, it was Anne who located a supply of blankets, who organized a rota of the homeless women to help with the extra cooking, cleaning and laundry, and who talked local firms into paying for a special bus to take the men to work once they had recovered from their ordeal. Above all, it was Anne who dealt with the inevitable disputes that arose amongst their distraught and overcrowded temporary guests.

Jocelin, representing his father, looked in to sympathize with them and to make them welcome. Anne saw him only briefly. He smiled and said he appreciated the extra work she was doing for these unfortunate people, but Anne thought he spoke more impersonally than he had done in the past and the feeling that he was merely performing a duty on behalf of the Company rankled with her. They had been closer than that once – or had she imagined it?

Evelyn's baby was born in the first week of February, an eight-pound boy who was christened George Jeffrey after Terry's dead father and his brother. The christening in March was the first opportunity Anne had had to meet Tessa. She looked very striking, in a bright blue dress and a fur jacket, with a dashing feather hat which clung close to her head and swept forward against one cheek.

Anne, seeing her standing alone and realizing that no one wanted to push themselves forward to speak to her, went up and introduced herself.

'You're the widow with the little girl, aren't you?' Tessa asked in her brusque way.

'Yes. Melanie is over there, as close to the baby as she can get. She's fascinated by him.'

'It's more than I am! Jeff's been hinting at starting our own dynasty, but I think it's a bloody awful prospect.'

She paused and smiled, the wide, frank grin that made her

so much more appealing. 'I must watch my tongue. He hates me to swear. He's frightfully old-fashioned. I suppose you've known him since you were in the cradle like this infant?'

'We grew up in the same village, but I hardly knew him until my sister married his brother.'

'I was livid when he told you Nanny Brewster's cottage was available, and then you only lived in it for a few months, so I might just as well have had it in the first place.'

'It served me a good turn,' Anne said, rather put out at having this old grievance dragged up.

'I suppose so since it got Jocelin interested in you and landed you your present job. I did wonder whether he was having an affair with you, but Jeff says not.'

'Certainly not!' Anne thought she sounded pompous and despised herself for the hot colour she could feel sweeping over her face.

'He's been dating one of my bridesmaids,' Tessa said inconsequently. 'Mummy is in ecstasies. She very much fancies having an Hon. in the family.'

Jeff came up to them. Anne thought that he looked wary when he saw them talking together, but Tessa did not seem to notice. She put her hand through his arm and held it tightly.

'Darling, haven't you done everything a godfather has to do?' she asked. 'We've cut the cake and drunk the ghastly infant's health. Can't we go?'

'In a few minutes. It will look rude if we make the first move.'

'I must drag Melanie away and take her home to bed,' Anne said.

'We'll give you a lift,' Tessa said quickly. 'All helpful and friendly, and no one will be offended.'

She made a little face at Jeff and the tip of her tongue peeped out for a moment between her lips. To Anne's surprise he laughed and agreed and since it would be a real help to be taken home by car Anne said goodbye and hurried Melanie into her coat, in spite of her protests that her little cousin wanted her to stay with him.

Anne saw a picture of Jocelin in a magazine a week later. 'The Hon. Penelope Carminster with Mr Jocelin Tyndall'.

The girl was tall and dark. She had turned her head to look at Jocelin so that it was difficult to see her features. Jocelin was smiling. It all looked very suitable. Anne closed the magazine and put it away from her with an irritable gesture. All these births and marriages and hints of romance; it made her feel as if she had been put on the shelf, and it was no comfort to realize that it was a shelf of her own choosing. If she had pushed her luck a bit harder with Jeff would he have married her in the end? Did she, just a bit, regret having been so firm with him? He could have given her the life she wanted. Even without the Tyndall connection Jeff had been going places. Now, with Tessa behind him, it looked as if the sky was the limit, while for Anne the future seemed to promise nothing but loneliness and hard work.

In April Wally was saddened by the death of an old friend who had risen to be Chief Engineer at Wallenshaw.

'Poor old Sid, I never thought to see him go off like that,' he said. 'Only a year or two older than me. They say it was his heart.'

'I thought the last time I saw him he was a funny colour,' Beryl said. 'He carried too much weight for a man of his age. You'll go to the funeral, Wal?'

'Those of us that knew him well are getting time off.'

It came as no great surprise to hear that Jeff had been promoted to the dead man's job and Wally was quick to disagree with hints that favouritism had been shown.

'Daft talk,' he said scornfully. 'Jeff's got the drive and the know-how to do the job. I won't say he couldn't have done with a few more years' experience, but unless they transfer someone from another works there's no one else at Wallenshaw who can take over from Sid. He'll do.'

Both Jeff and Jocelin knew that there was something going on in the Boardroom of S.V.T. which was not being disclosed to the staff, although wisps of rumours drifted out from time to time. They were being asked to produce an unusual volume of statistics on existing practices as well as feasibility studies for improving production, and the feeling of change in the air was vaguely unsettling for everyone.

At the beginning of June, on Coronation Day, when everyone

else's mind was fixed on Westminster Abbey, Sir Frederick suddenly took his son into his confidence. Lady Tyndall and Tessa were absorbed in watching the television set, but the long build up to the ceremony bored Sir Fred.

'Come and have a drink in the study with me,' he said to Jocelin. 'You can let me know when anything interesting starts to happen, Em.'

'I find it all interesting,' his wife said. 'Such a pity about the weather. Those poor people who've been out all night, they must be soaked.'

'I hope I'm as patriotic as the next man,' Sir Fred said to Jocelin as they left the room. 'But I see no sense in sitting out all night in the pouring rain. Here, have a whisky. I can't sit still staring at that box, I've got too much on my mind.'

'Something to do with the Works?' Jocelin asked.

'I suppose everyone knows. Impossible to keep these things quiet.'

'I began to guess when I ran into a chap from Supra Works,' Jocelin said slowly. 'I gathered they were doing the same exercise as we were. What is it to be? A straight choice between the two Works?'

'You've hit it. The Board has agreed in principle to a major expansion programme. The question is, where? To my mind Wallenshaw is the better site, but Supra has had money spent on it in the last five years and at the moment has the edge on efficiency.'

'What will happen to the Works which doesn't get the modernization programme?' Jocelin asked.

'While the present boom lasts we'll keep it in production. But you know we always say that demand for steel goes in cycles, and what goes up must come down. If we run into recession then the old-fashioned works will gradually be phased out.'

Jocelin crossed his long legs and looked at his father thoughtfully.

'Your own preference is for Wallenshaw?' he asked.

'Yes, and I don't think it's because I had the running of it. The trouble is, it's a gut reaction. I just feel in my bones that Wallenshaw is the better bet.'

There was a large-scale map hanging on the wall with all the S.V.T. steelworks marked on it. Jocelin got up and went to study it, his glass of whisky in his hand.

'Wallenshaw has room for development,' he said. 'Supra is hemmed in by housing.'

'A lot of the houses have been condemned and will have to be pulled down in any case.'

'Have you thought of offering Supra to one of the other steel companies? United Steel might find the ironmaking capacity useful.'

'Some of the Board members are a bit leary about doing that. Which ever of our competitors acquired it would have an advantage over us until the new capacity came in at Wallenshaw.'

'But we'd have cash in hand to play with,' Jocelin pointed out. 'How are you going to raise the finance?'

'Partly our own resources and we plan to apply to the Finance Corporation for about three million pounds.'

Jocelin's eyebrows rose. 'As much as that? You'll be lucky if you get it.'

'That's why the strategy has got to stand up to probing.'

'They've had labour problems at Supra, haven't they?'

'Yes, too much competition from other works nearby. The men can pick and choose.'

'If you're looking for arguments to swing opinion towards Wallenshaw then you could use that,' Jocelin pointed out. 'If you expand Supra you'll have to pull down houses and build new ones farther away, and you know how the average steelworker hates to live any distance from his place of work. If you enlarge Wallenshaw and run down Supra then it might be possible to shift some of the labour force and provide new homes for them round Wallenshaw.'

'It's a useful point,' Sir Fred agreed. 'Of course, in the end it's money that'll talk. Which one will it be cheapest to modernize and will it give us the return we're looking for?'

'Are you two going to stay in here talking secrets and miss the Coronation?' Tessa demanded from the doorway. 'The Queen's arrived at Westminster Abbey.'

Sir Fred drained his glass. 'I suppose we'd better go and see the lass crowned,' he said. 'I was born in the year Queen Victoria died so this makes my sixth monarch, if you count Edward VIII. I'm not likely to see another coronation in my lifetime.'

'Mummy's glued to the television set, looking for people she knows,' Tessa said. 'We spotted Lady Carminster amongst the peeresses, looking *exactly* like a horse. Penelope will be just like her when she's older. Mummy seems to think you're going to set up your own little stable with her, Jocelin?'

'I have no such intention.'

His father glanced at him quickly. 'It would be a useful connection,' he said.

'All that lovely money and Lord Carminster has influence in the City besides,' Tessa added helpfully. 'What have you got against Penny the hopeful filly?'

'I can't stand the way she has of calling me "Joz-lin",' Jocelin said.

He spoke flippantly, but both his father and his sister detected a degree of annoyance behind his words and Jocelin was conscious himself of a strong dislike of having his name linked with a young woman he had merely squired to parties a few times.

He thought about it as he sat and watched the slow ceremony of the crowning. Penelope was a pleasant companion, well-mannered, good-looking, fairly intelligent, but she lacked that essential spark which would have quickened his interest. It was a pity, because Jocelin had reached a point in his life when he was ready for a home of his own. The semi-independence he enjoyed in his parents' roomy house answered well enough, but he had grown dissatisfied with it. He had plenty of money and there was nothing to stop him moving into a place of his own, except that his parents would be sorry to lose his services as a useful caretaker at Upbridge Park while they were in London during the week, but he was looking for a more fundamental change than that.

There had always been plenty of women in his life, but such affairs as he indulged in were conducted in the discreet anonymity of London and he had never given rise to the sort of local gossip that had surrounded Jeff Blackmore. Penelope was no more than a friend, but there were other, more experienced women who were very ready to take Jocelin Tyndall into their bed. He moved amongst them lightly, never giving rise to any serious expectations and never becoming deeply involved. It was all very pleasant, very much on the surface. One woman, stung by a moment of inattention, had accused him of caring more about his wretched steelworks than about her and there was a grain of truth in what she said. She gave him no more than a quick gratification of the senses, enjoyable while it lasted and soon forgotten; his commitment to Wallenshaw went far deeper. His father had been right to detach him and send him to the United States for three months; he was growing too narrow in his approach and he owed it to the Company to take a wider view. All the same, when his father had spoken of making a choice between Supra and Wallenshaw Jocelin had felt an immediate apprehension in case Wallenshaw should be passed over. The Company had his allegiance, but it was Wallenshaw which touched his heart.

Jeff arrived to join them just as the crown was being lowered on Queen Elizabeth's head. Tessa looked round and made a grimace, but she patted the seat beside her and when Jeff sat down she moved so that her thigh rested against his. They were an odd couple, but there was something between them, an excitement, a mutual dependence, which Jocelin saw and envied.

He had not liked the idea when Tessa had first announced that she intended marrying Jeff, suspecting that Jeff was merely ambitious to marry the boss's daughter, but now he was not so sure. They acted as if they were in love, Jeff as much as Tessa.

The thing that had made Jocelin feel most uncomfortable was when he had found himself breaking the news to Anne Hardwick. Just for one moment she had looked stricken, then she had recovered and expressed an astonished pleasure so well simulated that he might have been taken in if he had not seen the way she was gripping the back of the kitchen chair.

It brought back to him the time when he had called on Anne in her old cottage and found Jeff there, very much at home. There had been a feeling of intimacy between Anne and

Jeff that day which had irked Jocelin, knowing, as he did, of Jeff's involvement with Tessa in London. A bit of a scoundrel, Jeff, when it came to his dealings with women, and by no means the brother-in-law Jocelin would have chosen, especially if he had behaved badly to Anne.

If he had not been leaving for New York the morning after Melanie and Peter's adventure Jocelin thought that he would have looked in on Anne again, if only because his sense of involvement with the Carless family had been heightened when he had driven Peter home. Sitting beside him, Peter had suddenly begun to talk, as one soldier to another, of his experiences in the Japanese camp. Jocelin had drawn his car in to the side of the road and let Pete talk himself out, listening in almost total silence to the dull, monotonous recital.

'I'll have to go and see Dave's mum and dad now,' Peter had concluded.

'Don't tell them!' Jocelin exclaimed.

'That I killed him? No, I won't do that. I'll just say I've remembered that I was with him and that he died quickly after having been wounded. I don't know why that should be a comfort to them, but it will be.'

He slumped lower in his seat. 'I'm that tired I could sleep for a week,' he complained.

By the time they reached his home Peter was so sound asleep that Jocelin and Wally were forced to carry him to his bed.

'Good job he's still sleeping downstairs,' Wally said. 'We're grateful to you, Mr Tyndall, though we're far off understanding what's happened today.'

'Shouldn't we wake him up?' Beryl asked nervously. 'It doesn't seem right, him sleeping like that.'

'Don't do that,' Jocelin said quickly. 'Pete has had an experience that has shaken him badly. Fortunately, he kept his head and rescued himself and little Melanie from what could have been a very nasty situation. It's brought back his memory of everything that happened to him as a prisoner-of-war and facing up to that has exhausted him. What I do urge is that he visits his doctor. He's been having psychiatric care, hasn't he?'

'Not really. There didn't seem to be anything they could do for him, not after all these years. But he's still in touch with the hospital,' Wally said.

'Do you think he'll go back to being his old self?' Beryl asked.

'I've no idea. The only thing I know is that your son has come back to life and it hurts. He may need to cover it all up again. That's why I say he must see the headshrinker.'

When Wally saw Jocelin to the door he asked abruptly, 'Will he tell us what he's told you?'

'I think not and it's better that he shouldn't. He talked to me because I was the first person he was alone with after getting out of the old mine and perhaps because he recognized me as someone who'd been through the war and seen some hard times. Let him shut the door on it, Wally.'

During his absence the impressions of that night had faded. Three months was a long time. Jocelin, not particularly relishing his tour of the American steel works, had made up his mind to get all the enjoyment possible out of his social life and had embarked on a whirlwind affair with a young woman who had needed very little wooing. Looking back, Jocelin felt a certain distaste. There had been an element of ruthless efficiency in the way he and Anna-Belinda had indulged their mutual lust which in the end had left him jaded. He had parted from her with a feeling that came close to relief. He had returned to England in a mood of melancholy and self-mockery and nothing that had happened since had made him feel any better.

When he had seen Anne at the time of the flood disaster he had only just remembered to ask after her brother and the little girl and her reply that they were both well had hardly registered with him.

A week after the Coronation Jocelin was driving along a country road near Wallenshaw. He had been working all day on a further report for the board and now that he knew that the future of the Works might depend on it he had put his entire energy into it. He was tired, but not too tired to notice a 'For Sale' sign on a tract of land by the side of the road. Because his mind was focused on making new housing available if Wallenshaw Works was expanded he saw immediately that this was a site which could not be ignored.

Everything depended on whether it could be used for building. Jocelin might not be a farmer, but he was country bred and he knew that it was land that had never been in good heart. What was more, it had been separated from the farm to which it belonged by the re-routing of a road. An idea came into his mind which made him smile in wry amusement. Temptation on a plate. If he bought the land and held on to it and the Company needed it for building he could make a small fortune. It would cause a nasty smell, though. 'Chairman's son in secret property deal'. He hadn't got the mentality to turn himself into a millionaire, it seemed. Nor the nerve either, he admitted. He would have to tell his father about it, but not until he had obtained all the details.

For no other reason than that he had to pass her door and was struck by the idea that she was a person he could trust to keep her mouth shut, Jocelin pulled up at the Gate House and told Anne about the land for sale.

'I'd like you to get in touch with the agents and get all the information,' he said. 'I've no objection to you using the name of the college, but I don't want to appear in the matter myself and I don't want the Company's name mentioned.'

'Why should S.V.T. be interested in a plot of land down that road?' Anne asked.

'That's the sort of question I want to avoid,' Jocelin said. 'Will you get me the particulars without mentioning it to anyone else and then forget about it?'

'Yes, of course.'

There was a touch of reserve in the way she spoke and Jocelin guessed the reason for it.

'I've got a nerve, coming and asking you to run errands for me when I've not been near you for months, is that what you're thinking?' he asked.

It was exactly what Anne had been thinking, but said out loud it embarrassed her.

'Not at all,' she said stiffly. 'Naturally I am prepared to accept any instructions you give me.'

'I'm not sure I like that. I'd rather you grumbled about it as you might to any other friend.'

'You certainly know how to charm the birds off the tree, don't you?' Anne asked in amusement and exasperation. 'Very well, Mr Tyndall, I think you're being very mysterious about a simple matter, but I'll get in touch with the agents and ask for the particulars you want.'

'I wish you'd call me Jocelin, Mrs Hardwick.'

'I wish you'd call me Anne – sir.'

Jocelin threw up one hand. 'Let's call off the hostilities. And let me make up for my neglect. Tell me how your brother is getting on.'

'He's doing marvellously well. He's still not the person he was before the war, but he always seems to know where he is now. He went round in a funny, dogged sort of way visiting all the places he used to go to as a boy, all the places he'd avoided since he came home, and it seems as if he's got his landmarks fixed again. Best of all, he's found a way of using the skill he picked up in the workshop at the Rehabilitation Centre. Look at this lovely dolls' house he made for Melanie. He's started making wooden toys and they've been really successful.'

'He sells them through a shop?'

'Two shops in Upbridge take all he can supply. He's had enquiries from farther away, but I doubt whether he will ever want to expand beyond what he does already. He seems contented and he's not ambitious.'

'Unlike his sister.' Jocelin picked up one of the books lying open on the table. 'Have you got your sights fixed on becoming Financial Director of S.V.T.?'

'Hardly that. What I do think is that once I've qualified I may want to move on from the College. I'm saving all the money I can so that if that day comes I may be in a position to buy a little house for Melanie and me.'

'You don't think you might marry again?'

Jocelin was looking down at the book on accounting and his question seemed absentminded.

'Shall we say that I'd consider the case on its merits?' Anne said.

'That's very cool! Obviously you have no one in mind.'

The man who would have suited me best married your sister; but Anne kept that bitter thought to herself.

'No one at all.'

Jocelin put the book down carefully. 'I must go. My dinner will be spoiling.'

'You look tired,' Anne said abruptly.

'I'm exhausted,' he admitted. 'There's a heavy workload at the moment.'

'My Dad's very suspicious; he thinks there's something going on the workforce aren't being told about.'

'What can I say to that except "No comment"?'

'That's as good as telling me that he's right. Not as diplomatic as usual, Mr Tyndall.'

'Jocelin. I told you I was tired.'

There was a line in the middle of his forehead which had not been there the last time she had looked at him closely and from his nose to the corner of his mouth the smile lines which gave his face its agreeable look of amused intelligence had deepened into permanent marks. His light brown hair needed cutting and flopped forward over his forehead. His look of weary vulnerability touched Anne as his usual self-sufficiency had never done. She had always thought of him as the effortless skier, swooping over the difficulties of life as he had once done over the snow to visit her. Never before had she felt this wish, almost a need, to reach out to him.

As they moved towards the door, with Anne seeming lost in thought, Jocelin asked, 'Shall I offer you a penny for them, or are your thoughts more precious than that?'

With a mixture of compassion and bravado she answered him, 'I was wishing there was something I could do to help you.'

She had surprised him; she saw that in the way his arching eyebrows rose and the way he began to smile.

'Dear Anne, you're very sweet,' he said, and the way he spoke led, without any thought about it at all, into a light touch under her chin and a quick, gentle kiss. She could feel his lips still smiling as his mouth rested on hers.

Anne stepped back. 'From Christian names to kisses in one evening is going rather too fast,' she said.

The frown was back on his face. 'I'm sorry, that was a mistake,' he said. He touched the tip of her nose with one long finger. 'Even though it was very pleasant.'

Thinking it over afterwards Anne resented him saying that. He had wanted to kiss her and the fleeting touch of his mouth on hers had given her a quick jolt of pleasure which he must have been aware of, in spite of what she had said. Why apologize? Unless he felt himself in the wrong for molesting one of the underlings – and that was a really unpalatable thought.

Anne went to some trouble to get the information Jocelin wanted about the land for sale and passed it to him with a business-like note. Jocelin gave the details to his father, but shortly afterwards Sir Fred reported that by the time the Finance Committee had decided on the purchase they had been too late: it had already been sold.

'I'm not altogether sorry,' Sir Fred told Jocelin. 'It would have meant tying money up in the land for some years, and I'm not sure we can afford to do that.'

'I was hoping possession of a suitable bit of land might tilt the scales in favour of Wallenshaw,' Jocelin admitted. 'I wonder who bought it. They seem to be as anonymous as we wished to be. It'll be interesting to see who builds on it, and what.'

Chapter Six

One thing Anne had always tried to do was to keep Melanie reminded that her father had been Canadian and that she had another set of grandparents in Alberta. Melanie could not remember Mel's parents, but they still sent her presents for Christmas and her birthday and Anne wrote and gave them news of herself and Melanie, if not very frequently at least often enough to quieten her conscience. She had sent them some photographs taken at her nephew's christening, not because they would be interested in him or in Evelyn, but because they included Melanie. She was growing up, Anne thought regretfully, losing her baby chubbiness and turning into a little girl. Her talk nowadays was all about going to real school in September, after her fifth birthday.

The birthday came and went and there was no parcel from Canada. Anne was in a quandary, not sure whether to write and ask if they had sent a present which had miscarried. The photographs had not been acknowledged either and that was not like her mother-in-law, who usually wrote back by return of post, leaving Anne with the disgruntled feeling that it was always her turn to write.

Two days after Melanie's birthday there was an Air Mail letter from Mrs Hardwick. Mel's father had suffered a massive heart attack at the beginning of July, he had been treated in hospital and had seemed to be recovering, only to succumb to a second attack which had killed him. Mrs Hardwick was not a woman to make a parade of her grief, her stoical reticence after Mel's death had seemed inhuman to Anne, but her letter revealed how deeply she felt her loss.

It was a shock and it came at a time when Anne was already

feeling depressed. Melanie was dismayed to see her mother wiping away tears. Anne explained that her grandfather in Canada had died and it made her sad.

'Died really dead, like my Daddy?' Melanie asked.

'Yes, dear. I must write to Granny and tell her how sorry we are.'

'You could tell her she didn't send me a birthday present,' Melanie suggested.

'She had other things to think about. She'll remember you another time.'

All day Anne was haunted by memories of her life in Canada and, in particular, of Mel. He had been fond of his father, more so than he was of his mother perhaps, that strange, silent woman. There had been times after Mel's death when Anne, catching a glimpse in the yard of his father's tall, upright figure, his black hair untouched by grey, his strongly marked features with their reminder of his Indian blood, had felt as if she were suffering from some mad hallucination and Mel had come back to her again. She would miss the thought of him, still there in the place where she had known Mel. It was one more link gone.

Until Melanie had gone to bed Anne managed to keep her sad recollections to the back of her mind, but once she was on her own she gave in not only to her sense of loss, but also to a furious feeling that her entire life had been misdirected. Everything was going wrong. It still rankled that Jeff had married another girl. Even the job which had given her so much satisfaction was turning sour on her.

She was standing with her back to the garden door, which stood open in the bright sunshine of the August evening, and when she heard a knock she hesitated before she turned to face her visitor, her head held high, daring whoever it was to notice that her face was mottled and her eyes were red.

It was Jocelin, the last person she wanted to see her looking like that, and far from passing it over in tactful silence, he said immediately, 'There's something wrong. What is it?'

'My father-in-law in Canada has died. Mel was very like his father. It brought it all back to me, made me remember . . .'

'I'm sorry. Do you want to talk about it?'

'No, I'd rather not.'

He made no attempt to probe any further. Instead, he held out the package he was carrying.

'I did remember Melanie's birthday,' he said. 'But I've been away all this week. This is for her.'

'How very kind of you.'

A silence fell between them. Anne searched her mind in vain for something to say. Her head ached, her body felt like lead. She had been a fool to let herself get so upset, just as if it was Mel who had died again.

'Why don't you go and wash your face and I'll make you a cup of tea,' Jocelin suggested.

'You . . . ?' Anne said disbelievingly.

'Why not? Go on, you'll feel better when you've freshened yourself up.'

She did as he suggested, washed her face, splashed cold water on her eyes, put on some lipstick, combed her hair, and it was true, it did make her feel more like her usual self.

'I didn't expect you to look so much at home with a kettle in your hand,' she said to Jocelin when she returned to the kitchen.

'I can cope if I have to. Are these the right cups?'

'They are the only cups,' Anne retorted. 'I'll pour it out.'

'How are things going with you, apart from this sadness over your father-in-law?'

'Oh . . . all right,' Anne said with a lack of enthusiasm that made Jocelin look at her attentively.

'Are you taking a holiday soon?' he asked.

'I'm off for the next two weeks, starting on Monday.'

'Where are you going?'

'I'm not going away. I might take Melanie to the coast for the day, that's all.'

'You ought to do more than that, have a proper holiday.'

Anne did not reply and Jocelin went on, 'Surely you could afford it? Your salary is quite good now and this place isn't expensive. I don't want to sound as if I'm trying to manage you, but I would suggest that money spent on a complete change would be an investment, both for you and Melanie.'

Anne concentrated on an odd tea leaf, floating on top of the tea in her cup.

'I think I told you I was saving up for a place of our own one day,' she said carefully.

'I thought that wasn't likely to be for some years?'

'It may have to be sooner than that.'

She sounded bothered, in a way that made Jocelin suspicious.

'You're thinking of leaving the college?'

'I don't know . . . yes, I might do that.'

'But why, Anne? I thought you were so well suited to the job and that the arrangements we've been able to make for you were helpful.'

'I know it must seem ungrateful,' Anne said hurriedly.

'Oh, damn gratitude! I don't want that. I do want to know why you're thinking of leaving. Is it money? Have you had a better offer?'

'Oh, no! I haven't anything else in view.'

'Then, if you'll forgive me saying so, you'd be a fool to leave.'

'Yes, but . . . things happen sometimes which make it necessary to . . . to make a change.'

'Do they indeed! What's gone wrong, Anne? Come on, you can tell me, surely?'

Anne shook her head, her expression a mixture of worry and embarrassment.

'No, I can't . . . I don't want to . . . I ought to be able to deal with it on my own,' she said in a rush.

Jocelin looked at her consideringly. 'It's not money,' he said. 'It's not the work, because Brian is always telling me how wonderful you are . . . oh, my God, it's not Brian?'

Anne pressed her hands to her cheeks. 'I didn't mean to tell you, since he's a friend of yours,' she said. 'He's got a grand wife and two lovely children and yet he doesn't seem to be able to leave me alone. I'm at my wits end to know how to choke him off without making a scene. I've begun to think the only thing to do is to leave, but that means giving up the Gate House and trying to find somewhere to live as well as looking for another job. It's all been rather wearing, and then when I got the news about Mel's dad it was the final straw and I made a right idiot of myself, as you saw.'

'I'll speak to Brian,' Jocelin said.

'No! I'd never be able to look him in the face again if he knew I'd talked to you about it.'

'I'll be more subtle than that, let him think I've noticed his behaviour myself. The trouble with Brian is that he was a bachelor for too long and he's never reconciled himself to settling down with one woman.' He shook his head in mock despair. 'No wonder my mother is always urging me to get married!'

'You don't seem to take it very seriously,' Anne said, not quite pleased by his easy handling of a problem which had been causing her so much aggravation.

'You're wrong, I do take it seriously. I could cheerfully knock Brian into the middle of next week, but that would cause just the kind of sensation you've been trying to avoid. I think it's best treated lightly. That way, we can save his face and make it possible for you to go on working together. You do want that, I take it?'

'Oh, yes! When I first started at the college I was so happy.'

'Then I'll do my best to put the clock back for you. And you must tell me if you have any more trouble.'

'Yes, all right,' Anne promised reluctantly.

She still wished she had not told him. It made her feel incompetent, not being able to cope with this mundane little problem. And it bothered her, the degree of relief she felt because Jocelin was taking it over for her.

'No wonder you were so annoyed when I made the mistake of kissing you,' Jocelin said.

'That was different,' Anne said quickly.

The only thing she had in her mind was that she could not bear him to think that she made no distinction between his cool little kiss and Brian's pawing hands. When she realized what she had said she went on hurriedly, 'After all, you're not married and you only meant it in a friendly way. I didn't really mind.'

'In that case, may I do it again?'

Anne was not at all sure she had heard him correctly. She

stared at him, with a feeling that her mouth must be dropping open. He was standing with his back to the door, very calm and collected, looking, Anne thought in wild amusement, every inch the English gentleman.

'Not if you'd rather not,' Jocelin said obligingly. 'No need to feel harassed. Not one step will I take towards you unless you say, "Yes, please, Jocelin".'

'It's s-so unsuitable,' Anne said uncertainly. 'Of course I'm very grateful to you . . .'

'Oh, Anne! Gratitude! The last thing I want. I can see you don't want to kiss me tonight, but keep it in mind. I shall ask you again.'

Keep it in mind! After he had gone she could think of nothing else. Jocelin Tyndall wanting to make love to her. It was enough to give any girl pause for thought, especially a girl brought up within sight of the steelworks his family controlled. How far did he want it to go? He was no inexperienced boy, not likely to stop short at a few kisses. Anne's stomach muscles contracted in a spasm of excitement at the thought of being in bed with Jocelin.

She poured herself out a cup of stewed tea and sat over it, her elbows on the table, lost in thought. She would have to be careful. An affair with Jocelin would soon be the talk of the neighbourhood. It would put paid to her chances of a second marriage to anyone local.

Since she had been forced to put the idea of marriage to Jeff out of her mind, Anne had refused to admit to the possibility of wanting any other man permanently in her life again. She had started out on her course of study in all sincerity, but what had once been an exciting choice had become a wearisome chore. She had stuck to it out of pride, but the truth was that she had reached a point where if she had to make a decision between a man and a career, she would take the man.

Marriage – to Jocelin? The idea followed on naturally from her train of thought. She doubted whether it was what Jocelin had in mind. What would she have to do to bring him round to it? Making love to Jeff had been a mistake, but Anne had the feeling that if she kept Jocelin at arm's length he would grow bored and bow out gracefully. She would have to gamble on making it so good for him that he would want her permanently. He could give her everything she had always wanted, not only for herself but, even more importantly, for Melanie, too. No more fears of poverty; they'd have a beautiful home, a good social position; and Jocelin would be a wonderful husband, streets ahead of anyone else Anne was likely to meet. Anne poured away the cold tea she had forgotten to drink, her mind made up: if Jocelin meant to pursue her she would make it easy for him.

The weather continued to be good and Anne and Melanie were able to start their holiday on Monday by taking a picnic into the fields. When they got home a note had been put through the door,

'If you and Melanie have no other plans for Wednesday, will you come to Skegness with me? I'll call for you at ten o'clock.

Jocelin'

'Is it a nice letter?' Melanie asked. 'You look all pleased.'

'Mr Tyndall is going to take us to the seaside on Wednesday,' Anne said.

For no particular reason she hugged her daughter to her and kissed her.

When Jocelin's car drew up on Wednesday they were ready and waiting, both wearing clean cotton frocks and sandals.

'Got your swim suits?' he asked, smiling at the sight of them waiting like a pair of expectant children by the garden gate.

'Yes, and a picnic,' Anne said.

She gave him a quick, shy look, taking in his casual elegance. Wretched man, he always looked as if he'd just been pressed and laundered, even in an open-necked shirt. Probably those beautiful lightweight slacks and the jacket flung carelessly on the back seat had cost more than Anne's entire wardrobe. The way she had been thinking about him made it difficult to act naturally and now that she was face to face with him Anne wondered how she had managed to persuade herself that Jocelin could be manipulated by any woman.

'I'll sit in front,' Melanie announced.

'Please *may* I sit in front,' Anne corrected her automatically.

She caught Jocelin's amused look and grimaced, reluctantly conceding that she sounded like every mother who had ever lived.

'Melanie will sit in front going and Anne will sit in front coming home,' Jocelin said.

'Now that I'm five I can call you Mr Tyndall,' Melanie told him, climbing into the seat beside him.

'Just as you like, but I'm quite fond of being Uncle Trindle.'

'No, it sounds like a baby. I'm going to start going to real school in September.'

'Will you like that?'

'Yes, she'll love it,' Anne said, with a warning frown. The last thing she wanted was for Melanie to get the idea that she might not like her new school.

'Sorry – tactless,' Jocelin murmured.

He began to realize as the day progressed how ceaselessly Anne's attention was focused on Melanie. Without apparently realizing it, while she was still talking to him, she would look round to check her daughter's whereabouts, and turn back satisfied if Melanie was playing happily nearby.

'You hardly take your eyes off her,' he remarked as they lay on the sand, stripped to their swimming costumes, while Melanie demolished the sandcastle Jocelin and Anne had helped to build.

'I try not to be over-protective,' Anne said quickly. 'But she's an adventurous child. It's difficult to strike a balance between letting her do things for herself and hauling her back from the edge of danger.'

'It's a fearsome thing, being a parent,' Jocelin said, looking round the beach. 'Something I've hardly thought about before. They're so little, and so vulnerable.'

'It limits your life in some ways,' Anne said carefully. 'There are many things I might like to do, but I always have to ask myself how it would affect Melanie.'

She wondered whether he had understood what she was trying to convey. If he did, he gave no sign of it.

'Is she like her father?' he asked.

'Very much so. She gets her black hair from Mel and some

of her ways – I find it almost unbelievable sometimes, considering she hardly knew him.'

'Tell me about him.'

'He was one of the most striking looking men I've ever seen,' Anne said slowly. 'Very tall, very dark – he had Red Indian blood in him. It's only recently that I've looked at our wedding photos and realized how young he was. He was brought up on a ranch in Alberta, very strictly brought up. He was extraordinarily shy when I first knew him. Being in the Army had driven him into himself rather than brought him out. We were attracted to one another right from the moment we met. I was a more outgoing person, a bit spoilt because I'd always been popular. Mel was deep and quiet and thoughtful, but not . . . I wouldn't call him a very *intellectual* person. He didn't have a lot to say in company, but we never stopped talking when we were alone. There's something very special in knowing that you are the one person another person can talk to.'

'You must have been very happy.'

'Until I spoilt it. I got terribly run down after Melanie was born and there were difficulties about our life in Canada. I couldn't settle, I was homesick; when I saw that we might be going to spend the rest of our lives on the ranch and – even worse – that it was what Mel wanted, I turned into a terrible nagger. Poor Mel, he didn't know how to cope with me. The worst of it was, I could see what I was doing, and yet I couldn't stop. Mel just withdrew. He never told me he was volunteering to go back into the Army until after he'd done it. And then he was killed.'

She bent her head over the handful of sand she was trickling through her fingers. Jocelin reached out and covered her hand in his, holding it in a warm clasp.

'I'm sorry,' he said.

'I've got over it now. It's only occasionally, like the other night after hearing that his father was dead, that it all comes back to me. But you do see, don't you, why I'm so careful of Melanie?'

'You feel guilty because you think you drove her father into the Army and so you must take special care of the part of him that has survived?'

'That's putting it in very plain terms,' Anne said, taken aback at being so thoroughly understood. 'I don't think like that all the time. I want Melanie to grow up happily for her own sake, not just to make up for my shortcomings.'

'You're doing a very good job.'

'It's good for her to have a man's company occasionally which is one reason why I'm grateful to you for this day out.'

'What about her mother?'

'It's good for her, too.'

He was lying by her side, wearing only brief swimming trunks, his lean body unexpectedly muscular, and very brown, but then he had already had a holiday abroad somewhere. For one breathless minute Anne was aware of every inch of him; his sleek brown head, his thin face with the mockingly arched eyebrows and veiled eyes, the fine lines of his arms and shoulders, his chest with a scattering of golden hairs, the taut muscles of his stomach, the swelling manhood under the brief trunks, his long legs coated in sand. She bent her head over the grains of sand, knowing that his eyes were on her, that he found her beautiful, that he desired her.

'Are you . . . are you going swimming?' she asked at random.

'I think I'd better.'

'You'll find the water cold, even in August.'

'Just what I need,' he said gravely.

Anne looked at him wildly, her face flushed, her expression desperately worried now that they had reached the point she had wanted.

Jocelin touched her cheek with a sandy hand. 'Don't look like that. I've told you before I won't do anything you don't like.'

He went down to the water and Anne looked round distractedly for Melanie, her mind in a complete turmoil. Just as well he couldn't read her thoughts. She had never wanted a man so much in her life, not even Mel. Not even . . . Jeff. She sat up, hugging her knees. I'd go with him now, this minute, if he asked me, she thought dismally, and no questions asked about what he intended for the future. Thank goodness we've got Melanie with us. And he was talking about me protecting her!

If Anne was more withdrawn for the rest of the day, Jocelin gave no sign of noticing it. He seemed to be more interested in playing with Melanie than in pursuing her mother. He insisted on taking them to what he called a 'reasonably civilized' hotel for tea, in spite of Anne's agitated objection that Melanie was grubby and covered in sand. She took her into the ladies' cloakroom, all imitation pink marble and gilded mirrors, and gave her a quick wash and a reminder to mind her manners. As she combed her own hair Anne looked at the reflection of her face, flushed from the sun, and thought that already she looked different, even though nothing had happened. Her eyes looked brighter, her mouth seemed softer and fuller. She closed her eyes and leaned her forehead against the cold glass.

'Have you got a headache, Mummy?' Melanie asked.

'No, dear. I just feel hot, that's all.'

The tea revived her, but it made Melanie sleepy. By the time they reached the Gate House she was sound asleep on the back seat of Jocelin's car.

'Shall I carry her in for you?' Jocelin asked.

'I'd be grateful. She's too heavy for me now. I'm sorry she's not awake to thank you for giving her such a lovely day.'

'It's been my pleasure.'

'I'm very grateful . . .'

'No more gratitude, Anne. Whatever I may have been able to do for you in the past is cancelled and forgotten. As from today we're making a fresh start.'

Anne looked straight ahead of her, at the roses she ought to have deadheaded, at one of Melanie's toys discarded on the grass with its wheels in the air, the bits of washing she had hung out before they left that morning.

'What is it you want from me?' she asked.

'Shall we say friendship, to begin with?'

He curled his fingers round her wrist, with a cool, light touch. Anne turned puzzled eyes on him, searching his face for some clue to his real feelings.

'Friendship?'

'To begin with.'

He opened the car door and got out and Anne followed him,

standing by while he carried Melanie indoors and up to her bedroom. She hardly stirred.

'She may wake when I undress her,' Anne said. 'Leave her for now.'

Downstairs again she faced him, willing him to go quickly, without touching her. It seemed as if Jocelin understood, because he made no attempt to linger. As soon as it was too late Anne felt a sickening disappointment. He was going, just as she had wanted, and she would have given anything to call him back.

She watched him walk the few steps to the gate, open his car door and then turn back again.

'Anne, your picnic bag,' he called.

He carried it into the house and put it down on the table. Again he made as if to go, but this time he said, 'My intentions are good, but there are times when I find it quite impossible to live up to them,' pulled her into his arms and began kissing her.

Anne's mouth was eager under his; she felt her body move, fitting itself against his. They swayed as they stood and Jocelin shifted his arms to hold her more comfortably as their lips parted and met again. Anne had no idea how long they stood together, holding one another so closely that they were almost one. Time had stood still for her and yet when they drew apart she was conscious not of the wild desire which had invaded her on the beach, but of a feeling of peace and happiness.

'So much for friendship,' Jocelin said.

He was smiling, but Anne thought his voice sounded unsteady and she was glad that he too, cool Jocelin, had been shaken off balance.

From upstairs a voice was calling her. 'Mummy! Mummy!'

'You must go,' Anne said. 'I can't . . .'

'No,' he agreed. 'I'll be in touch with you. Bear with me, Anne. I have to be in London for the rest of the week.'

He was gone for longer than that. Anne, watching constantly for his long grey car, lost a little of her happiness each day that it did not appear. The only thing she had to sustain her was a postcard saying, 'Detained in London, curse it. We must get you a telephone.' He signed it with nothing but an initial. Not a very lover-like message, but at least it told her the reason for his absence.

The next post brought Anne something she had never expected, an invitation from Lady Tyndall. She was not at all sure what it meant, 'Lady Tyndall At Home – 8 for 8.30' and scrawled in one corner, 'Black tie – Dancing'.

She was still debating how to reply when Tessa called to see her. She made no bones about telling Anne why she had come.

'I'm *devoured* with curiosity. I mean, I was there when Mummy asked Jocelin if there was anyone he wanted invited to her party and he said, "Yes, please, Mrs Hardwick". Mummy had completely forgotten who you were until I reminded her.'

'Is Jocelin home?' Anne asked.

'No, we were all in London.' Tessa's smile deepened. 'My dear, is this serious?'

'Certainly not. Jocelin has been kind to me, that's all.'

Anne could feel her cheeks burning and she knew she had not deceived Tessa for one moment.

'I doubt if I shall come,' she said.

'But you must! I want to see Jocelin and you together. You're frightfully pretty; there must be more to it than Jocelin doing his philanthropic act. He does rather go for married women, too. He bowls them over like ninepins in London.'

It cast a new and unwelcome light on Jocelin, that flippant remark from his sister. Of course, Anne had always known at the back of her mind that he must have had plenty of experience. He was bound to, a man of his age and background.

'If he thinks he's got an easy touch in me, then he can think again,' Anne said. 'He's not going to bowl *me* over.'

'That's the girl!'

Tessa looked at her admiringly. 'It's time someone stood up to Jocelin. I tried before I was married, but I never got anywhere. So you're not in love with him?'

On a sudden reckless impulse Anne told the truth.

'I could be. It wouldn't be difficult. But I can't have an affair with him. It wouldn't be fair to my little girl.'

She paused and then blurted out, 'I'd like to marry him.'

She thought that Tessa looked taken aback and Anne's heart

sank, but then Tessa pulled herself together and said thoughtfully, 'Why not? It's time he got married and no one else has managed to pull it off. Do you want me to help you?'

'Only in little ways. This invitation, for instance. I don't understand what it means.'

'We meet at about eight o'clock at Upbridge Park for drinks, then there'll be dinner and after dinner extra people will come in for dancing. You'll need a long dress. Have you got one?'

'Only a ballerina-length taffeta I bought for a students' dinner here. I've worn it three times already.'

'Get a new one. Look on it as an investment. If Jocelin is going to start taking you around you'll need it.'

'It's difficult for me to go out in the evenings. I've got Melanie to think about.'

'Can you make some arrangement for her, assuming you come to Mummy's do – which I really think you should.'

'My mother would have her for the night,' Anne said. 'I don't know . . . I'll feel awkward, arriving on my own.'

'As you're Jocelin's special guest he'll come and fetch you, of course. If he doesn't then Jeff and I will take you. I've always suspected Jeff had a bit of a thing about you. I wonder how he'll take it when he sees brother Jocelin walking off with you.'

'It hasn't happened yet.'

'It will, if you make up your mind to it. He's a frightfully good catch, you know, if you can stand his superior style. Get your hooks in him and drag him to the altar. What a hoot it'll be!'

'I don't intend to marry in order to give you a good laugh.'

'Now I've annoyed you. I tell you what I'll do: I'll meet you in Upbridge and take you to a dress shop I know. Upbridge isn't my favourite shopping centre, but there is one decent place and I'm quite thinking of getting myself something new for this party, so we could try them on together.'

When Anne continued to hesitate it never occurred to Tessa that it was because she was wondering how much she would have to draw out of the bank to pay for a dress from a shop recommended by Tessa.

'Look, this is going to be a big party with a lot of local

people there,' she said in her abrupt fashion. 'You can hold your own with any of them. I've got no use for that sort of false pride that creeps about being ever so 'umble and I don't think you have either.'

'I wish I could have spoken to Jocelin about it,' Anne said.

'Make up your own mind! Stand on your own feet! Do you want to come?'

'Yes, I do.'

'That's that, then. When shall we meet in Upbridge?'

'I could manage Thursday,' Anne said, capitulating. 'I'll park Melanie with Mum for the afternoon.'

The only glimpse Anne had of Jocelin was a hurried five minutes in her office.

'I'm lecturing here and then going straight off to catch a plane to Germany,' he said. 'I'll pick you up on the stroke of eight on the night of Mum's party.'

He glanced round quickly. 'Is the atmosphere here better?'

'It's like a different world. What did you say to Brian?'

'We've been friends for a long time. I gave him a few straight home truths. Don't worry, he thinks it was based on my own observation – and my interest in you.'

'Are you interested in me?' Anne asked.

'Is that a reproach because I've been neglecting you? I feel as hard done by as you do. Don't hold it against me. I've been run off my feet.'

He leaned towards her. 'If I kiss you now I shall forget everything I was going to say in my lecture.'

They looked at one another and then unwillingly Anne began to smile.

'That's better,' Jocelin said. 'I have to get you into a good mood because I'm going to ask you a favour. I'm bringing a couple of German industrialists back with me. If I arrange for them to sit at our table for dinner do you think you could remember enough of your German to help me keep the conversation going?'

That served her right for boasting that she spoke German, Anne thought with a sinking heart, but she managed to keep on smiling.

'They probably speak perfect English,' she said. 'If they don't, I'll do my best.'

Anne emphasized her usefulness as an interpreter when she asked her mother to have Melanie for the night of the party. Beryl took that in her stride, merely remarking that no doubt it would be a good night out and she had always wanted to see the inside of Upbridge Park herself, but she sniffed at the idea of Anne buying a new dress for it.

'What do you want with a long evening frock?' she demanded. 'When do you think you're going to wear it again? It'll hang up in the wardrobe gathering dust, that's what. Far better to spend the money on a nice warm coat for the winter. What's wrong with the pretty blue dress you bought last year?'

'I've worn it several times. Anyway, I've made up my mind to get a new one and Tessa is going to come and help me choose it.'

'It'll cost you a pretty penny then. That young madam's never been used to anything but the best.'

'I've got some money saved.' Anne hesitated and then added carefully, 'I want to look my best since it's Jocelin who's invited me and I'll be sitting with him.'

She saw her mother turning that over in her mind and braced herself for the inevitable comment.

'I don't know that I altogether like the way he's taken you up,' Beryl said. 'What's going to come of it? I'll tell you – nothing! You're a pretty girl and you always did have the boys after you! I dare say he's taken a fancy to you, but it'll do you no good in the long run. What you need, no matter how much you may talk about your career, is a husband for yourself and a father for Melanie. You'll not find a man of your own sort while you're running round with Jocelin Tyndall! What I said before I'll say again, Jeff Blackmore was the one you should have had.'

'Jeff didn't think so.'

'You could have had him if you'd wanted him. I saw the way he noticed you.'

Something about Anne's silence made her uneasy and she went on, 'You think it's none of my business and you don't thank me for interfering, I know that, but it's you I'm thinking about. Your dad would say Jocelin Tyndall's no better than any other man, but that's nonsense and we both know it. If you get a taste for the life he can show you you'll never settle down in the way you ought to.'

'I've got my head screwed on,' Anne said, trying to reassure herself as well as her mother. 'I'm not your daughter for nothing.'

Her mother's warnings and her own uncertainties reduced Anne to a state of frozen nerves on the night of the party. She looked beautiful, and slightly aloof, in a tight-fitting gown of fuchsia pink chiffon, swathed closely at the breast and waist and flaring out below the hips. It was a far more striking colour than Anne would have chosen without Tessa's encouragement, but Tessa had taken one look at her in the shop and groaned in envy.

'Hell! It's exactly what I would have chosen for myself if I hadn't seen it on you first. You must have it.'

And Anne, looking at the sophisticated beauty reflected in the long looking glass, had shut her mind to the voice of commonsense and written out a cheque for exactly twice the sum she had meant to spend.

Her conviction that she had made a profound mistake and would spend the evening regretting it, and in any case was not going to enjoy the party in the slightest, melted in the face of Jocelin's approval. He called for her, just as Tessa had said he would, looking as smooth and glossy as a model girl's escort in a fashion magazine, and totally out of place in the Gate House kitchen, but under this veneer he was still the Jocelin who had romped with Melanie on the beach, who had kissed Anne so wildly in that same kitchen.

He took both her cold hands in his, standing back to look her up and down with uninhibited satisfaction.

'I always knew you were lovely, but tonight you look dazzling. You will remember I was the one who asked you, won't you? I have first claim on you, no matter how fierce the competition may be.'

He raised first one hand and then the other to his lips, lightly kissing her fingers. There was something in his smile that hinted at better things to come and Anne found herself laughing in return, suddenly warm and confident.

After that everything went well. Anne was a success. She knew it and Jocelin told her so, not only in words, but by the way he looked at her, by the touch of his hand on her arm, by the way he held her when they danced. At dinner Anne sat with Jocelin on one side and one of the German visitors on the other. He was the elder of the two and spoke little English, while his younger companion was fluent. Anne, who had spent a frantic week poring over her old German grammar books, began by apologizing because her German was rusty, but under the influence of Herr Flischer's geniality she found it coming back to her.

Even Lady Tyndall, her vague manner concealing an eye that missed very little, went out of her way to say, 'My dear, you've been such a help with those heavy Germans. And how lovely you look! We must get to know one another better.'

She drifted away, cool and elegant in floating grey trimmed with fronds of ostrich feathers, her smile unshakeable, while her mind grappled with the realization that her favourite child was well on the way to disappointing all her hopes for him. Anne Hardwick was young, beautiful and undoubtedly intelligent, and it looked as if Jocelin was in love with her, but she was not what his mother would have chosen for him. Perhaps it would all blow over; one couldn't pretend that Jocelin hadn't had these little fancies before and nothing had come of them. Such a pity because he would make a delightful husband.

Anne tried to avoid Jeff, but that was impossible. She had to dance with him once. She felt herself stiffen as he pulled her into his arms.

'Relax, love, I'm not going to rape you with my ma-in-law watching, even though you look good enough to eat,' Jeff said in her ear.

'Your wife picked this dress out for me. She thought it did something for me,' Anne said, emphasizing her reference to Tessa.

'It certainly does something for me,' Jeff told her.

His big, strongly-muscled body was moving against hers. Anne tried to pull away from him.

'Don't hold me so tight. It's not decent.'

'Feels good though, doesn't it?' When she did not answer he repeated insistently, 'Doesn't it, Anne?'

Anne tilted her head back to look up into his face.

'I gave you my answer to that a long time ago. I don't want you, Jeff, and especially not now when you're married to Tessa.'

'Hunting different quarry?'

'If you want the truth, yes. If you can have Tessa, why shouldn't I have Jocelin?'

'No reason,' Jeff said. 'No reason, except that there's a little bit of you that'll always belong to me, whether you admit it or not.'

They finished the dance in silence, each of them annoyed with the other, and more disturbed by their proximity than either of them liked to admit. It was only thinking it over afterwards that Anne realized how telling it was that Jeff did not ask her to dance a second time.

It was nearly two o'clock before people started to leave. Jocelin came up to Anne and slipped an arm round her waist. 'My dance, and let's make it the last one,' he said. 'Have you had a good time?'

'Wonderful!'

'Better than you expected?'

'Much! Was it so obvious, that I dreaded feeling out of place?'

'I could see you expected to be eaten alive. People are people, Anne, no matter where you find them. And with your advantages you need never be afraid to go anywhere or do anything.'

Which was all very well, but what had made the evening memorable was that Jocelin had been there, always at her side when she needed him, dancing with her, introducing her to people, seeing that she was never without a drink, a partner, a topic of conversation. If only it could always be like that, what a wonderful life it would be.

It went on being delightful, the last blissful dance, the friendly goodbyes, the ride home in Jocelin's comfortable car. He hardly spoke as they drove along the quiet country roads, but he hummed the tune of the last dance under his breath and Anne let her head droop on the seat until it rested against his shoulder.

She turned towards him as they drew up outside the Gate House, but Jocelin did not touch her. He helped her out of the car, took her key and opened the front door. As he followed her in Anne realized that this was the way Jocelin had always meant the evening to end.

He took her little handbag out of her hand and removed her flimsy stole from her shoulders and then at last he drew her towards him and kissed her.

'Darling Anne,' he whispered. 'Lovely Anne. Wonderful Anne.'

His lips moved over her neck and shoulders, punctuating the repetition of her name with kisses. Anne stood with her eyes closed and her head thrown back, every nerve crawling with pleasure at the delicacy of his touch. When she felt him turn her towards the stairs, with an arm encircling her waist, Anne opened her eyes and said distractedly, 'Jocelin, I'm not sure I should do this.'

He twisted her towards him again and held her tightly.

'My darling, we can't turn back now. Don't talk, don't think, just feel. Let go and be guided by me. Trust me, Anne.'

He made it all seem easy, just as he had the whole evening. The sweet, insistent assault on her senses carried Anne far beyond the schemes she had made to tie Jocelin to her. She had thought in her ignorance that it would be up to her to make their lovemaking so good that he would not want to part with her, but now they were together it seemed as if she had never known a man before. They lay with their limbs so entwined that Anne scarcely knew which was her body and which was Jocelin's. Again and again she drifted to the edge of sleep and was called back by Jocelin's lips and hands to a pleasure so piercing that she heard herself cry out as if in pain. And when they were quiet she found that they could laugh together, a breathless acknowledgement of the extremes to which they had driven one another.

Anne woke at last from a haze of fatigue to find that it was light and Jocelin had left her side. She turned and saw that he was dressing.

'It's past six o'clock and broad daylight,' he said. 'I must go.'

He sat down on the edge of the bed and bent over her.

'Happy?'

Anne's head moved slowly on the pillow. 'So happy.'

'Good.' He bent down and kissed her lightly on the forehead. 'I'll come back and see you later in the day.'

'I have to go and fetch Melanie and Mum will expect me to spend the day with her,' Anne said.

'Damn. Tomorrow?'

'Melanie will be here. I can't . . .'

Again he kissed her. 'I know. Don't worry, I understand. But we must talk. I'll come tomorrow evening after she's gone to bed. Tonight perhaps it might be a good idea if we both got some sleep!'

Anne had no idea what her mother made of the state of dreaming delight in which she moved through the rest of the day. All Beryl said was, 'You look three parts asleep. Well, I'm glad you enjoyed yourself. Good job it was a Friday night and you didn't have to go to work this morning because you certainly don't look fit for it. Melanie's been very good, bless her. You'd better take her home straight after tea and put the pair of you to bed at the same time.'

By the time Jocelin arrived on Sunday night Anne had woken up. It had not gone as she had planned. It was Jocelin who was in control of their affair and Anne who was helpless. She loved him beyond all reason and not only for the physical pleasure he gave her. There were qualities in Jocelin which matched an ideal she had scarcely known she had. As for marriage, why should he bother, when she had fallen into bed with him at the first asking and was trembling with eagerness to do it again at any time he wanted?

When she let him in he was as smiling and confident as he had been when he left her, but he was quick to see that Anne was in a different mood.

'What's this?' he demanded. 'No smile for your demon lover?'

In spite of her qualms, Anne could not stop herself from laughing.

'That's better. Now kiss me, just to make sure I didn't imagine it ever happened.'

She clung to him, thankful to feel his arms round her once more and to know that he was unchanged.

'So you've spent the last twenty-four hours worrying about my wicked intentions, have you?' Jocelin said. 'Don't deny it, I can see it in your face.'

'If you spend the night with me regularly I'm going to be the talk of the neighbourhood. I won't like that, my family will be hurt, the day will come when I'll have to explain it to Melanie. I can't bear it, Jocelin.'

'I know, my love, I'm as alive to the difficulties as you are.'

It was not the response she had hoped for. Anne steeled herself and said in a voice flat with disappointment, 'We'll have to stop.'

'Not possible, darling. Just seeing you like this I'm frantic for you again. And you . . . ?'

Without putting his arms round her he moved closer, until their bodies were just touching. Anne shuddered and flung her arms round his neck, pressing herself against him, reckless of the consequences.

'Yes,' she said. 'I'll do anything you want.' Again she hardened herself to say, 'But I won't do it happily.'

'I don't want an unwilling lover,' Jocelin said. He tilted back her head to look down into her face. 'What is it you really want, Anne?'

With her lips scarcely moving, Anne said, 'Marry me.'

Jocelin was still looking at her intently, slightly frowning. 'I have thought of it,' he admitted. 'I was going to wait – see how things worked out. I've been in love before, my dear, but it's never lasted.'

'Because you always looked on it as a temporary arrangement,' Anne suggested. A feeling of hope was beginning to stir in her; at least he had not rejected her out of hand.

'Perhaps,' Jocelin admitted.

'Don't you want a proper home? Children of your own, like other men? I can give them to you.'

'I suppose – yes, of course I do.'

'Unless you commit yourself you'll never have them.'

'An act of faith?' He was beginning to look amused, but then his smile faded and he was watching her again with that strange intensity. 'Are you saying that unless we get married we've got to part?'

'No,' Anne said. 'I'm not strong enough for that. I love you.'

On an impulse that moved them both, they clung together, exchanging a long kiss.

'If you'd said "yes" I would have let you go,' Jocelin said. 'Desperately as I want you. I won't stand having a pistol held to my head. My own dear girl, I know you're right. I've teetered on the brink for too long. It's time I plunged into the water. If I wait for the rest of my life I'll never find anyone to match you, not just for beauty, but for courage and honesty, too. Will you marry me, Anne?'

'Yes, with all my heart.'

She felt dizzy, light-headed with relief. She'd pulled it off, and he still respected her. Not only that, but she was deliriously in love with him.

'Darling,' Jocelin said softly in her ear. 'Now that we're semi-respectable can we please go to bed?'

Chapter Seven

During the three months that he and Anne were engaged Jocelin bought a pleasant house standing in a large garden on the outskirts of Upbridge. Anne found it difficult to believe that it was really hers. Four big bedrooms, a lounge, a dining room, a study for Jocelin and a large, sunny kitchen. Two bathrooms! Never in her life had Anne imagined she would live in a house with two bathrooms. Only a few months before her highest ambition had been to have one proper one. She was slightly ashamed of her excitement and tried to hide it from Jocelin.

'You do like this house, don't you?' he asked when they had made a final inspection of the newly decorated rooms just before their wedding.

'Of course I do!' Anne replied.

'Sure? You've been very quiet about it today. You're not disappointed, now that you see it empty?'

'Disappointed?'

Anne quickly decided to tell him the truth.

'I'm afraid if I let you see how much I love it you might think that's why I'm marrying you.'

She was relieved when he laughed.

'And I've been worrying in case you felt that I was trying to play at being King Cophetua – you know, that chap who married the beggar maid? Not that you're a beggar maid, far from it. Let's be honest with one another, Anne. It must be a relief to you to know that I can provide you and Melanie with a decent home. I accept that. It makes me feel good. It's part of the satisfaction I'm getting out of marrying you. Inside of me there's a primitive man who wants to go around beating his chest and boasting about the fine dry cave he's found for his mate.'

'Idiot.'

They moved closer together and Anne closed her eyes as they kissed. Another hurdle was behind her, they had taken another step forward in their relationship. It was going to be good.

'Do you want to hang on to some of your independence?' Jocelin asked. 'Are you going on with your accountancy studies?'

Anne's first reaction was dismay that he should even suggest it.

'I've been finding the studying a burden,' she said carefully. 'And this is a big house to look after.'

'You'll need help in the house, of course,' Jocelin said, as if he had taken that for granted.

'Me, with a charlady? Goodness, that's something I hadn't thought of,' Anne admitted. 'Mum will come and give me a hand if I need it.'

'We can't employ your mother to do our cleaning,' Jocelin said. 'I think you should have someone who comes regularly – and preferably not from Brinthorpe.'

'I suppose you're right. Most of the women there have known me since I was born and it might be awkward, telling one of them what to do.'

They let the question of Anne resuming her classes drop, but the thought stayed in her mind and, with it, the suspicion that Jocelin would respect her more if she finished what she had started.

Although Anne explained to Melanie very carefully that she was going to marry Jocelin and they were all going to live together and be very happy it never occurred to her that Melanie would not realize that the quiet ceremony in Brinthorpe Church was the wedding. Brides, Melanie knew, wore long, white dresses and veils and they had bridesmaids. Melanie confidently expected to be Anne's bridesmaid. Going to church in her best clothes was something she did every now and again, but it did not, to Melanie's mind, make a wedding.

It was only after the service, when everyone was laughing

and talking and drinking toasts to Anne and Jocelin, that she began to get worried. She knew that she was to stay with her grandmother and grandfather, which was something she had done before, but never for more than one night. During the long two weeks while Anne and Jocelin were on their honeymoon Melanie grew pale and quiet; she refused to eat, she had inexplicable tantrums, but she never once asked when Anne was coming back because she was so much afraid that the answer would be that she had gone for good and Melanie would never see her again.

Her mother did come back, but she was subtly altered. To anyone else she might have looked like a young woman dazed with happiness; what Melanie noticed was that Anne no longer had eyes exclusively for her.

'She's been moping ever since you went away. It's been a real worry,' Beryl said. 'I don't know what came over her. She's been happy enough with us before.'

'Poor baby, was I gone too long?' Anne whispered, kneeling by Melanie's side and putting her arms round her. 'Never mind, my pet, I'm back now and step-daddy, too, and we're all going to live happy ever after.'

Melanie let herself be patted and kissed and something of her secret terror subsided, but over Anne's shoulder her eyes accused Jocelin. She knew very well who had taken her mother away and it would be a long time before she forgave him.

They ran into another difficulty two nights later when Anne was putting Melanie to bed. Melanie's room had been freshly papered and painted, all delicate pink and white and blue. She agreed, when Anne asked her, that it was pretty, but as Anne was tucking her up she said, 'Mummy when are we going home?'

'But, darling, we are home,' Anne said. 'This is where we are going to live all the time now. You remember, I explained to you we were going to live with step-daddy.'

'You said he was going to live with us,' Melanie accused her. 'I want to go home!'

In the storm of tears that followed there was nothing Anne could do but hold Melanie in her arms, rocking her gently as if she was a tiny baby.

When Anne went downstairs Jocelin had just come in after his first day back at work. He held out his arms and she went to him.

'Lovely, to come home and find you here,' he said contentedly. He looked down at her shadowed face and asked, 'What's wrong, darling?'

'Melanie still seems terribly mixed up about our marriage. Apparently she thought you were going to come and live with us in the Gate House! She insists she wants to go home.'

'Sit down and I'll fix you a drink.'

Sitting on the sofa, looking at his long back and deft hands among the bottles, Anne felt weak with love. Nothing could really spoil it, the wonderful happiness of her marriage to Jocelin, but all the same she could not help letting her thoughts drift back to her unhappy little daughter.

'I thought it was all going to work out so well,' she said. 'I thought she understood.'

'It's a lot for a five-year-old to take in,' Jocelin said. 'She'll come round in time. Is there anything I can do? Anything she'd like that would make her feel more at home?'

'It would be a mistake to try to win her over by giving her things,' Anne said. 'Just go on being yourself. She's always liked you; it's your new place in our lives she resents. She's jealous, of course, poor little mite, though she doesn't realize it. And quite without reason. I don't love her any the less because I love you too. Quite the opposite. At the moment I feel as if I love the whole world.'

'I'm rather pleased with life myself, and not only because of you. While we've been away the Board have at last reached a decision about the development programme.'

'It's going to be Wallenshaw? Darling, I'm so pleased. I know it's what you hoped for.'

'There are drawbacks,' he warned her. 'I'll be up to my eyes in work. I may have to leave you on your own far more than I'd like.'

'I think I'll take up that suggestion you made before we were married. I'll go on trying to qualify as a Company Accountant.'

'Good girl! You must learn to drive, too, then you can have a little car to run about in.'

'I can see my days will be full, even if you are going to neglect me,' Anne said.

Jocelin bent over her and kissed her quickly. 'Keep your nights free,' he whispered.

*

In her bewilderment Melanie turned to her Uncle Pete. She loved to visit him in the workshop he had set up in the garden shed at Brinthorpe, playing with the curling wood shavings and chattering away to him, not bothered that he said little himself because she knew he listened to every word she said as his craftsman's hands created a new toy or a miniature house. Her grandparents kept telling her what a lucky girl she was to have such a lovely new daddy; Uncle Pete said nothing. Melanie sensed his silent sympathy and used him to try out her ideas about the changes in her life.

'Mummy's married to Mr Tyndall,' she told Peter.

'I know. I was in church with you,' Peter reminded her.

'First of all he was Uncle Trindle, then he was Mr Tyndall and now Mummy says I can call him Daddy, but he's not my real daddy.'

'No,' Pete agreed.

'My real daddy's dead. He was ever such a brave soldier. Soldiers who get killed in the war don't come back, do they, Uncle Pete?'

For one moment Pete's busy hands were still amongst the woodshavings.

'No, lovey, they don't come back,' he said.

'Mummy still loves me,' Melanie said doubtfully.

'That's right. She wouldn't ever stop. And Mr Tyndall loves you, and I love you and Grannie and Grandad.'

'And Grannie in Canada.'

'And Auntie Evelyn and Uncle Terry.'

'And cousin Georgie.' Melanie paused for thought. 'Does Uncle Jeff love me?'

'Sure to. And Auntie Tessa.'

'*And* I've got a new Grannie and Grandad,' Melanie said importantly.

Like a small queen she let her mind run over this satisfactory array of subjects.

'And Mr Mann, the milkman, and Miss Thrower, my teacher, and my friend, Penny,' she improvised.

' "And Uncle Tom Cobbleigh an' all",' Pete said.

Melanie thought that was wildly funny.

'Sing it, Uncle Pete,' she begged. 'Sing about going to the Fair and they all come back dead!'

Gradually she came to accept the change in her life, until one day Anne overheard a snippet of conversation between Melanie and one of her little friends which she repeated that evening to Jocelin.

'He's not your *real* father, is he?' the other little girl asked.

'No,' Melanie agreed, and then she added, 'But he's all right.'

Jocelin joined in Anne's laughter. 'An accolade,' he said.

All the same, Anne was very cautious when she broke it to Melanie that she was pregnant but by that time a year had passed and Melanie took it in her stride.

She put her hand on Anne's stomach, just beginning to swell.

'Is he in there?' she asked.

'Mm. Very tiny yet. Later on, when he's really big, I may be able to let you feel him kicking me.'

But long before that stage Anne had other news to pass on.

Jocelin had been away attending a conference, fretting at leaving her, but powerless to avoid it. When he came home Anne said, 'I think you'd better sit down before I tell you what I've heard while you've been away.'

'Nothing wrong, I hope?' Jocelin flopped down in a large armchair, his long legs spread out. 'Lord, I'm tired!'

'This'll revitalize you. I'm having twins.'

She burst into a peal of laughter at the sight of his flabbergasted face. 'I can see you're delighted,' she mocked him.

'I'm stunned. Darling, what did the doctor say? Are you all right? I mean, it's a bit much, isn't it?'

'I couldn't be healthier and the babies are developing just as they ought.'

The twin boys were born on the 12th May 1955 and were christened Christopher and Timothy.

'I didn't particularly want *two* brothers,' Melanie objected. 'They aren't very pretty, are they?'

'They'll improve,' Anne said.

Melanie pressed closer against her. 'Do you still love me best in all the world?' she asked.

'Best of all the little girls in the world,' Anne said, scrupulously honest.

'Best of everybody,' Melanie urged.

Anne kissed her. 'You were my first baby, that's your special place,' she said. 'No one else can ever be *first* except you.'

When Pete heard of Anne's double event he made two identical cradles which made Tessa cry out in astonishment.

'Your brother made them? My dear, he's a genius! Really, Anne, something ought to be done about this. Some of the big London stores would be crazy about his stuff.'

Against Anne's advice she arranged for a friend from London to call and see Peter, but the store buyer retired baffled by his quiet obstinacy. Peter liked the way he lived and the way he worked and he had no intention of changing. All the same, the word got out and people from Upbridge with money to spare began calling at the little house in Brinthorpe to try to persuade him to make something for them – 'Really *not* expensive when you consider it's all solid wood and handmade and the children love the animals in their Noah's Ark. Such a delightful man, quite young, but a real character! If he's too busy he just says he can't take on any more work and he won't talk at all if he doesn't like you. They say he's turned down all sorts of offers, even Harrods.'

It was Peter who discovered the depth of Melanie's fascination with the prairies of Canada. He searched out old books he had read as a boy and found several about the Wild West. For her eighth birthday he made Melanie a miniature ranch, complete with cattle, horses and cowboys to ride them. The following Christmas he added an Indian encampment.

'I believe he's going to do the Mounties next,' Anne said to

Jocelin. 'I suppose it's a phase that will pass, but at the moment Melanie's got an absolute fixation about going to Canada and Pete encourages it.'

'We could take her over when the twins are old enough,' Jocelin said.

'It still takes my breath away when you say things like that,' Anne told him. 'When I said goodbye to Alberta I took it for granted that I would never go back.'

But before anything could be done about a visit from England to Canada Anne had a letter from Mrs Hardwick saying that she intended visiting England that summer and hoped to see both Anne and her grand-daughter.

'We must have her to stay,' Anne said. 'You won't mind, will you, darling? She's a strange woman, but she is Melanie's grandmother.'

'I'll be glad to think you've got some company. This is going to be a heavy year for me. We're rebuilding the furnaces, converting the last of them to all-basic, and after that the Rotor furnace for pre-refining hot metal will be installed.'

'You know you're talking double Dutch to me. What does it mean?'

'A highly complicated piece of organization! While each of the furnaces is out we'll have too little steel to keep the rolling mills busy, and once the operation is complete we'll have too much. So to begin with we'll be taking slabs from Supra to keep up our rolling production, then steelmaking at poor old Supra will start to be phased out and they will take slabs from us for rolling. The next stage will be to improve our rolling capacity at Wallenshaw.'

'And that means curtains for Supra?'

'Precisely. I'll make a steelworks manager of you yet.'

'Not while I've got two-year-old twins to look after! I wonder if they'll grow up to be as besotted about a dirty old steelworks as their father.'

'By the time they grow up it may be obsolete,' Jocelin commented. 'What we're doing at Wallenshaw is all very well and it gives me most of what I'd hoped for, but we're only putting patches on an old fabric. The people I really envy are the ones who'll be involved in building a new steelworks on a green field site.'

'Is there going to be one?'

'Oh, surely! Steel is still booming, S.V.T. is making good profits and so are the other companies. The time is ripe to cash in on it. The question is, where will it be? I think it ought to be Wales, but there's a strong feeling for Scotland, too.'

'Will S.V.T. be involved?'

'Unfortunately not. Richard Thomas & Baldwins, or possibly Colvilles, are more likely to be given the go-ahead.'

Anne discovered what he had meant about it being a heavy year when he started working seven days a week and rarely getting home before eight o'clock in the evening. She worried about him, but Jocelin seemed supremely happy, absorbed in his work, absentmindedly affectionate towards her and the children but, as Anne said in a moment of exasperation, with his mind always fixed on the men and machines he had left at Wallenshaw when he reluctantly came home to eat and sleep.

Tessa called in and complained bitterly about Jeff's neglect.

'At least you've got the children,' she said. 'You are lucky, Anne. I've been trying for three years to have a baby without any luck and you had two at one go.'

'I thought you didn't want a family,' Anne said.

'Oh, well, you feel sort of inadequate if you don't produce. Jeff would be pleased, though he's hardly going the right way about it at the moment. It's like being married to a bloody eunuch.'

She hunched her shoulders in her old slouch. 'I'm bored. I think I'll open a shop.'

'What sort of shop?'

'Not clothes, everyone does that. Children's things perhaps. Toys, if I can get your brother to do some work for me. Come in with me, Anne? I'll provide the money – I'm expecting to have some to spare shortly from some land I'm selling.'

Her eyes narrowed in malicious amusement.

'I've been saving that bit of land for years, ever since I heard Dad and Jocelin talking about expanding Wallenshaw on Coronation Day. Jeff thought I was mad, tying up money in poor agricultural land, but now the Company is clamouring for somewhere to build houses and I'm cashing in. I'd like to use the money to start a business of my own, if only to show Dad what he lost when he wouldn't take me into the firm like Jocelin.'

'Are you talking about the land along the Elford Road?' Anne asked. An uneasy memory came back to her, of Jocelin asking her to make enquiries and keep it to herself.

'That's right. I snapped it up while the Company was still dithering. There's been a bit of muttering since they found out I owned it, but land with building permission is hard to come by so they're biting on the bullet.'

'I wouldn't mind being involved in the business side,' Anne said. 'Keeping the books and that sort of thing. I'm entitled to call myself a Company Accountant, you know. I just managed to get through my finals before the twins started. It was a bit of a triumph for me and I regret not making any use of it. But I can't do anything until after Mel's mother has made her visit and gone back to Canada.'

Anne was nervous about the meeting with her former mother-in-law. They had parted in bitterness six years earlier and although they had written conscientiously in the intervening years there was no real warmth between them. When she saw Mrs Hardwick Anne's heart sank. It seemed to her that the older woman had not changed at all. Tall, thin, and flat-backed, her long black hair, streaked with grey, drawn back into a knot, her expression severe, she still looked like the woman who had disapproved of her son's marriage to the young English woman. She softened, though, when she saw Melanie.

'She's a fine child,' she said. 'Very like her father.'

There was a silence between the two women and then Anne said, a little desperately, 'I do try to keep him alive in her mind, but it's difficult when she never knew him.'

'It's a pity in many ways that she wasn't a boy,' Delia Hardwick said, ignoring this piece of sentiment.

'I wouldn't have her any different!'

'Maybe not, but it would make it easier for me to know what to do about the ranch.'

'That's something I've never thought about,' Anne admitted.

'I won't live for ever,' Mrs Hardwick said. 'It's a tidy little property, especially now.'

'You wrote and told me you were taking paying guests.'

Mrs Hardwick gave a curious little chuckle. 'I'm running a dude ranch! That's why I'm taking this holiday early in the year. Have to be back for the summer season. That's not what's bringing in the money. It's the oil.'

Anne remembered the Alberta oilfields and the strange little pumps the local people called 'Christmas trees' which clanked away all on their own in the middle of an empty landscape, pumping oil from far below ground into a network of pipelines. She remembered, too, that Mel had told her that an experimental borehole on a neighbour's property had been dry and that his father had refused to allow the test rig on his land.

'Vic had some queer notions,' Mrs Hardwick said, referring to her late husband. 'Didn't think it right to take the oil out of the ground, thought it would weaken the crust. He wouldn't let the oil company drill and he never parted with his mineral rights. He was a great one for holding on to what belonged to him. Anyways, he'd not been gone a year when they came round to try again. I considered in my heart what I should do and concluded I was free to make up my own mind. They found what they were looking for in the home valley, not more'n five hundred yards from the house.'

Anne had a vivid mental picture of the ranch: the old log cabin that had been built by Mel's homesteader grandfather and the house that had been added to it in the nineteen twenties; the scattered cabins which had housed the hands and their families in the days when it had been a working ranch; the corrals for the horses, the pens for the cattle when they were gathered for market, the stream which ran down the hillside and was piped into the house; the wide sweep of grass, the dirt road and the river in the distance. And now an oil pump, a 'Christmas tree' bringing the viscous black oil up out of the ground.

'It brings in a tidy sum,' Mrs Hardwick went on. 'I don't

spend a half, no, not a quarter of it. And I've no one in the world to leave it to but young Melanie.'

'There's no need to worry about it yet,' Anne said uneasily.

'I was thirty-nine when Mel was born, and many a cruel disappointment I'd had before I carried him full term. I'll be sixty-six this year. Nobody lives for ever. I wanted to see Melanie, and to see England before I got too old.'

She glanced round at the large, pleasant room full of spring sunshine.

'If this is what you were aiming at I'm not surprised the cabin you shared with Mel was a let down. It's been in my mind lately that if Vic hadn't been so adamant against letting the oil company in Mel might have had enough money to satisfy you and need never have been killed.'

'She left me speechless,' Anne told Jocelin later. 'I always thought she blamed me for Mel's death, but now it seems as if she holds his father partly responsible.'

'She's a formidable woman,' Jocelin said. 'Does this mean that Melanie is an heiress?'

'Something of the sort, though she didn't give me the slightest indication of how much money she was talking about. She said she'd like to take Melanie back to Canada with her for a few weeks. I've refused because I think she's too young. After all, she's only eight.'

'Nearly nine.'

'Not until August. You will back me up, won't you, darling?'

'Of course. Perhaps next summer we'll all go.'

With this vague promise Anne managed to stave off the invitation from her mother-in-law, but the visit had been mentioned in Melanie's hearing and the seed had been sown: nothing would satisfy Melanie now until she saw her dead father's home.

Tessa's idea of opening a shop became a reality in the autumn and to Anne's surprise it was a success. Tessa found premises in Upbridge and brought her sense of style to choosing the stock, but it was Anne who supplied the business knowledge which kept it from foundering in the first difficult months. Tessa had been fortunate in her timing; the small town was expanding, there was money about and a new influx of young people who were prepared to spend it on pretty baby clothes, on toys and nursery furniture.

'Are you sure you're not doing too much?' Jocelin asked Anne.

'Is that a complaint because I've had to give you a cold meal two nights running?'

'It's more of a worry because you're having to ask your mother to do so much babysitting for you.'

'She likes it and I know the children are safe with her. You didn't mind running her home, did you?'

'I could have done without it at the end of a busy day. If this heavy involvement is going to continue I think you should have permanent help. An au pair girl, perhaps.'

'No! I don't want my home invaded by a lot of servants.'

'One girl,' Jocelin said mildly. 'German-speaking perhaps, so that you can communicate with her.'

'Those girls are more trouble than they're worth. It doesn't seem right when the children's own granny is just down the road and willing to look after them.'

'Your mother's very good with them, no doubt, but it's a bit of an imposition, saddling her with three-year-old twins day after day.'

'I'll cut down on the time I spend at the shop,' Anne said reluctantly. 'I'm sorry, because I'm enjoying it. And I'd like to point out that you were the one who pushed me into getting a qualification that I've never used.'

'I like to see you happy and busy and I admire the way you've thrown yourself into Tessa's business. What I'm trying to point out is that you haven't really thought it through. If you're going to be a business woman you need more help with the children and house.'

'I'll put the boys into the nursery school Melanie used to go to, just for the moment, and I'll give up working in the afternoons. Does that satisfy you?'

'Don't let's quarrel about it, darling. You sound as if you resent what was meant to be a helpful suggestion.'

'You don't want my mother looking after your children,' Anne muttered.

'That's not true!'

Jocelin spoke quickly, conscious that while he had no objection to Beryl minding the children, he did find her constant presence in his home, waiting for him to drive her home night after night, something of an irritant. Just as she had once had a special voice for talking to Peter, Beryl had a manner she adopted towards Jocelin, forced and over-bright, which he found acutely trying. With Wally, Jocelin had no problems. They kept up the same guarded friendliness they had always shared, but with Beryl and Anne's sister, Evelyn, Jocelin found himself at a loss, unable to communicate with them without an embarrassment that was mostly of their making.

'Perhaps I'm being selfish,' he said. 'It's always meant so much to me, coming home and finding you waiting for me, sitting down for a chat and a drink to unwind. It's a bit of a facer having a wife who seems all set for a busy career. I thought perhaps we could get back some of the atmosphere we used to have if you had more help.'

'You always manage to sound so *reasonable*,' Anne said resentfully. 'All right, I admit it's not fair, making you turn the car round and drive to Brinthorpe and then come back and sit down to a meal that's already on the table. I'll try to get myself more organized. But no au pair girls.'

'Pity. I was looking forward to a sexy Continental about the house,' Jocelin said, trying her with a joke. He was relieved when Anne laughed.

'What really surprises me is that Tessa should be so enthusiastic,' he went on. 'The way she made the money for it rankles with me, but I have to admire the way she's buckled to and made a success of her first venture into commerce.'

'I think she needs a new interest,' Anne said. 'Have you seen much of Jeff lately?'

'Every day. Why?'

'Tessa talks about him as if they were hardly even living together.'

'He's been overwhelmingly busy, perhaps even more than I have. The engineering staff have been working at full stretch.'

'I hope that's all it is,' Anne said.

Her feeling that all was not well between Jeff and Tessa was confirmed when they met at Upbridge Park for Christmas Day. It was a wonderful setting for a family Christmas. The house was something of a nineteenth-century monstrosity from the outside, but inside the spacious rooms, decorated with branches of spicy-smelling pine festooned with gold and red, and warmed by large wood fires, breathed the very air of Christmas. Anne, knowing that her own mother and father and Jeff's widowed mother were spending the day with Evelyn and Terry, and that she and Jocelin were taking the children to visit Wally and Beryl on Boxing Day, was able to put her uneasy conscience to rest and forget that Beryl had really wanted to come to her for Christmas.

They had their Christmas dinner in the middle of the day for the sake of the children. Anna managed to keep the twins under reasonable restraint; Melanie, she noticed, was behaving like a little princess, in keeping with the splendour of her surroundings. The only thing that spoiled the meal was an undercurrent of ill-feeling, which from time to time broke out into open bickering, between Jeff and Tessa. It made everyone uncomfortable. Even Lady Tyndall lost her vagueness for a moment and murmured, 'Oh, Tessa, *dear* . . . it's Christmas Day', while Sir Fred, in an effort to restore the jovial mood in which he had sat down to the table, kept Jeff's glass refilled in a way which Anne thought unwise.

By six o'clock the twins were worn out by excitement and unusual food. Since they were staying the night, Anne scooped them up and took them off to bed. They were fractious, over-excited by their long day and the strange surroundings, but eventually they settled down, passing with the extraordinary facility of the very young from being two little bundles of energy to total oblivion, spreadeagled in sleep, long, dark lashes sweeping their flushed cheeks, two identical cockades of hair fanning out on the pillows. Anne bent over them, adoring them in their helpless abandon, and then, satisfied that they would not stir, she went back downstairs.

The stairs and hall were panelled in oak, in imitation of a Tudor mansion. Anne did not like the effect at other times of the year, but at Christmas the sombre walls made an effective background for the festoons of greenery hung with golden bells and glass balls. Anne paused halfway down the stairs to admire the decorations and found that she herself was being watched from the hallway.

'You look remarkably beautiful,' Jeff said. 'Come down and kiss me under the mistletoe.'

Anne ran down the remaining stairs. 'Since when did you need mistletoe?' she demanded lightly. 'I'm not going to kiss you, Jeff, even though it is Christmas.'

She would have gone past him, but he caught her arm and pulled her towards him. She began to suspect that he had still not sobered up from lunch time, or perhaps had been drinking Sir Fred's brandy since then.

'Do let me go,' she said. 'If you want to kiss anyone why not look for Tessa? She deserves an apology for the way you spoke to her over lunch.'

'I'll see her in hell first. Besides, it's you I want. Kiss me, Anne.'

Short of an undignified struggle there seemed to be no way Anne could get out of it. She stood still under his determined hands and raised her face. She had meant it to be no more than a token embrace, but as Jeff's mouth closed on hers she had a moment of blind panic. She remembered with extraordinary vividness the way she had felt years before, as if Jeff would swallow her up and nothing she could do would stop him. She pulled back, jerking her head to one side, and saw Jocelin standing in the doorway of the sitting room watching them.

'Let me go, Jeff,' she said in a fierce whisper, but Jeff still not realizing that they had been seen, merely laughed and held her more tightly, pinning her arms against her sides.

Jocelin spoke, in a voice which Anne scarcely recognized. 'Let go of my wife.'

Jeff's hands slackened and then fell away from Anne's arms. He staggered and put out one hand to steady himself against the carved wooden banister.

'She may be your wife,' he said, with a laugh that betrayed that he was far from sober. 'But I had her first.'

For one moment Anne thought that Jocelin was going to hit him. Instinctively, she stepped between the two men. With her hand lightly touching Jocelin's arm she said, 'It was nothing. Christmas spirit and mistletoe combined were too much for Jeff. Let's forget about it.'

Jeff looked at them, his face dark with resentment and unacknowledged shame.

'I'm going out for some fresh air,' he said.

There was a rush of cold air and then the front door crashed behind him and they heard his feet crunching on the gravel.

'He ought to have put on a coat,' Anne said, still trying to lighten the atmosphere.

'Nice of you to be concerned, but understandable in the circumstances, I suppose. Was it true?'

'What?' Anne said, knowing perfectly well what he meant but hoping to stave it off.

'Was Jeff your lover?'

'Put like that it sounds more important than it was,' Anne protested.

'But it was true?'

She was beginning to grow annoyed by his determination to cross-examine her.

'Yes,' she said shortly.

'I see. I suppose I should have guessed. He seems to have laid every other woman in the neighbourhood. Why not you, too? Why didn't you marry him?'

'Because he didn't ask me.'

Jocelin's eyebrows arched in the supercilious way that always made Anne want to hit him.

'What stopped you asking him?' he enquired.

A wave of humiliation swept over Anne. She could taste it in her mouth like the heartburn carrying the twins had given her.

She turned away, not trusting herself to answer, fighting against tears and determined not to give way to them, and she did not see the way Jocelin's hand flew out towards her as he realized the hurt he had dealt her.

If they had been in their own house the quarrel might have been resolved the same day, but at Upbridge Park, surrounded by people who were expecting them to be convivial, it was impossible to be alone, and by the time they went to bed they had both made up their minds not to be the first to give way.

Even Jeff, Anne thought rebelliously, had behaved better than Jocelin. He had come back, very cold and completely sober, and had said, quite simply, 'Anne, I'm sorry.'

'I could murder you,' Anne said bitterly.

'Shall I say anything to Jocelin?'

'Better not. Even seeing you speak to me is making him smoulder. If you want to make amends, go and patch things up with Tessa.'

From the grimace Jeff made Anne could see that he found that idea distasteful. Almost under his breath he said, 'Every now and again it comes over me how crazy I was to let you go when I could have had you for keeps.'

'Don't be a fool,' Anne said, alarmed by the note of sincerity in his voice. 'Go and talk to Tessa.'

During the four years of their marriage Anne and Jocelin had had disagreements, but this was the first time Anne had experienced Jocelin's cold, determined anger, which shut her off from him and left her feeling helpless and strangely afraid.

She waited for two days and then, coming into their bedroom from the bathroom and finding him reading a book in bed and refusing even to look at her, she yanked the tie at the waist of her pink satin dressing gown tighter in an angry gesture and said, 'Jocelin, this can't go on. I will not be made to feel guilty because Jeff spent one night with me years ago before you and I were important to one another.'

She thought he was going to ignore her, but as her words sank in he lowered the book and said, with a degree of uncertainty that made her feel better, 'One night? Is that all it was?'

'Yes, it was. And I'd like to remind you that you did the same before you condescended to marry me. Only, after Jeff, I felt angry with myself and humiliated and the next time he called I locked him out. I could never have done that to you.'

'When I saw you with him on Christmas Day it looked as if you were kissing him willingly.'

'It seemed better not to make a fuss. I attached no importance to it.'

Jocelin was silent for a long time and then he said carefully, 'I think I've been making a fool of myself.'

'You're dead right you have!' Anne agreed.

'I didn't "condescend" to marry you. Don't ever say that.'

'You reminded me that I was the one who did the asking. That hurt.'

'You only nudged me into doing something I already wanted. I've never thought about it since.'

'Haven't you? It came out very pat when you got upset. Perhaps it's been niggling at the back of your mind for the last four years.'

'I suppose I've always known that you wished I'd been the one to take the initiative,' Jocelin said slowly. 'Seeing you with Jeff got me on the raw and I deliberately said the most wounding thing that came into my head – as we all do when we're angry.'

Very deliberately he added, 'Every day of our marriage has been a blessing to me.'

They looked at one another, both willing to let their differences be forgotten, but still wary, frightened by the gulf that had opened between them for so little cause.

'What do I have to do to be forgiven?' Jocelin asked.

Anne slipped her arms out of the satin dressing gown. After a momentary hesitation her matching nightdress was tossed after it on to the floor.

'Tell me first that you're sorry and then that you still love me.'

*

The quarrel had blown over, but it did not make the two men like one another any better. Anne was conscious, as she had never been before, of an undercurrent of animosity between them and, in the spring of 1958, of a competition which only one of them could win.

She tried to cover up the fact that she did not know what he was talking about when her father said to her one day in March, 'Come on, Anne, let's have the news. Is it Jocelin or Jeff for General Manager?'

It took her a split second to think of an answer, but she managed to laugh and keep it diplomatic.

'I wouldn't tell you even if I knew!'

When she saw Jocelin that evening Anne asked, 'Are you in line for promotion?'

'Possibly.'

'You might have told me.'

'It's still confidential.'

Her hurt silence reproached him and he seemed to feel it because he went on, 'It's a delicate situation. We brought in the top man from Supra to run the new-style Wallenshaw and it's obvious now that he isn't up to it. He's likely to retire early, in which case there'll be a vacancy. I'm in the running for it, although I'm not yet thirty-seven and that's a bit younger than people are usually promoted to General Manager.'

'Do you know who else is being considered?'

'A chap from Wales, though there are doubts about how well he'd fit in. And Jeff.'

'It's between you and Jeff, isn't it?' Anne asked quietly. 'How badly do you want it?'

'Let's put it this way: I won't work under Jeff. If he becomes General Manager, I'll start looking for a transfer.'

'But . . . that would mean moving, giving up our lovely house, leaving our friends and family, taking Melanie away from her school.'

Anne's voice trailed away in dismay.

'All those things,' Jocelin agreed. 'Is it too much to ask?'

The carefully controlled question told Anne that she had blundered.

'No, of course not,' she said quickly. 'I go where you go. It's come as a shock to know that you'd got as far as thinking of such a possibility and not even mentioned it to me. What about Jeff? If you come out on top will he work for you?'

'Jeff will be able to rationalize it by assuming that I've been promoted because I'm the Chairman's son,' Jocelin said with a tight little smile. 'It takes a lot to dent Jeff's self esteem.'

'Tessa knows how to do it,' Anne said. 'Jocelin, she's your sister and I don't want to say anything against her, but she's really behaving very badly. Jeff came round looking for her the other evening . . .'

'Jeff came here? You didn't tell me.'

'I'm telling you now. He only stayed five minutes. I didn't say anything because . . .'

'You thought I might be jealous?'

'Because I didn't want to gossip about your sister!'

It was partly the truth, but not all of it, and Jeff had stayed longer than five minutes. For all that she held it against him that he had made trouble between her and Jocelin – trouble that still simmered below the surface even though they were reconciled – Anne had felt sorry for him.

'I've just got back from a visit to south Wales,' he had said. 'The house was all locked up and there's no sign of Tessa. Have you any idea where she is?'

'But, Jeff . . . surely you knew? She's gone to Paris. She's looking into the possibility of importing some children's clothes.'

'That's an excuse. She's gone to Paris to spite me. She wanted me to change all my arrangements and go gallivanting off across the Channel with her, not to buy for the shop but to go to some ball an old school friend of hers is giving. Not my line, but I would have gone if it had been any other week. I explained to her how impossible it was to get out of this south Wales trip.'

'Work comes first?' Anne asked with a certain ironic inflexion in her voice that made Jeff look at her quickly.

'You sound as if you've been on the receiving end, too,' he said. 'All right – barring emergencies, work comes first, both for me and for Jocelin. If Tessa is as ambitious for me as she's always pretended to be, then she ought to understand.'

'Tessa is a restless person. I think she's disappointed about not having had any children yet,' Anne said diffidently.

'Oh, hell! Anne, can I have a drink? Whisky, if you don't mind.'

Without meaning to Anne glanced at the clock.

'What's the matter? Afraid Jocelin will come home and find me here?' Jeff demanded.

'As a matter of fact, yes. He's never really got over what happened at Christmas.'

'It was a lousy thing to do, telling him about us. I feel a heel whenever I think about it. I don't know what got into me. Something about his damned, superior "unhand my wife, sir" attitude got under my skin.'

He took the glass Anne offered him with a muttered word of thanks.

'Do you ever regret marrying the Crown Prince?' he asked.

'No.'

'Never?'

Anne hesitated. 'We've had our difficult moments, as any married couple might. I've had to adapt.'

'Ah, that's the point. You've had to adapt to him, not the other way round. That's the way Tessa expects it to be, too. I give, she takes. Except that there's one thing I'm not going to be able to give her and how the hell I'm going to break it to her I don't know. I stopped off in London on my way home today to get the result of some tests. It seems I'm never likely to father a child.'

He gave a strange laugh while Anne was still grappling for something to say in response to such a disastrous revelation. 'When I think of the time I've wasted taking unnecessary precautions!'

He held out his glass. 'Come on, I may as well drown my sorrows in style. Jocelin keeps a very good brand of whisky.'

'You're not going to sit here and get drunk,' Anne said. 'I'm desperately sorry for you. Tessa will take it hard, I know. But it's not the end of the world, Jeff. Other marriages survive without children, why not yours?'

'You don't understand. I was confident that not having a child would turn out to be Tessa's fault. I needed that weapon against her, something that would keep her from getting the upper hand. Now it turns out to be another of my failings. I'm a disappointment to Tessa. She thinks I ought to have got on faster than I have.'

'But you've done so well!'

'Tessa doesn't understand that being a Chief Engineer is

not the same as being on the board. I advise on policy, I carry it out; I don't direct it. That's what she wants from me.'

'You're not yet forty!'

'Tessa likes quick results. I ought to have married you, Anne. You'd have had me, wouldn't you?'

'If you'd gone the right way about it,' Anne said carefully. 'But you let me see too clearly what you thought of me.'

'I was crazy about you!'

'To you I was a good lay, a nice bit of skirt, nothing more. I felt degraded.'

'Well, thank you very much! I'm a failed husband and a lousy lover. Perhaps I'll go and look for someone who appreciates me.'

'That'd be a disaster! Don't do something stupid because you're hurt. Share it with Tessa. Once she sees how grieved you are she'll surely rise above her own disappointment.'

'But Tessa's not there, is she? Gone off to Paris to dance with her smart friends. Just the sort of thing she would have despised when we were first married.'

'She's getting back at you because you've been neglecting her. She does care for you.'

'She's got a damn funny way of showing it,' Jeff muttered.

He was still twisting his empty glass round in his hand. Anne reached out and took it away from him.

'I don't want one of my best glasses smashed,' she said. 'And, no, you're not having any more whisky.'

'Haven't you got anything for me, Anne? Not one little bit of comfort?'

It had been a mistake to sit beside him on the couch. Anne moved back quickly, but his arms closed round her and he pushed her back against the soft cushions. She thought that he would try to kiss her, but instead Jeff bent his head until it rested against her shoulder.

'I feel bloody awful about it,' he said in a low, muffled voice. 'Me, sterile! It makes me sick.'

'Don't be daft!' Anne said. She shifted so that she could hold him more comfortably, her head resting against his dark hair. 'The way you're talking anyone would think you'd been castrated.'

Only too clearly she saw the reason for his anger at finding Tessa away from home. Outraged by something he saw as a reflection on his manhood, Jeff wanted a woman; his wife for preference, but failing her anyone else who happened to be around.

Not me, Anne thought. I'm not going to be used to prove that Jeff can still perform. All the same, she went on holding him, even when he moved his head and his lips brushed against the hollow at the base of her throat.

To hide the tremor of excitement that ran through her, Anne said quickly, 'The doctors aren't always right.'

'The specialist said no one could be a hundred per cent certain,' Jeff admitted.

The moment of despair which had made him lay his head on her shoulder seemed to be passing. He lifted his head and put his mouth on hers. His hand shifted until it rested on her breast. Anne lay back passive against the cushions until the moment when she heard his breathing change and he caught her to him more fiercely, then she tore herself away.

'No! I won't have it, Jeff. O.K., you still appeal to me. We both knew that already. But I'm not going to risk my marriage just to give your morale a boost.'

Jeff sat up, straightened his tie, ran a hand over his hair, gestures so automatic that Anne recognized with a spurt of amused annoyance that he had done it a hundred times before. Jeff, the buccaneer, back on form again.

All the same, when he put his arm round her waist as she went with him to the front door to let him out Anne did not move away, and when Jeff turned her to face him and said in an unexpectedly husky voice, 'One kiss, Anne. Just one to send me on my way,' she raised her head and put her arms round his neck.

They clung together, bodies closely engaged, lips and tongues moving in voluptuous pleasure. It was Jeff who broke away. He bit gently at the lobe of Anne's ear and said in a low voice, 'There'll always be something between us.'

It was true, Anne knew that. There was an affinity between her and Jeff that she did not share with Jocelin, that Jeff presumably did not share with Tessa. Something that went right back to their roots. With Jeff she could be basic woman and nothing else; with Jocelin, for all the love there was between them, she always tried to present herself in the best possible light.

She did not reply to Jeff's remark, but because she recognized the truth of it, Anne said as she saw him out of the door: 'Don't come and see me again, Jeff.'

'Perhaps you're right,' he agreed. A reluctant and bitter smile twisted his lips. 'I'd really despise myself if I started hankering after something I'd thrown away!'

Remembering that visit, and the way she had washed Jeff's glass and put it away because she did not want to tell Jocelin that he had been there, Anne found herself in two minds about the contest between the two men for the General Manager's job. She wanted Jocelin to get it, of course she did, especially since it might mean moving if he were unsuccessful, but the realization that achieving this step might be essential to the survival of Jeff and Tessa's marriage made her feel regretful that Jocelin's success might be at their expense.

She had been disturbed by Tessa's brittle gaiety in the weeks following her visit to Paris. Anne assumed that Jeff had told her his unfortunate news, but it was not a thing she could talk about unless Tessa confided in her. It was something of a relief when Tessa spoke quite openly about the ball she had attended in Paris.

'A super party! Lots and lots of lovely Frenchmen, all dancing attendance like mad. I had a wonderful time.'

'A pity Jeff couldn't go,' Anne suggested.

Tessa pretended to think about it, her head on one side, but smiling in a way Anne did not like.

'Oh, I don't know. Husbands and wives should make little sorties on their own occasionally, don't you think? It stops one from getting stale.'

The interviews for the General Manager's post were held in London in March. The night before, feeling Jocelin lying tense and wakeful by her side, Anne moved closer to him and said, 'Darling, you must try to relax. Does it mean so much to you, this wretched job?'

Jocelin turned and settled himself more comfortably against her.

'I look upon it as an absolutely necessary step in my career. Both Dad and I take a pride in having come up through the works, just like all the Tyndalls since the eighteenth century. I may have spent only a few weeks on the shop floor, but I did my stint. Your father will tell you, he didn't have to spare me while he was my boss. I was a Shift Manager and when I got promotion it was because I'd earned it. I've pushed for the improvements at Wallenshaw and I want to be the man in charge now that we're beginning to reap the benefit of them. But more than that: one day I'm going to be Chairman of S.V.T. – a *steelmaker* Chairman in an industry that's dominated nowadays by accountants. To achieve that I need to be General Manager now – and if it's not at Wallenshaw I shall go after the next opportunity that crops up no matter where it is – and then Director of a steelmaking group within the Company. After that it's a logical step one day to Chairman.'

'But why do you have to be in such a hurry, darling?'

'Dad will be fifty-nine this year. I'm thirty-seven. There's no absolute requirement for him to retire at sixty-five. If he stays on two or three extra years until, say, 1967, when I'll be forty-six, then I think I stand a good chance of succeeding him.'

'Chairman of a huge concern like S.V.T. at forty-six?'

'I've got the background, I've got a financial stake in the Company, I'm a Tyndall. Given nine or ten years of the right experience I can be ready.'

'I knew you were ambitious, but I never realized the extent of it,' Anne said slowly.

'I don't look upon it as ambition. More as if it was my birth right.'

'The Crown Prince,' Anne said, remembering Jeff's words.

Jocelin took it as a joke. 'More or less,' he admitted.

'You should have married a princess,' Anne said, still following the same train of thought. 'Made an alliance with another great steelmaking family.'

'I looked the field over and none of them appealed to me,' Jocelin reminded her. 'I fell in love with a different kind of girl, one who helps me keep my feet on the ground.' He gathered her closer. 'A girl who's going to be very kind to me,' he whispered in her ear. 'Because I simply must relax and get some sleep.'

He came back from the interview not knowing the result, but cautiously confident of having made a good impression. Two days later he came home and shouted for Anne in a boisterous way that was quite out of the ordinary for him. When she came out to join him in the hall he put his arms round her and whirled her round, lifting her off the ground in his exuberance.

'What would you like? A diamond bracelet, a fur coat, a Rolls Royce?'

'I'd settle for a decent holiday,' Anne said. 'You've got the job? Darling, congratulations! Well done!'

She went to the shop the next day nervously concocting ways of talking to Tessa about it, but Tessa merely smiled with creamy complacency.

'It's a bore and a nuisance and I hate Jeff being pipped to the post by rotten old Jocelin,' she said. 'But nothing can touch me: I'm pregnant!'

Chapter Eight

In the five years she had been married to Jocelin Anne had learnt that his air of unconcern masked a capacity for grinding hard work that at times seemed inhuman. If he strolled into a committee meeting with two minutes to spare looking as if his mind was on the golf course it was because he had spent the previous day, and usually the evening as well, mastering every aspect of the agenda and supplying himself with information which could be used to achieve the end he had in mind. He was never more dangerous than when he leaned back in his chair, doodling idly on his note pad, apparently only half attending to the business in hand. He would look up and pose the one question that exposed the weakness of an argument and then more often than not go on to supply the answer as well.

He had always been formidable, and he became more so when he took up his position as General Manager of Wallenshaw. More than that, he expected from his colleagues the same dedication that he had himself.

'The man's a bloody machine,' one of his disgruntled managers grumbled, but Jocelin was not a machine and the regime he imposed on himself took its toll.

Anne, remembering the days when Jocelin had arrived home in time to romp with the twins before they went to bed, the evenings they had spent talking to one another, the weekends when they had been able to get away for a couple of days of relaxation, was first of all regretful and then remembering, too, the effort she had made to preserve the leisure time he had said was important to him, resentful.

He seemed to have fallen into a routine of arriving home

late, eating what was put in front of him without apparently noticing what was on his plate, and then disappearing into his study with a briefcase full of papers. Sometimes that was the last Anne saw of him until after she had gone to bed, when he would slide in beside her, kiss her and fall asleep.

Anne exercised all the patience of which she was capable and put up with this for the first few difficult months of his new job and then she acted. She gave him an hour one evening to work on the papers he had brought home with him, then she went into his study.

'I'm thinking of taking a lover,' she said.

'Mm?' Jocelin looked up, but it was obvious that he had not taken in what she had said.

'I'm a young woman of twenty-nine. I love my husband, but unfortunately he's got a mistress and he loves her more than he does me. I can't think why because she's a noisy, ugly, dirty thing. So I think I'll retaliate.'

Jocelin pushed his chair back from the desk. 'I see I have a crisis on my hands,' he said.

He held out his arms and Anne went and settled herself on his lap. 'You certainly have,' she said. 'When did you last make love to me?'

'Er . . .'

'You can't remember.' She pressed her lips softly to his temple, in the place where a few grey hairs were beginning to show amongst the mouse brown hair. 'It used to be memorable, didn't it?'

'It certainly did. And still is.' He turned his head against her throat. 'You're still my best girl, Anne. Things are difficult at the moment, that's all.'

'The trouble with you is, you're a perfectionist. When I think that I used to imagine that you sailed effortlessly through life! Darling, you're killing yourself with overwork. Also, you're becoming extremely boring to live with.'

'I've taken over the Works at a bad time. The boom years seem to be coming to an end and we're having to fight hard for our markets. I'm not too happy about the Cabinet decision to allow two new works to be built. One, yes – but to give one to Wales and one to Scotland is a real judgement of Solomon –

split the baby down the middle and please nobody! There's an election looming, too, and I'm worried about the outcome. Wallenshaw has to be able to show a good record or it could be in jeopardy, in spite of the millions that have been spent on it.'

'If I'd known about that I might have felt less hard done by. But you didn't tell me, did you?'

'I suppose . . . I haven't been talking to you much,' Jocelin admitted.

'Tonight you said "Sorry I'm late, darling; I'll be with you in a minute", when you came in; while we were eating I told you what the twins had been getting up to and you said, "Little devils"; after dinner you said, "Give me a cup of coffee and I'll take it into the study",' Anne recited meticulously. 'Not exactly a scintillating evening's conversation.'

'You're exaggerating!'

Already Jocelin was looking wistfully over her shoulder at the papers strewn on his desk.

'Not very much. Tell me, where are we going for our holiday this year?'

'The children enjoyed Cornwall last year, didn't they? Why not book up for the same place again?'

'What about our trip to Canada?'

'Oh, darling, not this year! Unless you'd like to take Melanie on your own and leave the twins behind?'

'No, thank you. I'd be worrying about them all the time. I suppose you feel the same way about Wallenshaw, though with rather less cause because there are plenty of people to run the Works while you're out of the way. Jeff's pulling his weight, isn't he?'

It was a question she particularly wanted to ask and she hoped Jocelin would not realize how she had dragged it into the conversation.

'Jeff's too good at his job to do it badly,' Jocelin said. 'All the same, he's changed. He drinks too much for one thing. Not to excess, not yet, but more than is good for him. I know he was disappointed when I became General Manager, but I would have expected Jeff to be more resilient. He's always bounced back in the past and you'd think he'd be on top of the world just now, with this baby he and Tessa have wanted so long coming along.'

For one moment Anne considered telling Jocelin about Jeff's confidences about his sterility, but the difficulties were too great. Jocelin would certainly resent Jeff having talked to her about such a private matter – and rightly. Thinking about that episode, the way she had given in to the long-standing attraction between her and Jeff, Anne doubted whether she could talk about it to Jocelin without betraying the uneasy guilt she felt. Even worse, it might start him wondering, as Anne had been wondering ever since Tessa announced her pregnancy, as Jeff must be, about the legitimacy of Tessa's child.

She turned her mind resolutely away from Tessa and Jeff and said, 'Before I leave this room tonight I want an absolutely firm promise from you that you'll take three full weeks' holiday this year – in Cornwall if you insist – with no contact with Wallenshaw whatsoever.'

'I'll do my best.'

'That's not good enough. Promise!'

'You're a managing woman. All right, I promise.' Again he looked at the papers on his desk. 'I must get through this lot tonight, but it won't take more than another half hour.'

Anne got up from his lap regretfully. 'I'll probably go to bed with a good book,' she said with resignation.

'Don't go to sleep,' Jocelin said with the smile that could still make her stomach churn.

'Is that a promise too?' Anne asked hopefully.

'It certainly is. And if I keep you awake all night, remember you asked for it!'

*

Tessa's baby was born in September, a little boy with the long bones of a Tyndall and what appeared to be his father's dark hair and eyes. Tessa was triumphant.

'I knew he would be a boy,' she said. 'Maximilian Frederick Jeffrey.'

'Sounds like an exiled king from Ruritania,' her brother

commented. 'If I'd known his name was going to be such a mouthful I might not have agreed to be godfather.'

Tessa insisted on having an enormous party for the christening, just before Christmas. Anne thought that Jeff was noticeably silent, but perhaps it was only by contrast to Tessa's exuberance. She had scarcely set eyes on him since that night he had come looking for Tessa, but when they found themselves standing apart from the crowd he said, with an abruptness that, to Anne, betrayed how much he regretted having confided in her, 'I went back to that doctor and he pointed out that he'd only ever said that it was *unlikely* that I would have a child. Apparently it's possible for one lucky little sperm to be in the right place at the right time and the woman gets pregnant.'

'It must have seemed like a miracle, just when you'd given up hope,' Anne said gently.

'I never told Tessa,' Jeff went on, as if he had not heard her. 'We had a furious row after she got back from Paris, then we made it up. Tessa dates her pregnancy from that.'

The way he spoke dared Anne to wonder just what Tessa had got up to in the three nights she had spent in Paris. Jeff must have thought about it. No wonder Jocelin had noticed a change in him. Because, behind his defiant manner, Anne detected a desperate need for reassurance, she said, 'You've got a beautiful little boy. He looks just like you.'

'Does he?' Jeff's cynical smile showed that he had understood her intention, and perhaps resented her too quick understanding of his own misgivings.

'The absolute image,' Anne insisted.

She grew to believe it herself as time went by and Max grew into a leggy little boy with smooth dark hair and round black eyes. Tessa idolized him, to an extent which Anne thought unreasonable.

'A pity he's an only child,' Jocelin commented when Max was nearly four years old. 'Tessa pays far too much attention to his whims and fancies. She ought to have had half a dozen to keep her occupied.'

'Two would do,' Anne said. 'Jocelin, my love, the time has come when you will have to take more of a hand with the twins. They're getting beyond me. You may remember we were going to have the back door painted a beautiful shade of green?'

'The paint got diverted?' Jocelin guessed with the glimmer of a smile.

'We have a green potting shed, a green back fence and we did have two green-spotted children until I cleaned them up and packed them off to bed.'

'I'll have a short, sharp word with them in the morning,' Jocelin said. 'I'll tell them that unless they're good they won't come with us to Canada this summer.'

'Jocelin! We're actually going, after all these years and years of putting it off?'

'I promise. That last letter you had from Mrs Hardwick made me feel guilty. You can even tell Melanie.'

Melanie would be fourteen in August. She was tall for her age, a thin child, all arms and legs, and gawky in a way that Anne had never been, but she still had her wild rose complexion and hair like a raven's wing. She had become more withdrawn as she grew older, less of the outgoing child who had chatted to strangers on the bus, and Anne no longer felt that Melanie told her everything. She thought that it was only natural, she remembered going through a phase herself when it had seemed better to conceal her thoughts because her mother and father would not understand them, but she suspected, too, that Melanie felt that the seven-year-old twins absorbed too much of her mother's attention and left little over for her.

It grieved Anne to see the way Melanie controlled her delight when she was told about the visit to Canada. A lovely pink flush covered her face, she began to smile, and then she looked down and said, 'I expect he'll change his mind before August.'

For the first time it seemed to Anne that she should have done what Jocelin had suggested years before and taken Melanie to Canada on her own. The way Melanie had spoken was disturbing, reminiscent of her resentment of Jocelin when she had been a small child.

'Not this time,' Anne said. 'We're definitely going.'

They spent the whole month of August at the Hardwick Ranch, the longest holiday Jocelin had taken in the last ten years. It seemed to Anne that every day he grew a little younger, shedding the grey look that worried her, growing leaner and fitter, his face and arms brown from long hours on horseback. They all rode, Jocelin and the children with easy confidence, and Anne more cautiously, secretly glad of the Western saddle and the high pommel she could grab when she felt unsafe.

'You should grip with your knees, Mummy,' Christopher told her severely.

The twins formed a deep attachment for old Tom, who looked after the horses, and who had been at the ranch in the days when Mel had been alive. They were more obedient to a laconic word from Tom than to any amount of pleading from their mother, running round after him, grooming the horses for the people they learned to refer to scornfully as 'the dudes', rarely standing still long enough for Anne to catch them and wash them. They were supremely happy, their only ambition being to be able to spit with the same accuracy as old Tom. And Melanie fell in love.

He was seventeen, a tall, brown-haired boy from Toronto, who had spent two previous vacations at the ranch with his parents and this year was there for the summer, working for his keep before going to college in the fall. His name was Richard, but he was always known as Ricky.

'He seems a pleasant lad,' Jocelin said. 'Though not perhaps the paragon that Melanie seems to think.'

'Poor little mite! I suppose she thinks no one notices the way she moons about after him,' Anne said. 'At least he doesn't snub her. How old were you when you first fell in love, Jocelin?'

'I seem to remember lusting after the gym mistress when I was about ten.'

'Precocious! It's a complication I hadn't bargained for with Melanie, not for a year or two yet. It makes me feel old.'

Because Anne had said she was tired of horses they had left the ranch and climbed the hill behind it, leaving the children behind. Now they were resting, sprawled in the long grass that was full of late summer flowers and just beginning to show a hint of the yellow that in a few weeks would turn the prairie into a sea of gold. Anne was wearing shorts and a loose cotton shirt, carelessly unbuttoned at the neck. Jocelin looked at her long bare legs and the voluptuous curve of her breast showing at the open neck of her shirt and laughed.

'Poor old woman! Come here and let me see if I can make you feel young again.'

Anne put her arms round his neck and pulled him down to kiss her, but when she felt his hands on the buttons at the waist of her shorts she tried to squirm away from him.

'Jocelin, we can't! Not here! We'll be seen!'

'No, we won't. Anyway, who cares?'

'I do!'

He put his hands under her shirt and began to tickle her and Anne snorted with laughter, wriggling against him in protest, knowing that she was only exciting him more, knowing that she was going to capitulate as soon as she sensed that he could stand her evasion no longer.

Melanie, meandering by on a solitary ride, heard their laughter, saw two bodies closely entwined in the long grass, and went on her way, her face burning, her adolescent body full of strange urges which had suddenly found an outlet in her hopeless love for Ricky. She felt a faint, puritanical disgust at the antics she had glimpsed, but all the same, watching her mother that evening, seeing the way she had to bite her lip to stop herself from laughing out loud when she caught Jocelin's eye, she longed to know what it was really all about. A happy thing, it seemed, this love between a man and a woman, and yet the way she felt about Ricky made her miserable. She went to bed and cried quietly into her pillow because he had only spoken to her once that evening and never recognized how much she was luxuriating in her own despair. She woke up once in the night with a cry that fortunately disturbed no one and realized that she had been dreaming that it had been herself and Ricky embracing on the hillside.

Anne tried to help her, but although she had always spoken frankly to Melanie about sex and her physical development, she found it a more delicate matter to deal with the emotional side of adolescence. Melanie, inhibited by her new awareness of the relations between her mother and Jocelin, shied away from her and would not listen.

Ricky was an uncomplicated boy who had been dating girls since he was thirteen, and would have been incredulous if he had known how Melanie suffered when he neglected her. He thought she was a nice kid, and different from Canadian girls. Not better, just different. He liked the whole family. Jocelin was a great guy, Anne was a real looker, for an older woman – and only Jocelin noticed with secret amusement Ricky's surreptitious admiration of Anne's beautiful body – the twins were holy terrors, but full of spunk, and Melanie, she was . . . he searched his mind and could only come up with the same description that had occurred to him before . . . she was different.

He thought he had discovered the reason for that difference when Melanie told him about her ancestry. He was even more sure of it when they rode over to an Indian encampment and he saw her deep interest in the way the Indians lived.

'Mostly they live in houses now,' Ricky pointed out. 'The teepees are for showing to the tourists.'

'No, they only pretend that it's for the tourists so that they can keep it all alive,' Melanie said with an assurance that surprised Ricky.

She stood, very straight and tall, her black hair lifting in the breeze, her face serious as she watched the assured hands of a Blackfoot Indian woman weaving a basket, and Ricky thought in astonishment, 'She's one of them! For crying out loud! I never saw it before, even though she told me.'

It made her more interesting in his eyes, this sudden identification with her Indian ancestors. For Melanie it was a moment of profound significance. Very tentatively she asked to be allowed to try the basket weaving. The Indian woman smilingly agreed. She put the lengths of dried grass into Melanie's small, deft hands and almost without having to think about it Melanie began to imitate the movements she had been watching. It was as if she had always known this skill. She felt breathless with achievement as the basket took shape.

The Indian woman watched, her face impassive. Melanie

looked up and said, 'My great-grandmother was a Blackfoot Indian.'

'I know.' The Indian woman was completely unsurprised. 'She was of our tribe – the Blood Indians. Her name was Running Woman. She married the white man, Jacob Hardwick, and bore him a son. And the son grew up on the homestead and had a son in his turn, but he was killed in the war. Now there is no one at the ranch but the old woman.'

'And me. I'm Melvin Hardwick's daughter. One day,' Melanie said, knowing for the first time that it was true, 'one day the ranch will belong to me.'

'And will our people still be welcome to make camp here as we have done since the days of Running Woman?'

'Always,' Melanie said. 'I promise.'

The woman bowed her head gravely. 'You will be held to that promise. Remember it.'

It was Ricky who told everyone about the visit to the Indian camp.

'I thought Melanie was going to stick a feather in her hair and go live amongst the teepees,' he said. 'Gee, you should have heard the way she talked to that old Indian woman. She must have been about ninety and I could smell her from where I stood, but Melanie treated her like she was a queen or something. Is it really true that this spread will belong to Melanie one day?'

'That's a right tactless question,' Mrs Hardwick said drily. 'I'm still in the land of the living and the way I make my Will is no concern of yours, young Ricky. All the same, Melanie is my only grandchild and I'm not likely to forget her when the time comes.'

She and Melanie looked at one another and they both knew that there was no real doubt about her intentions.

'I'd like to come back again next year,' Melanie said. 'Can I, Grandma?'

'Depends on your mother. It's taken you long enough to make your first visit. You'll be welcome as far as I'm concerned.'

'I could come on my own,' Melanie said, and something about the determination in her voice kept Anne silent.

There was a change in Ricky's attitude towards Melanie after that visit. She was still not much more than a child in his eyes, but her eagerness to be with him touched his young male vanity. He was patronizingly kind, in a way that set Anne's teeth on edge, and the last two weeks of Melanie's holiday passed for her in a dream of happiness.

On their last evening Melanie and Ricky lingered at the corral after all the horses had been unsaddled and shut in for the night. They sat side by side on the top rail, watching the sun go down, fiery red.

As the light in the west faded Ricky slipped his arm round Melanie's slight waist.

'Will you be sorry to say goodbye to me tomorrow?' he demanded.

'Oh, I will!' Melanie said. 'But I'm coming back next year. Will you be here, Ricky?'

'Hard to say. Depends how things go when I start college in the fall. I guess I might, if I need a job in the vacation.'

'Do come,' Melanie said, so intent on persuading him that she forgot her shyness and leaned unselfconsciously towards him.

Ricky laughed and bent his head and kissed her. The feel of her soft lips, half open and wholly innocent, excited him. He put his other arm round her and held her tightly against him. 'You're a sweet kid,' he whispered.

They drew apart, Ricky slightly ashamed of making love to a mere babe, Melanie trembling with shock and delight.

'Will you write to me?' she whispered. 'Please, Ricky, please.'

He promised, only half intending to do as she wished, but during the year he did answer her long letters and if his replies were short Melanie could forgive that since he was naturally busy in his first year at university.

It surprised Anne at first, the tenacity with which Melanie clung to the memory of Ricky, until she began to suspect that there was something defensive about it. It was very convenient to have a boyfriend on the other side of the Atlantic who made no demands beyond an occasional letter and who could be used as an excuse for not competing for someone closer at hand. From remarks that were dropped Anne gathered that it gave Melanie a special standing amongst her school friends.

'These poor children,' Anne said in exasperation. 'I was thought to be precocious because I started taking an interest in boys when I was sixteen. Now they seem to think they're on the shelf if they're not having regular dates as soon as puberty sets in. I really don't like it; I feel they're being robbed of their childhood. Melanie's obsession with Ricky may be foolish, but at least it keeps her at home in the evenings and saves me from constantly telling her she can't go out.'

Since nothing would satisfy Melanie next summer but another visit to Canada, Anne allowed her to go to her grandmother on her own. The twins were packed off to a camp in Wales for a couple of weeks and Anne and Jocelin took a holiday alone.

'Help Granny in the house,' Anne instructed Melanie as she kissed her goodbye at the airport. 'Remember she's seventy-two and it's to see her that you're going all this way, not to spend every day riding with Ricky – if he's going to be there.'

'He is,' Melanie said, with the lovely flush in her cheeks which gave away how much it mattered to her.

Anne's heart misgave her as she sent her young daughter off on her first long journey alone. She thought Melanie looked forlorn amongst the hurrying crowd, scared and trying to hide it under a jaunty air. She was only fifteen after all, perhaps it was too soon to let her go away on her own, but it was not as if she was going to a strange place and her grandmother would keep an eye on her.

Melanie had changed during the year. She still had the touchingly vulnerable look of a young colt, but her breasts had developed, firm and round, and the slacks which had hung loosely from her thin waist were now stretched tightly over her taut stomach and curving hips. Her face, too, had begun to lose its childish contours and it was obvious to others beside her mother that Melanie was going to be a beautiful woman.

Anne and Jocelin took the car over to France and meandered around from place to place, enjoying the sunshine and the delicious food, without plans or itinerary, happy to be alone together, although nothing could stop Anne ringing home every couple of days for news of the children.

By September they were all home again. The boys were full of the adventures they had had, but Melanie was very quiet. Anne tried probing gently, but she could get nothing out of her except that the ranch had been lovely, that Grandma had been well, that she had done a lot of riding, that everything had been super, Mummy, really super. When Anne mentioned Ricky Melanie jerked her head away and Anne thought she had discovered the reason for the change in her daughter: Ricky had found someone else and Melanie had been neglected. It would have been a hard lesson for a fifteen-year-old to take, especially when she had had her mind so set on him, but she would get over it in time.

The weeks went by, but Melanie did not recover either her looks or her happiness. Anne guessed that she had been writing to Ricky because she saw an air mail envelope in her daughter's satchel as she went to school one day, but although Melanie looked up every day when the post arrived there was no letter from Canada for her until the beginning of October. When she saw the envelope with the Canadian stamp her face lit up, she seized it and ran back up the stairs to her own room.

Anne waited, but when Melanie did not come down to breakfast she went to the stairs and called, 'Melanie, come along! You'll be late for school.'

There was no reply. Anne went up to Melanie's room and opened the door. Melanie was lying face down on her bed; the torn envelope and crumpled letter were on the floor. Quickly Anne went across the room and put her arm round Melanie's shoulders.

'It was from *Granny*!' Melanie whispered.

'Sit up, darling. Let's talk about it. I know you've been unhappy since you came back from Canada.'

Very slowly Melanie obeyed her. She had not been crying. On her white, set face there was a look of such suffering that Anne was shocked. Instinctively she put her arms round Melanie and pulled her close, hiding that despairing look against her shoulder.

'It's Ricky, isn't it?' she asked. 'He's given you up and you find it hard to bear. My precious, we all go through it and honestly one does recover. You think you've fallen in love but, pet, you've got years and years in front of you for all that. You're too young for all this steamy emotion. Chalk it up to experience. Nasty, hurtful experience, but part of growing up.'

'I hate him,' Melanie said. Her clenched fist moved against Anne's shoulder as if she would have hit her. 'I hate him. Oh, Mummy, what am I going to do?'

As Anne took in the quality of that desperate question she began to feel herself go cold. She recognized now what lay behind the look on Melanie's face: it was fear. She forced herself to start asking the necessary questions.

'Melanie, what happened between you and Ricky this summer?'

There was no reply, only a long shudder through Melanie's body, pressed against hers.

'He made love to you?' Anne persisted.

There was a small movement of Melanie's head against her shoulder.

'All the way?'

Again that slight affirmative motion. This time Anne paused, but it had to be said.

'Melanie, are you pregnant?'

The tears came then, in a storm that left Melanie limp, and Anne recognized that behind her shame and unhappiness there was relief, too, that at last the worst was known.

'He said everybody did it. He said all the girls he knew . . . And I loved him. I thought he loved me, too. I couldn't help being too young. I thought if we really belonged to one another it would mean that we'd be *committed*, like being engaged. But afterwards, it was awful. He didn't want to know me. Another girl came and he did it with her, too, I know he did.'

The tears burst out again at the recollection of her humiliation. Anne held her tightly, trying to soothe her.

'When did you know . . . about the baby?' she asked.

'The first week I was home. I wrote to Ricky and told him, but he didn't answer. I . . . I've missed again this month. It's the second time. It must be true. I wish I was dead.'

'No, darling, that's a silly way to talk. We'll find some way to cope.'

She was surprised to hear how sensibly she was speaking, out of the desolation inside her.

'The first thing we must do is see Dr Charter.'

'No! He knows me!'

'All the better. He'll understand that you're a good little girl who's made a silly mistake.'

'Will he help me get rid of it?'

It shook Anne, that question. She had not got as far as thinking about abortion and it chilled her that Melanie should suggest it, but of course the poor child had been facing the situation for the past month and it had only burst on Anne in the last few minutes.

'I can't bear the thought of it,' Melanie was saying. 'Growing inside me. I feel filthy. I won't have it. I'll kill myself.'

The hysteria in her voice alarmed Anne. She gave her a little shake. 'I won't have you talking like that. You've got everything to live for. Whatever Dr Charter says Daddy and I will do all we can to help you.'

'Don't tell Daddy!'

'I must. I can't keep something like this from him.'

'He doesn't need to know. It's not as if he was my real father.'

'He's my husband. I need his support. I . . . it's painful for me, too, Melanie.'

Anne remembered saying that when she told Jocelin that evening. She had gone through the day in a daze of misery, scarcely knowing what she was doing. At one moment she found herself sitting with an old photograph in her hand, a picture of herself and Mel, with Melanie in his arms, taken at the ranch before he had gone off to Korea. Where did I go wrong? Anne asked herself. What did I leave out when I told Melanie about growing up? What warning could I have given her that would have stopped her getting into this mess? My lovely little girl. She bowed her head over the photograph in desperate grief, but by the time she spoke to Jocelin she had recovered and was able to tell him calmly.

'Apparently there are loopholes in the law,' she said. 'The

most Dr Charter could do was to recommend me to a clinic, but he made it fairly clear that they would arrange a termination on the grounds of her youth and mental state. I gather it will be expensive, but I've made an appointment to take her there.'

'Is that the best solution?' Jocelin asked, his eyes on her ravaged face.

'I have terrible qualms about it,' Anne said wearily. 'I've thought of every possible alternative: persuading Melanie to have the child and giving it for adoption, or bring it up ourselves; I even considered taking her back to Canada and giving out that I was pregnant and bringing it back here as mine.'

'Leaving me and the boys on our own for six or seven months?'

'It was a wild idea; I've dropped it. What it all comes down to in the end is that Melanie doesn't want to go on with it. She gets hysterical at the idea.'

It all went ahead very smoothly. In her heart Anne was shocked, even revolted, by the ease with which an abortion could be arranged if one had the money to pay for it. The official story was that Melanie was having a minor gynaecological operation to ease difficult periods and that was what Anne told Tessa as an excuse for not going in to the shop on the day that she had to deliver Melanie to the clinic.

Tessa's eyebrows shot up nearly to her hairline. 'That clinic? Never say so! What has your little Melanie been getting up to?'

'I don't understand you,' Anne said, but with a sinking heart.

'Oh, come on, Anne. Everyone knows what goes on there. At least one of my school friends went there to get rid of a little mistake.'

'They do other gynaecological work as well,' Anne said obstinately.

Tessa gave her a piercing look. 'All right, if you say so,' she said obligingly. 'But I'd keep the name of the clinic quiet, if I were you, at least in front of anyone who might be in the know.'

What Anne had not anticipated was that Tessa and Jeff, paying one of their rare and, on Tessa's part, reluctant visits to Jeff's mother would mention this item of news, though not Tessa's interpretation of it, and that Mrs Blackmore would remark on it to Anne's mother, who promptly came round to see what was happening.

'What's all this about our little Melanie going into hospital and not a word to me?' she demanded. 'I would have thought her own grandmother might have been told, not left to hear it from a neighbour.'

'It's only a minor thing,' Anne said. 'She'll be home tomorrow.'

'I never knew she'd been having trouble. She always looked healthy enough, especially since she began to fill out. Bless her, I would have gone in to see her if I'd known.'

'The clinic is a long way away. Too far for you to go without a lift.'

'If it's such a little thing she's having done why couldn't she have gone into one of the local hospitals? Aren't they good enough for you?'

'It's not that.' Anne turned her head away, fighting against tears.

'There's something wrong,' Beryl said in an altered voice. 'You're keeping something from me. There's more the matter with the little lass than you're letting on.'

Anne struggled for a moment and then she gave in and told her mother the whole story. She had not realized until that moment how much of a relief it would be to pour it all out. Jocelin had been loving and sympathetic, but what Anne needed was a woman who had borne children, someone who could enter into her worry for her daughter and her repugnance at the ending of a life.

'Poor little girl,' Beryl said. 'Eh, poor wee mite. He wants shooting.'

'I'd have killed him with my bare hands if I could have got hold of him,' Anne said.

'No need for anyone to know,' Beryl said. 'I'll not talk, not even to Wally. Jocelin knows, of course. Good job he can afford to pay for it.'

'Mum, how can you? I feel sick at the thought of what we're doing.'

'You'd not be so soft if you'd seen as many unwanted children come into the world as I have. What do you think I'd have done if you'd fallen for a baby before you were married? Tried to rid you of it, that's what. Little Melanie's too young to be saddled with a responsibility like that for the rest of her life.'

Her robust and practical view eased Anne's sore conscience slightly, but only slightly. Seeing her doubtful expression, Beryl added, 'What right have you to indulge your nice feelings at Melanie's expense?'

It was a point of view Anne had not considered. 'Put like that I suppose we may be doing the right thing,' she admitted. 'What I keep asking myself is how it could have happened? I thought I'd brought her up so carefully.'

'She's your daughter, that's what,' Beryl said. 'Look back a year or two, my girl. Do you think I don't know what you and Mel got up to, long before there was talk of a wedding? Sick with worry I used to be, and you'd been brought up strict enough, goodness knows.'

'I was older,' Anne said weakly.

'Three years, not much more. There was the war, I'll give you that, but if you ask me the only thing wrong with Melanie is that she's got too much of her mother in her!'

It was not particularly palatable, coming from her mother, but it helped Anne to talk to Melanie again when she came home, looking thin and hollow-eyed, but perfectly composed.

'You must put this behind you,' Anne said carefully. 'You made a mistake, but you mustn't feel guilty or let it spoil you for falling in love in the future. We pretend that most girls are still virgins when they get married, but it isn't always so. I was only eighteen when I first knew your father and we made love to one another before he went off to the war. It made us both very happy and I've never regretted it. If he'd been killed we would never have got married but I would still have been glad of what I'd done.'

'I didn't feel like that,' Melanie said. 'I didn't even like it. I thought it was horrible.'

In the face of that bleak confession Anne felt completely helpless.

'You were too young and Ricky was just a selfish boy,' she said. 'Making love is a happy thing, darling, truly it is.'

It seemed to Anne as the months went by that Melanie was trying, whether consciously or not Anne could not tell, to put back the clock. Whereas before her visit to Canada she had begun to take a shy pride in her appearance, experimenting with cosmetics, wanting high-heeled shoes, complaining about being made to wear school uniform, now she rarely bothered to change when she came home from school, she stopped clamouring to have her hair cut in the latest style and wore it long and straight, pushed back behind her ears. She was clean, neat and tidy, Anne saw to that, but the bathroom no longer billowed with clouds of scented steam when Melanie took a bath.

'It'll pass,' Jocelin said absentmindedly when Anne tried to talk to him about this new austerity.

'You didn't even hear what I said,' Anne accused him.

'Yes, I did.'

He looked up from his newspaper and asked, 'She's eating all right, isn't she? One of our chaps is having terrible trouble with his teenage daughter who seems to be trying to starve herself to death.'

'Melanie hasn't thought of that, thank goodness. And tying her hair back with a bit of string and not painting her nails won't stop her from growing and changing.'

'Nor from becoming beautiful, like her mother. I think you are going to have to face the fact that Melanie will probably always have a stormy love life,' Jocelin said.

'I suppose she will fall in love properly one day. I hope she does. But not yet,' Anne said hastily.

'She's got a quality that she shares with you that will pull the young men to her. And it's all the more potent because neither of you exercises it consciously.'

'Sex appeal,' Anne said gloomily.

'A garden of delights,' Jocelin said. He looked at her with interest. 'My dear, can I really make you blush after ten years of marriage?'

Anne pressed her hands against her hot cheeks. 'You always did have a silver tongue,' she said. 'Go back to your rotten old *Financial Times*.'

As she had done in the past when she was unhappy, Melanie turned to the comforting, silent presence of her Uncle Pete, but she did more now than hang about watching him as he worked; she started using the tools herself and discovered an exciting new talent which began to lift her out of the depths into which she had fallen.

It surprised Peter to realize that it was the girl of the family who liked working with her hands, but he was a patient, willing teacher and the pleasure he took in passing on his skill added a new dimension to the affection between himself and his niece.

He knew, somewhere in the recesses of his mind, that there was something wrong with Melanie, but he had no idea what it was. Beryl had not quite kept her word to Anne – she had not been able to stop herself from telling Wally what had happened – but it was not a thing she would have dreamed of discussing with Pete, and so he remained in ignorance and, more than that, went on looking on Melanie as a child.

It was not until Anne's birthday that Melanie revealed what had been keeping her busy, and comparatively happy, as the spring advanced. With a look that reminded Anne of the way she used to wait as a child for her mother to open the present she had got for her, Melanie handed over an oblong parcel. Inside was a polished wooden box, decorated on the lid with a carved spray of ivy leaves.

'It's nothing much, but I did make it all myself,' Melanie said in an offhand way. 'I thought you could use it for a jewel box or something.'

'Darling, it's absolutely splendid!' Anne exclaimed. 'Do you mean you really made it yourself? This lovely decoration, too?'

Melanie nodded, her face pink with pleasure.

'Never mind the decoration, what I admire are the beautifully fitting joints,' Jocelin said, taking the box from Anne. 'Melanie, you're a craftsman!'

'I like making things with my hands. Uncle Pete showed me

how. The first one I made wasn't very good, so I kept it in the workshop and didn't say anything.'

She looked at her mother anxiously. 'You will use it, won't you, Mum?'

'Indeed I will!'

'Do you look on it as a hobby or is it something you'd like to take up as a career?' Jocelin asked, watching Melanie, suddenly flushed and animated and young again.

Melanie bent her head, the long fall of her hair hiding her face. 'I haven't thought much about what I want to do,' she said.

She looked up and met his intent look, but said nothing, mutely pleading for understanding.

'There is going to be a future for you, you know,' Jocelin said gently. 'Art School, perhaps? We could look round for one that specializes in wood carving.'

Melanie nodded, her eyes bright with tears, her lips trembling, but with the beginning of a new hope in her face.

No inkling of the calamity that had befallen her granddaughter seemed to have seeped through to Mrs Hardwick. She continued to write, rather more frequently than she had before the two visits to Canada. She was asking whether Melanie would go out to her again in 1964, but when Anne asked her daughter Melanie shook her head with a look of the old, sick horror.

'Not this year,' she said. 'I couldn't. I will go again – some time. You can think of an excuse for me, can't you, Mum?'

Anne wrote back diplomatically, saying that she would prefer the family to have a holiday together that year and Canada was a little too far and too expensive for all of them to come again so soon. By return of post Mrs Hardwick wrote offering to pay all expenses for the whole family.

'Something of a facer,' Jocelin said when Anne showed him the letter.

'It's not like her,' Anne said with a worried frown. 'I hope she's all right. I'm determined not to go. It's really too much to expect Melanie to face. I can't have anything upsetting her when she's showing signs of coming back to life again.'

'Tell Mrs Hardwick we've already taken a villa abroad for the summer,' Jocelin said.

'Have we?'

'We could. Have a look at the advertisements. There's bound to be something that appeals to you.'

'Expenses no object?'

'No need to be sarcastic. As a director of S.V.T. I can afford to give my family a few of the luxuries of life.'

'Jocelin! Is it really going to happen?'

'In the autumn. Jeff will take over from me as General Manager at Wallenshaw. He'll be good, perhaps better than I've been. I'll be Director of the Semi-Finished Products Division.'

'Where will you be based?' Anne asked.

'In Scunthorpe. Don't worry, I'm not going to ask you to move. It will mean a longer drive to work each day, that's all. However, as I get a chauffeur-driven car . . .'

'Cor!'

'Talking of moving, there's something you ought to start thinking about. When Dad retires, and especially if I take over as Chairman, he may very well ask if we'll take on Upbridge Park.'

'*Live* there?' Anne asked. 'Goodness . . . you really have floored me. I do so love this house.'

'It's adequate, but it may not be large enough in the future. You're going to have to start doing some entertaining for me, darling. Not just family and colleagues from the Works, but overseas visitors and people like that.'

'Do you remember that dance your mother gave?' Anne asked, her mind going off at a tangent. 'The one you took me to and I wore my bright pink dress.'

'And I took you home afterwards,' Jocelin said. 'The best night's work I ever did.'

Anne went and sat down on the hearth rug by his feet. 'We've had a good marriage,' she said. 'These changes – they won't make any real difference will they?'

Behind her question lay an uneasiness she suspected Jocelin did not understand. Becoming a Tyndall had carried burdens Anne had not been prepared for when she had entered so thankfully into her marriage. After ten years she had grown accustomed to the social occasions in which they were involved, but she knew that her mother-in-law thought she did not do enough either in the way of entertaining or of voluntary work. Anne loved giving parties for the children and she was happy to have a few friends in for a drink and a meal. What she had avoided, giving her involvement with Tessa's business as an excuse, was the round of big, impersonal parties and Lady Tyndall's charity work. Taking on Upbridge Park would mean more than moving into a big, old-fashioned house; it was all too likely to carry obligations towards the W.V.S., the Red Cross, the local hospital, the almshouses – all the duties Lady Tyndall took for granted but which seemed to Anne to bear no relation to her own life.

'We may have to let the world into our home rather more than we have done in the past,' Jocelin was saying. 'Anne, the time has come when you've really got to make up your mind to allow the boys to go away to school.'

Anne sat up. 'No,' she said. 'I won't have it. They belong at home. I need to keep an eye on them. Look what happened when I let Melanie go off on her own.'

'That's not a problem that's going to arise with the boys,' Jocelin said mildly.

'Don't be funny about it. You know what I mean – getting into trouble generally. And anyway, you hear such things about boarding schools!'

'I emerged from school with only the vaguest idea of what a homosexual attachment meant,' Jocelin said. 'My education was first class and I met . . .'

'People of your own sort,' Anne interrupted him. 'You've kept up with them, haven't you? The Old Boys' Network. You make me feel like running up the Red Flag when you talk like that.'

Jocelin said nothing, but the hand that had been lightly touching her hair was withdrawn. Anne began to feel uneasy. They had had this conversation before, but in the past it had all seemed too far away to be taken seriously. Now the twins were nine and it was true that some thought must be given to their future, but not boarding school, that Anne was determined on.

'You knew I'd put their names down for Eton,' Jocelin reminded her.

'You haven't said anything about it for ages. I hoped you'd dropped the idea.'

'When I discovered how passionately you felt against it I let it ride, thinking you'd come round in time. I'm going to overrule you on this, Anne. The boys will go to my old school and learn to love it, just as I did.'

'They'll learn to despise me and my family, that's what they'll do! They get on fine with Mum and Dad now, but what'd it be like when they come home in their namby-pamby Eton suits and started looking down their noses at them?'

'They'd get the hiding of their lives! Do you really imagine I'd put up with that? When did I ever patronize your mother and father?'

'You're a grown man,' Anne muttered. 'But there is a difference, you know there is. They don't feel really at home with you, not like they do with Terry, for instance.'

'Nor do you feel at home with my mother and father,' Jocelin said gently. 'I've often regretted that you're not closer to them, especially now when I think you might be glad of some help from Mum.'

'Meaning that I'm not up to entertaining your grand friends now that you're going up in the world?' Anne asked.

'Nothing of the sort! But you might make it easier for yourself if you'd accept a few tips from Mum. You won't, will you? You're too proud. It's another kind of snobbery, Anne.'

'We're wandering off the point. I absolutely categorically refuse to allow the boys to go to Eton.'

'Only a few minutes ago we were saying what a fine marriage we've had,' Jocelin said. 'Surely we can reach some compromise over this, darling?'

'I won't compromise when it's a question of my babies' lives.'

'They're not babies,' Jocelin pointed out. 'They're rapidly growing boys and a fine handful at that. When they are the right age I want them at Eton, learning some of the lessons I learnt, not just from books but from rubbing along with other people.'

'They can do that at the local grammar school.'

'It's not a bad school,' Jocelin admitted. 'But it won't give them the opportunities I want for them.'

'I'll never give in and you won't get them there without me helping you, buying all their clothes and all that.'

'I could send them to London for the day with my secretary and tell her to get them outfitted,' Jocelin said.

'I'd never forgive you!'

'Then be sensible and see the advantages as well as the drawbacks.'

It shook Anne, that casual suggestion of high-handedness. He wouldn't really do it, it would be too outrageous, but she had the feeling that this time Jocelin was not to be turned away from the path he had chosen for his boys and that in the end she was going to be defeated. Unspoken between them was Jocelin's criticisms of Melanie's local school. He thought that the tone of the school had been bad for his step-daughter and it was difficult for Anne to refute that judgement since the outcome had been so disastrous.

Not for the first time, Anne found herself pouring out her troubles to her mother.

'You must be mad,' Beryl said flatly. 'You want the best for them, don't you? Eh, I'd get a thrill, that I would, telling the Mothers' Union about my grandsons at Eton!'

'You're no help,' Anne said. 'I bet Dad is on my side.'

'I'm none so sure,' Wally said when she put it to him. 'They're gentry-born when all's said and done. They might as well learn how to get on with the nobs while they're little.'

'What about equality?' Anne demanded.

'I'd like to see working class lads going with them,' Wally said mildly. 'I'm not one of the Reds who want to see all the good old schools abolished. Levelling up, not levelling down, that's my motto.'

Jocelin played his strongest card when he suggested that Christopher and Timothy had a right to express an opinion. To Anne's hurt disappointment they were wholeheartedly in favour of going away to school. She shed a few tears, turned a cold shoulder on Jocelin when he tried to patch up the quarrel between them, and continued to refuse to admit that it was really going to happen.

They took a villa in Majorca for three weeks in the summer. It was a delightful place in the northern, rocky part of the island, with a riot of pink geraniums cascading from the terrace and lemon trees in the garden. Jocelin taught the boys to water-ski and Anne, watching him each day as his lean body turned a darker shade of brown, seeing the gay, adventurous spirit of the two small boys who were growing up so like him, felt herself weakening. They were his sons, he had a right to a say in their upbringing; but it was such a large slice of their lives; they would grow away from her; it would make them change.

They gave a small party for some of their neighbours one evening in their third week. Anne, as always, had a few minutes of stage fright beforehand. Jocelin seemed to be immune to the misgivings that always attacked her before a party, especially when she was the hostess. She dressed carefully, reassured as she had often been in the past by her own good appearance. She saw Jocelin looking at her, but whereas he usually commented, this time he turned away without saying anything and she missed the boost his admiration would have given her.

The holiday had not brought them to better terms with one another. Jocelin had made overtures and Anne had refused to be won over. Watching him as he moved amongst their guests, smiling and courteous, with a word for everybody, and looking, thought Anne resentfully, absolutely devastating, she knew she could keep it up no longer. She had been wrong to carry their disagreement about the boys into the bedroom. It had been a petty, mean-spirited thing to do. Besides, she wanted him too much to go on with it. She felt wild with impatience for the guests to go so that she could let him know that even though she still disagreed with him there was no need for the love between them to be denied.

The party spread out into the garden. The guests carried their plates and glasses out into the warm night and sat at the white tables Anne had had set out on the grass. She lost sight of Jocelin and then saw that he was looking after Bianca, a sleek, black-haired Italian woman whose husband was something high up in international banking. She was a voluptuous creature and the tight green sheath she wore made the most of her splendid body. Anne thought it vulgar, especially after she had seen Jocelin balancing on the arm of Bianca's chair and leaning towards her. He must be getting a good eyeful, Anne thought. She was surprised by the depth of her resentment. After all, no one knew better than Jocelin how to handle a light, momentary flirtation. She had seen him do it a dozen times, had teased him about it, feeling smugly contented that the other women who coveted him didn't have a look in.

She was admired herself and it meant nothing, but that evening, as Anne smilingly accepted compliments and slipped away from hands that were laid on her arm to detain her, she suddenly felt impatient with it all. She left the chattering crowd and walked away, just for a minute or two, to a darker, more solitary part of the garden.

She thought she was alone, but as her eyes grew accustomed to the darkness she saw two figures at the far end of the terrace. A breath of air moved the branch of a tree and threw a shaft of moonlight on them. Jocelin and Bianca. As Anne watched the two figures melted into one and they began to kiss.

Her sandals made no sound on the rough, thick grass. She turned and went back. Outwardly she was still the charming hostess, but her eyes searched the crowd constantly until she saw Jocelin and Bianca return. Jocelin was as inscrutable as ever, but Bianca was smiling and a strand of her smooth black hair had escaped from its chignon and fallen forward against her cheek.

Anne told herself that the dignified thing to do was to ignore the whole incident, but that was more than she could manage. As soon as she was alone with Jocelin her indignation burst out.

'I saw you kissing Bianca in the garden!'

Jocelin was undoing his tie. She thought he looked slightly wary, but all he said was, 'Are you surprised?'

'I suppose I shouldn't be,' Anne said. 'She has the reputation of putting it about a bit.'

She was furious when Jocelin laughed. 'She's a fiery girl,' he agreed.

'You enjoyed it?' Anne enquired, politely bitter.

'Up to a point, yes. You've spoilt me for other women, Anne, but if you reject me then I'm going to be tempted to turn to someone who's more willing, even though it's second best for me.'

They stood looking at one another across the width of the double bed in which they had slept chastely all through the holiday.

'I started thinking this evening that I'd been wrong about the way I've been treating you,' Anne said abruptly. 'But now I'm so angry that I'd hit you if you touched me.'

'Because I kissed Bianca? Not a very heinous offence, darling.'

'I can't stand it when you drawl in that affected way. I suppose it wasn't the first time. Have you been unfaithful to me since we've been married?' ·

'No, as a matter of fact I haven't. But you're going the right way to drive me to it.'

'I'm sure you'll find plenty of women ready to co-operate. You used to have quite a reputation, didn't you? Married women were your speciality, I understand. Is that the sort of thing they taught you in your upper class school?'

She was too angry at first to understand the conflicting emotions that chased across Jocelin's face until at last his lips quivered and he said in an unsteady voice, 'Adultery wasn't actually on the curriculum.' Then she saw that he was trying not to laugh.

Totally exasperated, Anne stormed round to the other side of the bed and slapped him hard across the face. For a moment they stood looking at one another and then Anne backed away, her eyes widening in horror as she saw the red mark she had made on Jocelin's cheek.

'Possibly I deserved that,' he said, tenderly touching his jaw. 'I apologize about Bianca. A foolish thing to have done. Were you really feeling more kindly towards me until I lapsed from grace?'

'Stupid of me, wasn't it? You needn't think you're going to get round me now,' Anne said.

She turned her back on him and began pulling off her clothes, careless of where they fell, fighting against a desire to throw her arms round him and beg him to forgive her. Jocelin neither spoke nor made any attempt to touch her, even though he must have known that she was longing to make it up and the smallest gesture would have taken her into his arms.

She was lying on the far edge of the bed with her back obstinately turned when Jocelin got in beside her. When he put his hand on her bare shoulder she hunched it away petulantly.

'The way I see it, you've got yourself into a corner from which you can't retreat without losing face,' Jocelin said. 'Talking has got us nowhere. Would it help if I forced you?'

'No, it would not! How dare you even think of such a thing!'

'Darling, I've been thinking about it with monotonous regularity every night for the last three weeks.'

The plaintive way he spoke made Anne bury her face deeper in the pillow, hiding her unwilling smile. His lips were touching her shoulder, his hand was feeling round the front of her nightdress, seeking for her breasts.

'Turn round,' he whispered in her ear. 'If you don't, I'll attack you from the rear.'

Anne turned. 'Damn you, there are times when I hate your guts,' she said. 'You can talk me into anything, and make me like it, and it's not fair. Where did you learn to be so all-fire beguiling?'

'Union negotiations,' Jocelin said. He slid the straps of her nightdress lower. 'We don't really need this, do we?'

It ended in laughter and a renewal of the passion that held them together, but it was a defeat for Anne. The boys would go away to school and Jocelin had got his own way again, as it seemed he always did except, perhaps, in the one thing that mattered most to him: the Labour Party was back in power and the threat of nationalization was renewed.

For the time being the Government had too small a majority to go ahead with nationalization of the steel industry, but in the year after Jocelin took up his new position he worked like a demon to push up falling profits and all the time at the back of his mind was the knowledge that the ultimate reward might be withheld from him.

Chapter Nine

❦

The shop which Tessa had opened in Upbridge had continued to flourish and she had never lost her interest in it, even
during her pregnancy and while Max was a baby. Indeed,
she had been adroit in exploiting her newly acquired knowledge of the clothes and requirements of young children to
improve the stock in the shop. In the early spring of 1965 she
opened a branch in Lincoln.

'I've been meaning to do it ever since Max started school,'
she said. 'But it's been difficult to find the right premises.'

'I suppose I'll be able to find time to go to Lincoln,' Anne
said doubtfully, thinking of the way she had been doing the
book-keeping ever since the shop in Upbridge had opened.

'As a matter of fact, darling, I'm going to employ a proper
accountant to look after both shops. I'm terribly grateful for
all the help you've given me in the past, but if I'm to go on
expanding then I ought to employ someone full time.'

Anne smiled and joked about being given the sack, but in
her heart she was hurt by the casual way Tessa discarded her
when her usefulness was at an end. With the boys going away
to school in the autumn she was likely to find herself with
time on her hands and it would not have been difficult then
to drive to Lincoln and provide the same service for the
second shop as she had done for the first.

'You'll probably be frightfully busy, entertaining for Jocelin
and that sort of thing,' Tessa said vaguely.

Anne grimaced. 'I'd give anything to get out of the dinner
for the Japanese next week. The war may be twenty years
behind us, but it makes my flesh crawl to think of sitting
down to eat with them.'

The emergence of Japan as one of the major steelmaking countries of the world was one of the great surprises of the post-war years. With no raw materials of their own they had built large new works on the edge of deep water and imported coal and ore in large carriers at advantageous prices. Because they were starting from scratch they were able to incorporate all the latest technology and their productivity record was the envy of the older steelmaking countries. Impeccably dressed, polyglot and unremittingly polite they toured the European steel works.

'Goodness knows why,' Jocelin remarked. 'There's not much we can teach them. Still, they're here on my patch this week and no matter how you feel I'm afraid we've got to entertain them.'

'Not under my roof,' Anne said. Her mouth set obstinately.

'Dinner at a local restaurant,' Jocelin conceded. 'Sorry, darling, but it's got to be done.'

The dinner went off reasonably well. If Anne, wearing black in a deliberate gesture of rebellion, was slightly frosty, the small, elderly man with round spectacles who sat next to her did not seem to notice.

It was Wally, delegated to explain some points of procedure during the tour of Wallenshaw Works, who dug in his heels and refused to have any dealings with the Japanese.

'I applied to change shifts,' he said. 'Jeff wasn't best pleased 'cause he was expecting to see me at my post when he came round with them little slit-eyed monkeys. He gave me a right bollocking when he found out I'd given them the go by.'

A reluctant smile appeared on his face. 'He's got a fine flow of language,' he said admiringly.

'Does he make a good General Manager?' Anne asked curiously.

'He does that! I won't say he's better than Jocelin, but being a Tyndall, Jocelin always had his mind wandering round the corner to what was happening in the rest of the Company, if you see what I mean. Jeff keeps his eye fixed on the Works and we never know where he's likely to turn up next.'

Anne repeated the gist of this conversation to Jocelin, more out of interest in his reaction than anything.

'It's true, but I didn't realize it was so obvious,' he admitted. 'I've felt myself expanding since I became a director. It suits me, being able to see the larger picture. I only hope I can hang on to it.'

'There's no fresh news?'

'A lot of agitated to-ing and fro-ing behind the scenes. The Government would nationalize if it could get enough backing, but while they have a majority of three we must be safe.'

For once Anne held her tongue, though in the past she had not hesitated to challenge Jocelin when he had spoken of being 'safe'. The conviction in which she had been brought up, that nationalization must necessarily be a good thing, had been eroded by her marriage, but she had not been able to bring herself to vote anything but Labour in the 1964 election. She felt absurdly guilty about it, as if she were letting Jocelin down, and it was something of a relief that the result had been so inconclusive.

Anne had had a letter that day which troubled her. Mrs Hardwick had written to say that she had taken on a manager for the ranch since she was no longer able to run it single-handed. He was an American and his name was Steve Tracey; apart from that she volunteered no information. She was after all coming up for seventy-four, Anne reasoned; it was only natural that she should begin to need help.

A week or two later Anne heard direct from Steve Tracey and knew that her vague uneasiness had been justified. He wrote, in a firm black script which looked clear and proved unexpectedly difficult to read, that Mrs Hardwick had gone into hospital for a major operation. Since he understood that Anne was her only family connection he had written to warn her that the outcome was doubtful.

'I ought to go over,' Anne said, but the operation proved successful and her mother-in-law was released from hospital after only three weeks. She wrote reassuringly and Anne contented herself with planning a visit later in the year.

'Will you take Melanie?' Jocelin asked.

'I don't know. I'll see how she feels about it when the time comes.'

Before these plans could be carried out Anne heard again from Steve Tracey and this time he had to tell her that her mother-in-law was sinking fast.

'I must go, even though I know I can do nothing,' Anne said to Melanie. 'I think you ought to come with me, darling. I know it will be painful for you, but you are the only actual blood relation she has in the world and that does mean something.'

'It won't hurt me in the way you imagine,' Melanie said. 'When I think back to that time with Ricky it all seems to be blotted out. There's a sort of black mist in my memory. It must be like Uncle Pete and the way he forgot what happened in the prisoner-of-war camp.'

It was not a particularly reassuring simile, but since it would enable Melanie to visit her grandmother Anne tried to be glad about it.

With the memory of the outcome of Melanie's last visit at the front of her mind, Anne had a moment of bitterness as she stood at the bedside of the dying woman. Her body was so thin that its outline barely disturbed the rigid hospital sheets. Her cheeks had fallen in and her hair, whiter than the last time Anne had seen her, had been plaited. The two meagre braids lay straight on either side of her throat and the tasselled ends rose and fell with the effort of her breathing.

Mrs Hardwick opened her eyes and looked up at Anne and a flicker of recognition showed in them. Her lips parted and she said, in a hoarse and difficult whisper, 'Melanie?'

'She's here.'

Anne drew Melanie forward and watched as her daughter, awestruck and a little frightened, bent over her grandmother. Seeing the flood of inarticulate love that rose in her mother-in-law's face, Anne felt both pity and rage. If you loved her so much why didn't you take better care of her? she silently asked. Were you so blind? And, of course she knew, even as the thought came into her mind, that Mrs Hardwick had indeed been unable to conceive that her fifteen-year-old grand-daughter could be capable of the sort of behaviour she would have condemned in a woman twice her age.

Mrs Hardwick died three days later. Anne had known that the job of going through her mother-in-law's possessions would fall on her and she had dreaded the task, but Mrs Hardwick had lived a life of Spartan simplicity and it proved surprisingly easy. Everything had been left in perfect order, including a copy of her Will, which, as Anne had expected, left everything to Melanie, to be held in trust for her until she was twenty-one.

Steve Tracey had made himself known to them as soon as they arrived, coming to the airport to meet them. He was younger than Anne had expected. Mrs Hardwick had given her no personal details about him at all and somehow Anne had built up a mental picture of a grizzled man in his fifties. It was disconcerting to discover that he was in his early twenties. Anne found out more about him when she went through her mother-in-law's correspondence. He was twenty-three, the son of a rancher, and he came from Montana, just south of the Canadian border. He was also a college graduate who had majored in English Literature and Geography, which seemed a strange combination for the manager of a small homestead in Canada.

Because she was curious, Anne probed gently into his background. Steve was perfectly ready to supply the missing details.

'I quarrelled with my old man,' he said. 'Dad wanted me to settle down and follow in his footsteps.'

He glanced sideways at Anne with a look of mischief on his face. 'To tell the truth, he wanted me to marry the girl next door. A dynastic marriage to combine the two spreads, just like old-time royalty. Waal, she was a nice enough girl, but I didn't see things quite that way, so I shook the dust from my feet and took off to see the world. I bummed around – sorry, that's a rude word in England, isn't it? – I *worked* my way round the country, doin' anything that came handy – dishwashing, garage hand, a bit of wrangling with horses, rode in a few rodeos, ended up here helping Mrs Hardwick out last summer and she offered to keep me on. That suited me just fine and here I am.'

He was immensely attractive. Tall and thin, with legs that seemed endless, broad shoulders tapering down to a waist that hardly supported the skin-tight jeans he wore sliding down his slim hips. His hair was brown flecked with gold and it had a tendency to curl which he seemed to deprecate; he had a way of flattening it down with his hand as he talked, so ingrained that he was obviously unconscious of it. His eyes were blue and could assume a guileless look which Anne wholly distrusted, especially once she had taken in the obstinate determination betrayed by his mouth and chin. A young man with a lot of charm, a really likeable boy, but she had grave doubts about leaving him in sole charge of the Hardwick Ranch. What she needed was a staid, middle-aged man, not this glamorous, footloose youngster with his wicked smile and disconcerting way of looking her over with undisguised approval.

Steve had no qualms about asking for what he wanted.

'I'd sure like to stay on here,' he said earnestly. 'Will you take me on as manager until Melanie comes of age?'

'Or until it suits you to move on?' Anne asked.

'Whichever comes first,' Steve agreed obligingly.

He studied her doubtful face and went on, 'I see I'll have to come clean. All this bumming – moving – around is just an excuse. I want to be a writer. That's what my old man couldn't stomach. He thinks it's no profession for a real man. I've written one novel, which no one will publish. Now I want to get down to something fresh. It's all in my mind. I'm mad to get started, but I need a roof over my head. This job is just right. I can get plenty of fresh air and exercise and a bit of company in the summer, and come winter I'll settle down and put the words on paper. I won't mind being alone, in fact I'll welcome it. Come on, Anne, do your bit for the literature of the world – give me a livin'.'

'Literature of the world, indeed!' Anne said, weakening but not quite ready to give way. 'You don't lack for cheek! What makes you think your writing is any good?'

For one moment all the laughter went out of Steve's face. Austere and unsmiling he looked like a different man.

'I can write,' he said. 'I will write better. I've given up my family and a mighty comfortable life because I won't compromise about it. I'm willing to settle down in this one-horse place and earn my keep, but only because it'll give me somewhere to go on writing. OK, so you don't think I can be trusted – I'll move on and find somewhere else, but it won't be as good.'

'Wait a minute,' Anne protested. 'Don't start packing your bags before I've made up my mind. Melanie and I will be here for at least another week.'

'Fine, that'll give you a chance to judge how I handle things. You don't want the dudes put off because of Mrs Hardwick's death, do you?'

'The . . . ? Oh, the visitors! No, let them come. It would be unfair to spoil holidays which are already arranged, and besides I have to consider Melanie's interests – the profits will be hers!'

She was curious to know what Melanie made of him.

'What do you think?' she asked her daughter. 'Is he a person we can leave in charge here? After all, darling, if he turns out to be untrustworthy it's you who will be the loser.'

'Granny trusted him,' Melanie pointed out. 'I don't think he'll run away with the takings.'

'Do you like him?' Anne persisted.

'He's all right. What does it matter whether I like him or not? He hardly knows I exist. You're the one he looks at all the time.'

It was an ungracious answer. Anne suspected that Melanie's attitude contained a hint of jealousy. It would hardly be surprising if she resented being overlooked by such an attractive young man in favour of her mother, but although Anne watched carefully she could see no sign of Melanie taking any particular interest in Steve. Perhaps it was just as well. She would not be seventeen until August and Anne had no wish to see her risking further heartache. There was plenty of time for Melanie to put her past unfortunate experience behind her and fall in love properly.

Melanie knew she was being watched and she resented it, misunderstanding the reason for Anne's vigilance. Did her mother really think that she was not to be trusted in the company of a young man? He was attractive, Melanie saw that, but she saw it with the dispassionate interest of a spectator. She would have liked to have tried to draw him, or better still to have felt the wood coming alive under her hands as she carved out a figure that conveyed something of his vitality, especially on horseback. As a man he did not touch her at all.

She was just beginning to realize it, this indifference she had developed towards the opposite sex. From being an outgoing child, friends with all the world, Melanie had grown into a lonely girl, distanced by one devastating experience not only from male company but from the friendship of other girls as well because she shrank from sharing the confidences they exchanged. Separated from her mother, too. Anne tried to hide it, but to Melanie it seemed that her sense of guilt over the abortion she had arranged for her daughter put a barrier between them.

Melanie was impatient with the laughing, semi-flirtatious relationship that developed between her mother and Steve, and she blamed Anne for not giving him a sharp rebuff. Her mother might shake her head at his blatant admiration, but Melanie saw that she could not stop herself from smiling, that her colour would rise and her eyes sparkle when Steve helped her down from her horse and leaned towards her with an outrageous compliment.

Anne herself was beginning to feel slightly guilty about the way her friendship with Steve was progressing. It meant nothing, of course; he was so many years younger than her that she could only laugh at his audacity. All the same, although she kept emphasizing both to herself and to him the difference in age between them, in her heart she knew that a man of twenty-three was not a boy. She really would have to stop giving in to a weakness for long legs and a wicked grin.

But when she tried to put their relationship on a more formal footing Steve turned the tables on her.

'Gee, it's cold in here tonight,' he said on an evening when

Anne had responded to all his sallies with polite indifference. 'Don't you think so, Melanie?'

'I think it's warm,' she said, but she looked at him sharply as he sat with his elbows on the kitchen table after their evening meal.

'Maybe it doesn't affect you, but the frost warnings are sure out for me.'

The dancing light in his blue eyes challenged Anne to understand him. She looked down, biting her lip to stop herself from responding.

Melanie got up. 'I'm going to take my sketching pad down to the river,' she said.

'You'll be eaten alive by mosquitoes,' Anne warned her.

'They don't bother me.'

She went out and Anne looked after her with worried eyes.

'I guess she doesn't like me chatting up her mother,' Steve suggested.

'I don't like it either,' Anne said, swiftly deciding that the time had come to put an end to it. 'I'm fourteen years older than you, Steve, happily married and the mother of a seventeen-year-old daughter . . .'

'Seventeen? Is Melanie really as old as that? I would have given her at least two years less. She's not as precocious as my fourteen-year-old sister was the last time I set eyes on her.'

'Melanie isn't quite seventeen and in some ways she's young for her age,' Anne admitted, and not for the first time she felt a chill at the way her young daughter's development had been stunted. 'In other ways . . .'

'She's as old as the hills. There's an area of darkness in her. Did something bad happen to Melanie?'

'She had . . . an unfortunate experience,' Anne admitted cautiously. She was disturbed by his unexpected insight.

'Sometimes I understand things with the inside of my mind and don't know how I picked up the message,' Steve said, with a hint of apology. 'I guess it's because I watch people. Melanie . . . yes, now that I know how old she is I can see the reason for the tension in her. She's trying to hold herself back. If she ever lets go, wow! The dam will sure burst. And with those looks . . . she's got it in her to become a real femme fatale. You're one hell of an attractive woman yourself, but you'd never be destructive.'

'Neither will Melanie!' Anne exclaimed.

'Mm, well, I'm not so sure. I see now why I've never managed to get through to her. She's got a grudge against men. Heaven help us if she ever decides to take her revenge.'

'No, no, no!'

Anne pushed back her chair and stood up, bitterly distressed by this reading of her daughter's character. Steve followed her and put his arm round her shoulders.

'Gee, I'm sorry. I write fiction. I make things up. It need not be that way at all.'

'It won't be.'

Anne looked up at him, tears standing on the end of her lashes, her wide, soft mouth quivering. Steve leaned towards her and kissed her. Anne put her hands flat against his chest, meaning to push him away, but Steve was holding her too strongly. She felt it rising in him, the urgent tide of sexual need, and her own response, and then she broke away from him.

In a frightened rush she said, 'Steve, this has got to stop.'

'Yeah, I guess so,' he agreed. 'Damn. I meant to keep it light.' His smile was lopsided and not entirely convincing. 'A meaningful experience with an older woman.'

He turned away from her, looking blindly out of the window. On the far side of the meadow he saw a small figure, a girl with her black hair lifting in the evening breeze, her face turned towards the lighted window.

Since Anne was not aware that Melanie had seen her in Steve's arms she did not realize the reason for her daughter's increasing withdrawal from her. She told herself that Melanie was grieving for her grandmother, that the ranch was still a painful place for her to be, that everything would be all right when they got home.

She was wild to get back to England, but there were legal requirements which could be more easily dealt with while they were on the spot and so she forced herself to be patient, to suppress her longing to get back to Jocelin and away from

Steve, who was now avoiding her in a way which Anne thought must make their mutual attraction only too apparent.

It was the beginning of June when they got home. Jocelin was waiting for them at the airport. For one moment he looked like a stranger, then it seemed to Anne as if something clicked back into place and the old, familiar love flooded through her.

'We got most of the business settled,' she told him that evening when they were alone. 'I had a shock over the size of Melanie's inheritance. A quarter of a million!'

'Pounds or dollars?'

'Pounds! And, of course, it will be even more by the time she's twenty-one.' She yawned hugely and flopped her head back against the armchair.

'Come on, sweetheart, you're suffering from jet lag. Bed for you.'

They wandered upstairs with their arms round one another.

'Lovely to be home,' Anne said contentedly. 'Have you missed me?'

'I've noticed you weren't around.' As they entered their bedroom his lips brushed her forehead. 'Silly question.'

'I missed you, too,' Anne said.

'Have you been a good girl while you've been away?'

It jerked Anne out of her drowsy stupor. 'Oh, Jocelin! Not altogether. That Steve, he was such a lovely young man and he did rather fancy me.'

'So I gathered from your letters.'

'He kissed me.'

'How shocking.'

Anne hid her face against his shoulder. 'And I liked it!'

'Never darken my doors again.'

She looked up and joined in his amused laughter. 'Oh, darling, do you think there's any way I can get it across to Melanie that the most important thing about being in love is being able to laugh?'

At the back of her mind a thought occurred: she had told Jocelin about Steve and they had both treated it as unimportant but what about similar incidents in the past with Jeff? Not for all the world would Anne have spoken to Jocelin about them. Steve did not matter, but Jeff constituted a threat, unacknowledged but there just the same, something that could break up her marriage, whereas Steve and that Italian woman – Bianca – were nothing but tiny scratches on the surface.

*

School seemed like an alien world when Melanie went back to it. Her reception from her teachers was frosty. Her long absence in the middle of term was not approved of, even though it was because of a death in the family.

'They keep on saying we have to be able to study on our own once we're in the Sixth Form, but when I said I took some of my books with me and studied while I was away I could see no one believed me,' Melanie complained.

'You're looking forward to leaving, aren't you?' Anne asked.

She thought that her daughter was looking less strained. There was a better colour in her cheeks and she seemed to be holding up her head again. *Femme fatale*, indeed; what nonsense that boy did talk.

'I haven't any real friends at school,' Melanie was saying. 'No one I want to bring home or go around with. It was all right until . . .' She tilted her chin and looked at Anne with deliberate jauntiness. '. . . until my little mistake. After that I always felt I had something to hide. Going to Art School will be like a fresh start. It'll be more grown up, more . . .'

'Congenial,' Anne supplied.

She felt immensely cheered by this evidence that Melanie was looking forward hopefully to the future and even more delighted when Melanie reported that she thought she had done well in her final examinations.

'I got annoyed when everyone kept taking it for granted that I would fail because I'd been to Canada,' Melanie said. 'I put in an extra spurt and I think the results are going to surprise them. Now I can relax and enjoy the last couple of weeks. We're being given a real treat next week – a visit to Wallenshaw!'

'To the Works? Heavens above, couldn't they have thought of something more glamorous than that?'

'It'll be interesting,' Melanie said. 'I've never seen the inside and after all our lives do depend on the Works, don't they? I'm going to smuggle in my sketch pad and try to do some drawings.'

Melanie had always taken for granted the size and importance of Wallenshaw Works. The great mass had always been there, just as it had been for Anne in her childhood, but Anne had been closer to it, not only because of the proximity of the Works to her home, but because her father was physically involved in the business of steelmaking. To Anne, Wallenshaw had been a vibration in the air, a billow of smoke on the near horizon, an actual presence just the other side of the Beck. Melanie had had no such intimate acquaintance with it and she was overwhelmed by the feeling of power that came to her as they were conducted round.

They saw from a distance the cokemaking plant, with the red-hot coke cascading out into the waiting hoppers, the sinter plant where the ore was prepared, and the blast furnaces where the iron was melted and purified, and gasped as they saw the molten stream of slag poured off, only a few feet from where they stood.

The melting shop, where the iron was turned into steel, was even more impressive. The furnaces were like great sullen animals waiting to be fed, digesting their meals in a roar of flame, barely held in control by the puny figures of the men who tended them.

'Don't look at the melt without your eye shields,' they were warned and they all held the strips of darkened glass in front of their eyes and watched respectfully as a lad in a white overall probed into the furnace, removing a sample of liquid steel which he poured into a miniature ladle for despatch to the laboratory.

'Time was when the quality of the steel depended on the judgement of the foreman,' their guide told them. 'He looked into the furnace and when he thought it was ready the steel was tapped. But things were slower then and a few minutes here and there weren't critical. Now, we rush the sample to the lab and as soon as we know it's up to standard the word is given to start tapping.'

He looked at the group of girls in a slightly baffled way, not sure how much of what he was saying was getting through to them.

'After stripping in the melting shop bay, casts of hot steel are delivered to the soaking pit by diesel locomotive. Casts are nominally one hundred and ten tons and are top poured or bottom poured according to steel quality,' he said, but it was obvious that he had lost them.

The thing that woke them up and made them laugh was seeing tea being made between the soaking pit and the rolling mill. As the steel ingot, fading from white hot to dull red, moved along the roller table one of the operatives stepped up to it with a kettle in his hand and placed it casually on the glowing metal. Before the ingot reached the rollers the kettle was boiling. He lifted it off, poured the boiling water into an enamel tea pot and a couple of minutes later was handing out mugs of tea.

As they congregated outside after the visit was over, chattering excitedly, Jeff came across the yard towards them, to say a few words. There was an amused quirk to his mouth as he began to speak. It made a change, having a gaggle of girls about the place, instead of the usual class of boys. From force of habit he gave them the quick once over, and his smile deepened as he saw the way some of them responded to that rapid, challenging glance.

'I say, not bad!' the girl next to Melanie breathed.

Silly idiot, Melanie thought distastefully. 'He's my uncle,' she said.

'Lucky you! Real uncle, or just married to someone?'

'He's married to my stepfather's sister. Do be quiet, I want to hear what he's saying.'

It was a speech Jeff had delivered many times before: hoping they had enjoyed their visit, pointing out the importance of Wallenshaw to the local community, making a graceful reference to the fact that some of them might have family connections with the steelworks, and finally suggesting that they should all be taken to the canteen for a cup of tea.

Towards the end he caught Melanie's eye and gave her a tiny conspiratorial wink.

'Mm, dishy!' Melanie's neighbour sighed as he strode away, glad that it was over, impatient to be back at the centre of things.

His long legs carried him swiftly away from them. There was something about him that exactly fitted his environment. In his square cut donkey jacket, his safety helmet worn at a cocky angle, its whiteness setting off his dark good looks, he looked every inch a steel man. They sensed in him, though none of them could have put it into words, a power that could be dangerous, and they were excited by it, as they had been by the might of the throbbing furnaces.

When they clattered down the stairs from the canteen to their coach Jeff's car was also at the gate. He wound down the window and called, 'Melanie! I'm on my way to Scunthorpe for a meeting with your dad and I'll be passing your house. Do you want a lift?'

Melanie glanced at the schoolmistress in charge of the party. 'May I? It will save me going into Upbridge and out again.'

As she got into the car with Jeff she knew that her schoolmates were looking after her with envious eyes. Their reaction to him had surprised her, but then she had never thought of Jeff except as a member of the family. And after all he was quite old. She took a quick sideways look at him. Jeff was leaner than he had been and it suited him. Unlike Jocelin, he had no trace of grey in his hair. He was, she supposed, a good looking man.

'Enjoy your visit?' Jeff was asking.

'I'm stunned,' Melanie said. 'I didn't realize it would be so . . .' she paused, frowning as she searched for a suitable word. 'Impressive,' she ended lamely.

'It gets you, doesn't it? I still get a thrill when I see a furnace tapped, even after all these years, even when she's acting up, like Number Four was today, the old cow.'

'Some cow!' Melanie commented. 'More like a prehistoric monster.'

'A dragon, breathing fire and slaughter?'

'Do you ever feel they might break loose and start stomping round the countryside?'

'Like the walking drag line in the open cast mine? No, that's one nightmare I've been spared, and I wish you hadn't put it into my head, young Melanie.'

He was undeniably attractive when he was laughing.

'We've got the beasts under control, I assure you,' Jeff said. 'I'll give Number Four a new lining and she'll start purring like a kitten again.'

'That's the thing I'll remember most,' Melanie said quickly. 'That you – that the men in the Works – were able to manage all that brute force and make it work for you.'

'It's brains that does it,' Jeff said. 'We know what we're doing, that's all.'

That was the quality she liked about Jeff, Melanie decided. He knew what he was doing. There seemed to be no doubts or dark corners in him. That was the advantage of age, of course. He had none of the uncertainties of the boys she knew.

'Give my love to your mother,' Jeff said as he dropped her off.

Melanie wandered indoors, lost in thought. She had had a very interesting afternoon, she told Anne. No, she hadn't done many sketches; the light had been poor and they had hardly ever stood still. Uncle Jeff had given her a lift home. He had sent his love.

Melanie went upstairs to wash away the grime of the steel works. She tossed her sketching pad on the bed and the leaves fluttered open. Almost the only complete drawing she had been able to make had been of Jeff, dashed off quickly while he had been talking to them. It was quite good, she decided. She had got his sharp profile, the angle of his steel helmet, a hint of his challenging smile, something of the arrogance of the man who was sure that he was in charge. She tore the sheet out of the pad and put it away in a drawer, under a pile of underclothes.

'I've had a letter from Steve,' Anne told her when she went downstairs. 'Very gloomy about American troops being committed to Vietnam. He seems to think he might get called up himself. His novel's been turned down again, too, poor lad. Here, you'd better read it; there's a message for you in it. Something I don't understand about some Indians camping at the ranch in the summer months.'

'I promised they could go on doing that,' Melanie said quickly. 'Because of Running Woman – my great-grand-mother. I must write to Steve myself and make sure he understands, because it's important.'

*

Melanie was accepted for Art School, but her course was not to start until October. Anne, blissfully reunited with her rapscallion boys, hardly noticed at first how much at a loose end her daughter was. They all went away to Brittany for two weeks right at the start of the school holidays.

'That really is all I can manage,' Jocelin said apologetically. 'I'm up to my neck in S.V.T.'s part in the new negotiations with the Government.'

The Government's White Paper on Steel Nationalization had been published in April and debated in May, but they were still not in a position to put their plans into operation.

'It's given us a bit of lee-way,' Jocelin said. 'The Government can't go ahead with something so controversial while it's hanging on to power by its finger nails. In the meantime, the industry is putting forward fresh proposals. One is for the replacement of the Iron and Steel Board with an Authority that would have more positive powers of control – the Board has never had any teeth – the other suggestion is for Government participation as a major shareholder, possibly by as much as fifty per cent.'

'Will they accept?' Anne asked, her eyes on his tired face.

'I don't know. It's coming up to crunch point. If they turn us down flat then there's no way ahead at all. It'll be outright nationalization.'

'And what will happen to you?'

Jocelin rubbed his hand over his forehead and yawned. 'They can't sack all the managers overnight. Someone has to go on running the industry. I'll still have a job.'

When Anne woke up to the way Melanie was mooning

about the house, not doing anything constructive, not even visiting Pete as she usually did in her holidays, she suggested she should get herself a job.

'Perhaps Tessa could use you in the shop,' she said.

'I'm not frightfully keen on that,' Melanie said, wrinkling her nose. 'The place I'd like to work is Wallenshaw. I was fascinated when I went on that visit.'

'You'd better talk to your Uncle Jeff,' Anne said absently.

She hardly expected anything to come of it, but Jeff reported that there was a temporary vacancy in the mail room and if Melanie had no objection to sorting letters and doing up parcels they would be happy to take her on.

With careless good nature he accepted that if Melanie happened to be around when he was leaving the Works he would give her a lift home. It was only after this had been going on for a week or two that he woke up to the amount of time she was spending in his company, not only riding home with him, but turning up in the evenings and at weekends to swim in the pool Tessa had had dug in the garden of their house.

Melanie, in a minute green bikini, her body smooth and brown, with her long legs, her flat stomach and full, pointed breasts, was a sight to give any man pleasure. Sitting by his side in the car, talking and laughing, full of eager questions about the Works, tossing back her long black hair, twisting towards him with her face alight with interest, she was enough to turn the head of any man who didn't happen to be nearly thirty years her senior and adept at getting out of awkward corners.

Tickled, flattered and horrified, Jeff finally admitted that Anne's young daughter was making a play for him. What a situation! She would have to be choked off, of course. He might have his faults, but cradle snatching was something he had never gone in for. Sweet, silly, lovely little idiot. He'd always had a soft spot for her, and an even softer one for her mother. Anne would blame him if she saw what was happening and for once his conscience was clear. He felt injured at being put on the spot and, deep down inside, regretful that he could not take advantage of the advances of this delicious young creature. Her youth drew him as much as her beauty – and Melanie was beautiful. She had grace in every line of her warm, rounded body, her hair was like a skein of silk, her full mouth hinted at a capacity for passion, unconscious but waiting to be discovered.

Tessa was woman enough for any man, when they were getting on, but they had hit a bad patch that summer. They were jaded with one another and they both enjoyed the stimulus of novelty. Tessa was disappearing to London 'on business' too often and Jeff suspected there was something going on. Nothing serious, he was pretty sure about that, but she was inclined to come back with an extra sparkle about her that showed she was basking in some other man's admiration. She was still damned attractive, but she no longer had the exquisite freshness of seventeen-year-old Melanie.

As they were driving home one day Melanie began to realize his deliberate refusal to respond to her presence. She turned her head to study him, but Jeff kept his eyes fixed on the road. And yet, beneath the surface, Melanie sensed that he was intensely aware of her. His hands gripped the wheel, strong and square with blunt-tipped fingers, a scattering of dark hairs across the back. Melanie reached out and put one of her own hands on top of his.

Jeff said something under his breath and pulled up abruptly by the side of the country road.

'If you do things like that we're going to have a crash,' he said. 'In more ways than one.'

Melanie leaned towards him, her eyes searching his face, her wistful mouth so inviting that Jeff pulled her head down against his shoulder to hide it.

'You've reached the age when girls start trying out their attractions to see what reaction they get,' he said. 'But you mustn't experiment with your wicked old uncle, sweetheart. It isn't fair.'

'I'm not experimenting!'

'Find yourself a nice boy your own age,' Jeff said firmly, but his lips brushed the satin skin at her temples and his free hand cupped itself over her shoulder, caressing its roundness beneath her cotton shirt. Looking back afterwards he was not at all sure that he had been as discouraging as he had meant to be.

To Anne's delight Lady Tyndall suggested giving a party at Upbridge Park for Melanie's birthday in August.

'A grown-up dance,' Anne said. 'Because you are seventeen, you've left school, and things are so unsettled who knows what may have happened by this time next year?'

'Dad won't be out of work if the steel industry is nationalized, will he?' Melanie asked incredulously.

'He thinks not, but it's going to come very hard on him, losing control of the Company. We'll have our party this year while we're still feeling fairly safe.'

'Can I have a really gorgeous new dress?' Melanie asked.

The days when Melanie took no interest in her appearance had passed. Now she demanded new clothes, studied the fashion magazines and washed her hair every other day. Just like any other teenager, Anne thought thankfully. What a lovely girl she had turned out to be. It was a pleasure to go shopping with her when everything she tried on was so becoming.

'But not black velvet, darling,' she said firmly. 'It's not at all suitable and besides it will be too hot. Something light and summery and young.'

'I'm tired of being treated like a kid,' Melanie complained.

She twisted in front of the mirror, admiring the effect of her white skin against the black velvet.

'I liked you in that floaty green thing,' Anne said.

'Oh, Mummy, it's positively antediluvian! If I can't have the velvet, and perhaps it would be too hot, I'll have the silver one.'

Anne opened her mouth to protest and closed it again. The stark little tunic, ending well above Melanie's knees, might seem like a strange choice for a party dress to her, but it was very modern and right in fashion. When Melanie was finally kitted out in silver mesh tights and boots ('for *dancing?*' Anne protested, but in vain) with her hair caught up behind in what Jocelin described as a cut-off from a steel tube, she looked like some exquisite visitor from another planet.

Looking round Upbridge Park on the night of the party Anne remembered what Jocelin had said about taking it over if his father retired. Would it ever happen? If Jocelin were not to become Chairman of S.V.T. would there be any point in retaining this large house with its acres of garden? She had never really wanted it, but all the same it made a splendid setting for a party. She could not help feeling glad that, just for once, Melanie and the boys were able to see it being used as it was meant to be used.

It was a hot night. The doors to the terrace stood open and people wandered out with glasses in their hands for a breath of air. The youngsters who had been invited for Melanie's benefit seemed impervious to the heat. The insidious beat of the music they preferred vibrated through the air. Melanie appeared to be enjoying herself. Anne had a momentary qualm as she saw the way the shimmering silver dress showed off her body as she twisted and turned.

'Come and dance with me, Jeff,' Melanie demanded. 'Come on, it's an old-fashioned thing you ought to be able to do.'

'Uncle Jeff to you, young Melanie.'

'I've decided to drop that now that I'm grown up.'

'Grown up! You're just a little silver fish who doesn't even know her way down the river.'

Melanie tilted her head back to look up into his face.

'I know the river, but I think I need someone to teach me how to swim,' she said. 'Come into the garden and talk to me about it.'

Jeff's heart sank as he saw the glittering excitement in her eyes. The silly little chump was going to give herself away in front of all her friends if he didn't prevent it. What was he to do? Tessa might be cruel if he told her about Melanie's infatuation and he wouldn't stand for that. As for Anne, how did a man tell a woman he'd made love to, that her baby daughter fancied him?

'I'll get you a cold drink and we'll go on the terrace, and no farther,' he said. 'And that's only because I'm fair sweltering in here.'

'I'll have champagne,' Melanie said.

'You'll have iced lemonade and like it,' Jeff retorted, but he got a stiff whisky for himself; he felt he needed it.

There were four other couples on the terrace, he was glad to see. Melanie had retreated to the far end, under the shadow of an overhanging tree, balancing on the wide stone balustrade. He could just see her silver dress glimmering in the darkness.

'Now then, young Melanie, I've got a few straight words to say to you,' he began.

'I'm the one who's going to do the talking,' Melanie said. 'I'm in love with you.'

'By heck . . .' Jeff said weakly. 'You mustn't say things like that!'

'You're married, you're older than me . . .'

'Twenty-seven years! I'm old enough to be . . .'

'My father. Do you feel like a father to me?'

'I feel like an uncle,' Jeff said firmly.

'We're barely related at all. The other day, in the car, you were only pretending. If I put my arms round your neck, like this, and kissed you, I could make you forget that silly age business.'

'I won't say you're wrong,' Jeff said, disentangling himself. 'When it comes to women I'm easily tempted and you're the choicest morsel that's come my way for a long time. All the same – no!'

It hurt him to see the way she wilted. Her head drooped and she said in a whisper, 'You don't understand. I was unhappy, so terribly unhappy, until you came along.'

'I've always been here.'

'I didn't notice. Suddenly I did and I thought . . . you could make it all come right for me.'

She took his hand in both of hers and held it tightly. 'I'm not the inexperienced little fish you think. I had an abortion when I was fifteen.'

'I know.'

Melanie dropped his hand. 'Did Mummy tell you?'

'Tessa guessed. She knew someone who'd been in the same clinic.'

'It was awful. Nothing else that ever happens to me can be

as bad as that. And I hated Ricky – the boy. When I look at boys of my own age I remember and I feel sick. I couldn't let one of them touch me. That's why it was so wonderful when I began to feel like this about you and why I had to nerve myself to tell you. I wouldn't mind making love with you.'

'God almighty, you're only seventeen! You haven't even begun to grow up. You've got years and years in front of you before you need start worrying about whether you enjoy sex or not.'

'But suppose I never do? It frightens me, looking into the future and thinking perhaps I'll always be alone.'

'Poor little love. Why don't you talk it over with Anne?'

'I can't. She's so happy, so successful with men. Daddy's nuts about her, even though they've been married all this time. And there was a man at the ranch in Canada. He kissed her and she just laughed.'

'Surely that would make it easier for her to advise you?'

'I don't think she'd understand if I told her I was in love with you.'

'I'm darn sure she wouldn't! But the other business, you could tell her that.'

'No.'

Jeff felt more helpless than he ever had before in all his dealings with women. He was intensely sorry for her. It was very hard not to take her in his arms and comfort her.

'You'll get over this in time,' he said gently.

To his relief she seemed to accept what he said.

'You think I'm just being silly. I'm not, but I won't make a spectacle of myself, so you needn't be worried. I won't run after you if you really don't want me.'

Jeff picked up his glass from the balustrade and swallowed the rest of his whisky. He felt enormously relieved, as if he had just passed through a great crisis.

'Jeff,' Melanie said in a small voice. 'Would you kiss me, just once, so that I can have one little thing to remember?'

Jeff glanced over his shoulder. The last of the four couples was just disappearing through the door. They were alone. He felt compassion for her, and affection, and beneath that a current of urgent lust of which he was deeply ashamed. He

took her in his arms, with great gentleness and all the skill he
had learnt over his mis-spent years. Melanie slid her arms
round his neck and raised her face.

It was like holding a mermaid, a quivering creature of the
sea, but warmblooded and sweet beyond imagining. And her
mouth learned quickly, tutored by his own experience. There
was nothing she would not give him and the longer he held
her the more he wanted.

It was the sound of his glass, shattering on the flagstones,
that brought Jeff back to his senses. He put her away from
him with a violence that gave away the effort it cost him.

He could hear his own breathing, rasping in his chest. It
seemed an age before he could speak, but when he did he
was still grimly hanging on to his control.

'That's that then,' he said. 'That's the end of it, Melanie.'

'It's just beginning,' Melanie said. 'Because now I know
you feel the same way about me.'

Chapter Ten

'Will you divorce Tessa?' Melanie asked.

She twisted a strand of Jeff's hair round her finger, tugging at it to rouse him.

His head moved against her shoulder. 'No.'

'Why not? You love me, not her.'

'I've told you before, this won't last. You'll get over it, I'll get over it – or so I hope.'

He rolled away from her, feeling on the bedside table for his cigarettes.

'Anyway, I've got no grounds for divorcing Tessa – as far as I know,' he said. 'The boot's on the other foot. I'm the guilty one.'

'Would she divorce you if she knew about me?'

Jeff lay on his back, his arm under his head, and blew a cloud of smoke into the air. As he watched it wreathing away above his head he said, 'No, I don't think she would.'

He turned his head to look at Melanie again and added deliberately, 'She never has before. This isn't the first time I've been unfaithful to her.'

'But the way we feel about one another is special,' Melanie protested. 'It is, isn't it?'

'Special? I'd call it freakish.'

'You're always like this after we've made love,' Melanie complained. 'Why?'

'Remorse.'

With all the singlemindedness with which she had clung to her infatuation for Ricky, Melanie had pursued her new obsession for Jeff, sure that he was the answer to the lack she felt in her life. Amongst her contemporaries in what had started to be called the Swinging Sixties, Melanie moved in an uneasy limbo, inhibited from experimenting with boys of her own age, frightened by her lack of response to them. The boys retreated, puzzled by their failure with her, and the girls left her alone because she shared none of their emotional ups and downs. Her imagination had seized on Jeff. In spite of the extreme difference in their ages he was still a glamorous figure. His dark good looks, his powerful sexual attraction, the hints she had garnered of his dubious reputation, all these fed Melanie's craving.

She refused to believe that Jeff could be indifferent to her, and he was not. With all the force of his indulged senses he felt the tug of desire for this wilful child who threw herself in his way. When, fighting to preserve some sense of proportion, he had tried to laugh her out of her folly, Melanie looked at him with such desperate, wounded eyes that he caught her in his arms to comfort her. There were more kisses, longer sessions of the petting that drove Jeff mad and left Melanie bright-eyed and sure that he did love her and was only holding back because of his old-fashioned scruples.

'It's not as if you and Tessa got on well,' she said, in the days when Jeff was still standing out against her. 'You've always had rows, ever since I can remember.'

'But we're still together,' Jeff said.

That was one of the meetings from which Melanie had retreated dispirited and hurt. For a short time Jeff had believed that he had succeeded in discouraging her, but only a few days later she turned up on his doorstep, disconcertingly frank about the fact that she knew Tessa had taken Max to London for a couple of nights. She lifted her face to him with an innocent wantonness that floored Jeff completely.

'I don't see how you can possibly pretend you're not in love with me when you kiss me like that,' Melanie said, leaning against him contentedly.

'A man can make love without being *in* love,' Jeff told her.

'Don't you care for me at all?'

'You're the loveliest thing that ever lived,' Jeff said unsteadily. 'I'm much too fond of you to do you an injury. Now go home. Where does your mother think you are?'

'Visiting a school friend in Upbridge.' Melanie wrinkled her nose. 'I don't like telling lies,' she admitted.

'I'm glad you have some moral sense! How about chasing a married man, doesn't that make you feel guilty?'

'No, because I love you so much.'

She walked past him into the lounge, sat down on the couch and patted the seat by her side. Jeff sat down at a safe distance, but when Melanie changed her place and leaned against him he put his arm round her. He had no illusions about the nature of her feelings for him, nor about his for her. What Melanie was seeking was the reassurance of a physical relationship. Because she was young and inexperienced she had dressed it up in the trappings of romantic love, but Jeff was cynically aware of his own crude craving for her body.

He tried that evening to shock her out of her muddled dream.

'I'm no Fairy Prince,' he said. 'I'm a randy middle-aged man who's being teased by a naughty schoolgirl. To me you're just a gorgeous lump of flesh. What I feel about you is rude and nasty and vulgar. I'd like to strip you naked and ram you until you screamed.'

For one moment he thought his deliberate brutality had paid off. Her expression wavered, a look of doubt crossed her face. Then she laid the palm of her hand against his cheek.

'You wouldn't hurt me, I know you wouldn't. You'd make it wonderful for me.'

Putting his desire into words had excited him almost unbearably. He caught her up and held her tight. 'Melanie, you're going too far. Every man has his breaking point and I'm near to mine.'

'Good. Darling Jeff, I do love you so very much.'

They grappled together on the wide, soft couch, but after a minute or two Jeff got up.

'I'm past the age for wallowing on a sofa. Come upstairs. You've asked for it and, by heck, you're going to get it.'

The only thing that betrayed to Jeff, as their affair progressed, that Melanie did not really believe that it was going to be permanent was the care she took to keep it secret. To him it seemed incredible that no one saw through the screen of lies with which they protected themselves, but Anne was serenely trusting, believing that Melanie was involved in events at her new Art College, Jocelin was preoccupied, and Tessa was indifferent. Jeff suspected that she might be carrying on an affair in London herself, but that was something he never spoke about to Melanie and even to himself Jeff did not admit how much of his response to Melanie arose from the poor relations between himself and Tessa. It shook him when Melanie raised the question of divorce. That had never been on the cards as far as Jeff was concerned.

Their opportunities for meeting were infrequent, but Jeff had not indulged in liaisons in the past without learning the ropes. There were always places where one could take a girl with a bit of wangling and a willingness to spend money. Throughout the autumn and winter they contrived to meet and make love.

Occasionally, when Tessa was away, they were able to meet at his own house, as they had on the chilly February day when Melanie had started talking about divorce. They avoided the room he shared with Tessa and made use of a guest room with a choice of two narrow single beds. It was not particularly comfortable and they had to be careful to clear away signs of their occupation. There was a lot to be said, Jeff thought as he lay and smoked, for the restful convenience of a wife and a large double bed.

'I'm getting old,' he said out loud.

'I haven't noticed it,' Melanie said.

She climbed over him and began pottering about the room, finding the clothes she had discarded in a wild flurry. Her naked body was so perfect that it made Jeff's heart ache.

I'm going to end it, he suddenly thought. I've had her, she's wonderful, no man could have had a more perfect experience. If only she wasn't so young, if only I didn't feel so damn bad about it. I've made her happy. Sweet idiot, imagining she might not find a man to rouse her when the truth is she was made for love. It can't go on. If we're found out the end will be sordid and that will spoil anything good she's got out of it.

He followed Melanie's example and began to get dressed.

As he buttoned his shirt he said, 'Sweetheart, that was the last time.'

'You can't be serious,' Melanie said, half smiling and half doubtful.

'Now's the time to stop, while it's still a secret.'

'Oh, *you*! You always get qualms when it's too late. You'll be just as mad about me next time we meet.'

'This time I mean it.'

'That's what you always say.'

He did not reply and Melanie said, 'Jeff . . . ? You're not really serious? Honestly, I don't care if everyone knows. I've been trying to find out if it would be legal for me to marry you and I think it would.'

He was appalled. 'I'm not going to marry you,' he exclaimed. 'Good God! Come downstairs. I could do with a drink.'

'I must do my hair. I'll be down in a minute.'

When she joined him Jeff was standing by the fire in the lounge, a glass in his hand.

'Have you really thought what it would be like if everyone knew what we'd been up to?' he demanded.

'Mummy would stand by me. And Daddy, too.'

'Could you face your grandparents? Your Uncle Pete? What about my brother and your Aunt Evelyn? Would you really like them talking it over between themselves?'

He saw from the shiver of distaste that ran through her that he had scored a point. He pressed his advantage relentlessly.

'Your father's my boss. We couldn't go on working together if he knew I'd been fucking his little daughter.'

Melanie put her hands over her ears. 'Don't use words like that! Not about us. And he's only my stepfather.'

'Don't split hairs, either about Jocelin or about what we've been doing. Face facts, Melanie. We've given one another a damn good time. You're fantastic in bed. And not just because I've shown you how; you've got a natural talent for it. You'll never have any difficulty in finding a man to make love to you, nor in responding to him. But from now on you're on your own. Next time you take a lover it's got to be a boy of your own age.'

Melanie shook her head helplessly. 'Is that really all it's been?' she asked in a whisper.

'That's all,' Jeff said. He only wished that it was true, that she hadn't got into his heart, so that breaking with her was like tearing out a part of himself.

Tessa came home the following evening, chatting brightly about visiting Max at his school, discreetly silent about why it had been necessary for her to stay overnight in London.

'Any visitors while I've been away?' she asked.

It was better not to tell unnecessary lies. 'Young Melanie looked in,' Jeff said.

'As she so often does when I'm not around.'

Tessa was dangerous when she spoke in that silky way. She seemed to be expecting an answer, but Jeff merely grunted and to his relief she let it pass.

The following day Tessa called to see Jocelin in his office. It occurred to Jocelin as she was shown in that it was some time since they had met. She and Jeff had taken Max abroad for Christmas and he had certainly not set eyes on her since their return.

'You look very opulent,' he remarked as Tessa loosened her fur coat.

'I bought it myself,' she said. 'I won't waste any time, Jocelin. I'd rather come straight out with what I've got to say and get it over. You and Anne seem to be completely blind to what's going on between Jeff and Melanie.'

Jocelin sat up with a jerk. 'Melanie?' he said incredulously.

'Your little step-daughter is my husband's mistress.'

The appalling thing was, he knew immediately that it was true. He had noticed the teasing, flirtatious relationship that had developed between Melanie and Jeff last summer, had been irritated by it and had seen it, as he thought, disappear. Now he knew with absolute certainty that it had been replaced by something more serious. All the same, he was not going to admit that to Tessa.

'Have you any proof?' he asked coldly.

'I can get it. She was at our house this weekend. She left me a message in one of the guest rooms.'

Tessa held out her hand. On the palm lay one of the tortoiseshell combs Melanie used to hold back her hair.

'She didn't leave it behind by accident,' Tessa said. 'Oh, no! Melanie is too clever for that. She meant me to find it. Little bitch.'

'It's hardly proof of adultery,' Jocelin said.

'It's not the first time she's been there while I've been out of the way. Jeff thinks he's clever at hiding the traces, but those long black hairs are difficult to get rid of. If I had enquiries made I dare say I could find other evidence. I'm thinking of getting a divorce and citing Melanie.'

'Tessa, for God's sake! If you want a divorce find some other reason. She's only a child.'

'A precocious child. If it comes to a divorce I shall have to mention her previous abortion.'

The smile on her face was not pleasant as she saw how deeply she had shocked him.

'I could be persuaded to change my mind,' she said.

'How?'

'I'll strike a bargain with you. I want Upbridge Park to begin with.'

'That's up to Dad.'

'He and Mummy don't want it. Nor does Anne, not really. Dear Anne is a suburban housewife at heart – that's why it's going to come hard on her to learn that her daughter is having an affair with her uncle.'

'Very well, you can have Upbridge Park. Though what you want with that great white elephant of a place I really don't know.'

'It makes a suitable home for the Chairman of S.V.T.'

Jocelin stared at her and then he burst out laughing.

'Oh, Tessa! Jeff – Chairman of S.V.T.? The Board would never wear that.'

'They might if you were out of the way. I don't care how you work it – resignation, a request to be transferred to other duties, anything you like. Then recommend Jeff to replace you. Once he's on the Board I'll work on Dad to nominate him to be the next Chairman.'

'I don't think you will. You talk as if the Company belonged to the family. It's more complicated than that, little sister. Dad and I have a duty to the shareholders.'

Tessa smiled again. 'It's been astonishingly easy to buy shares in S.V.T. lately. With nationalization in everyone's mind the smaller shareholders have been only too glad to part with their holdings. And I had plenty of money to play with from my shops. Jeff is really in a very strong position if he can get the present Chairman's nomination plus the support of his brother-in-law, especially since his wife is a major shareholder. And, of course, he's known. I've seen to that, though it's damn little thanks I've got for it.'

'You're completely out of your mind! With nationalization round the corner it doesn't matter a tinker's toss who becomes Chairman of S.V.T.'

'I don't think I can lose either way. If there's an election and Labour gets in with a bigger majority we'll have nationalization. In that case, as Chairman, or Chairman-elect, Jeff must be in a good position for a top job in the new organization. He'll be new, you see, not one of the old guard, and it's known that his sympathies are with nationalization. The men at the top of the industry at the moment have fought too hard against it – as you have yourself, brother dear. But Jeff, still young, dynamic, a natural leader, newly promoted to a top job in one of the larger steel companies – oh, yes, I think we'd be laughing. And, of course, if there's no nationalization I'd still win.'

'All this because one silly little girl lets herself be seduced by a man old enough to be her father.'

'I'm not sure who was the seducer,' Tessa said. 'I suspect Melanie made most of the running. It'll be a juicy case if it comes to Court.'

She watched his unyielding expression for a moment and then she said, 'Anne will hate it.'

'You'd better leave me before I forget we're brother and sister,' Jocelin said. 'Your plan is ridiculous, of course, but I'd like time to think about it.'

'Anyone else would be raving round the room,' Tessa said, almost enviously. 'You're so cool you make me wonder whether you've got any blood in your veins at all. I'll give you until the end of the week – and that's generous.'

When she had gone Jocelin sat at his desk fighting to preserve the calm of which she had accused him. Was it possible for the scheme Tessa had proposed to be carried out? No, he was sure it was not. The trouble with Tessa was that she was fundamentally a stupid woman. He remembered her as a girl, always demanding something she couldn't have, but not prepared to work towards an achievable goal. He felt nothing but disgust for her devious and unworkable plot.

As for the other two, if Melanie had walked into the room at that moment he would have blasted her to ashes with the white hot blaze of his anger, and Jeff – his hands clenched, but coming to blows with Jeff was a luxury he couldn't allow himself. As he considered the damage Tessa could do, Jocelin began to see that the one person he had to talk to was Jeff.

Jeff received him cheerfully, surprised by Jocelin's unexpected visit to him at Wallenshaw, but wholly unsuspecting. He was feeling good; it was a relief to have pulled himself together and broken with Melanie and it certainly made it easier to look Jocelin in the face, unencumbered by the nagging sense of guilt which had plagued him for the last five months.

'Did you know Tessa had been buying up stock in S.V.T.?' Jocelin asked.

It was so remote from anything Jeff had thought he might ask that he was taken completely by surprise.

'What on earth is she thinking of?' he asked. 'It can hardly be a good investment – and that's not like Tessa. She usually manages her affairs better than that.'

'Talking of affairs,' Jocelin said. 'Have you been bedding young Melanie?'

He saw the horror in Jeff's face, the sick dismay, and knew he was going to lie.

'No, of course not!'

'Tessa thinks you have.'

'*Tessa* knows . . . ?'

'It's true, isn't it?'

Jeff nodded, without looking at Jocelin.

'I'll just run through the proposition that's been made to

me,' Jocelin said in the same equable tone he had preserved so far.

When he had finished Jeff was sweating. He pulled out his handkerchief and wiped his forehead.

'Tessa's out of her mind,' he said.

'So I think. I told her I needed time to think it over, but of course I don't. None of us could push through a deal like that, and the fact that it's impossible makes Tessa all the more dangerous, because if she doesn't get what she wants she may carry out her threat. I may as well tell you, I would never support you for the top job in this organization. I'll do you the justice to admit that you're a first class General Manager at Wallenshaw, I even think you could run a larger complex, but Chairman – no! Leaving on one side your total lack of morals . . .'

'It wasn't all my fault,' Jeff said quickly.

'That's one defence I'd rather not hear – that you succumbed to the advances of a seventeen-year-old girl,' Jocelin said, and the light contempt in his voice cut Jeff to the quick.

'As I say, quite apart from that aspect of your character, I don't think you've got the stature for high office.'

'And you have, I suppose?'

Jocelin did not hesitate. 'Yes, I would have been a good Chairman. You'll notice I say "would have been"; I have very little hope of getting there now.'

'If Tessa doesn't get what she wants . . .' Jeff said slowly.

'Then the divorce goes ahead, Melanie is sacrificed, Anne will be heartbroken, and you, Jeff, will be out of a job.'

'You'd have me sacked,' Jeff said.

'Of course I would! Gross personal misconduct. If my father and I took our outraged feelings to the Board and said that there was no possibility of our co-operating with you in the future I think we'd get a sympathetic hearing. No doubt something civilized could be arranged. You would be allowed to resign, there'd be a golden handshake for you.'

'And I'd be out of work – now, when the whole industry is in a state of flux!'

'Obviously Tessa never considered that. You could, of course, resign immediately . . .'

'I'm damned if I will!'

'I won't press for it because Tessa might go ahead with the divorce if I do. It's up to you to find some way of stopping her. It's your mess, Jeff. I'm handing you the chance of getting out of it. God knows how! The only suggestion I can come up with is to play on her feelings for Max. A messy divorce would be very nasty for him.'

'Max,' Jeff said. 'There's one card I could play, but it's a damned dirty one.'

'You're hands aren't noticeably clean,' Jocelin said. 'God in heaven, man, did you have to have both of them – mother and daughter? That's what will kill Anne if she ever finds out.'

For the first time he allowed the full force of his disgust to show. Jeff's eyes glittered and a dark red flush rose in his face. To have incurred Jocelin's anger and to know that it was justified, that was bitter. He would have liked to have struck out wildly at Jocelin, to have throttled Tessa, even to have hurt Melanie, anything to relieve the frustration of knowing he had sinned and had been found out.

It made him brutal when he dealt with Tessa that evening.

'You fool, to think you could outwit Jocelin!' he said. 'I'll tell you something: if it really came to the crunch he'd sacrifice Melanie. God help him, I think he'd even sacrifice Anne, just so long as his beloved Company came out unscathed. As for me, he'd trample me into the ground.'

'I could have dealt with him if you hadn't crumpled up,' Tessa said. 'This is the first time I've ever had a really strong hand . . .'

'A strong hand! A silly,. unrealistic, *woman's* idea,' Jeff said scathingly. 'Damn you, I don't need your meddling. I'm making my own way up the ladder – or I was. Unless you drop this divorce I'm going to be out on my ear.'

'Why should I care? If I can't put you at the top of S.V.T. I'll make do with a scandal that'll raise the roof.'

'You have no proof,' Jeff said. 'I may have been indiscreet – I'll admit to no more than that. Melanie has a childish crush on me, that's true, but I've already told her that I won't let her ruin her life over something she'll have forgotten by this time next year.'

'She'll remember it for longer than that by the time I've finished dredging up the evidence.'

'I could retaliate.'

Tessa shrugged with apparent indifference. 'Go ahead. There's nothing you can find out about me that matches having an affair with your seventeen-year-old niece.'

'I could ask for a blood test on Max.'

Tessa went as still as if he had hit her, as he had so much wanted to do. When she spoke it was in a hoarse whisper.

'After all these years . . .'

'I've never been sure he was mine.'

She rallied and began to protest. 'How can you say such a thing? Of course he's yours. There's never been any doubt about it. You've never hinted at it until now.'

'I wanted to believe he was my son. But there's something I've never told you, not even when you complained about him being an only child. I'm sterile. I found out while you were off on that trip to France just before you said Max was conceived – or did some Frog give him to you while you were away?'

'It's not true,' Tessa said.

She looked down, hiding the flicker of fear she felt. She had wondered sometimes whether it was possible . . . Only the faintest recollection of the Frenchman came back to her – thin, dark, intense, and a damn good lover – she had forgotten his name . . . Bernard, that was it. It had been after the ball, she had been half drunk and careless. But she had pushed the idea to the back of her mind, telling herself that there could be no doubt that Max was Jeff's.

She lifted her head. 'I wasn't unfaithful during that visit to Paris,' she said. 'I swear it.'

'I'm prepared to believe you, provided you believe I haven't been to bed with Melanie. Otherwise I'll set about proving that Max is a bastard.'

'You couldn't do that to him! Poor little devil, why should he suffer?'

'He can't help suffering if we divorce one another, especially if it's the sort of juicy case you have in mind.'

'Those blood tests aren't conclusive.'

'And there's a million to one chance that I fathered the boy.

I'm damned fond of the little chap. As far as I'm concerned, he's my son – as long as you stay my wife.'

'Bloody blackmail,' Tessa muttered.

'That's good, coming from you. What was your scheme but a crude attempt at blackmail? Christ, Tessa, did you really think you could get away with it? That I'd agree? That I'd go on living with you? At Upbridge Park, too – I like that touch!'

'Damn you, I was doing it for you!'

'It was your ambition you were feeding, not mine.'

Tessa was crouching on the sofa, the same soft couch where Melanie had offered him her sweet temptation.

'What are we going to do now?' Tessa asked, her voice sullen with defeat.

'Damned if I know.'

'I've been having an affair with one of my designers in London.'

'I thought you had.'

She got up and began to pour herself a drink, the clattering of the glass betraying how her hands were shaking. Over her shoulder she said, 'It was bloody humiliating, being thrown over for a teenager I've known since she was a baby.'

'I've told you – it's over. Melanie knows it. She was trying to force my hand when she left that comb for you to find.'

There was no reply. After a minute Jeff said, 'You might fix me a drink, too.'

Tessa hunched her shoulders in her old, petulant fashion, but when she did as he asked Jeff knew that he had won. As she put the glass into his hand he said, 'We deserve one another, you and I, but we could do better than we have recently.'

'Darling! You'll be saying "let's make a fresh start" next!' Tessa mocked him.

'Yes, that's what I'm going to say. You're a lousy wife, but I'd rather have you than anyone else.'

'And you're a bloody awful husband.'

'But . . . ?'

Tessa shrugged. 'I nearly spat blood when I began to suspect about Melanie. Jeff, how *could* you?'

'I've never had any difficulty about giving into temptation,'

Jeff said drily. 'Do you still want a divorce? It could be fixed – without bringing Melanie into it – if you wanted to marry your designer.'

'Him? No, thanks! I was just using him to work off my spleen.'

'That must have been a whole lot of fun.'

Tessa caught her breath in an involuntary laugh and then, wholly unexpectedly, her face crumpled and she began to cry in an angry, uncertain way. Jeff handed her his handkerchief and she blew her nose loudly.

'Damn, damn, damn,' she said.

'There's still something between us,' Jeff said, watching her. 'If there hadn't been, you would have gone straight for the divorce, without bothering about being the Chairman's lady. You wanted the position, the prestige, but you wanted me, too. You still do.'

'You're so conceited you make me sick! I don't want you. I'd just as soon never set eyes on you again.'

'A separation?'

Tessa did not answer. Instead, she asked, 'What will happen between you and Jocelin?'

'We'll paper over the cracks. If there's to be no scandal we've got no excuse to do anything else. Besides, he needs me at Wallenshaw. It won't make that much difference; he's never liked me ever since he began to suspect I was making love to you before we were married, even less since he found out I'd slept with his wife . . .'

'*Anne*, too?' Tessa said incredulously.

'I forgot you didn't know about that.'

She began to laugh wildly, rocking backwards and forwards, the tears streaming down her face at the same time. Jeff smacked her, very deliberately, first on one cheek and then on the other. Tessa gasped, choked and began to cry in earnest, but without the hysteria. Jeff put his arms round her, holding her tightly, hiding her face against his shoulder.

'The real reason we're still together is because we each know the worst about the other – and we wouldn't like making the same revelations to anyone else,' he said. 'We've put up with one another for fourteen years, that must count for something.'

'I could kill you.'

'I could kill myself. If you think you've been humiliated, just imagine how I feel, having Jocelin tongue-lash me and knowing I deserved it.'

Almost under her breath, Tessa said, 'About Max . . .'

Jeff tilted her head back and stared into her flushed, tear-distorted face. 'Max is mine. That's the way I want it. I've got your word for it that there's no reason for me to doubt that I'm his father?'

Without taking her eyes from his, Tessa said, 'Yes.'

'Then we'll take it from there and start again. I'm . . .' It was not easy to get it out, but he made an effort and did it. 'I'm asking you to forgive me.'

He got no answer, but he had not expected one. To lighten the atmosphere he said, 'And from now on, consult me before you meddle with my career. I know my way about the jungle better than you do.'

Chapter Eleven

When Jocelin first confronted Melanie with his knowledge of her affair with Jeff she was defiant.

'I love him,' she said. 'And he loves me.'

There was a shade of uncertainty behind that second statement which Jocelin was quick to recognize.

'Jeff and Tessa are going to stay together,' he said gently. 'And it's right that they should. You've behaved badly, Melanie. You could have caused a lot of trouble which would have affected all our lives.'

Very briefly, he told her about Tessa's ultimatum. Melanie stared at the floor, sick with humiliation. Jeff had given her up because Tessa had threatened divorce and scandal. Melanie had only half believed him when he had said the time had come to part, but now she saw that he had meant it. She had left her hair comb behind, just as Tessa had suggested, as an act of defiance, to force Jeff into acknowledging her openly. It had all gone wrong. Jeff had never loved her, not in the way she still loved him.

'It can't be over, not just like that,' she pleaded. 'If I could see Jeff . . .'

'No!'

The way Jocelin spoke made Melanie jump.

'I know you believed you had fallen in love,' he went on more quietly. 'That's no excuse for coming between a man and his wife. If you ever put yourself in Jeff's way again I'll send you into exile.'

He saw from Melanie's stare that she had no idea what he meant.

'I'll pack you off to Canada. The only thing that stops me

from doing it now is that it would mean telling your mother. At the moment she knows nothing and I mean to keep it that way. Don't give yourself the luxury of confessing, Melanie. It would hurt her too much. You're a woman now; keep your mouth shut about your misdeeds and learn to live with them.'

It was galling to have to go on working with Jeff as if nothing had happened, but Jocelin gritted his teeth and did it. In any case, what was happening in the political arena was so momentous that it overshadowed his family difficulties.

In March 1966 another election was held and the Labour Government got back into power with a greatly increased majority. The 'steel barons', still fighting a rearguard action, set up a Development Co-ordinating Committee under the chairmanship of Sir Henry Benson to make further proposals for nationalizing the industry, but everyone knew it was a hopeless exercise. The Government produced its Iron and Steel Bill in June and the Second Reading took place in July.

'That's it, then,' Jocelin said blankly to Anne. 'We've lost.'

'Who will be the Chairman of the new Corporation?' Anne asked.

'A man from outside the industry, I imagine. It would be very difficult to put any of the present top men in charge – even if one of them could be persuaded to accept the job.'

'Are you very upset?' she asked, watching his tired face.

'It's been hanging over our heads for so long that it's a relief to get it settled. There are things to be said in favour of nationalization. The industry's top heavy, over-manned, under-developed, not really competitive in a modern world. No one has been keen to make changes, knowing they might be throwing their money down the drain. Perhaps now we can make a fresh start.'

When the name of the new Chairman was announced Wally, for one, could scarcely believe it.

'A merchant banker? And a Conservative peer at that!' he said disbelievingly. 'Lord Melchett! What does he know about steelmaking?'

'Jocelin was surprised, but he thinks it could turn out to be a good appointment,' Anne said.

'Aye, he would, wouldn't he? He's one of them,' Wally said.

'Went to the same school an' all. Eh, it's not what I expected, I tell you straight it's not.'

'He seems to be making a whirlwind start with his Organizing Committee. Jocelin is impressed. He thinks he might stand a chance of pulling it all together.'

'Early days yet,' Wally conceded. 'Have to let him show what he's made of, I suppose, but if you ask me they'd have done better to appoint somebody that knew a blast furnace from a rolling mill.'

Anne repeated this to Jocelin, who agreed that the appointment had been received without enthusiasm on the shop floor.

'What they don't realize is that Julian Melchett will spend his time negotiating at Government level on finance and policy,' he said.

'Did you know him at Eton?' Anne asked.

'Not that I can recollect. He's a year or two younger than me and he was at a different house. The boys may know his son. I must remember to ask them.'

Because she was preoccupied with Jocelin, Anne paid little attention to the change in Melanie, from excited, almost frenetic gaiety, back to the moodiness she had shown in the past. And Melanie, bewildered by Jeff's abrupt desertion, hugged her misery to her and did her best to keep it hidden from her mother. She tried not to think about Jeff, but in the unguarded moments between sleeping and waking the memory of him would come back and she would twist and turn, unable to sleep, burying her face in the pillow to stifle the tears that stung her eyes and made her throat ache.

Gradually, the first desperation faded. Melanie still refused to accept that she might get over falling in love with Jeff, but once it was no longer necessary to keep herself free in case he could spare time to be with her she began to join in the social life at the Art College and to learn from the frankness with which the other students discussed their chaotic love lives that she was not alone in making mistakes. There were even times when she felt relieved to be free of her liaison. There had been a heady thrill in deceiving everyone, but it had not been a healthy excitement; looking back, Melanie grew to feel ashamed of it.

She did not, as Jeff half thought she would, immediately start a new affair with a fellow student. Instead, she continued to hold herself aloof. There was an air of mystery about her. Her smile beckoned, her body looked sensuous, but she was not to be had. She became one of the most sought after girls of her year, but no one could boast of having so much as held her hand.

Occasionally she wrote to Steve Tracey in Canada. It had started when Steve sent a letter to Melanie, instead of to Anne as he usually did, about her ancestor, the Blackfoot Indian woman.

'I've scrapped the novel I was working on,' he wrote. 'Even I can see it's no good. Instead, I've been talking to that old Indian woman who camps at the ranch each summer. I think there's a good story behind your great-grandmother's marriage to Jacob Hardwick. Do you mind if I write it? Better still, have you got any information or a photograph of her?'

There was one photograph, a strange, brown print of a dark-faced woman staring impassively at the camera. She was wearing European dress, but her hair lay in heavy braids over her shoulders. Melanie could gather nothing from her expression. She sent the photograph off to Steve and from time to time he dropped her a line to let her know how his research was going. He told her, too, something of his inner conflict over the struggle in Vietnam. It had been an accident that he had been in Canada when the war began to escalate; now he was faced with the choice of remaining in exile or going home to be drafted. Steve, deeply troubled but persuaded in his own mind that his country was tackling the situation in the wrong way, did not feel prepared to fight for a cause in which he had no faith.

Jocelin never discovered how Jeff had persuaded Tessa to drop both the divorce proceedings and her bizarre ambitions, but one of her conditions must have been that there should be no meetings with Melanie because there was even less contact between the two families than there had been in the past. Jocelin witnessed only one encounter between Jeff and Melanie in the summer months of 1966 and it troubled him considerably.

Each year Lady Tyndall lent her garden for a fête in aid of the local hospital. There had been a feeling that the National Health Act would make charitable fund raising unnecessary, but there always seemed to be something for which extra money was needed and so the party went on, with amateur side shows and a tea tent and heartfelt prayers for a fine day.

There was a cricket match, too, in which Jocelin and both his sons were playing against a hospital side. The sight of the three of them in their white flannels, the boys suddenly so tall and like their father, Jocelin with his easy elegance, made Anne blink and sniff into her handkerchief.

'What's making you weepy?' Melanie asked in amusement.

'They're so *beautiful*,' Anne said. 'Don't tell them I said so!'

They all met at tea and that was when they bumped into Tessa and Jeff. Tessa, thinner and noticeably well dressed, was a different creature from the girl who had once shrugged on her clothes anyhow. Her brusqueness had hardened into a brittle social manner. Jocelin, carefully watchful, thought that her high-pitched chatter, the restless movement of her hands, the way she looked past the person to whom she was talking to spy out what was happening elsewhere all betrayed an inner dissatisfaction that would probably never be cured. Ambition without ability, that had always been Tessa's dilemma. Jeff had not quite achieved the heights she had planned for him. She laid a possessive hand on her son's arm and the thought came to Jocelin that the poor boy was going to have a hard life unless he managed to break away from her.

Tessa spoke to Anne, but ignored Melanie. Fortunately, Anne did not seem to notice. Jocelin saw Melanie glance once at Jeff. A wave of colour swept over her face and receded, leaving her unusually pale, but as far as Jocelin could tell her reaction was nothing more than acute embarrassment.

'I promised to go and help serve teas to the bigwigs at four o'clock,' she said in a breathless rush.

Jocelin watched her as she ran across the lawn and he saw that Jeff was doing the same. For one moment he saw an expression on the other man's face that shocked him into unwilling pity. Poor devil, caught in an entanglement he had meant to be trivial which had turned into a craving for which there was no release. And Melanie? She no longer cared, not in the way that Jeff so obviously did.

It was this meeting that prompted Melanie to say to Jocelin, 'You never told Mummy, did you?'

'No.'

'How could you keep a secret like that from her? You always seem to share everything. Doesn't it worry you that she'd be terribly hurt if she ever found out you'd kept it from her?'

'I share my own secrets with her, not necessarily other peoples'.'

'It's my fault that you've got something to hide,' Melanie said. 'I'm sorry.'

He only smiled in an absentminded way, but to Melanie it seemed that she owed him a debt. It was in a fumbling attempt to repay him that she said abruptly to Anne one day in the autumn, 'Daddy looks dead tired. Aren't you worried about him?'

'I am,' Anne admitted. 'I was cross that he didn't take a proper holiday, but there was so much going on in July and August that I had to accept it when he said he couldn't come away with us.'

'Couldn't you twist his arm to take a week or two off now?'

'Possibly, but what about you? I wouldn't leave you alone in this big house.'

'I could go and stay with Granny and Grandpa. I haven't seen much of them recently. I'd like to catch up on some work with Uncle Pete, too. Granny would have me, wouldn't she?'

'My dear, she'd be over the moon! I'll see what I can arrange.'

Neither of them said it, but they both knew that Anne's parents thought she saw less of them than she might. It had been a gradual process, but it was true that she had grown away from them. She felt guilty about it without being able to see how she could change her life in order to give them a larger part in it. It would please both of them, her mother in particular, to have Melanie to stay.

'I dare say we can make her comfortable,' Beryl said.

'Don't spoil her too much. It won't do her any harm to give you a hand in the house,' Anne said.

'She's grown into a lovely girl, really lovely,' Beryl said. 'The way she walks, so straight! It puts me in mind of young Mel the first time I met him.'

'Me, too,' Anne said.

'She's put all that other nasty business behind her?' her mother asked.

'I don't think she'll ever forget. I was a bit worried about her when she first left school, she seemed so restless and excitable, but that's passed. She's really grown up in the past year. This holiday with Jocelin was her idea.'

Melanie settled down well in the little house where her mother had been born and submitted with nothing more than an inward grimace to the cosseting her grandmother lavished on her.

'Yes, I *am* going to cycle to College every day,' she said firmly. 'I'll be as round as a barrel by the time Mummy comes home if I don't get some exercise.'

'You don't eat enough to keep a sparrow flying,' her grandmother complained. 'Lancashire hotpot and treacle tart tonight, love, so don't go filling yourself up with nasty shop cakes mid-day.'

At the end of the first week Melanie went out to the workshop on Saturday afternoon while Pete stayed indoors to watch a football match on the television. She was working at the bench with her back to the door. When she heard it open she assumed that Pete had come out to join her.

'Wasn't the game any good?' she asked.

Getting no reply she glanced over her shoulder. It was Jeff. He shut the door behind him and stood leaning against it.

'I came to visit my mother and she sent me on here with a message for your grandmother,' he said. 'How are you keeping, Melanie?'

'I'm all right,' she said. She could feel her colour rising. It was disturbing, to have him so near, staring at her in that fixed way.

'It's more than I can say about myself,' Jeff said. 'Do you have any idea what it's been costing me, keeping out of your way?'

Melanie edged farther away. 'I thought you'd made it up with Tessa.'

'I made a bargain with her. I've kept to it, but it's been damned hard.'

She had backed up against the work bench. Jeff went and put his hands down on the bench on either side of her, not touching her, but preventing her from getting away.

'We may never get another chance like this,' he said. 'Isn't there anything left for me, sweetheart? One kiss? Just one?'

She turned her head to one side, but Jeff put his arms round her and laughed as she tried to struggle, exulting in the way her body twisted against his, enjoying using his strength against her.

'Let me go, Jeff,' Melanie said in a low, fierce whisper. 'It's not the same now. I won't be treated like this. I won't . . .'

They were too absorbed to notice that the door had opened. As Jeff's mouth came down on Melanie's a hand caught him by the shoulder and spun him round. His face dark with anger, Pete swung up his fist and delivered a punch to the point of Jeff's chin that had all his strength behind it. Jeff staggered, his head jerking backwards. He lost his balance and fell, and his head hit the edge of the bench with a sickening thud.

Melanie was standing pressed hard against the angle of the bench and the wall, both hands over her mouth to stop herself from screaming. Pete backed away, a look of such horror on his face that Melanie abandoned Jeff and went to him.

'It wasn't your fault,' she said urgently. 'You were trying to help me.'

She shook his arm and Pete looked at her with dazed eyes.

'I've killed him,' he said in a whisper.

'Nonsense! Look, he's coming round already.'

She knelt by Jeff's side. He opened his eyes and looked up at her in a dazed fashion. A sickening realization of all that might come out if the full story were told suddenly hit Melanie. She went back to Pete again.

'He slipped and fell,' she said. 'You understand, Uncle Pete?'

'I hit him.'

'You mustn't tell anyone that. Think how horrible it would be for me if they all had to know what happened.'

A saner look came back into his eyes. 'Nasty!' he said with a grimace. He looked down at the floor. 'He slipped on the wood shavings,' he agreed.

Jeff was stirring, trying to prop himself up on one elbow.

'Did you hear that?' Melanie asked. 'You slipped and hit your head on the bench. No need for anything else to be said.'

Jeff put a hand to the back of his head and winced as he felt the bump that was already rising.

'Whatever you say,' he agreed. 'I must have been mad.'

There was blood on his hand where he had touched the back of his head. He wiped it off impatiently with his handkerchief and refused Melanie's nervous offer to bathe the graze.

'I'm going,' he said. 'I don't want a lot of fuss. The best thing we can do is pretend this never happened.'

He let himself out of the back gate to avoid having to see Beryl and Wally as he went through the house. His car was parked in the road outside. He got in, slamming the door so hard that the car body shook. His face was suffused with a dark, angry flush. He was furiously humiliated, shocked by his own lack of control and, although he would not admit it, bitterly hurt by Melanie's rejection of him. Only a few months ago she had been all over him, the little bitch.

He should have gone straight home, but he was in no mood to face Tessa's suspicious eyes. The truce between them held, but only just. Let her get wind of a scrimmage between him and Pete, with Melanie involved, and she would soon guess the truth.

He turned his car towards Wallenshaw. There was sure to be something there for him to do, not the administrative work which irked him, but a practical problem on which he could give advice. He'd heard a mention of some trouble in the cooling system in the blast furnace building. Mustn't let that get out of hand. He might be able to put his finger on the difficulty. There was one thing everyone had to admit about him: he was a damn good engineer. The thought soothed his battered ego and his temper began to subside.

He parked his car in the bay reserved for him and then, automatically, without having to think about it, he reached over to the back seat for his safety helmet. He jammed it on his head and winced as the rim caught the bruised welt at the base of his skull. He took the hat off and carried it dangling from his hand. He had a thumping headache. Perhaps he'd go along to the Medical Centre and get them to put something soothing on the bump.

Number One blast furnace was being tapped. Jeff stood and watched the molten metal streaming towards the ladle. The young shift manager was on hand. He nodded to Jeff and came over to him.

'Afternoon,' Jeff said. 'I hear you've been getting a leakage from the cooling system.'

He saw a flash of exasperation, mixed with admiration, in the boy's eyes and again it made him feel better. Jeff knew his reputation for getting around and seeing things his staff would rather he didn't know about. Apparently it never occurred to them that he found it a relief to leave his office and get down on the shop floor.

'Not exactly a leakage,' the shift manager protested. 'But there is a bit of seepage of water round the plugs. Not bad, a sort of sweating.'

Jeff frowned and then wished he hadn't as a stab of pain flashed across his head.

'The system should be watertight,' he said. 'If it touches the molten iron you'll get metal spitting all over the place. Keep a close eye on it. Are the plugs due for a change?'

'They shouldn't be. We're still well within their theoretical life.'

'I can't remember having this trouble in the past,' Jeff said, casting his mind back.

'We certainly never had any problems with the old brass plugs,' the shift manager said.

'Jack isn't in today, is he?' Jeff asked, referring to the Blast Furnace Manager.

'No, he's been off sick again.'

'If he's in on Monday ask him to give me a ring.'

Jeff's headache had become a dull, persistent throb. He

would go and see the medical people. At the very least they could give him a couple of aspirins. Jeff swung away towards the far exit. High above him on a cross-girder a workman carrying out repairs reached forward for the heavy steel spanner he had laid down.

Below him, lost in thought, still dangling his safety helmet by its strap, Jeff was brought to a standstill by a sudden appalled thought. What was it that boy had said about the cooler plugs? They'd never had trouble with the old brass ones. Christ! Surely the young idiot hadn't meant to imply that the present plugs were made of anything else but brass? He turned back.

Up above, the workman swore softly as the spanner slid out of his reach on the smooth surface. He made a desperate grab and missed it. It teetered on the edge and fell. Just his bloody luck, with the guv'nor walking about on the shop floor, now he'd be slated for using loose tools. He shouted a warning, but Jeff did not look up. The spanner plummeted downwards, straight for his defenceless head.

Jeff was not aware of having been hit, only that the headache which had been painful had become excruciating. It was splitting his skull open. He was face downwards on the floor, his mouth in the dust, everything was black. His fingers scrabbled helplessly on the gritty surface. In his mind was a message that had to be passed on.

When they turned him over his eyes were sightless, but his lips still moved.

'Cop . . . cop . . .' He fought to get it out. The word exploded in his head. Copper! And then there was nothing.

'Poor bastard was trying to say he'd copped it, and I reckon he has,' someone muttered.

He died in the ambulance on the way to the hospital, with his warning undelivered.

*

There was an inquest and Melanie was afraid that either she or Peter would have to give evidence about the first blow Jeff had received. Melanie was determined that it should not be

Pete. She had already had to exert all the force of her will to prevent him telling the truth about that incident.

He went around dazed and silent, but to Melanie he said, 'I killed him. If I hadn't hit him he would have been wearing his safety helmet.'

'He slipped and fell,' Melanie said. 'You know we agreed to say that, Uncle Pete. You mustn't change the story now. It will do no good.'

'It was my fault,' Pete persisted miserably.

'It was Jeff's fault for trying to kiss me,' Melanie said, but in her heart she thought that she was a hundred times more guilty than Pete, or even Jeff. She had run after Jeff, she had insisted that her love would never change and then, after only a few short months, it had dissipated, just as he had told her it would. His attempt to kiss her had filled her with shame as she had realized how unwelcome it was.

Since Pete was still looking unconvinced she made another desperate effort.

'Think of Aunt Tessa,' she said. 'She's got enough to bear without the extra unhappiness of knowing that Jeff was . . . was playing the fool with me just before he died.'

'That's true,' Pete acknowledged. 'But if we have to go to the inquest, Melanie? Suppose we have to take an oath? We can't lie about it then.'

'I can,' Melanie said. 'Don't worry, I'll see you're not called.'

In the end neither of them was asked to attend. The medical evidence showed that there had been a previous blow, which the doctor found entirely compatible with the story he had been given, and since it had not contributed to the death – except that it might be the reason why Jeff had not worn his protective hat – no one else was required to speak about it.

It worried Melanie that Pete insisted on going to the funeral, but although he continued to look sick and shaken and seemed to have fallen into something of his old withdrawn lethargy, he did nothing to cause her any anxiety. As for Melanie, she was living in a nightmare that seemed to have no end. Anne, seeing how strained she was looking, suggested gently that it was not necessary for her to go through the ordeal of attending the funeral, but Melanie, knowing that she must be on hand to keep an eye on Pete, insisted on going with the rest of the family. She was worried by the way Pete kept repeating that he had sworn he would never kill anyone again, and now he had broken his word. No matter how often she told him that he had not killed Jeff, Pete still clung to a belief in his own guilt. To Melanie, thinking he had his war service in mind, it began to seem morbid, but Pete was remembering the death of a friend and the way a knife had slipped into familiar flesh. Now he had been the cause of another man's death, and nothing that Melanie, untouched by war and the horror of killing, could say to him gave him any comfort.

The sight of Tessa, wild-eyed and distraught, filled Melanie with horror. All through her affair with Jeff she had discounted his marriage. Tessa, with her drawl and her offhand manner and the way she immersed herself in her business, did not count. But now Melanie saw Tessa, dressed in black, her bony face ugly with grief as she followed her husband's coffin to the grave, and knew that Tessa in her way had loved Jeff far more than Melanie had ever done.

As the earth thudded on the coffin Melanie tried to shut her mind against the memory of Jeff, his strong, muscular body, the way the dark hair grew across his chest, the touch of his searching, experienced hands, the feel of his lips on her nipples. She closed her eyes, fighting against a spasm of nausea. When she opened them she saw Tessa looking at her from the other side of the grave. Melanie stood, unable to take her eyes away from Tessa's face, until Tessa pressed her handkerchief against her lips and looked down at the ground.

Tessa was staying with her parents and Sir Fred and Lady Tyndall expected everyone to go back to Upbridge Park after the funeral, but Melanie said to Anne, 'Mum, I think this has been too much for Uncle Pete. Shall I take him home?'

'Yes, do that, darling,' Anne said, with a worried look at her brother, standing apart with a look of dull withdrawal on his face. 'It will be good for you to get away, too. I'll see you at home later.'

Melanie took Peter back to Brinthorpe, settled him in his father's armchair in the kitchen, and made some tea. Then she put to him a plan which had been forming in her mind for some time and now seemed more desirable than ever.

'Uncle Pete, would you come to Canada with me?' she asked.

'Canada?'

He looked at her in a dazed fashion, as if she had been speaking of the far side of the moon.

'Yes, to the ranch.'

'For a visit?'

'No, to live. Look, we both like working with our hands. They tell me at college that I'm more of a craftsman than an artist and I think they're right. There's a good house on the ranch and it's surrounded by cabins. We could set up a workshop and make things to sell. What I'd really like to do once we were launched is to bring in other people with different talents, to make up a little colony of people like us.'

She was thankful to see from the way he began to look alive again that she had caught his interest.

'I'll talk to Dad about it,' she promised. Almost under her breath she added, 'I want to get away.'

Melanie went home with the intention of sounding out Jocelin first about her plan and asking for his help in persuading her mother. She knew that they were back because she saw Jocelin's car in the drive, but when she went in the house was strangely silent.

She found Anne and Jocelin in the lounge, not speaking to one another. The feeling of an argument which had been broken off, but not resolved, hung heavily in the air.

Anne looked at Melanie as she came in with such intentness that Melanie was almost prepared for what she was going to say.

'Tell me it's not true,' Anne said. 'You and Jeff . . . it's not possible.'

Instinctively, Melanie looked at Jocelin for guidance.

'Tessa made a scene,' he said wearily.

There had been a cold buffet at Upbridge Park. No one had been very hungry, but they had gathered in the dining room, talking in subdued voices. Tessa had come up to Anne and

Jocelin, a glass in her hand, her eyes glittering in her ravaged face.

'Has the other little widow decided she's had enough?' she asked.

She saw that Anne did not understand her and gave a jarring laugh.

'Anne, do you mean to say you still don't know your daughter and my husband – my *late* husband – were carrying on the most torrid affair you can imagine all last winter?'

'Tessa, that's enough,' Jocelin said sharply.

Again she laughed. 'I damn near blackmailed Jocelin into putting Jeff up for Chairman of S.V.T. on the strength of it.'

She looked towards the other side of the room, to where her son, very thin and dark, was talking awkwardly to his grandmother.

'I'd have divorced him, the swine, if it hadn't been for Max.' Her face crumpled grotesquely. 'He said we needed one another and he was right. What am I going to do without him?'

She was crying hysterically. Jocelin took the glass out of her hand as the liquid in it threatened to spill over the edge.

'You won't cure your troubles with the gin bottle,' he said. 'Come on, you'll be better out of this. I think Mum should take you up to your room.'

When he went back to Anne she was still standing in the same place.

'It can't be true,' she said, as she had gone on saying ever since.

'It's true,' Jocelin said.

'You *knew* – and didn't tell me?'

'This isn't the place to discuss it.'

'You're right! Take me home.'

Anne spoke only once in the car going home.

'How could you keep such a thing from me?' she asked in a scarcely audible whisper.

'I knew how much it would hurt you,' Jocelin said cautiously.

'She's *my* daughter! I had a right to know.'

Jocelin did not reply and Anne subsided into hurt, bewildered silence. As soon as they were indoors she turned on him once more.

'Last winter! She was only a child. It's disgusting, horrible! An affair with Jeff! Of all the people in the world, Jeff!'

'She was seventeen. Old enough to know what she was doing.'

'That you should have kept it from me for nearly a year! I can't believe it, Jocelin.'

'Melanie wanted to keep it from you. It was over before I found out about it.'

Very briefly he told her the whole story as far as he knew it.

'You went on working with Jeff as if nothing had happened,' Anne said.

'I had to if there was to be no scandal.'

'You mean nothing that would harm S.V.T.! You weren't trying to spare me, or Melanie. You wanted to make sure you kept control of your precious Company. It didn't do you much good, did it? I'm glad it's been nationalized. You've lost, and it serves you right!'

When Melanie walked in and Anne saw the way she looked towards Jocelin for guidance it was an added bitterness.

'You covered it up between you,' she said. 'What made you think I had to be protected? I've faced unpleasant truths about Melanie before this, haven't I?'

'It was because of that other . . . thing about Ricky that I wanted to spare you when I made a fool of myself a second time,' Melanie said. 'Not that I thought I was being a fool while it was going on. I did believe I loved him, Mum, truly I did.'

'A man old enough to be your father! He ought to have been prosecuted.'

'He's dead,' Melanie said in a low voice.

'Do you know what Tessa called you? "The other little widow"! If she goes on talking like that everyone will know. Perhaps they do already? Am I the only one in the dark?'

'No one else heard Tessa and I'll make her keep quiet,' Jocelin said.

'Of course. Your speciality, isn't it? Hushing things up.'

'There's something else you'd better know,' Melanie said.

'I was hoping not to have to tell you, but I can't be sure that Uncle Pete will keep it to himself and I don't want to go through this again.'

As she described the scene in Peter's workshop she saw from Jocelin's frown that he shared her disquiet.

'I thought Peter was looking more than usually strained,' he said. 'He doesn't realize . . . ?'

'That at one time I wouldn't have fought Jeff off? No, that's not occurred to him.'

She seemed to grow whiter every minute. Looking at Jocelin she said, 'Uncle Pete blames himself for Jeff's death, but I know I'm the guilty one.'

She swayed where she stood and Jocelin put a hand on her shoulder and pushed her roughly into a chair.

'Put your head down,' Anne said, without making a move to touch her daughter.

Melanie straightened up. 'I'm all right,' she said. 'But I'm worried about the effect this has had on Uncle Pete. I want to take him away. To Canada.'

She looked towards Jocelin once more. 'You said that if I didn't behave myself you'd send me into exile. I think the time has come for me to go.'

'That's for your mother to decide.'

Anne gave a bitter little laugh. 'Is it? You and Melanie between you seem to be quite capable of deciding her future. Why bring me into it?'

'Mum, please . . .' Melanie said in an agonized whisper. 'Don't turn away from me. I've behaved badly, I know that. It was like an illness. I was out of my mind. But I did think I loved him.'

The composure she had been hanging on to suddenly broke. She began to cry wildly, the tears streaming unheeded down her face. Jocelin made a move towards her and checked it. Anne got up, moving awkwardly, as if her muscles were stiff. She put her arms round Melanie and pulled her head down to her shoulder.

'Damn him,' she said. 'If I'd known I would have killed him.'

Over Melanie's head her eyes met Jocelin's and he saw that

although she might unbend towards her daughter, he was unforgiven.

Day after day Anne moved about the house, whitefaced and silent. If it had been anyone but Jeff she would have been just as horrified that Melanie had once again involved herself so young with an unsuitable partner, but the thought of her daughter in Jeff's arms was nauseating. The memory of the passages there had been between herself and Jeff in the past rose up and confronted her and, more than that, the realization that she had cherished a false idea of him. Always, at the back of her mind she had thought of Jeff as the man she ought really to have married. In spite of the love she felt for Jocelin, in spite of the happy years of their marriage, in spite of the beautiful children he had given her, still she thought of him as someone slightly alien, a little apart from real life, the life of struggle and hardship. It was part of his attraction, this element of strangeness. With Jeff she had shared the same roots, there were common experiences between them which didn't need putting into words. She had resented his promiscuity and refused to become one of the herd, but in her heart she had admired his rampant masculinity. Now Anne saw that what she had thought of as strength had been a weakness. She accepted that Melanie had thrown herself in his way, but Jeff had not been able to resist the temptation she offered.

Jocelin would never have allowed himself to commit so gross a folly. An inner core of fastidiousness, a clearsighted understanding of the rights and wrongs of the situation would have preserved him. And he had not told Anne about the affair because he knew the way she thought about Jeff. That was what humiliated Anne to the ground. He had guessed and he had wanted to spare her. Far more than the revelation about Melanie, Anne was stricken to the heart by the failure of confidence between herself and Jocelin and by the knowledge that she had deserved it. He was a better man than Jeff. Now, after all these years, she knew it. What made her writhe was the realization that if Jocelin had been completely sure of her undivided love he would have made Melanie confess to her mother.

To Melanie, Anne hardly spoke and the reason was that she

was afraid of saying too much. The bitter reproaches that came into her mind were better not put into words.

'She's taken it even worse than I thought she would,' Melanie said to Jocelin.

'She blames me, not you,' Jocelin said.

'That makes it worse. Has she said anything to you about my Canadian plan?'

'No,' Jocelin said, suppressing the fact that Anne had scarcely spoken to him at all for days.

'I can't do it unless she agrees. Will you . . .?'

'No, it will come better from you.'

When Melanie, speaking in a nervous hurry, explained her plan about setting up a workshop in one of the cabins at the ranch, Anne listened in silence and then acquiesced without even taking time to think it over.

'When are you planning to go?' she asked.

'As soon as possible.' Melanie caught her mother's eye and added deliberately, 'I think it's best, don't you?'

For once Anne's stony composure faltered. She looked away without replying.

'It will be good for Uncle Pete, too,' Melanie said. 'He's still brooding over what happened. Besides, he does such splendid work and he lives like a hermit. He ought to get out and see the world.'

'You'll know what it's like to live like a hermit when you've spent a winter on the Hardwick Ranch,' Anne said drily.

Beryl and Wally were at first totally disbelieving when they heard that Peter wanted to go to Canada. He had lived at home for so long, quiet, unassuming, apparently happy in the life he had made for himself, that it was difficult for them to believe that he was prepared to make so drastic a change.

'What'll you do without me to watch after you?' Beryl demanded. 'You know you suffer with your chest and how you're going to weather those winters Anne told us about I'm sure I don't know. You'll be laid up with bronchitis and young Melanie won't know what to do.'

'There are doctors in Canada,' Peter said mildly. 'Melanie is giving me the chance to do something I've been pondering about for a long time. I'm not a young man any longer, but

I'm young enough to make a change. A few more years and it'll be too late.'

'You ought to have found yourself a nice girl and got married,' his mother said.

Peter smiled, a curious, resigned smile. 'There's not many round here that would have me,' he said. 'To them I'm Peter Carless, who used to be queer in his head and hasn't ever settled down and done a decent job. Not a good prospect as a husband.'

'You earn as much as any man in the village and God knows you've been a good son to me and your father. We'll miss you, that we will.'

'It's hard to tear myself away,' Pete admitted. 'You and Dad ought to come over and see me when Dad retires.'

'What! Cross the Atlantic at our time of life?' Beryl demanded. 'And what about the expense?'

'You never know, we might do it,' Wally said unexpectedly. 'If you make a go of it and decide to settle, we'll think of making a visit to see your new home.'

To Melanie it seemed that in the period before she and Pete left she was moving in a dream, travelling inexorably towards a point of departure which would change her whole life, either for good or ill. If anything had happened to prevent her plan she thought that she would have cracked and broken down.

Her mother continued to talk calmly about her departure, but the air of remoteness about her still frightened Melanie. It held up until they said goodbye at the airport and then, right at the last moment, when it was almost too late, Anne suddenly clung to her, her face wet with tears, and muttered, 'Look after yourself, darling. My precious, I shouldn't have let you go! Change your mind! Come back . . .'

'No, Mum.' Melanie hugged her so hard that all the breath went out of Anne. 'It's better like this. It will work out, you'll see.'

The flight was delayed by fog and they were four hours late arriving at Calgary Airport. Steve Tracey was waiting for them, bored and slightly exasperated by this unexpected development in the life he had carved out for himself at the Hardwick Ranch.

He still thought of Melanie as the immature young girl who had been with Anne eighteen months earlier and his first sight of her when she and Pete arrived did nothing to change his opinion. Melanie had lost weight in the weeks before leaving England, her clothes hung on her loosely, and her face was sallow with fatigue.

Melanie sensed the reserve behind Steve's welcoming words and it made her stiff with him. He thought her as prickly and difficult as she had been when they last met: a spoilt kid with a crazy notion of running what sounded like a weird hippy settlement. He was glad that he had a means of getting away from the ranch and he lost no time in speaking about it.

'This isn't the best time of year for you to come to Alberta,' he said as they drove away from the airport. 'But it suits me fine as it happens. My novel's been accepted and my publisher wants me to go and see him. It'll have to be in Toronto. If you and Pete can keep an eye on the horses while I'm away it'll save me a lot of worry.'

'I expect we can manage. When is your book coming out?' Melanie asked.

'Not until the spring. They seem to think quite well of it,' Steve spoke in an offhand way, trying to conceal his pride and excitement.

'Congratulations,' Melanie said, but she was too tired to enter into his feelings. She wished that she was sitting in the back of the car with Pete and could doze off without having to make conversation.

'Do you still want to go on living at the ranch?' she asked with a yawn that Steve interpreted as a bored lack of interest in his plans.

'For the time being,' he said. After that he did not make much attempt to keep up the conversation.

He had broadened a little since Melanie had last seen him, but he still dressed in exaggerated cowboy style and he had the wide shoulders and lean horseman's hips to carry it off. As the big car sped through the night on the eighty mile journey from Calgary Melanie noticed his hands on the wheel, long-fingered, strong and competent. Not the hands one would have expected of a writer; more like her Uncle Pete's hands, used to working with tools. But then, presumably, Steve was still doing the day-to-day chores about the ranch as well as bashing a typewriter in his spare time.

'Have we got any other men working at the ranch just now?' she asked.

'Old Tom is still around. I guess he's a fixture. I've got a woman working in the house. I hope that's O.K. with you? I took her on in the summer and she made herself so useful I kept her on to look after me.'

'A young woman?' Melanie asked.

'About forty.' Something of her suspicion got through to him and he turned his head and said, 'No, we're not.'

'What?'

'Living together. She's too old for me.'

'I thought you went for older women.'

He caught the drift of her thoughts, the recollection of his attraction to her mother, but he wasn't going to let her know it.

'A kid of your age shouldn't have such ideas,' he said austerely.

She made a curious little sound, half gasp, half laugh, but said nothing. She had always been a queer kid. He remembered that from her last visit. Her mother, now, she'd been a really exciting woman, and what a looker!

With his mind on Anne and the way he had felt about her on that visit he said, 'Is your mother well?'

'Very well, thank you. She sends you her kind regards.'

Steve gave a yelp of laughter that made Pete stir in the back seat.

'Kind regards! Gee, that sounds so British! How does she feel about this venture of yours?'

'She didn't do anything to stop me coming,' Melanie said carefully. 'I think she's relying on you to keep an eye on me.'

'I'm a horse wrangler, not a nursemaid.'

'I'm glad we agree about that. A horse wrangler I need, a nursemaid I don't.'

For the first time it really got home to Steve that she was his boss. Under age, of course, but still – the ranch belonged to her. What a weird set up! A teenage girl who could give him orders. Except that the first time she tried it he'd pack his bags and leave.

'Did you keep to your idea of writing about my great-grandmother?' Melanie was asking.

'Yeah, it's her story,' Steve said.

He was surprised when Melanie said, 'I'm glad about that. It gives her a sort of immortality.'

It was a pity that she paused for so long before she added, 'I shall look forward to reading it.'

'It didn't turn out too bad,' Steve said. 'I'll give you a copy when it comes out – if you're still here.'

This time it was Melanie's turn to try to make out his face in the darkness. After she had studied his profile for a minute or two she said, 'You don't think I'll stick it, do you?'

'No, I don't,' Steve said frankly. 'It sounds to me like you've come out here on a wild impulse, dragging your uncle with you, and what the pair of you are going to do with yourselves all through the winter months is more than I can fathom.'

'We'll be working. All the cabins have electricity now, don't they? Before you go off to Toronto I shall want to settle with you which of them we can turn into a workshop. When do you want to leave?'

'The sooner the better.' And she could interpret that how she liked. 'The day after tomorrow?'

'Very well.' Melanie's curt agreement concealed her dismay at being left on her own so soon after her arrival. But he would be coming back, or so he said.

The car ride seemed interminable. Coming on top of their delayed flight and the emotional upheaval of the last few weeks it reduced Melanie to a state of fatigue in which everything took on a hallucinatory quality. The car sped on, but Melanie had the strange idea that they were sitting motionless while the dark, empty landscape rushed by them. It was not until the last few difficult miles that she spoke again as they lurched along the dirt track.

'This road hasn't improved,' she said.

'No, thank goodness,' Steve said crisply. 'The day we get a tarmac road the whole quality of the valley will disappear.'

'At the moment I'd settle for a smooth surface and civiliz-
ation,' Melanie said as she was thrown against him.

'That's why I think you won't stick out the winter,' he said.

He turned the car into the gateway. There were lights in the
distance on the hill. They had reached the end of their journey.
Melanie looked over her shoulder and saw that the rough ride
had woken Pete.

As they reached the top of the rise Steve sounded his horn.
The front door of the house was flung open and a shaft of light
shone out. A figure appeared in the doorway, a small,
darkhaired woman.

Melanie climbed out stiffly, so tired that she felt her legs
would scarcely hold her up. Her uncle got out of the back of
the car, still dazed with sleep, and came and stood by her side.
He looked past Melanie at the woman on the porch. She stood
with her hands folded in front of her and made a small, polite
bow.

'Where have you brought me?' Pete asked hoarsely.

She was Japanese.

Chapter Twelve

Steve began to change his mind about Melanie when he saw the way she coped with the nervous crisis that attacked her uncle when he first set eyes on Yoshiko Moru. Steve lacked the background knowledge which would have explained the way the older man shook from head to foot and had to be coaxed into the house. What he did see was that it was Melanie who was in charge of Pete, not the other way round.

He expected, once he knew the reason for Pete's revulsion, that Yoshiko would be dismissed, but Melanie would not hear of it.

'Uncle Pete admits that if he hadn't been half asleep he wouldn't have been so upset,' she said. 'He'd been dreaming about the last long journey he took, which was during the war. It hardly seems fair to send the poor woman away just because of an unfortunate dream. Besides, I need her.'

'Not accustomed to housework?' Steve drawled.

'As a matter of fact, no. I'd manage if I had to, but Yoshiko's standards are so high I'd be ashamed to take over from her.'

By the time Steve returned from his visit to Toronto Melanie and Pete had settled in. He noticed that Pete went out of his way to avoid speaking to Yoshiko, but the Japanese woman gave no sign of awareness of his attitude. She had always been a silent creature, something for which Steve, immersed in hours of writing and emerging only to eat the food she put in front of him, had been grateful.

'Was your visit to your publisher satisfactory?' Melanie asked, conscientiously making conversation over the evening meal they shared on the day of Steve's return.

'It went O.K.,' he said.

A tremor of excitement went through him. The visit had been more than satisfactory, it had been unbelievable.

'Have you written a bestseller?' Melanie asked idly.

'It might turn out that way,' Steve said.

He tried to speak coolly, but Melanie caught the triumph behind his noncommittal reply and was surprised into astonished pleasure.

'Steve! You haven't really? How thrilling! What is it called?'

'I called it after your great-grandmother – *Running Woman*. It turned out quite well.' He gave in to his euphoria and, with a wide, triumphant grin, he said, 'It's good. I'm besotted about it. What's more the publishers are crazy about it, too. It looks as if I've maybe hit the jackpot.'

'When can I read it?' Melanie demanded.

'Not for a month or two yet.'

He looked at her flushed, smiling face, the generous curve of her mouth, her shining eyes and thought disbelievingly: but she's beautiful!

Steve had been away just over a week, long enough for Melanie to recover from the extremes of fatigue that had almost overwhelmed her on arrival. She had got back her colour, had even begun to regain a little flesh on her lovely bones. She had been out in the cold autumn air every day and the exercise and the feeling of having settled had been good for her. It had needed a conscious act of will to get Pete stabilized and she had risen to necessity and been successful. He would not give in again to the irrational fear that had attacked him and Melanie thought that in time she would be able to persuade him into friendship with Yoshiko.

She had got him working, that was the most important thing. They had set up a workbench in one of the cabins, his tools had arrived, Melanie had got hold of a supply of wood, and Pete had begun to make a model of the ranch.

'Hey, this is great!' Steve said, picking up a spirited horse. 'Pete, I didn't know you did this kind of thing.'

'That one's mine,' Melanie said. 'We want to get a few things done in time to sell them locally for Christmas. Look, each of the riders will fit on to any of the horses.'

'Shouldn't have any difficulty in selling these,' Steve said.

'Will you be here for Christmas?' Pete asked.

'I guess so.'

Something about the way Steve spoke made Melanie look at him suspiciously.

'Don't you want to go home and see your family?' she asked.

'You haven't quite grasped the situation. If I enter the United States I'm liable to be arrested. That's why the meeting with my publisher had to be in Toronto. I'm a draft dodger, honey. By rights I ought to be fighting in Vietnam.'

'You've quarrelled with your father again,' Melanie said slowly.

'My old man fought in the Second World War. He can't understand anyone opting out. "My country, right or wrong" is his attitude. I happen to think that it's up to people like me to make a stand against something we think is, at the very least, misguided.'

'Do they know where you are?' Pete asked.

'They do, but I've cut myself right off. We aren't communicating.'

'It seems hard on your mother.'

'Let's not get sentimental,' Steve said crisply. 'It's hard on a lot of people, including some of my old school friends who happen to have got themselves killed. Maybe I could have saved a life if I'd been around. On the other hand, I might be dead myself. Or worse.'

'Mutilated, do you mean?' Melanie asked.

'Possibly that, but I was thinking of a different kind of maiming. Getting used to the killing, taking it for granted; dead inside. Pete, you know what I mean.'

'I've seen it happen,' Pete admitted.

'That's not for me.' Steve spoke decisively, but he was watching Pete and to Melanie it seemed that it was more reassuring than it should have been when the older man nodded his head. If Steve was so sure about the stand he was taking why did he need Pete to agree with him?

*

By the time Christmas came they had had their first snow. It lay on the ground, smooth and white, but not as yet very thick.

'We're stuck with it now,' Steve said. 'This won't melt, not unless there's a Chinook.'

'What's that?' Pete asked.

'A warm wind that comes up quite unexpectedly in the middle of winter. The first you know of it is when you see the Chinook arch – an arc of cloud with blue sky behind it. They say that in a good Chinook you can start out for Calgary with runners on your sledge and have to change to wheels before you get there.'

He kept a straight face, but Pete laughed. 'We tell tall stories like that back home, too,' he said.

'How're you settling down, Pete?' Steve asked curiously. 'It seems to me that young Melanie has dragged you half way across the world just for a whim of her own. Does it suit you?'

'Melanie acted for the best, for both of us,' Pete said with a quietness that made Steve suspect, not for the first time, that there was more behind this sudden move than he had been told.

They had been cutting logs for the fire out by the horse corral. Pete looked round at the empty expanse of whiteness in a puzzled way.

'I've settled in as if I'd always been here,' he said. 'It's the strangest feeling. As if I'd come home.'

*

It was a restless time for Steve, waiting in limbo for his book to appear, and with too much time on his hands to brood over the way the war in Vietnam was going. He had not yet started a new book. That there would be a new one he no longer doubted. Something would happen to get him started again, but somehow he could not give his mind to it. He drifted along from day to day, doing the chores around the homestead, letting his imagination lie fallow, and keeping very quiet about the increasingly troubling war reports.

Christmas came and went with the five of them – Steve, Melanie, Pete, Yoshiko and old Tom – spending the day together. Steve had still not been in touch with his family. He felt uncomfortable about it, especially when there were telephone calls from England for Melanie and Pete. He thought that Melanie looked unhappy again, in the way she had when they first arrived, but she shook it off, and made them all join in carols round the log fire. A bossy kid, and yet she was the one who held them together and made the day go well.

The New Year brought the real snow and the biting cold. Steve discovered that Melanie could ski, but she had never tried to use snow shoes and he taught both her and Pete, covering the ground with long, swinging strides. He saw that Melanie worried about her uncle, particularly when the temperature dropped to forty below, but to Steve it seemed that the older man was gaining in strength and he could see no signs of the bronchitis he had been told had plagued him in the past.

'It's not good for anyone to exert themselves when the temperature drops this low,' Steve told Melanie. 'But there's something happening outside that you ought to see. Come and watch the Sun Dogs dance!'

She followed him outside, huddled in a thick parka with a fur-lined hood. On either side of the red sun, low on the horizon, two bars of light quivered and shook.

'What causes it?' she asked.

'Ice particles in the air, I think,' he answered doubtfully. 'As to what it *means*, you'll have to ask your Indian ancestors.'

He had been teasing her, but Melanie said seriously, 'That's one of the things I mean to do – study Indian legends. Did the old woman come and camp again last summer?'

'She did, but she was very feeble. I'm not sure she'll make it this year.'

'I'll go to the reservation when the weather gets warmer and enquire after her. I want to find someone to teach me some of the Indian crafts.'

'Yoshiko does a nice line in paper folding,' Steve said idly. 'You ought to get her to show you that.'

'Paper folding?' Melanie said in a mystified way, but when she asked Yoshiko and saw the delicate skill with which the Japanese woman manipulated a sheet of paper into the likeness of a bird she exclaimed in pleasure.

'It's not the correct paper,' Yoshiko said apologetically. 'With proper Japanese paper I can do better.'

'I think it's enchanting! Look, Pete, isn't it clever?'

She was deliberately bringing him into the conversation and Pete knew it. He looked at the paper bird and said in a flat voice that it was very pretty. Yoshiko gave him one quick glance and then she lowered her eyes, her face impassive. He felt ashamed and impatient; she expected too much of him, they all did. He would tolerate her in the house, but he was not to be persuaded into friendship.

'Do you play chess?' Steve asked Melanie one dark evening when everyone seemed to have something to do except him. 'No? I'll teach you.'

'You mean, "Melanie, would you *like* to learn to play chess?",' she corrected him.

Steve grinned unrepentantly. 'Yeah, I guess that's what I mean. Come on, put down that whittlin' and amuse me instead.'

'Whittling, indeed! My beautiful snow goose.' She looked at her work critically. 'Perhaps it would be better if I left it alone for a while,' she admitted.

'What about skating? Have you ever learned to do that?'

'No, I haven't, and I'd love to,' Melanie said. 'Is there a skating rink near here?'

'I heard some folk down the valley were going to flood a field and smooth it over. Want to go along and try it?'

The visit to the improvised skating rink enlarged Melanie's circle of friends. After dark the young people circled the field with a ring of cars, switched on the headlights and danced on the ice. Someone lit a bonfire and roasted potatoes and what Melanie called sausages and everyone else called weenies.

'You skate really well,' she said admiringly to Steve.

'I'm no great shakes at the fancy stuff. Speed skating used to be my thing. I played ice hockey for my college.'

'It's a very rough game, isn't it?'

'Honey, I'm a very rough fella,' Steve said solemnly.

He tried to put his arm round her when they were on their way home, but Melanie shrugged it off and he knew that he had made a mistake. He had no special feeling about it, it was just that they had had a good time, he was exhilarated by the exercise and the cold, stinging air and he would have had no objection to winding up the evening with a few kisses from a pretty girl. He ought to have known better than to try it on with the little princess. Melanie's air of aloofness both amused and annoyed him. She had a mighty high opinion of herself, did young Melanie, and while she was a beautiful creature Steve had no intention of joining the court that began to gather round her.

*

The Christmas that had made Melanie realize how far she was still estranged from her mother had brought no lessening of the tension between Anne and Jocelin. Anne had felt obliged to invite her mother and father to join them on Christmas Day, more because she thought Beryl expected it than because she really wanted them.

'You're looking peaky,' Beryl remarked. 'Missing young Melanie, I suppose. I don't know what you're moping about. You've still got Jocelin and the boys. You don't hear me and your dad complaining because Pete's gone off and left us.'

'I'm not complaining,' Anne said.

'Not much, you're not! Going about with a face as long as a wet week. Cheer up, for goodness sake. It's Christmas!'

She gave her daughter a long, shrewd look.

'Nothing wrong between you and Jocelin, is there?' she asked.

'Of course not.'

'I thought you were a bit snappy with him, that's all. Well, they all try our patience at times. Jocelin must have a lot on his plate, losing Jeff an' all.'

'I suppose so.'

'Wally says they've still only got a stand-in for General Manager. According to him, the man who ought to have got the job is the one who's been Blast Furnace Manager, but he's been away ill since goodness knows when.'

She looked up as Wally and Jocelin came into the room after taking Timothy and Christopher out to try out the new bicycles they had been given for Christmas.

'Isn't that right, Wal? You think Jack will be General Manager of Wallenshaw when he comes back?'

'If he comes back,' Wally said. 'I've heard it's cancer.'

He glanced at Jocelin and after a brief hesitation Jocelin nodded.

'He went back into hospital yesterday,' he said. 'It can only be a matter of weeks, if not days.'

'Poor soul!' Beryl exclaimed. 'It'll be a sad Christmas for his wife, just as it must be for your sister, Jocelin. Has she gone to your mum and dad?'

'Tessa and Max have gone to visit friends in Austria. It seemed a good idea. Max will enjoy the ski-ing.'

'And Tessa will enjoy the instructors,' Anne said.

It struck a jarring note. She saw her mother look at her with a frown. Jocelin's face was expressionless. Perhaps it was because of her remark that he went on talking shop with Wally.

'I wish I could have spent more time at Wallenshaw in the last few months,' he said. 'The blast furnaces in particular seem to be plagued with problems.'

'They are that,' Wally agreed. 'Jack would have sorted them out if he'd been a fit man and I dare say Jeff would have put his finger on the trouble in a jiffy. He was down there having a word the day he died, poor devil. I tell you what, Jocelin, you need a new Blast Furnace Manager, and right soon at that, plus a man at the top with a firm hand.'

'It's been difficult to make new appointments with everything in such a state of flux, and replacing Jack would have been as good as telling him he wasn't going to recover.'

'He's past caring now, so you can get a move on.'

'You'll see some changes in the New Year,' Jocelin promised with a smile.

'Do we have to talk about Wallenshaw on the only day in the year when it's closed?' Anne asked, and again her mother looked at her, noting the shrewish tone in her voice.

Beryl spoke about it to Wally when they got home that night.

'There's something wrong there,' she said. 'I'll have to sort Anne out the next time I've got her on my own. A better husband she couldn't wish to have, for all his uppercrust ways, and always as good as gold to you an' me, which I didn't look for when she married him.'

'You'd do better to leave well alone,' Wally said, but without any real hope of deterring Beryl.

There was no opportunity for Beryl to see her daughter between Christmas and the New Year, but shortly after New Year's Day, having seen Wally off to work, she cast her mind over her household affairs, decided that there was nothing that couldn't wait and made up her mind to visit Anne without warning and probe into the reason for the discord she had detected over Christmas.

She washed out her tea towel after doing the breakfast dishes and went to hang it on the clothes line in the garden. Passing Pete's empty workshop gave her a pang, as it always did. She missed him, more than she'd ever admitted, even to Wally. Her next door neighbour called to her, but Beryl would not stop.

'I've got wet hands,' she said. 'And I'll get that chapped if I stand about in this cold wind.'

As she turned away the air shook with an enormous explosion. Instinctively, both women turned towards Wallenshaw. On the horizon a column of black smoke drifted into the air.

'I've not heard the like of that for many a long day,' the other woman said.

'Not since the war,' Beryl said. 'The bombs in the war.'

*

Wally had been walking across the yard, not hurrying. The shifts would be changing shortly, but he had time in hand. The familiar, comfortable atmosphere settled round him. It had been a hard life, but a good one, working at Wallenshaw. He was due to retire later in the year and he secretly wondered how he was going to get on, being at home all day. Beryl was looking for him to decorate the house, which would take him over the first few weeks, but he'd miss his mates and the use of the skill he'd acquired over the years.

The blast of the explosion knocked him off his feet. His hands went up and covered his head as bricks and debris showered round him. A searing pain shot into one hand. Looking at it wildly Wally saw that it had been burnt to the bone by the splash of molten metal.

A cranedriver, caught in the path of the white hot iron, leapt frantically for his cab. A wave of flame engulfed it. Wally could see the man's white face, his mouth opening and shutting soundlessly, as he beat against the windows and then collapsed.

Wally could hear the terrible, inhuman screams of other men who had been closer to the source of the explosion. A lad from the laboratory ran out, his arms spread wide, the back of his white coat blazing. Wally got to his feet. Stumbling in his heavy boots, he ran towards the boy. He took him in his arms and thrust him to the ground. With his face close to the boy's chest he could smell his burnt flesh.

Wally raised his head and looked round. It was like a scene out of hell. Huge flames shot into the sky, wisps of black smoke drifted across the shattered walls and twisted pipework, and the deadly streams of metal ran like water into every crevice, lighting fresh fires as they moved.

In one golden pool Wally saw a black outline; the charred remains of a human body, already beyond recognition. With his damaged hands clasped to his heaving stomach he tried to force himself towards the devastated building. There was a roar as another section of the roof collapsed, letting in more air to feed the fire. The flames surged forward. A big vertical pipe, its support destroyed, buckled in the heat like crumpled paper, and then with a grinding, wrenching noise it collapsed. Wally looked around and saw that his only way of escape was across the molten iron. As he hesitated, the wall seemed to sigh and give up. With slow inevitability it leaned towards him, broke and covered him up.

*

It was the worst disaster in the entire history of Wallenshaw. Seven men died and eleven were injured. The young boy Wally had tried to help lingered for two days and then he too joined the list of the dead.

Jocelin was on his way to the Works as soon as the news

reached him, but the first that Anne heard of the explosion was when her mother telephoned from a call box.

'I've heard nothing,' Anne said. 'No, I didn't know there's been an explosion.'

'Two or three of us put on our coats and walked over,' Beryl said, her voice hoarse with worry. 'But we couldn't get anywhere near. It's bad, that's all I know. There's ambulances and fire engines all over the place. Your dad hadn't been gone more than a few minutes. He hasn't come back so I don't know whether he's stayed to help or . . .'

'Nothing's happened to him, of course it hasn't,' Anne said quickly. 'I'll ring Jocelin's office and see if there's any news. Stay where you are and I'll ring you back.'

But although Jocelin's secretary confirmed that there had been a bad accident at Wallenshaw and that Jocelin had gone over there she could tell Anne nothing more.

It was another two hours before Jocelin came home, his face and hands streaked with dirt, his eyes red from fumes and smoke.

'There was nothing I could do,' he said. 'There'll have to be an enquiry, but we already think we know how it happened. A plug from one of the cooling pipes failed, water jetted out and hit a ladle of molten iron. In the ordinary way it would have boiled off straight away, but the ladle was being moved, the crust on top broke and the water got below the surface. When it touched the metal it formed steam which couldn't escape and the whole ladle full of white hot metal exploded.'

He rubbed a grubby hand across his forehead. 'Anne, my dear, I think you should go to your mother.'

'Not Dad,' Anne said. 'Oh, no, Jocelin, not Dad.'

'I'm afraid so. We haven't got him out yet, but he was seen . . . I can't pretend there's any hope of finding him alive.'

Beneath the dirt his face was grey with fatigue and shock.

'My place is with you,' Anne said.

'Is it?'

'When you look like that, when I see you in trouble – then I know that you come first, always.'

She went and put her arms round him. Jocelin held her

tightly. For a moment he closed his eyes and rested his cheek against the top of her head.

'Seven men,' he said. 'I know we've lost at least seven. And the injuries are frightful, not all of them will survive.'

He drew a deep, shuddering breath and put her away from him.

'I'll have a bath and a drink and pull myself together,' he said. 'Go and fetch your mother. Bring her back here and I'll tell her all I can.'

Still Anne hesitated. 'She'll talk,' she said. 'When she's upset she can't stop.'

'I know. It's a small price to pay to do *something* to help one of our people.'

'You aren't responsible,' Anne said. 'Not personally responsible.'

'In a disaster as great as this responsibility lies at the top,' Jocelin said quietly. 'We've pussy-footed around since Jeff died, jockeying for position, trying not to have someone foisted on us from outside the old Company. And I delayed appointing a new Blast Furnace Manager because I didn't want Jack to know he was dying. All right, the man who created the conditions that led to the explosion is the one who used steel plugs in a copper vessel without having the basic commonsense to realize that they would react against one another and the plugs would corrode, but there were warning signs – vague, inconclusive, but there if anyone with sufficient understanding and experience had been around to recognize them. I can't walk away from the knowledge that some part of the blame is mine.'

'I'll go and get Mum,' Anne said. She passed an unsteady hand over her eyes. 'I can't drive. I'll take a taxi.'

*

'I knew as soon as the taxi drew up there was bad news,' Beryl said. 'I thought it must be from the Works, sending to fetch me to the hospital. I knew something had happened to him, not hearing a word all this time and some of the men already home. I'm all ready. I've been standing by ever since it happened. If anything was wrong Wally was bound to be in the thick of it. Which hospital is he in?'

'Mum . . . it's worse than that,' Anne said.

'He's not dead,' Beryl said. 'No, you'll never tell me my Wally's dead. He'd not had time to get to work before the balloon went up. And it was the blast furnace, I already knew that. He didn't work in the blast furnace, so he wouldn't have any call to be in there.'

Anne shook her head, her throat working convulsively, incapable of speech.

'He's not dead,' Beryl said in a desperate whisper. 'That's daft, that is, my Wally getting himself killed in a place he'd no right to be.'

'Come with me,' Anne pleaded. 'Jocelin will tell you . . .'

By the time they reached the house Beryl was convinced. A faint spark of hope was roused in her when Jocelin admitted that Wally's body had not yet been found, but he steadfastly refused to let her imagine that Wally might be brought out alive.

'You're a hard man,' Beryl accused him.

'A strong man,' Anne said, almost under her breath.

Jocelin glanced at her and for a brief second he almost smiled. She clung to him in bed that night in a storm of grief for her father and Jocelin held her close as much from his own need for comfort as from his desire to help her, until Anne, putting up her hand to wipe her eyes, brushed it against his cheek and knew that the wetness she felt was not from her own tears.

Anne found the next day that her mother was taking it for granted that Peter and Melanie would come back to England at least for the funeral, if not to stay, but when they telephoned Canada with the news they found that Pete was not well enough to travel.

'Bronchitis!' Beryl said. 'I knew it! I told him before he went. "You'll go down with your chest", I said. There's no one knows better than me how it lays him low. A fine thing, laid up sick on the other side of the world and not able to come to his father's funeral.'

Her voice wobbled and her eyes filled with tears once more.

'I was counting on him being here with me,' she said.

'You'll have me, and Evelyn and Terry,' Anne said. 'And Jocelin. Don't cry any more, Mum, please.'

'Why shouldn't I cry?' Beryl demanded, wiping her eyes. 'I've lost a good man. It's hard not to have my only son by my side at a time like this.'

She paused and looked hard at Anne. 'You'll bring the boys home from school,' she said.

'Oh, Mum, I hardly think . . .'

'It's a mark of respect. Wally was just as much their grandfather as Sir Frederick Tyndall.'

Unexpectedly, Jocelin agreed with his mother-in-law.

'Wally was very highly regarded,' he said. 'There'll be a big attendance at his funeral. I'd like Timothy and Christopher to be there, not only for family reasons but because it may be the last chance to let them see something of the old Company spirit.'

'Must you drag S.V.T. even into my father's funeral?'

'It can't be avoided,' Jocelin pointed out. 'The Unions will want to be represented, Wally's workmates, the management. We're doing the same for the other men who died.'

In Canada, on the day Wally was being buried, Melanie crept into Pete's room and sat with her hand in his, not wanting to talk, just to be with him. The only sound in the room was his laboured breathing. Yoshiko paused by the open door and saw them and went quietly away again.

Later in the day Steve went out to the rough wooden building that served for stables for the half dozen horses they kept at the ranch during the winter. He paused in the doorway and stamped his feet to get rid of some of the snow he had picked up on his way over from the house. The building smelt of horses and their droppings, of straw and the leather tackle he had greased and hung up for the winter. The horses shifted and snorted; even indoors the breath from their nostrils hung white in the air on that bitter day. Steve did not at first see Melanie sitting on a pile of clean straw at the far end, her head bent and her shoulders bowed.

She looked up as he came in and straightened her shoulders

as if she was picking up a burden she had temporarily laid down.

'I guess you're feeling pretty blue,' Steve said. 'But you shouldn't be out here in the cold, honey.'

'I'm warm enough,' Melanie said.

He dropped down on the straw by her side, ready to offer sympathy if she needed it.

'Did you ever hear that saying about "For want of a nail the shoe was lost; for want of a shoe the horse was lost . . ." going right on to the loss of a battle and the loss of a kingdom?' Melanie asked.

'Sure I did.'

'I've been thinking about the way one thing leads to another. If I hadn't made a fool of myself with a man he might still be alive. If he'd been alive he might just possibly have prevented this terrible accident that's killed my grandfather.'

'There's an awful lot of "ifs" in that,' Steve said gently.

'It's like a chain reaction,' Melanie said, ignoring him. 'The sort of thing they talk about with atom bombs. Everything I do seems to cause harm.'

'So that's why you decided to come and live at the ranch?'

She shivered suddenly. 'I thought it would be safe here. And it is safe – for me. But the consequences still go on.'

'Blaming yourself for a technical failure in a steelworks thousands of miles away is just plain morbid,' Steve told her. 'You're feeling miserable, which I understand, and you're chilled to the bone, which is very bad for the morale. I suggest you give me a hand to muck out the stables. Now there's a job that'll drive away the blues.'

It got him a perfunctory smile, but the haunted look in her eyes troubled him. He took hold of her hands and hauled her to her feet.

At least he had given her thoughts a different turn. 'I ought to help you more,' Melanie said. 'You've been very good, not complaining about doing work like this when you ought to be writing a new book.'

'You're the lady owner and I'm the hired help,' Steve said. 'I'm not writing at the moment. I've not got even the beginnings of an idea, which is why I'm attending to the stables instead of leaving it to old Tom. Something basic, like mucking out, keeps the body warm and stirs up the mind.'

He was not surprised when, a couple of days after her chilly sojourn in the stables, Melanie went down with the cold that had laid Pete low. It was a relief when Yoshiko took charge of her.

'You cannot go into your uncle while you sneeze all the time,' she said. 'I will take his food and see to his needs.'

'Oh, but . . .' Melanie stopped, looking bothered, trying to find some tactful way of conveying that Yoshiko's ministrations would not be welcome to Pete.

Yoshiko smiled, a very small, mirthless smile. 'He does not like me because I am Japanese woman,' she said. 'When man is ill colour of nurse not important. You will see.'

She was small and neat, deft in all her movements. It fretted Pete to have to accept her help, but she was a far better nurse than Melanie. She was older for one thing and even though he shrank from her touch it was easier to let a woman in her forties help him to get out of bed than it was to have to lean on little Melanie.

When the cough racked him in the night he turned with gratitude to the hot drink Yoshiko brought in. It burned in his chest and eased the tight band that was stifling him. She plumped up his pillows and raised him up so that he could lie against them more easily. When she left he felt warm and comfortable and sleepy.

'I'm sorry I disturbed your sleep last night,' he said stiffly the next morning. 'I'm feeling better today so I hope it won't happen again.'

'If you need me I will come,' Yoshiko said with the serenity they had all come to accept as part of her.

'You've been kind to me,' Pete admitted, more because he felt the acknowledgement was due to her than because he wanted to say it.

Something about the way she bowed her head with a small, ironic smile irritated him.

'I've got good reason not to like your people,' he said abruptly.

'I, too,' Yoshiko said. 'I have good reason not to like your people.'

'I was in a prisoner-of-war camp. I was treated atrociously.'

'If you are truly feeling better I will tell you my story,' Yoshiko said. 'I was married when I was eighteen years old and I had a baby, a fine son. In 1945 I heard that my husband had been killed fighting the Americans. When my first grief was over I wished to visit his parents, but my baby I left with my own mother. On the sixth of August, 1945 I was in Tokyo.'

She paused, with the same mirthless smile. 'The date means nothing to you, does it? Already it is forgotten. Perhaps you will remember when I tell you that my home was in Hiroshima.'

'The atom bomb . . .' Pete said.

Yoshiko bowed her head. 'I lost my baby, my mother and father, three brothers and a sister, my mother's sister and all her family, my grandparents, and many, many friends. My home and all my possessions disappeared as if they had never been. My little baby has no grave.'

'I'm sorry.' It was an inadequate response, but what else could he say?

Pete told Melanie the bare outline of Yoshiko's story the next day and she asked Steve if he had known.

'Yeah – at least, I knew she'd lost her family. I didn't know there was a kid involved. It makes me feel as guilty as hell.'

'The war in Vietnam is killing women and children, too.'

'No need to remind me. Do you think I haven't got it on my mind?'

Melanie noticed a change in her uncle's attitude towards Yoshiko once he had recovered from his bronchitis. Instead of avoiding her he seemed to seek her out, he made a point of helping her with heavy chores and he tried, in his inarticulate way, to draw her into the conversation when they sat around the open log fire in the evenings. Yoshiko accepted his new friendliness with the same serenity as she had his former coldness, but there was a gentleness between them which had not been there before.

Steve, too, seemed to be less critical than he had been when Melanie and Pete first came to the ranch. Unconsciously,

Melanie had begun to lean on him, if not physically then certainly for moral support. He received some advance copies of his book towards the end of February, while the snow was still thick on the ground and the deceptive sunlight sparkled coldly on the icicles hanging from the roof of the house. He opened the parcel and gave a whoop that brought them all into the kitchen to see what was happening.

Steve seized Melanie by the shoulders and whirled her round the kitchen table. He took hold of Yoshiko and kissed her on both cheeks.

'We must have a party,' Melanie said. 'A launching party!'

'Just us,' Steve said quickly. 'I don't want a lot of fuss. My publishers have been on to me to go and visit them in New York, which of course I can't do.'

He glanced quickly at Melanie and looked away again. His mouth set obstinately. 'I don't see why me standin' around with a drink in my hand should sell any more copies than if I stayed right here and let them get on with it.'

It might help with the women, Melanie thought. He was immensely attractive, with his long, lean body, and his lopsided grin, especially as he was then with his blue eyes alight with excitement and his hair curling wildly as if there was a new electricity in every strand. She looked down at the book in her hand. On the cover a black-haired Indian girl with haunted eyes and a wistful mouth stared back and superimposed on the background were the figures of a modern couple, another darkhaired girl and a young man in the sort of outfit Steve wore.

Melanie started reading *Running Woman* that night and didn't put it down until the early hours of the morning. When she met Steve the next day she looked at him with new eyes.

'You're not the person I thought you were,' she accused him. 'What are you doing playing around at being a ranchhand when you can write like this?'

'You liked it?'

'I thought it was remarkable. Come on, Steve, no false modesty. You must know it's good.'

'It sort of took me over. That makes it difficult to judge. Fitting the modern story against the nineteenth century one was difficult. There were times when I wasn't quite sure I'd brought it off.'

'I didn't realize until about halfway through that you'd taken the name of my great-grandmother and made it mean more than it seemed at first. The Indian girl turning her back on her own people, the modern girl running away from reality – it was very clever.'

Steve was looking at her with a strange intentness. 'I was writing about you, wasn't I?' he asked. 'I've only just realized it. I don't mean I took you as a model, but there's a similarity, isn't there?'

'I didn't run, I withdrew from a situation that became unbearable. What about you, Steve? When are you going to stop running away from your family?'

'I guess the time has come to try and make my peace. It's been on my mind lately.'

'I could see something was weighing on you.'

Steve looked up quickly. 'You don't miss much, do you? Yeah, I'm troubled in my mind, Melanie. Don't seem to be able to see which way to move.'

He shook his head, as if to clear away his difficult thoughts.

'The publicity men want to come to the ranch to take some pictures. Is that O.K.?'

'As long as you keep me out of it!'

But that was more than Steve was able to achieve once it became known that Melanie was a descendant of the real Running Woman. She was young and beautiful and she was the new writer's boss. It was an intriguing situation, it was newsworthy, it just had to be exploited.

'How about romance?' the publicity man asked hopefully.

Steve and Melanie spoke with one voice. 'No!'

'Well, O.K.! No need to jump down my throat.'

The publicity man looked after Melanie as she walked away, slender and long-legged in jeans and a checked shirt. He shook his head in disbelief.

'I guess I have to take your word for it,' he said to Steve. 'But, boy, are you slow off the mark!'

What Steve had not foreseen was that the publicity would bring his father to the ranch. Mr Tracey arrived one afternoon, without any warning, breathing fire and slaughter, but unable to hide his mixture of pride and amazement that his son should actually have got himself into print. He was shorter and stockier than Steve, but he had the same blue eyes and the same curling hair, frosted with white and receding from his sunburnt forehead.

'Got yourself a mite of notoriety since we last met, haven't you?' he demanded.

'Guess I have,' Steve admitted cautiously.

'How do you think your mother felt, seeing your picture plastered all over the newspaper and not a word to us about writin' a book and gettin' it published?'

'Pleased?' Steve suggested.

'Pleased! Shocked, that's what! You'd have thought a son would've come home and had his picture taken with his own folks if it was goin' to get into the papers.' He gave his son a withering look. 'If he hadn't been dodgin' from the law, that is.'

Steve ignored that. 'Why didn't Mom come with you?' he asked. 'Is she O.K.?'

Mr Tracey looked away, avoiding Steve's eye. 'She's . . . all right,' he said. 'Sure she is! She'll come another time.'

Even to Melanie it sounded unconvincing. She was not surprised when Steve asked suspiciously, 'Are you sure there's nothing wrong?'

'Oh, heck! I'm no hand at lyin', as you well know. I knew I wouldn't be able to keep it to myself. Your mother made me promise not to tell you, but she's been sick, real sick. An operation.'

'What for?'

'She had a breast removed.'

'Cancer?'

Mr Stacey nodded. For a moment his belligerent manner wavered. 'They say they got it all away,' he said. 'They say she'll be O.K.'

'I ought to have been told.'

'She thought if you knew you might come home and be caught for the draft. She didn't want that. We don't see eye to eye on that question, but I couldn't go against her at such a time.'

From the fixed way Steve was staring at his father Melanie could see how shocked he was. She saw, too, that both men had forgotten she was there.

'Steve, why don't you take your father into the living room,' she said quietly. 'There's a fire in there and you can have a good talk.'

When Steve emerged hours later he found Melanie in the kitchen. She thought he looked exhausted. It came as no great surprise when he said, 'I'm going home.'

'I thought you probably would.'

'It's not just the news about Mom – though that shook me. It's a decision I've been moving towards for a long time. My publishers wanting me to go to New York and not being able to do it, I hated that. The feeling of having gone into exile, permanently for all I know.'

'I thought you were happy here.'

'I am . . . but it's not my own country. I thought I despised old-fashioned nationalism, but there's still a pull.'

'It's a rotten war you're getting yourself into.'

'I know that. If we'd been winning I could still have turned my back on it, but when my own side is losing then I want to get in there and help.'

'Do you think one man is going to turn the tide?'

'No, but I know I have to go. Something Pop said this afternoon crystallized everything I'd been thinking myself. He asked me how I could write about real life if I hadn't experienced what was going on in Vietnam.'

'It seems a trivial reason for getting yourself killed.'

'Not to me. As soon as he said it I knew he was right. I've got to write about it, and how can I do that unless I've been in the fight myself?'

'What about killing other people? Can you cope with that?'

'I'm going to try for some sort of non-combatant job.'

'And if you don't succeed?'

There was no reply from Steve. 'You're just like every other man,' Melanie said. 'If you're given a gun you'll use it. I don't

❧ 267 ❧

agree with you over this, Steve. I think it would have been stronger to stand by what you believed.'

'If I was absolutely sure I was right . . . but I *don't* agree with the Reds taking over a country without opposition; I can see a case for putting up a fight against them.'

'Was the regime they wanted to overthrow worth saving?' Melanie asked quietly.

'We're committed to it now,' Steve said wearily. 'We'd better agree to differ, you an' me, Melanie.'

'When will you be leaving?'

'Tomorrow, when Pop goes. I'm sorry. I feel I'm letting you down.'

'I'll survive. The question is, will you?'

There was a large flat parcel on the table by Steve's chair at the dinner table that night.

'Uncle Pete and I have been working on a present for you, to mark your publication day,' Melanie said. 'We didn't get it finished quite in time, but now it can be a goodbye present.'

There was a wooden box inside the wrapping paper. It opened out to form a chess board, with the pieces concealed in miniature drawers under the two flaps. The Kings were Indian Chiefs in feathered war bonnets, the Queens were two versions of Running Woman, the pawns were teepees.

'A stockaded fort was the best we could think of for castles,' Melanie said, watching his face. 'And the Bishops have become Medicine Men.'

'It's the best present I've ever had,' Steve said. 'You designed it?'

'Yes, and made most of the pieces. Uncle Pete did some of the others and the box. I'm glad you like it, but when we were working on it I didn't expect you to take it away to war.'

Steve did not comment on that. Carefully replacing the pawns in the box he said, 'I'll try to get up to see you again before I go overseas.'

It had all happened so quickly that it was difficult to take in. One day Steve was there and the next he had gone, and Melanie felt his absence more than was comfortable. Uncle Pete was still her dear friend, as he always had been, and Yoshiko was unfailingly kind, but they were both silent people.

Melanie missed the quick exchange of views she got from Steve, his light-hearted commentary on everything they did together, the companionship of another young person.

Running Woman did everything Steve's publishers had hoped. It was well reviewed and it was popular. During the months following Steve's departure it became a bestseller.

It was April and there was at last a hint of warmth in the air when Steve came back for a fleeting visit. He was in uniform and he was different, not just because his unruly hair had been subdued and he had lost his easy, loping way of walking; there was a tension in him that had not been there before.

'Congratulations on the success of your book,' Melanie said, trying to keep off the subject of his posting overseas.

'Yeah, I seem to be making quite a bit of money,' he admitted. 'I've got a plan for spending it and that's one reason I wanted to see you before I go. I'd like to buy the ranch from you.'

He had not been prepared for the look of horror on Melanie's face.

'Oh, no!' she said breathlessly. 'No, Steve. I can't part with the ranch.'

'I'll give up the idea if you feel so strongly about it,' Steve said. 'It's just that for me it's come to seem like home.'

'I thought you'd decided your home was the other side of the border.'

'It was being compelled to live in Canada that went against the grain with me. If I were free to come and go I'd like to settle here. I'd like to think of it as the place I was coming back to. I'd make some improvements to the house, keep a few horses and raise some cattle, just enough to give me an interest when I'm not writing. No more visitors, of course, except my own friends. I've had it in my mind for a long time. I know just the way I'd like it to be.'

'I like it the way it is now. You don't understand how much it means to me.'

'I think I do. The ranch is your refuge, the place you've run away to – just like the girl in my story – but, honey, it's not going to work for you any more than it did for her.'

'It seems to me that it's working very well. At least in the last few months I haven't done anyone any harm.'

'That's a negative way to live – and it won't last. There's something you're going to have to face up to, Melanie: wherever you live men are going to beat a path to your door.'

'I'll send them away.'

'You're not yet nineteen and that's too young to make up your mind to live like a nun. The day's going to come when you'll start feeling lonely.'

'I've got Uncle Pete to look after.'

'Yoshiko may take over from you there. Have you really not noticed the way they've started to turn to one another?'

She had seen it, of course, but she had not put the same interpretation on it as Steve had. Now she saw that it was possible that her uncle and Yoshiko might make a life together.

'They'd still want to go on living here,' she said. 'Once and for all, Steve, I'm not parting with Hardwick Ranch.'

'O.K., I won't press you. Don't look so worried, I can't buy it unless you say so. I guess I'm crazy to let a place come to mean so much to me.'

They had dropped the subject, but Melanie had been shaken. She had come to the ranch intending to make it her permanent home and with no thought of any altered circumstances. She told herself now that if it should ever happen, strange as the idea seemed, that Pete should want to marry Yoshiko, then she would build them a little house of their own and they would all go on living in exactly the same way, but she felt chilled at the idea of living in the old ranchhouse on her own.

Steve watched her, wishing he had not told her about his ambition to own the ranch at a time when he could, in any case, do nothing about it; wishing too, with a violence that would have startled Melanie, that he was not about to go away. She troubled his mind in a way no woman had ever done and yet there seemed no way of getting through to her. She was too damn young, she was maddeningly standoffish, she was beautiful; she was impulsive and generous and she was deliberately trying to stifle a temperament that was meant for love. Poor kid, he could show her what love ought to be if she'd only let him, but not now when he might be just about to get himself killed. Anything between them now could only be a temporary arrangement and Steve guessed that would be a disaster for Melanie.

'The ice on the river must be just about ready to break,' he said later on in the afternoon. 'Want to come down and see it?'

'Is it worth seeing?' Melanie asked.

'If you catch it at the right moment. Walk to the river with me and I'll show you.'

He pulled on an old parka with a hood he had worn all through the previous winter and suddenly looked more like the Steve Melanie had grown used to seeing around the ranch.

On the river bank the piled-up snow had begun to recede. There were patches of mud, even a few straggling blades of frost-blighted grass to be seen and there was a constant drip of water. Across the ice on the river there were deep fissures, jagged black lines on the surface which had been smooth and white all through the winter.

'She's beginning to go,' Steve said. 'Listen!'

There was a crack like a pistol shot, followed by a rasping noise which rose in pitch until it sounded like a squeal. The ice floes in front of them began to move and because there was nowhere for them to go they reared up, the great slabs of ice sliding and crashing across one another. Imperceptibly they drifted away, yielding to the irresistible surge of the newly melted snow water.

'Even the thickest ice melts when the spring comes,' Steve said.

So casually that Melanie did not realize what he was doing he turned her to face him, cupped his hand round her cheek and lifted her face so that he could kiss her. Melanie's protest was strangled in her throat by his warm mouth against hers.

'Winter's over, honey,' Steve said at last. 'Time to come back to life.'

She struggled out of his grasp, furious with him and with herself for not seeing it coming.

'I suppose you think you're entitled to kiss the girls goodbye,' she said. 'Well, as far as I'm concerned you can keep your

soldier's farewell, Private Tracey. I'm still of the same opinion
– you're wrong to go and fight in a war you don't believe in.'

'We've been through this before,' Steve said. 'I've got the
same misgivings I always had, but I've still got to go.'

'Pride, that's all it is! It irks you to see your side losing.'

She looked down the river, to where the thin spring sunlight
caught the fractured blocks of ice and turned them blue and
green. The colours blurred and sparkled like jewels through
the tears she refused to shed.

'Pete almost lost his reason in the last World War, my father
was killed in Korea,' she said. 'Now you . . . and all the young
men like you. Are we never going to have any peace?'

Chapter Thirteen

※⚜️※

In April 1967 Sir Frederick Tyndall announced his retirement, but he was frustrated in his dearest ambition: to hand over the Chairmanship of Smithson, Venner & Tyndall to his son. At his retirement party he made a speech which made Jocelin wince. He managed to keep on smiling, but a reporter from the local paper who asked for Jocelin's comments on Sir Fred's description of the British Steel Corporation as a misconceived abortion which would enjoy a short life got his head bitten off.

Two nights later Anne woke up and found Jocelin's place beside her empty. She sat up and switched on the bedside lamp. It was after two o'clock. She could hear nothing so she got up and went to the top of the stairs. Below her, in Jocelin's study, she could see a light.

When she got down there she found Jocelin sitting at his desk with a glass in front of him.

'Sorry if I woke you,' he said. 'I couldn't sleep so I came down and got myself a drink, but it tastes foul at this time in the morning.'

'I'll make some tea,' Anne said.

When she returned with the tray Jocelin was still sitting in the same position. His hair, normally so sleek, was sticking up in spikes, his shoulders were bowed. On his face was a look of brooding unhappiness. Anne switched on the electric fire and poured out the tea.

'What's the matter, love?' she asked.

'Oh . . . things,' Jocelin said comprehensively.

He sipped slowly at the hot tea and some of the tension seemed to go out of him.

'Your dad's speech?' Anne suggested.

'If I'd had my wits about me I'd have nobbled that reporter. Of course, Dad didn't expect a few remarks made at a semi-private dinner to get into the national Press.'

'Is he sorry for all the fuss he's caused?'

'Not him! If it wasn't for the fact that I'm being made to share the blame he'd glory in it!'

'It wasn't your fault. I expect he'd had a fair amount to drink.'

'He was fairly well tanked up. I could have put out a statement repudiating what he said, but I'm damned if I'll do that to my own father. So now I'm accused of being disloyal to the new Corporation.'

'It'll blow over,' Anne suggested.

'It could hardly have been more badly timed. The report on the Wallenshaw disaster will be out this week. It's pretty scathing about our shortcomings. They're looking for a scape-goat, Anne.'

'Not you! That would be monstrously unfair!'

'Perhaps I said once too often, and to the wrong person, that I felt personally responsible. I meant it, but I didn't expect it to lead to murmurs about resignation.'

Anne had a feeling of panic. Jocelin, on the scrapheap before he was fifty – it was unthinkable.

'You must fight against it,' she urged.

'I've been asking myself whether I really want to put up a fight. That's why I can't sleep, turning it over in my mind, trying to reach a decision.'

'I thought you'd come to terms with nationalization,' Anne said.

'Now that Dad has gone we're carrying out some of the alterations he wouldn't allow while he was still around. As I came through the gates tonight I saw a man painting out the name of the firm. "Smithson" had already gone, he was just tackling "Venner". I sat in the car and watched while he blotted out "Tyndall". It's a strange sensation, seeing your own name disappear.'

He bent his head and went on in a carefully controlled voice, 'We've been in the business so long! Ever since we started digging up iron in a small way two hundred years ago. Tyndall & Sons joined up with Venners in the nineteenth century and that brought in the Welsh interest. My grandfather got a knighthood for the work he did in the First World War. He was the Tyndall who negotiated the deal with Alexander Smithson which brought us Wallenshaw. A bit of a buccaneer, but every inch a steel man. I just remember him. Dad carried on and was knighted, too. He worked like a slave all through the last war. And I . . . I was going to be next.'

He picked up his cup and drank thirstily. 'I know all the arguments in favour of nationalization,' he said. 'I even agree with them to a certain extent. Steel is too important to be left in private hands – there's something in that, though most of us are responsible people; the finance required to expand nowadays is so vast that only the Government has the resources required and if the Government provides the money why shouldn't it have a say in the running of the business? And it's true that bulk steelmaking is in the hands of just a few large companies, so we have a monopoly situation already. I *know* all that, and yet . . . my whole life has been a preparation for carrying on in Dad's place even though we've long since ceased to be just a family concern. We've got – we had – hundreds of shareholders, the Bank had a seat on the Board, but in my heart I always thought of S.V.T. as *mine* and it's been taken away from me. Nothing can ever make up to me for that.'

With every fibre of her being Anne knew that it would be a disaster for Jocelin to throw in his hand and leave the steel industry. Desperately, she sought for a way to convince him, too.

'I can understand that after such a crippling disappointment you might feel you didn't want to carry on,' she said. 'But to go out under a cloud – oh, no, Jocelin! You can't do it, not after all the years and years you've given to the Company.'

'What company?' Jocelin asked, and the way he said it summed up all his bitterness. 'I'd rather resign of my own accord than be given the push.'

'I don't agree with you. If these new people are going to be stupid enough to part with one of the best men they've got then you should make it as difficult for them as you possibly can.'

'They aren't new people, my dear. They're the same old ones wearing different hats, and some of them would be just as glad to see the back of me.'

'I've never thought of you as a man with enemies,' Anne said, startled.

'Not enemies. Rivals. There are fewer jobs at the top now and we all want them. My departure would leave a vacancy there'd be a scramble to fill.'

'I still think you should put up a fight. Dignity is all very well, but survival is more important.'

Very carefully, Jocelin said, 'I've made provision for a calamity like this. We'd be reasonably all right for money. I wouldn't have to ask you to make drastic changes in your life. In any case, Dad is still a comparatively rich man and he'd help . . .'

'That's not what's in my mind!' Anne said. She sounded indignant, even though she had had a moment of panic at the idea of Jocelin without a job and their comfortable life being threatened.

'It's you I'm thinking of,' she insisted. 'You said just now that you'd given your life to steel. What else could you do? You'd be like a fish out of water in any other environment.'

'I'll adapt if I had to. All right, I'll soldier on – provided I'm given the chance. There's to be a meeting in London on Thursday to discuss the report on the explosion. After that I'll know what's going to happen.'

'You'll tell me as soon as you know?'

'Of course.'

'There's no "of course" about it,' Anne said tartly. 'You've been keeping all this bottled up inside you, not talking to me about it, haven't you?'

They looked at one another steadily across the width of Jocelin's desk and then Anne flushed and looked down.

'We haven't been very close in the last year,' Jocelin said

deliberately. 'At the time Wally was killed I thought we'd come back together again, but it didn't last.'

When Anne didn't answer, he went on, 'You've never forgiven me for not telling you about Melanie and Jeff.'

'It was very hard to bear,' Anne said.

She spoke defensively, knowing that her long resentment had been unreasonable. Knowing, too, that there was more behind it than they had ever put into words.

'I took it out of you because of the way I felt towards Melanie,' she admitted, striving for honesty. 'I didn't know it was possible to feel such revulsion towards my own flesh and blood.'

Without looking at Jocelin, she added in a low voice, 'You know why.'

'Because Jeff had once been your lover, too. My dear, that was why I kept it from you. I thought it would be unbearable for you . . . as it was.'

'I believe you meant it for the best,' Anne admitted reluctantly. 'You're right, we've been living separate lives this last year. It mustn't happen again, not when you've got problems that could affect all of us.'

Looking at his tired face, she said, 'Come on, darling, let's go back to bed. You look exhausted. Do you think you can sleep now?'

'I think so,' Jocelin said, getting stiffly to his feet. 'After all, I've got a lot to be thankful for – not least that I've got a wife who gets up and makes tea for me in the middle of the night.'

He fell asleep almost as soon as they were back in bed, and it was Anne who lay awake. They were reconciled, and this time it would hold, but even now Jocelin did not understand the shock of grief she had felt when Jeff had died, and it was better that he should not. She loved Jocelin, as strongly as when they had first come together, but theirs had not been a marriage of equals. There was a fairy-tale element about it which would not have been present in a marriage between Anne and Jeff. That would have had its roots in the soil they both shared. Even now there were times when Jocelin's way of thinking was alien to Anne. Jocelin could contemplate throwing up a lifetime's work out of pride or to defend a principle, whereas Anne would fight tooth and nail to keep what belonged to her, as Jeff would have done in Jocelin's place. Anne and Jeff had shared a common background and in other circumstances they would have been an ideal match for one another. When he had died Anne had felt a sense of loss out of all proportion to his place in her life. It was her consciousness of this that had made her recoil in sick disgust when she had discovered that he had taken her own daughter as his mistress. Unfair, to have taken it out on Melanie; even worse to have blamed Jocelin. There were tears in Anne's eyes. As she wiped them away she knew that they were the last she would shed for Jeff.

Jocelin went off to London on Thursday to attend the meeting about the findings on the Wallenshaw explosion. Anne waited on tenterhooks all day, knowing how much depended on it. To her relief he came back looking more relaxed.

'We've accepted collective responsibility,' he said. 'No one will be asked to go. The man who was responsible for the original error is dead. I suggested there was no point in having a witch hunt and the Chairman supported me, which I didn't expect.'

'So you'll carry on?'

'I'll carry on and make the best of things,' he agreed. 'It may not be too bad.'

'The next most important thing, as far as I'm concerned, is to put things right with Melanie,' Anne said. 'Is there any chance of our spending our holiday in Canada this year?'

'Not a hope, darling. I'm sorry, but it's more than I can do. Go on your own.'

'And leave you alone? Not likely! We'll leave it until we can go together. If I work on her a bit longer Mum may agree to come, too.'

In spite of his retirement, Sir Fred expected to be kept informed about what was going on. When the first Organization Report of the new British Steel Corporation was issued in August he demanded a copy as soon as it was available.

'They've decided to go for regional groupings,' Jocelin said. 'We'll be in the Midlands Group.'

'When you say "we", you mean the bit of S.V.T. you've been a director of,' Sir Fred said. 'What about the Welsh Works?'

'They fall into the South Wales Division,' Jocelin admitted.

'So we're being split in half straight away,' his father said.

'What does it matter? We've lost over-all control even though our own men are still running things locally. It makes no difference what you call the group.'

'Any more news about your own position?'

'Essentially I'll be doing the same job, but as part of a far larger whole. It could be exciting. The British Steel Corporation will be one of the largest steel concerns in the world. We'll be in a stronger position internationally than we've ever been in before.'

He spoke with deliberate cheerfulness, sticking to his resolve to come to terms with the new regime; knowing, too, that anything he said to his father was likely to be repeated around the circle of his old colleagues.

There were still minor sacrifices to be borne. He mentioned briefly to Anne that a decision had been made to close the offices where he had been working and to take him and all his staff into the new Group Headquarters, but it was only when she pressed him that he admitted that it would be a wrench to leave the building which had been associated for so long with S.V.T.

'How far away are your new offices?' Anne asked.

'Don't worry, not far enough to make it necessary to move. I'm losing my director title and my chauffeur, but I'm still entitled to a company – I mean a Corporation – car.'

'That seems unfair when you're still doing much the same job as before.'

'I'm a small frog now and the pond is very, very big. Unwieldy, in my opinion. This regional grouping isn't going to work. There are too many old company rivalries still being fought out, as I discovered at the time of the disaster enquiry. I'm as bad as anyone else; when I hear someone from Stewarts & Lloyds or Colvilles criticize something we did at

S.V.T. I feel my hackles rise, and I'm by no means the most partisan of the old guard.'

He was only forty-six, but the grey in Jocelin's hair was spreading. Anne brooded over him, noticing the deepening of the lines of his face. They had been married thirteen years and apart from the one year in which they had been so profoundly alienated it had been a good marriage. If only she could be sure that one day Melanie would find the same happiness. Anne had sometimes wondered whether she might discover it with Steve, until he went off to Vietnam. From the way Melanie wrote about that it sounded as if they had had a profound disagreement about it, even an outright quarrel.

And then, in the autumn of 1967, Melanie wrote to say that Steve had been wounded. She had few details beyond the fact that he had been injured in both legs and was in a Military Hospital, but she promised to let Anne know if she received any further news. Anne scanned the letter, searching for any hint of feeling beyond a natural concern over the illness of a friend, but the words conveyed nothing beyond the bare facts as Melanie knew them. Not that she would have admitted in a letter to her mother that Steve's misfortune had caused her distress; she kept their correspondence to a strict recital of what was going on at the ranch. Anne sighed over it, knowing that the only way to restore their old loving relationship was to go and see her daughter, but determined not to leave Jocelin while he needed her support.

It was not Jocelin's health but the new Chairman's which gave way. Just after Christmas it became known that he had suffered a severe coronary thrombosis.

'It's a disaster,' Jocelin said. 'Both for him, poor chap, and for the Corporation. If he resigns I don't know who the Government will find to replace him.'

But Lord Melchett did not resign. After a minimum period of rest he carried on working from his hospital bed, even though it was months before his doctors would allow him back to the Corporation's new headquarters in Grosvenor Place.

'There's a feeling of re-organization ahead,' Jocelin told

Anne. 'They say the Chairman was influenced towards the idea of centralization by his visit to the United States before he fell ill.'

'What do you think about that?'

'I'm not keen, but what I think doesn't count. I favour smaller units and a degree of local autonomy, but then I would because it's what I've been used to.'

'I hope nothing's going to prevent you taking a proper holiday this year. Darling, I do so want to go to Canada. It's been eighteen months. I ought to see Melanie.'

'I can manage three weeks in August,' Jocelin offered. 'What about your mother?'

'I've talked her into coming with us.' Anne sighed. 'I'm hoping it will cure her of her belief that what Pete really wants to do is to come home. Myself, I think he would have come back by now if Canada didn't suit him.'

She wrote to Melanie and the answer she got back was so enthusiastic that Anne wondered just how much Melanie was really enjoying her life on the ranch. It was the most spontaneous letter Anne had had from her daughter since she went away.

'There'll be plenty of room,' Melanie wrote. 'I took on a married couple to help me when Steve went away, but they live in one of the cabins. I've heard from Steve that he's been repatriated, but he's still in and out of hospital, having operations on his leg. He says he'll come for a visit when he can walk on his own two feet, but so far there's no sign of him. Considering he's a writer he's a very poor correspondent.'

Melanie was not looking forward to the summer influx of visitors, not without Steve to jolly them along. She had stuck to her plan of arranging an informal summer school for artists and craftsmen to meet at the ranch and the previous year she and Yoshiko had worked hard, keeping them fed, organizing the arrivals and departures, the classes and demonstrations, the piles of laundry, the excursions and daily rides. It had been a novelty then. This year the responsibility would fall more heavily on her.

With the promise of a respite for the whole of August

Melanie was able to deal successfully with her early summer visitors, even the extra people who arrived for the Calgary Stampede, but she was not sorry to have a calmer week after they had gone.

She was in the kitchen, putting together a salad for the evening meal, when there was a step in the doorway behind her and a long shadow fell across the table.

'Anywhere around here where a fellow can park a type-writer?'

Melanie whirled round so fast that her salad bowl rocked and nearly fell on the floor.

'Steve! Steve, it's really you!'

'Sure is. Hey, you look great! How does a fellow say hello to a girl who gets three times more beautiful every time he turns his back?'

'You could kiss her,' Melanie said, holding up a face that was alight with laughter.

'I could do that,' Steve agreed, but Melanie was not quite prepared for the leisurely way he took her in his arms, nor for the long, slow kiss he gave her, and she broke away from him with heightened colour and an embarrassed laugh.

'I didn't mean a movie-style clinch,' she protested, then she looked up into his face and caught her breath at the change in him. It was not just the lines scored on his face by months of pain, nor the thin, white scar down one cheek; it was the look in his eyes, old and tired and sick. Without saying anything Melanie laid her hand against the mark on his face.

'It was bad,' Steve said, answering her unspoken question. 'Worse than anything I had ever imagined. Not just the fighting. The corruption, the feeling of sickness in the air. None of us who went to Vietnam will ever be the same again.'

'Do you regret your decision to go?'

'Are you kidding? With my legs held together by steel pins? All the same . . . if I'd still been sitting here, safe and wondering whether I was doing the right thing, I'd probably be regretting that, too. All I know is, I've got a book out of it.'

'Already?'

'I've been in and out of hospital for the last eight months,' Steve pointed out. 'Writing it all down helped to get it out of my system. I was one of the lucky ones, out of the battle zone six months after I landed, and I can still walk, drive a car, ride a horse.'

'You're out of the Army?'

'Yes, they've decided they don't want me any more. Just as well, it leaves me free to publish my book. It's rather different from *Running Woman*.'

'I'm sure it is,' Melanie said with another searching look at him. 'How are things at home?'

'Oh, fine! Mom's not had any more trouble since her operation. Pop's a bit conscience-stricken about me getting blown up. He fusses round me like an old hen, much worse than Mom. I've just spent a couple of weeks with them.'

'It didn't occur to you to write and say you were coming to Canada?'

'I wanted to take you by surprise,' Steve explained. 'Have you missed me?'

'I have when we've been cleaning out the stables or rubbing down the horses.'

'I'll start giving you a hand again tomorrow. That is, if I can stay?'

'Of course you can,' Melanie said, carefully suppressing any enquiry about his fitness for work. 'Your old room is ready for you any time. Why don't you go up now?'

She cast a harassed look at the clock. 'Uncle Pete's still got a few woodcarving students here and I've got an awful lot to do if I'm not to be late with the evening meal. We can talk this evening.'

Steve paused by the door. With his head turned away from her he said, 'Not about Vietnam.'

'Not if you don't want to,' Melanie said.

The old foursome gathered on the porch that evening – Pete and Yoshiko, Melanie and Steve – talking together as they had in the past, but with something added, a newness because they had all changed during Steve's absence, Melanie and Steve most of all.

Steve and Melanie lingered after the other two had gone inside. When Melanie finally got up she paused by Steve's chair before she went in.

'It's good to have you back,' she said.

'It's good to be back.'

*

Steve insisted on taking Melanie into Calgary to meet the flight from England.

'I'm a friend of the family,' he pointed out. 'I already know your mother and I'm looking forward to meeting everyone else.'

He caught Melanie's swift look when he mentioned her mother and guessed what she was thinking.

'Honey, it was nothing,' he said gently. 'I was a callow kid making a pass at a beautiful woman. Anne quite rightly slapped me down. Forget about it. I'm sure she has.'

Certainly any recollection of Steve's attraction was far from the front of Anne's mind when she saw him waiting behind Melanie at the barrier. It was her daughter who claimed all her attention.

'Darling, you look wonderful!' she exclaimed. 'So beautiful! It's breathtaking. Oh, it's lovely to see you.'

There was one brief moment of hesitation and then she was holding Melanie tight. When she let her go she felt in her handbag for a handkerchief.

'I knew you'd cry,' Melanie said, blinking hard.

'Silly old Mum,' Anne agreed. 'And Steve! It's so good to see you again. I didn't know you would be here.'

'There wasn't time to let you know,' Melanie explained. 'He walked in a few days ago – without a word of warning.'

Anne looked quickly from Melanie to Steve. Melanie was different. She was suntanned and her hair was shorter than it had been when Anne had last seen her, but it wasn't that. There was a look of serene, clear-eyed contentment about her, a peace that had certainly been lacking when she left home. As for Steve, Anne caught her breath as she realized the change in him and when she saw his slow, limping walk as he helped Jocelin with the luggage her eyes misted over again.

'They make a good-looking couple,' Beryl remarked when they were settled in at the ranchhouse. 'A pity about his disability and about him being an American, though I suppose if Melanie is determined to stay on this side of the world she might just as well take up with an American as a Canadian.'

'Don't talk about him like that to Melanie,' Anne said in alarm. 'In fact, don't say anything to her about him at all.'

'I hope I've got more sense,' her mother said in an offended way. 'She's as contrary as you ever were and it only needs someone to tell her she's doing the right thing to put her off it.'

The twins were wild with excitement at being back at the ranch.

'We were only babies when we came before,' Christopher told Steve. 'This time we can appreciate it properly. Which horse am I going to ride?'

'Come and choose,' Steve said goodnaturedly.

He took the two of them off to the corral, helped them capture a couple of horses, and ended by taking them out for a ride almost before the unpacking was done.

'I do think Melanie's lucky, being left an interesting ranch,' Timothy said enviously. 'All we've got in the family is mucky old steel – and we haven't even got that now.'

'Don't say that in front of Dad,' Christopher warned him.

''Course not.'

He aimed a blow at Christopher which his brother countered, but the threatened battle was cut short by a peremptory order from Steve.

'No fighting on horseback! I don't care what you do to one another, but I won't have you frightening the horses.'

They subsided, grinning surreptitiously at one another. Steve was a decent sort, though it was disappointing how little he would tell them about being wounded. With unspoken accord they decided to cultivate his company.

'You mustn't let my kid brothers be a nuisance to you,'

Melanie said to Steve, noticing the way they dogged his footsteps.

'Don't worry, we're getting along just fine. I need someone to ride with me, the way you've been shut up in the house with the womenfolk.'

'I'm glad my brothers make an acceptable substitute.'

Steve's smile deepened. 'That I didn't say,' he drawled.

There was one thing Anne had to brace herself to tell Melanie before she could feel completely at ease with her again. She meant to bring it up tactfully, but they were so rarely alone that in the end she had to seize her opportunity and blurt it out, for fear of Beryl getting in first with the news.

'Teresa's getting married again,' she said. Melanie seemed to freeze, but all she said was, 'So soon.'

'It's been two years.'

They fell silent, both grappling with the realization that Jeff had been dead that long.

'Someone suitable?'

'I suppose so. Plenty of money, at any rate. But he's divorced, with a family of his own.'

'Does Tessa seem happy?'

'On top of the world. Slightly overdoing it, I thought. She's become very social, forever dashing off to first nights and charity balls. Max has a thin time, in my opinion. It may be an advantage to him, having a step-brother and sister.'

'Poor Max,' Melanie said. 'The one person none of us considered.'

'I did,' Anne said, with the recollection of Max's dubious parentage in her mind. 'He's growing up fast. Sometimes he seems more mature than the twins.'

'Perhaps as a result of losing his father,' Melanie said in an even voice.

'Perhaps.'

They looked at one another helplessly, until Melanie said, 'There's nothing more we can say about it, is there?'

'Nothing,' Anne agreed, knowing that her daughter was not referring either to Tessa or to Max.

As Anne had feared, Beryl made no secret of her belief that Pete would do far better to return to England.

'It's all right here, I suppose,' she said. 'The scenery's grand, if you like that sort of thing.'

'But you don't?' Anne asked with a smile.

'You couldn't call it homely, could you? Too big. I wish Wally could have seen it. He said more than once that we'd try and come over when he retired. I never thought I'd come on my own.'

'You're not alone,' Anne pointed out.

'It's not the same. Perhaps you've forgotten what it's like to be a widow. Even now I keep looking round for him, and he's not there. The house is that quiet . . . If Pete came back at least there'd be a man about the place again.'

'He might come back to England, but not to Brinthorpe,' Anne suggested.

'That'd be a daft thing to do. He's always had a good home.'

She looked out of the window and saw her son walking towards the river with Yoshiko.

'As for that Japanese woman, I'd never have believed he'd be so friendly with her. A nice enough person, I grant you, and looks after him well, but Pete and a Jap! I wouldn't have thought it possible.'

By the river's edge Peter and Yoshiko paused and looked at the reflection of the golden sunset. There was something in Pete's mind that needed saying, but he did not know how to begin.

As if she sensed his difficulty Yoshiko broke the silence.

'I am happy for you that so many of your family are here,' she said.

Pete made a restless movement with his hand.

'I'm pleased to see them, of course, but the place seems crowded.'

'Not as crowded as during the summer school,' Yoshiko pointed out.

'They didn't get on top of me in the same way. I'm glad to get away for a few minutes down here with you.'

Without taking his eyes from the glittering river he went on, 'Mum wants me to go home.'

'And you? Is that what you want?'

'She's lonely. I can understand that.'

Yoshiko said nothing. Pete picked up a stone and skimmed it across the surface of the water.

'If I went back she'd have someone living in the house for the rest of her life. I'd not move again.'

'She would like that?'

'I think she's counting on it.' Very carefully he added, 'All those long years after the war when I wasn't myself, she looked after me as if I was a child again.'

Something in the quality of Yoshiko's silent understanding encouraged him to turn and look at her. In her face he saw a delicate distress neither of them would put into words.

'Brinthorpe isn't a place I'd take anyone to who wasn't born there,' Pete said. 'A little village. People who don't take easily to strangers. Sharing a house with Mum.'

Yoshiko bowed her head in acquiescence at his decision. Neither of them spoke again as they walked back towards the house.

The next time Beryl spoke of Pete's return to England it was as if it were a settled thing. She was in the kitchen, as she usually was every morning.

'You're not having a holiday at all,' Melanie protested.

'I'm not one for sitting around doing nothing. Time hangs when you've got no occupation. That's why I'll be glad to have Pete back.'

Melanie glanced round quickly to check that Yoshiko had gone out of the room.

'Has Uncle Pete said he'll go home?' she asked.

'Not in so many words, but he'll come all right. It's the sensible thing to do.'

'Are you sure it's what he wants? He's been happy here.'

'It suits you to think so! The winters don't agree with him. Look at that bronchitis he had when your grandfather died.'

'He was perfectly well last winter. To me, Uncle Pete seems more alive: even, in a strange sort of way, younger, since he came to Canada.'

Beryl's floury hands moved restlessly over the pastry board.

'I can't see it! Anyway, it's not for you to decide, Melanie. I don't want you persuading him to stay against his better judgement just because you need him. Find yourself a nice young man and get married. If you ask me, Steve would have you if you encouraged him.'

She thought she had silenced her grand-daughter when she saw the way her face coloured up, but Melanie persisted.

'If Uncle Pete stays here I think he'll marry Yoshiko,' she said. 'But he'll be a bachelor all his life if he goes back to Brinthorpe. Do you want that? What will happen when you die?'

'I've a few years left in me yet,' Beryl said.

She rinsed her hands under the tap and left the kitchen, looking hot and annoyed.

On the landing upstairs she found Yoshiko putting clean sheets away in the linen cupboard.

'Melanie's been putting my back up, suggesting Pete doesn't want to come back to England,' Beryl said abruptly.

She looked suspiciously at the Japanese woman, taking in her smooth black head, her round face the colour of old ivory, her neat figure, the small, deft hands sorting the linen. She must be in her forties, but she looked younger than that.

'A man has duty towards his aged parent; Peter knows that,' Yoshiko said.

She had a funny way of saying his name, 'Petah'.

'I'm not *that* old,' Beryl said, irritated.

She didn't like the sound of that word 'duty', as if Pete would be making a sacrifice in living with her.

'Is he happy here?' she asked.

'Oh, yes.' Yoshiko looked faintly surprised. 'But he would not be happy knowing he had disappointed you. He will come with you when you go, I think.'

It was all vaguely unsatisfactory. In the days that followed Beryl said nothing more about her plans for her son, but she started watching him and what she saw did not reassure her.

Towards the end of the second week of their holiday Jocelin received a long, typewritten letter from England. He glanced at it quickly and then put it back in the envelope to read later.

'That looks suspiciously official,' Anne said. 'You promised me there'd be no business while we were away.'

• 'I need to keep up with the news,' Jocelin said. 'Are you coming riding with me and the twins this morning?'

'You're very quick to change the subject. Are you keeping something from me?'

'I'll tell you later.'

Steve thought that Jocelin was unusually quiet when he rode out with him and the twins. He glanced at the older man, admiring the way he rode, loose and easy in the saddle. The two boys rode round them, excited and a little wild. Steve kept a tolerant eye on them, but he had given up worrying about them now that they had been out with him every day for two weeks.

'Tell me,' he said to Jocelin. 'Do I have to get permission from you or her mother before I marry Melanie?'

'Anne is her guardian, I'm merely a trustee of her grandmother's will,' Jocelin said, jerked out of the train of thought he had been following. 'Anne is the one to give permission until she's twenty-one. You've taken me by surprise. I didn't know things had progressed that far.'

'Melanie hasn't come round to it yet, but she will,' Steve said. 'You don't think Anne will object because I'm a bit of a crock?'

'You've overcome it very well. Perhaps I appreciate more than she does how much it's cost you. I'll see she doesn't raise that objection.'

'I'll be grateful for your help. Melanie's my woman and before the summer's over I'm going to get her to admit it. I was nearly sure before I went away, and since I've been back . . . well, you know how it is, she's got me tied up so tight I'll never break free, nor want to either.'

'What can I say, except to wish you luck? She's a lovely girl, and not only in looks.'

'That she is,' Steve agreed. 'I'd like to get it settled before you all go home. The time's coming when I'm going to have to crash through the last barrier Melanie's put up around herself. I only hope I don't make a hash of it.'

'I won't try to give you any advice,' Jocelin said. 'You'll have to use your own judgement. All I can say is that you've got my blessing, for what it's worth.'

'It's a step in the right direction. Now, what are those two fool boys up to? They'll be riding into a swamp if they go that way.'

He set off after the twins, rounding them up like a couple of wayward steers, while Jocelin followed more slowly, momentarily diverted by Steve's confidences, but soon lapsing into the abstraction that had fallen on him ever since he read his letter from England.

The other three were far ahead of him. Jocelin touched his heels to his horse's flanks and increased his pace. He was galloping easily across the yellowing grass of the prairie when the horse stumbled and fell. Jocelin, riding a little too slackly, was tossed over its head. The sun-baked ground seemed to rush up to meet him. He landed, with a jolt that went right through his body, on the point of his shoulder. Pain shot through his arm and back. He tried to sit up and felt the grinding of broken bones.

It was a minute or two before Steve realized that Jocelin was not following on behind. He wheeled round, searching for him, and saw his horse, standing quietly with its head drooping and one leg lifted, as if in pain.

By the time Steve reached him Jocelin was making a second attempt to sit up.

'My collarbone's gone,' he said. 'I don't know what I was thinking about, to take a toss like that.'

'Your horse put his foot down a gopher hole,' Steve said. 'Damn bad luck. And we're a long way from home. If I fix you up with a pad and a sling do you think you can get back on horseback so that I can lead you home? It's the quickest thing to do, but it'll hurt like hell.'

He was already undoing his own bright red plaid shirt.

'I picked up a bit of rough and ready medicine around the rodeos,' he said. 'I won't say I can make you comfortable, but I can immobilize the arm. As soon as we get back to the ranch I'll put you in the back of my car and take you into Calgary to the hospital.'

Chris and Tim stood by, their faces solemn at the sight of their father's helplessness.

'Shall we ride ahead and tell Mum?' Christopher asked.

'No point,' Steve said. 'There's nothing she can do. And I don't want you two riding off hell for leather and having another accident. Stay close. If your father looks like passing out I may need you to hold him in the saddle.'

Getting up on Steve's horse was excruciatingly painful, but Jocelin had the high pommel of the Western saddle to hang on to with his good hand and with a boost from Steve he managed it.

'How do you feel?' Steve asked.

'Sick.'

'Yeah, I guess,' Steve said sympathetically. 'Think you can make it?'

Jocelin straightened his back. 'I'll be all right.'

He smiled faintly at his wide-eyed sons. 'When I feel better you can tell me what a stupid idiot I was. All right, troops, let's get started.'

It was Pete who was the first to see the little procession because he was up on top of a ladder taking a look at a piece of faulty guttering.

'It looks as if there's been an accident,' he called down. He put up his hand to shield his eyes. 'I can't see properly, the sun's right in my eyes. I don't think it's either of the boys. It might be Jocelin riding and Steve leading him and a lame horse, or it might be the other way round, but the one riding is wearing a red shirt and he's on the white horse.'

'Steve!' Melanie said.

She was gone in a whirl of movement that carried her over the parched ground towards the riders, running hard with no thought in her mind except that Steve was hurt and she must get to him. She was almost on top of them before she realized that it was Steve who was walking and her stepfather who was swaying in the saddle. She stopped dead.

'Don't worry, only a broken collarbone,' Steve called out.

As they drew nearer he looked with concern at Melanie's white face.

'I thought it was you,' Melanie whispered, too shocked to be anything but truthful.

Steve began to smile. Melanie looked at him helplessly, brilliant colour coming back to her pale cheeks. Steve held out his free arm and she fell into step by his side with his arm round her shoulders.

When Jocelin was settled on the back seat of Steve's car and Anne in the front, ready to be driven to the nearest hospital, Steve turned to Melanie with a look of rueful regret.

'I have to go, honey. It's the only thing I can do.'

'Of course.'

Melanie lifted her head and looked at him steadily.

'I'll see you later,' Steve promised.

All day Melanie waited in a state of dreaming expectancy. It was evening before Steve returned, and he was alone.

'Jocelin's O.K.,' he said. 'But Anne didn't think he was up to a second eighty-mile drive so they're staying the night in Calgary. I'll pick them up tomorrow. Where's Melanie?'

'Mooning about somewhere,' Beryl said, sounding both anxious and cross. 'We've scarcely had a word out of her all day. I don't know what's the matter with her.'

'I do,' Steve said. 'You leave Melanie to me.'

He found her sitting on the corral fence, looking lonely and slightly forlorn.

'What's this?' Steve asked. 'You don't look as happy as you did when I left you this morning.'

'I've had time to think since then,' Melanie said.

'We'd better have a talk. I've scarcely had a bite to eat today so I've asked Yoshiko to put a few things in a basket for us. We'll have one of our picnics. Be ready in five minutes.'

'It's nearly dark. It'll be too chilly to eat out of doors,' Melanie protested.

'We'll build a fire.' There was so much understanding in Steve's face that Melanie began to smile, a little uncertainly but definitely a smile. He cupped his hand round her cheek. It felt big and warm and gentle. 'I don't intend you ever to feel cold again,' he said.

They lit their fire on a pile of stones in a hollow not far from the river. Nothing had ever tasted quite so good as the lamb chops they laid on a grill over the glowing embers. All of a sudden Melanie was ravenously hungry. Above them the sky was black and moonless, but brilliant with stars. They were completely alone in a world where a small wind rustled through the grass and the orange flames leapt upwards from the hearth they had built together.

When they had finished eating Steve shifted nearer, so that his shoulder was just behind Melanie's and she could feel the warmth of his body.

'Ready to start talking?' he asked.

'Not much to talk about, is there? You must have guessed the way I feel about you.'

'You've fallen in love with me. But, honey, it didn't really happen like a flash of lightning. It's been going on for a long time.'

'I shut my mind to it, perhaps because I didn't want to spoil the way things were between us.'

'It couldn't go on. I love you, too, and my patience was wearing mighty thin.'

'There are some things I ought to tell you about myself,' Melanie said.

'Only if you feel you must. I don't need to know.'

'It will help me – if you don't mind listening. No, Steve, don't touch me, not until I've done.'

With her eyes on the fire she told him about Ricky, about her abortion, about Jeff and her terrible feeling of guilt for his death; a bald recital of facts, but Steve sensed the pain behind the words.

'My poor little love,' he said when she had finished. 'You started too young with a silly boy and it was fiendish bad luck after that to fall in with a man prepared to take advantage of a schoolgirl infatuation.'

'You mustn't say that,' Melanie interrupted him. 'Jeff got all the blame, but it was my fault. I did a lot of harm, that was why I came away.'

'Did you think you could come here and live in a vacuum? It's not possible. Everything we do affects other people as well as ourselves, sometimes for good, sometimes not. Coming to Canada was a good decision. Let's build on that.'

'Do you still feel the same way about me?' Melanie asked.

'Of course I do. I'm a full-grown man. I've knocked about the world. I've been to war and when you read my book you'll realize that I've committed a few sins of my own. I've seen myself becoming brutal and degraded and pulled myself back from the brink just in time. I've even come to see that perhaps I was saved from something worse by treading on a boobytrap mine. I'm not about to cast any stones because your feelings ran away with you when you were just a kid.'

'I'm not a child any longer,' Melanie said. 'I'm twenty.' She sounded surprised, as if she had suddenly become an adult without noticing it.

'Do you feel ready to marry me? Think before you answer. I'm partly crippled and always will be. I still suffer some pain and it could get worse. I may turn into a grouchy old man.'

'I'll take that risk! Yes, I'll marry you, if you're sure that's what you really want?'

'I'm sure,' Steve said.

She turned to him then and he took her in his arms and pulled her down to lie by his side on the sun-dried grass. All the excitement she remembered from Jeff's lovemaking was there, the vivid sexual urge she had suppressed since she lost him, but this was Steve and it was different; he was entirely himself, there was no need to be afraid of ghosts from the past. When he ran his hand down the length of her body Melanie shuddered and clung to him, kissing him with urgent passion that subsided into tenderness.

Steve laughed under his breath and loosened his hold on her. 'That's what I've been waiting for,' he said. 'Now I'm sure you love me.'

'I do. So much. Nobody could love anyone more than I love you. And I wouldn't even admit it until today. We've been such good companions. That will go on, won't it?'

'Of course. No reason why we can't be friends as well as lovers. We'll make our home here at the ranch . . .'

'Oh, that's why you want to marry me! So that you can get the ranch!'

'Only way I could do it. No more paying guests, but I think your summer school ought to go on and you must keep up your woodcarving. I'll need to do some travelling, sweetheart. You won't mind that?'

'It'll be exciting. Anything, so long as we can be together.'

She lifted her face and they kissed again, savouring the pleasure they gave one another.

'We're going to have a proper old-fashioned engagement, with a ring and everything,' Steve said. 'We'll buy it tomorrow when I go into Calgary to fetch Jocelin. And I'm not going to make love to you until after we're married.'

'That's more old-fashioned than I'd expected,' Melanie said. 'Is it going to be a long engagement?'

'How about a wedding next week, before your folks go home?'

'Steve, we can't!' Melanie collapsed against him, warm with laughter.

'Why not? We know what we want, there's nothing to stop us. And anyway, that's about as long as I reckon I can hold out.'

The news that Melanie and Steve were engaged to be married hardly came as a surprise to any of her family, but the idea of a hurried marriage did worry Anne.

'I think you should agree,' Jocelin said. 'It's not as if they'd only just met. They've known one another on and off for years. They've got a home ready-made for them and plenty of money. Steve is successful – and a very likeable person, surely? Melanie appears to be head over heels in love with him, and he with her.'

Jocelin was back at the ranch, his injured shoulder strapped up, apparently none the worse for his misfortune beyond the inconvenience and a degree of pain, but there was something worrying him. Anne knew it and meant to get to the bottom of it as soon as she had reached a decision about Melanie's future.

'If you refuse your consent they'll only live together for a year and then get married,' Jocelin went on. 'I think Melanie needs a more stable relationship than that.'

'You're right. Of course they must get married if they want to,' Anne capitulated.

The prospect of a wedding gave a boost to Beryl's spirits as nothing else could have done.

'I've said all along Steve was the one for our Melanie,' she said. 'There'll be a lot to do if it's to be next week, but I dare say we'll manage.'

'Melanie won't need me any more,' Pete said deliberately. 'If I can get a seat I'll come home on the same flight as you, Mum.'

'That you will not!'

Beryl straightened her shoulders and her mouth tightened into an obstinate line.

'I'll not deny I had it in my mind when I came out here, but I've had second thoughts. I've got used to having the place to myself. They say you get selfish if you live alone, but I think I'm entitled to indulge myself at my age. That woodwork of yours, scrape, scrape, scrape, it fair gets on my nerves. Come back if you must, but I'll tell you to your face I don't want you, Pete.'

She glared at him, daring him to argue with her, and Peter, completely thrown by her about-turn, could find nothing to say. It was Yoshiko who spoke to Beryl later when they were alone.

'You are a good woman,' she said in her quiet way.

'I only hope I've done the right thing,' Beryl said.

'Once I, too, had a little son and there was no sacrifice I would not have made for him.'

'Sacrifice, indeed! Highfalutin talk!' She blew her nose with a loud, defiant noise. 'Just you look after him, that's all.'

In the rush of activity before the wedding Anne did not lose sight of her intention to find out what was bothering Jocelin, but she put it on one side until after the ceremony. When Steve and Melanie had gone off on their unconventional honeymoon on horseback to camp in wild country, Anne found time to walk quietly away from the ranch with Jocelin.

'Feeling melancholy?' he asked with a glance at her thoughtful face.

'Not really. Steve is so right for Melanie that I can't feel sad about it. I have been remembering, though – Mel, and the time we spent here together when she was a tiny baby. So long ago! A different life.'

She slipped her hand through his good arm and they strolled together towards the far end of the paddock.

'I've been neglecting you for the past week,' Anne said. 'And you've got things on your mind, haven't you? That letter you had. There was something in it that worried you.'

'You won't approve of this,' Jocelin warned her, with the smile that never failed to bring out an answering gleam from her. 'The old boy network still operates! I was promised advance warning by my old colleagues farther up the line and this is it. Lord Melchett has been having talks with the present Managing Directors about reorganizing into Product Units instead of on a regional basis.'

'You thought that would happen!'

'I thought it inevitable – the regions are being too damned independent by half for a Chairman who sees our salvation in a central organization. I don't know yet exactly how our part of the industry will be split up, but probably we'll be formed into a Heavy Steels Division. It will need a new Managing Director.'

'Jocelin! You don't mean . . . you?'

'Apparently the Chairman was favourably impressed when we met to discuss the disaster report. You were right when you urged me to defend myself.'

'It's splendid news – if it's what you want?'

'I suppose in terms of size of the job it's equivalent to the one that got away. Not so personal as being Chairman of S.V.T., but equally important. Yes, I want it.'

'Then why have you been going round with a frown on your face for the last week?'

'Wallenshaw is to close.'

'Oh, no! Not Wallenshaw!'

Anne's shocked exclamation made Jocelin grimace.

'It won't happen overnight. We're being given two years to run it down.'

Anne looked out over the sun-parched prairie of Canada to where the river ran and there was a distant gleam of snow on the heights of the Rocky Mountains, but in her mind she saw the long, heavy mass of buildings and chimneys which had formed the skyline of her childhood. The belching chimneys would be smokeless, the mills would fall silent, the furnaces would go cold, bricks would crumble and weeds grow where the locomotives had shunted.

'Is that what Dad died for?' she asked. 'So that it could all close down and come to an end?'

'It's a blow,' Jocelin admitted. 'I've said in the past that Wallenshaw was outdated and ought to be shut down, but I was thinking in terms of rebuilding. That won't happen now.'

'You're already coming to terms with it,' Anne accused him. 'Jocelin, it's a horrible decision. Why don't you fight against it?'

'Unless I take the post of Managing Director I have no authority, and if I accept it then I have to give my loyalty to the Chairman and his policy.'

'But the whole village where I grew up depends on the steelworks for a living!'

'Jobs will be found for as many people as possible at other works. Anne, I don't know all the details, and won't until my appointment is confirmed.'

'Don't accept it. Throw up your job and put yourself heart and soul into fighting against the closure of Wallenshaw.'

'Would you stand by me if I did that? It would mean the end of your comfortable life, my dear.'

'I wouldn't care. All right, when I married you it was partly because of what you could give me . . .'

'I've always known that,' Jocelin said quietly. 'It's never seemed important, not compared with what you gave me in return. Love, companionship, a settled home, two beautiful sons.'

'Quite a lot of problems.'

'Any family has those. We seem to have come through them quite successfully.'

'I love you more now than I did fourteen years ago. I value you more. I can't bear to stand by and see you compromising on something you feel strongly about, not for the sake of a grand position and money in the bank. Give it up.'

'I can't. Anne, this is the job I was trained for, these are the decisions I would have had to make as Chairman of S.V.T. Agonisingly difficult, especially knowing the people involved so well, but unless I am in a position of power I'll have no influence at all.'

'You've already thought it all out and made up your mind what you're going to do,' Anne said in a low voice.

'Protesting against the closure of Wallenshaw from outside the Corporation will have no effect – and why just Wallenshaw? To be consistent I'd need to rally support against all the closures. That would only be feasible if I went into politics – and I'm not cut out for that.'

When Anne did not reply, Jocelin went on, 'I wish I could persuade you that what I am choosing is the more difficult way. And it's not for money or position, it's because I believe I'm the best man for the job.'

'You'll do it very well,' Anne agreed. 'As you say, it's what you were brought up for.'

'I'll need your help,' Jocelin said.

'Will you? My opinion seems to count for very little. I think you're taking the easy way out.'

'No, the easy thing would be to be poor, self-righteous and popular. It's much harder to be rich, powerful and unpopular.'

'If it wasn't for your broken collarbone I'd *hit* you!' Anne said heatedly. 'I don't know why you don't go in for politics; you've certainly got the tongue for it! All right, I accept that you believe you're doing the right thing and that your motives are pure as the driven snow. Where does that leave me?'

'Standing by your own opinion if you want to, but still loving me, I hope.'

'I don't know why I ever bother to get into an argument with you,' Anne said bitterly. 'I always lose.'

Jocelin put his uninjured arm round her shoulders. 'The most important thing that's been said in the last ten minutes is that you love me more now than you did fourteen years ago,' he said. 'Did you mean it?'

'I suppose so.' Anne's head shifted to rest against his shoulder. 'Yes, of course I did. It'll take more than a difference of opinion to change me now.'

'I wonder if you have any idea how much I depend on you?' Jocelin said quietly. 'To know that amongst all the shifting sands I have to negotiate there is one person whose loving support is like a rock, that gives me something I can get from nobody else. There's a painful, difficult time ahead of us. I shall need you as I never have before.'

'I'll be there,' Anne said. 'Disagreeing with you in private, perhaps, but needing you and wanting you just as much as you need and want me. Come on, darling, let's walk back. I must finish packing if we're to leave for home tomorrow. Oh, Jocelin, just think! This time next year I might be a grand-mother!'